W9-BVB-074

RAVE REVIEWS FOR EDWARD LEE!

"A horror extravaganza . . . Lee's twisted tale has an outrageously paranoid surprise that will keep fans of cover-ups and conspiracy theories reading to the final sentence."

—*Publishers Weekly* on *Monstrosity*

"The living legend of literary mayhem. Edward Lee writes with gusto, guts, and brains. Read him if you dare."

—Richard Laymon, internationally bestselling author of *Darkness, Tell Us*

DISCARDED

"The hardest of the hardcore horror writers."

—*Cemetery Dance*

"Lee has penned some of the wettest, bravest terror this side of the asylum."

—*Hellnotes*

"A demented Henry Miller of horror."

—Douglas Clegg, award-winning author of *The Hour Before Dark*

"Adventures galore."

—*Publishers Weekly* on *City Infernal*

"Utterly intriguing."

—*Horror World* on *City Infernal*

"Lee is a writer you can bank on for tales so extreme they should come with a warning label."

—T. Winter-Damon, co-author of *Duet for the Devil*

"Lee pulls no punches."

—*Fangoria*

THE THING IN THE LAKE

Caleb suddenly stopped, hip-deep in the water. Something *real big* brushed against him. *Don't panic*. He stood stock-still, hands poised. Behind him, again, something big swam against him.

He turned very slowly, so as not to agitate the water, raised one foot to take the first step forward back to the shore, and—

WHAP!

The water surged. Foot-wide jaws hit Caleb right in the crotch and clamped down. He fell over, screaming, splashing, reeling a frantic circle in the water as his predator reeled with him: a huge eel. The great jaws locked down harder; Caleb was paralyzed in agony.

He would never fish again. He would never make love to Kari Ann again, and he had slapped his last high-five with his good friend Jory.

Then—a hand grabbed his collar and pulled him from the water.

"Jory, thank God! Get this thing off me!"

The eel let go, the gnawing gristly pain abated, and Caleb heaved breaths in nearly mindless relief. Back on shore, he collapsed in exhaustion, looked up at Jory, and . . . it wasn't Jory.

Caleb wished he were back in the water again with the eel when he got a look at the face of the thing that had pulled him out.

Other *Leisure* books by Edward Lee:

CITY INFERNAL

EDWARD LEE

MONSTROSITY

LEISURE BOOKS  NEW YORK CITY

For Dave Barnett

A LEISURE BOOK®

April 2003

Published by

Dorchester Publishing Co., Inc.
276 Fifth Avenue
New York, NY 10001

If you purchased this book without a cover you should be aware that this book is stolen property. It was reported as "unsold and destroyed" to the publisher and neither the author nor the publisher has received any payment for this "stripped book."

Copyright © 2002 by Edward Lee

All rights reserved. No part of this book may be reproduced or transmitted in any form or by any electronic or mechanical means, including photocopying, recording or by any information storage and retrieval system, without the written permission of the publisher, except where permitted by law.

ISBN 0-8439-5075-7

The name "Leisure Books" and the stylized "L" with design are trademarks of Dorchester Publishing Co., Inc.

Printed in the United States of America.

Visit us on the web at www.dorchesterpub.com.

ACKNOWLEDGMENTS

As always, the author is in debt to many, but particular thank-yous are due to: Rich Chizmar, Doug Clegg, Don D'Auria, Dallas Mayr, Tim McGinnis, and Tom Piccirilli. I need to thank some of the staff at Bay Pines Med Center for seeing to it that I will live to write still more horror novels: Dr. Durr, Kent Bown, Steve in ER, Dr. Lopez, and Dr. Nash. More thanks to Amy and Scott (for stomaching a number of my books), Christy & Bill (it's a good thing we're not drinkin'), Julie (for still speaking to me after reading *Creekers*), Stephanie (for the name of the lake and for being the only person on the beach who knows who Rothko is), and Susan (for interesting shooter names) & R.J. (for disliking the Red Sox as much as I do), and everyone else at Philthy Phils. Thanks, too, to Tony and Kim at Camelot, and, as always to Bob Strauss; and to Rob Stevens and Bruce Thomas.

MONSTROSITY

Prologue

Federal Land Grid S27-0078
Central Florida
June 1995

The bodies lay in pieces. They'd been expertly dismembered.

And they were over 10,000 years old.

Professor Fredrick's team had finally gotten the vault open an hour ago. It was Fredrick himself who'd ordered the MMD scan; the circle of stone benches he'd initially discovered were of a typical Ponoye congregational alignment. The Ponoye Indians were the rage now in archaeological circles, and Fredrick was the one who'd discovered them. This dig should be the one that made him famous.

I'm almost seventy now, he thought. *I've earned the right to be famous, damn it*. Yes, he'd discovered this obscure offshoot Indian tribe but no one had yet discovered one of their locations of worship. Fredrick had long learned that the secrets of ancient races were always unlocked by analysis of their system of religion. He could feel his old pulse jumping with excitement.

"Lower," he said into the microphone. "Ten more feet and I'll be on the floor." He waited, hanging in the harness, for his command to be met. The flashlight swung around, revealing more brief slices of wonder. Fredrick couldn't wait to kneel before them, to revel in them like a child at the foot of the Christmas tree. The excitement was overwhelming him, his heart racing beneath the dusty khaki field shirt. *Don't have a heart attack*, he warned himself. *Have a heart attack tomorrow. But you've got to see what's in this vault first . . .*

His booted feet dangled in the air, just a few feet over what would probably turn out to be the most important find of his life.

Then his body began to rise. They were pulling him back up.

"Damn it, what are you doing?" he shouted into his mike. "Down! Down!"

But back up he went, reeled up and out of this newfound heart of darkness. Before he was fully out of the vault, however, his flashlight fell for one final moment back on the very first things he'd glimpsed:

The bodies. The dismembered bodies, preserved by time and happenstance to near perfection . . .

"Sorry, Prof," Dales said. Dales was Fredrick's senior teaching assistant: young, brash, but very good. This was the third dig he'd accompanied Fredrick on, and the boy knew the ropes. He had the bad habit of stuffing Gummy Bears in his cheek like chewing tobacco, and he had a smart ass to go along with his academic prowess. But in secret, Fredrick could now almost regard him as a son, and he hoped the boy would go on in his much older footsteps.

Dales continued his hasty explanation as to why he'd so quickly extracted Fredrick from the belly of the cenote.

"It's the testing equipment. It's all our stuff, remember? It's from the college inventory. The feds may be paying for this dig but they're not buying us any new testing gear."

Fredrick stomped out of his lift harness, practically having a tantrum there in the dell. "What are you talking about!"

"The air probe."

"What!"

"It's a first series Becton-Dystal, Prof. It's practically as old as . . ."

Fredrick's baggy eyes narrowed at his associate's clipped pause. He jabbed a finger. "You're a cocky young punk, you know that? You were about to say it's practically as old as me."

Dales grinned through a mouthful of Gummy Bears. "Naw, Prof, I meant it's as old as the hills—and let's face it. That's pretty much the same thing. And before you have your fourth coronary of your career, let me explain. When we first dropped the probe, it came back green, so then we dropped you in. After you're down there, the probe goes red. The goddamn thing's so old and rusty it was giving us a false positive, took five minutes for the real reading to log in the chromatograph. When you were down there, Prof, you were breathing a couple thousand parts per million of methane, CO^2 , and radon. Five more minutes in that hole and you'd be dead . . . and I don't care *what* the rest of the faculty says, Prof. The world's better off with you than without you."

Fredrick made a reciprocating gesture with his middle

finger, but after a few grumbles and a quick cough, he said, "Good work, son. Thank you."

Dales laughed. "So now I get an A on my thesis, right?"

"Don't push it." Fredrick finally shucked off the rest of the clumsy harness. A racket rose as several other enthusiastic students dropped the white vent hose into the hole. Dales feigned concern, grabbed Fredrick's shoulders, and turned him away from the sight. "Don't look, Professor. It'll bring back traumatic memories—of your last colonoscopy!"

"You're a regular comedian today, Dales. What we *should* do is throw *you* into that hole. Just sit down there and talk about yourself for five minutes—all that hot air will surely blow out any toxic fumes."

"Hee-haw, boss! That's a real knee-slapper!"

Fredrick frowned against the high sun. All the activity of the site was beginning to annoy him: the clatter of dredger engines, the trucks barreling in out of the dell, the endless grate of shovels biting into stony earth. "How long will it take to vent?"

Dales sat down on an unearthed chunk of black granite whose divets indicated that it was probably once used as a beheading abutment. "Could be a lot of cubic yards of space down there," he pointed out. "You know the drill. How big is the cenote?"

The question duped him. "Impossible to say. I only caught a few brief glimpses with my flashlight before I was pulled back. I couldn't even estimate as to the interior perimeter."

Dales shrugged. "Could take an hour, could take a month."

The possibility filled him with the most shocking despair.

He wanted to get back in there.

Now.

"And you're sure you saw *bodies?*" Dales asked.

"*Dismembered* bodies," Fredrick said. "Bodies dismembered at the hips and shoulders."

"Hmm." Dales thought about this. "Bones, you mean. Ossified imprints?"

"Limbs, incredibly well preserved. Essentially intact—"

"—after 10,000 years?" Dales went on. "Shit a brick, this is some co-inky-dink, huh? High nitrogen, an unadulterated thermal flux of methane and carbon dioxide, and since the cenote's been so well-sealed, all the radonite gas the shale was leaking never vented out. Every archaeologist's ultimate hard-on."

Dales's less-than-technical terminology proved accurate nonetheless. A monumental fluke had provided an absolutely pre-eminent environmental condition for archaeological preservation. Simple good fortune had seen to it that the bodies in the cenote would be flawlessly mummified.

Ten millennia old, Fredrick realized. *And still intact . . .*

Dales was chuckling. "I can't wait to see the looks on the faces of the schmucks who've been laughing at you all this time. I mean, Christ, this isn't some peat bog in the Andes or a melted piedmont in Nepal. This in Florida, boss. You've discovered that an offshoot Indian tribe was practicing a systematized religion before any systematized religion existed. You kick ass, you know that? You fuckin' rock."

Though Fredrick appreciated the encouraging remarks—however coarse—he knew that none of his discovery would be accepted as credible if what he *thought* he'd seen in the vault turned out to be some optical illusion. Lower oxygen content could very easily account for such a hallucination. And at Fredrick's age, so could wishful thinking, he supposed. But he felt so *sure*. He felt *sure* he'd seen the bodies, and he felt sure he'd seen the—

"What about the heads?" Dales asked now, as if intercepting a thought. But what an odd thing to ask. "Was it just the arms and legs separated from the torsos, or the heads too?"

"The heads too," Fredrick enlightened.

"So you were right all along. All this time you've been saying that the Ponoye were ritually sacrificial."

Fredrick saw his point at once, then quickly corrected: "Oh, no, I don't think the bodies were sacrifice victims. They were lying askew on the vault's floor. No pattern, no order. And they were priests."

"You're kidding me."

Fredrick shook his head so vigorously some dust sifted out. "Their ritual dress had sufficiently oxidized, of course, but I could still make out the remnants very well. These men were wearing albs and stoles, intricate cassocks. There were four bodies, Dales, and I saw what appeared to be four headdresses oxidized on the floor as well."

Dales winked. "Got'cha. Stupid me. The headdress doesn't usually stay on the head when the head's cut off."

"Yes, and I don't think they were *cut* off."

Now Dales was beginning to lose some of his wit. "What, you mean they somehow came detached after mummification? A tremor, earthquake?"

"No, no, no," Fredrick insisted, straining the memory of his vision. "I'm talking about the morphology of the heads—peri-mortal, not post-mortal. Just the way the necks looked. The heads weren't cut off, Dales. They were pulled off."

Dales spat out his Gummy Bears and glared back at Fredrick. "Okay, boss. Now you're starting to freak me out. Usually it's the priests who do the sacrificing. But you're telling me that 10,000 years ago, someone went down there and sacrificed the priests?"

Despite the sun's fierce blaze, he shivered in the humid air. The site made him think of violations, of rape. A line of zealous students tore at the face of the ridge with 20-pound pickaxes. Others turned shovels around amorphous shapes of things that the last six days of excavation had raised from the oblivion of ages. Dust rose in billows. The hectic sound of metal striking rock rang as a familiar song. Fredrick had spent his life doing this: disgorging smothered civilizations from the thick skin of the earth. Yet he'd never felt this way before. He felt like a trespasser.

He looked down at his clay-flecked leather boots, the same he'd worn on countless digs. From Galli to Nineveh, from Jericho to Troy to Knossos. He abstracted, wanting to smile. He thought of himself as a specter of the future. All these cities, once great, had been predestined to be trod upon by Fredrick's old boots a millennia later. Time buried. Whole civilizations locked in layers of clay. He was walking on worlds, and someday, he realized, someone like him would walk on his.

But not today . . .

Today Fredrick would be the herald between the present and the dimmest past.

Alone now, he stared at the ingress.

Cenote, he thought. Yes, what anyone else would simply call a hole in the ground, men like Fredrick would call a cenote. Cenotes and ziggurats. Tower and tunnel. Up and down. They were universal. All ancient civilizations conformed to some similar spiritual ideology.

Heaven was up. Hell was down.

The Tower of Babel, for instance, was a ziggurat, a sanctified structure whose deliberate height meant to bring the priests closer to heaven.

Fredrick, at this isolated, tropical dell, had found the counterpart—a ceremonial cenote—whose depth meant to bring the priests closer to the underworld.

Closer to devils.

The Ponoyes. The obscure Indian tribe's ancient tabletries spoke of a holy cenote—the *cennana*—and it looked like Fredrick had found one. Just like the ancient cenotes of, say, Mesopotamia, except—

This cenote had to have been dug 5000 years earlier than the oldest Mesopotamian cenote, Fredrick thought.

Proof of an ascensional religious system existing eight thousand years before the birth of Christ?

In North America?

It'll turn the modern archaeological community on its ear . . .

The image in the flashlight beam snapped back to his mind's eye; Fredrick was sure the bodies in the vault were Ponoye priests. The cenote's unlikely environment had preserved their regalia perfectly: the pectoral jewelry. The armlets and wristbands. The headdresses—more like the peaked miters of the Assyrian smoke-diviners than anything that could be thought typical of Native American ceremonial garb. The Ponoyes were unique in many ways: first, they had an exclusive, intricate written language, and were transcribing religious script at about the same time the Egyptian aristocracy was writing on pressed papyrus. Second, they wrote hieretically: only the clergy were allowed to partake in writing. Third, they weren't nature worshippers. They were *descentional theologics*.

In other words, the Ponoyes did not worship a god on high. They worshiped "lower" gods.

Fredrick's bottled-up excitement was making him shake now. His old joints began to ache just from pacing back and forth before the ringed safety rail around the cenote's mouth. After a while he realized that the sun was beginning to set and he hadn't even realized it. One student quickly loped by, waving him over: "Chow truck's here, Professor. Come and get it!" and then the rest of the excavation team began to break off. Suddenly, the site fell silent save for the steady chug of the ventilator's small gas-powered engine. Only when he was totally alone did Fredrick notice the old-series air-probe's display panel.

The light was green.

It had been hours now; surely the cenote's vault had vented by now. Dales was nowhere to be seen, standing in the chow truck line no doubt.

Damn it, Fredrick thought.

He couldn't wait any longer.

He began to strap himself into the descent harness.

"To hell with the winch," he was muttering to himself next. "I'll do it the good old fashioned way . . ." Safety precaution and simple common sense had eluded him; he was done screwing around. A couple dozen yards below his feet, straight down into the ground, a 10,000-year-old mystery was waiting for him with open arms.

It would wait no longer.

The drop line tightly gripped to his chest, Fredrick began to lower himself down into the hole. The metal bites on his boot tips helped him steady his pace, and in a few moments, the old man was working his way down the narrow sinkhole with the skill of an expert. *Careful of the edge*, he reminded himself when he'd gone along for a while. The "topwall"—the ceiling—of the vault should be coming up soon.

His boot tip scuffed down, measuring, feeling for the end. *Don't screw up now, you old crank!* he warned himself. True, in his past, he'd rappeled countless hundreds of times, but he was seventy now. Even a free-drop of only a few feet could break a hip or blow out a knee.

Careful, careful . . .

Now he was lowering his full body weight by the strength of his arms alone. The vault's absolute darkness seemed to swallow him whole.

Lower . . .

Where's the damn floorwall!

. . . and lower still. The total blackness leeched all sense of dimension; to some primordial part of his psyche, his feet could be dangling over a mile-deep shaft. That mental image—compounded by the darkness which now just seemed to get *darker*—caused his heart to buck again. He knew he wasn't strong enough to pull himself back up into the confines of the sinkhole where at least he could brace himself. Now his arms trembled, and he realized his only recourse: let go and free-drop.

He didn't have to command his hands to release the drop line. All strength in his gloved hands gave way, and he fell—

Please, God! Save me!

—all of maybe eight inches before his feet landed on the cenote's floor.

Idiot. Crazy old fool.

But he thanked God nonetheless.

He stood still in the blackness, letting his heart beat down a little, regaining his true senses. *I'm here. Finally.* The impact of that fact eventually struck him:

I'm the first human being to set foot in this place . . . in ten thousand years . . .

He reached down, felt for the line he'd tied his flashlight to, then gripped it in his hands. He waited a moment, then—some tawdry sense of dramatics—the flash-light poised but still unlit. *When I turn this on, I will see a fragment of what just might be the most arcane history ever discovered in North America . . .*

Then: "Enough melodrama," he told himself aloud. "Instead of standing here like some seventy-year-old retirement-home kook, turn on the goddamn flashlight."

But a few more seconds ticked by, and he didn't.

He could only guess. It was historical human nature to be afraid of the dark but right now, it seemed, Fredrick was afraid of the light.

Why?

There are dismembered bodies on the floor, he thought. *Hierarchal Ponoye Indian priests. How did they come to be dismembered?*

He was afraid.

What sheer horror went on here back when the last Ice Age was ending?

These were generally not the typical trepidations of an historical scientist. Men like Fredrick thought in terms of carbon dating, soil stratifications, of weights and measurements and core samples. His world existed in terms of objective features, not—

Not emotional, illogical notions like fear.

After all, what did he have to be afraid of?

Whatever had perpetrated the gruesome atrocity that

had taken place here was surely long gone. There were no ghosts in Fredrick's cold, sensible, scientific world. There were no devils. The Ponoye worshiped lower demons out of the same mechanics of formative superstition that influenced all species of early man. They believed in them, yes.

But demons did not exist.

When Professor Fredrick turned on the flashlight, he saw that he was clearly wrong.

Demons *did* exist.

And one such demon was reaching for him now. . . .

Part One

Chapter One

(I)

It was always brightly lit. It was always so silent.

It was always the same.

Clare knew it was a dream but somehow that fact never occurred to her while she was having it, which made it all the more cruel. Being raped was like remembering your own murder after being resuscitated. Hadn't enough things in her life gone wrong? Why did fate see fit to curse her with the damnable thrice-weekly dream?

In the nightmare she was as paralyzed as when it had actually happened: he'd injected her with something. She couldn't move but she could feel everything. The most chilling words she'd ever heard resounded now in their slurring, retardate horror: "Duh-duh-don't worry, Clare. I wuh-wuh-won't hurt you till I'm done." He grasped the scratch-awl in his bizarrely deformed right hand, just a thumb and forefinger—a birth defect, she'd been told. The left hand was normal. For some reason, the details of the event—in recollection—were never as disturbing as that single image—the deformed hand.

Then the hand did things to her, caressed her, prodded her in places—she just wanted to jump up and scream, fight back as viciously as any woman could, *kill* him, but of course none of that had happened. The drug had paralyzed her as effectively as a broken back.

She couldn't flinch. She couldn't even squirm.

All she could do was lie there and watch, see everything, *feel* . . . everything.

He'd chosen to rape her in the base autopsy suite, the examination lights bright in her face, the skin on her bare back shriveling against the cold steel table. Then . . . the simple, awful silence. The only thing she could hear was his lips smacking and her heart hammering. He'd bitten her several times too, each clamp of his teeth like electricity shooting through her flesh.

She'd been used as a piece of meat, her precious life and body vandalized for this pervert's amusement. It didn't matter that he hadn't actually injured her—the bites had barely broken the skin—and it didn't matter that after he'd had his way, the post guard had come in before he could start to work on her with the awl. What shocked Clare was the attitude of the JAG office, the look on all their faces that said "She was asking for it." The rest of the outrage played out over humiliating months, with headlines in the base newspaper every week like: "Arraignment Testimony Suggests That 'Raped' Lieutenant Was Lying," then "Judge Says No Rape Trial For Lt. Prentiss; Court Martial Instead." The perpetrator had an alibi, the duty guard was paid off, the semen test came back negative, and she failed every polygraph.

It was all a setup.

After "Tailhook," the sex scandal at Aberdeen Proving Grounds, the "Rapist Drill Sergeants" of Fort

Letterwood, etc., Uncle Sam would not tolerate any more damning national headlines.

And neither would Colonel Harold T. Winster, the research corp commander . . . because the perpetrator was Winster's son.

Instead, good old-fashioned corruption and sexism had kicked Clare right off the scales of justice.

She sat up groggily on the narrow-mattressed bed. The barest traces of dawn were filtering in through bent window blinds. *Another day, another handout*, she thought. The room she awoke in didn't smell very good; homeless shelters never did. The light snoring from the other bunks rose and fell in a constant flutter. Clare awoke like this every morning: in shock, in disbelief. And mad as hell.

That's not me! she thought when she looked at the other women asleep in their racks. *This isn't me! I DO NOT belong here!*

She didn't. But she was here anyway, and had been for months now.

Sky-high SAT scores and a college education with a 3.9 GPA didn't matter at all, nor did the military security clearance classification of Secret-SI. Her discharge from the U.S. Air Force, in fancy Gothic letters, read DISHONORABLE along the top. Any employer who ran a basic criminal-background and credit check was immediately greeted with her discharge status. Her degree in Criminal Justice was worth less than a roll of toilet paper now; no police department or security firm in the country would touch her. Her outstanding service record before her court martial was moot, and so were the commendations and the valor medal. In every way, shape, and form, Clare Prentiss's name was proverbial mud.

Even the most basic minimum wage jobs were not available to her; the Tampa Bay area's tourist-dollar economy was very competitive. Trying to get a job working in the popcorn stand on the St. Pete Pier required an application and interview process that would eventually unveil her dishonorable separation from the military. It was ridiculous. Janitorial positions, dishwashing, garbage removal—the jobs were out there, but no one would hire her. She'd applied for one job with a contractor that cleaned dumpsters. "Hiring you is asking for trouble," he'd told her. "Why should I hire you when the next person in line *doesn't* have a dishonorable discharge?" The employer's point couldn't be denied, but—*Dumpsters, for God's sake! They won't even hire me to clean dumpsters!* The oyster-shucking job faired as well. "This is a job for morons, honey, but I need *honest* morons. Sorry, you're too great a risk," the boss had said. Clare had just about lost it. "What's the risk?" she'd countered. "Because I have a dishonorable discharge, you're afraid I'm gonna do what? Steal *oysters?* I'm gonna stick a few in my pocket every night and walk out with them? Sell them on the street for crack money? Jesus Christ, can't somebody give me a break?" The proprietor just shrugged: "I'm a business man. I got no obligation to give you a break. The fact of the matter is you got a shitty background, so I'm not gonna hire you. Sure, it sucks a girl with your education can't get a job shucking oysters . . . but you should've thought about that before you fucked up your life." Clare wanted to take him down right then and there, three-point him on the floor till he started crying. Instead, she walked out.

"I did not fuck up my life," she whispered to herself

now, in the ratty homeless-shelter bed. "I was set up and I was ripped off."

But no one wanted to hear *that*. That was the story for every woman down on her luck. It was *someone else's* fault. They believed that one about as much as they believed that any convict you ask is really innocent.

That's what the world was saying to her now: *Tough luck, honey*.

The sweat on her skin felt like slug slime. She squinted at her watch in the meager morning light: 04:57. The fine mil-spec chronomatic watch only reminded her that she'd have to give it up very soon. Four hundred dollars retail but she'd be lucky to get fifty for it from the St. Pete pawn-shop shylocks. Her security platoon at the base had given it to her when she'd made 1st LT . . . back when she was somebody, back when she was respected and liked. Back when she had a life.

The shelter staff would be coming in in an hour to wake them up. The nightmare had foiled any chance of a decent night's rest, and there was no point in trying to fall back to sleep now—the deformed hand of her rapist would be waiting for her, she knew. Why give it the satisfaction? *Time to un-ass this place*, she thought. The buses wouldn't start running out of Williams Park for another hour, and if she was lucky she could catch the Missionaries of Charity truck on 4th Street for a free sandwich. She grabbed her clothes off the metal fold-down chair by the bed and whisked herself quietly to the latrine. The Florida heat was bad enough, and the shelter was not air-conditioned. Clare felt gross, her bra and panties sticking to her. A nice cool shower was what she needed. Maybe that would improve her mood.

Then again, maybe not.

Aaaaaaaaaaaaaaaaw, damn it! she thought. *The deodorant test!*

True, she was a bum by any standard now, but with no drug or alcohol dependencies, she at least qualified for private product testing. The money wasn't much but it was better than nothing. Today, of all things, she was testing a new roll-on deodorant, with an ungainly stipulation: she wasn't allowed to shower for twenty-four hours. *Charming. It's going to be high nineties today*. Another kick in the tail.

Don't bellyache, she resolved. *Just go with it*.

She tried washing her hair in the sink but the faucet was too short and the basin too shallow. She had to settle for just a hand and face wash; then she pulled on her clothes and rushed out of the shelter onto the street.

Downtown St. Petersburg was beautiful in the morning . . . if you looked to the east, toward the water. Looking west provided an abundant display of stained-brick bum motels, pawn shops, and alchy bars. She clenched her fists so hard her nails nearly drew blood in her palms when she arrived in Williams Park and saw all the winos and transients sitting calmly in the grass eating sandwiches. The sandwich truck was driving away.

She stood at the corner, foot tapping, tempering herself, *demanding* of herself: *I will not cry. I will not scream. I will not lose it. There are tons of women in the world a hundred times worse off than you, so . . .* DEAL WITH IT, CLARE! *It just so happens, for whatever friggin' reason, that you're having a bad day. Just . . .* DEAL WITH IT.

Sometimes she actually believed it might be some defect in her spirituality, that some deity—God, Buddha, Whomever—was punishing her for squandering a life once rife with opportunities, for just not resolving to be a good person.

Yes, sometimes she actually considered that possibility.

"Damn it," she whispered aloud. "I *am* a good person. There's nothing wrong with me. I'm gonna pick myself up and fix my life."

She had exactly five quarters in her pocket. That would get her on the No. 35 bus to 66th street. There were no transfers here so she'd have to walk the thirty blocks from there to the Hillover Products Testing building.

Fine. It would be hard but she was going to do it.

Just do it and quit griping. One step at a time.

Through the plexiglass of the bus shelter she gasped when she saw the scrawny, destitute woman with chopped blond hair and sunken eyes standing there. Scuffed jump boots for shoes, crumpled khaki pants several sizes too large, and the soiled olive-drab t-shirt that read U.S. AIR FORCE TOP PISTOL TEAM—MACDILL AFB. The woman, of course, was herself, her reflection in the plexiglass.

Clare's lower lip trembled when she stared harder at the truth of what was really happening to her. She was starving, emaciated. Her whole life was going down the drain.

A tear glimmered in her eye.

In the garbage can she noticed a brown paper bag—carry-out Chinese food. The half-eaten egg roll in the opened white container looked mighty tempting, but she just wasn't there yet. There were ants in it. *I'm not going to eat garbage*, she thought with conviction.

Wait, what's—

She reached into the bottom of the bag and nearly

squealed when she found several plastic packets of duck sauce and hot mustard. They hadn't been opened. And, better yet, one cellophane-wrapped fortune cookie.

She felt ashamed that others were seeing her like this; nevertheless, the condiment packs tasted succulent. She crunched down the fortune cookie. Delicious.

Then she read her fortune:

SOMETHING VERY GOOD WILL HAPPEN TO YOU TODAY.

(II)

Kari Ann's next climax seemed to flatten her. Yes, she was being *crushed* by her passion, she was being *compressed* by her need. A dropout in the fourth grade, Kari Ann Wells wasn't really educationally furnished with a clinical understanding as to why this might be . . . and she really didn't care, either. For instance, it would never have occurred to her that the long-term crystal meth habit might have something to do with it. She preferred to think of herself, instead, as a passionate woman who pursued her physical desires in a feminine, natural way, not a societal urchin hopelessly addicted to variant amphetamines and subsequently given to rampant sexual excess due to a subjugating environment and a connected dependency to the unnatural stimulation of certain chemical receptors in her soon-to-be-if-not-already damaged brain.

Kari Ann was a trailer tramp, in other words, an "ice" junkie and a whore, whose facility for free will was long given over to the tragedy of substance abuse. In her own mind, though, she was a vibrant, happy woman who loved to be loved.

And right now, Jory Kane was giving her some formidable love indeed.

The woods were a cacophony, the crush of night-sounds almost tactile as Jory bulled into her. Caleb had sent them back to the boat for more tackle, but they weren't heading down the path for two minutes before Jory's hand had found its way down her cut-offs. The response was almost automatic, it was ingrained in her. She pulled off her top at once, dragged him down into the nearest stand of palm trees.

"Whatever you do," she whispered, "don't tell Caleb . . ."

"Shit on Caleb," he muttered and crudely peeled her shorts off. He lowered his jeans just as quickly, then pushed her knees back into her face.

Kari was ready; she was *always* ready. But— "Aren't you going to put on a—"

Ummph!

No, the next gesture told her. He wasn't.

"Bet Caleb don't give it to you like this . . ."

Kari Ann sucked in a great breath through her teeth.

No. Caleb didn't.

God, he's huge, was all she had time to think, and then she was being skewered. But the discomfort was delicious, the abrupt penetration reaching right into her and turning on all her sexual senses at once. Like a light switch—*snap!*—and she was on and running, a hot, ticking appliance, ready to be used. Jory used her well.

The worst image winked in her mind: Caleb crunching down the path, wondering what was taking them so long, and—

Finding them.

It wasn't that Kari Ann feared the likes of physical abuse—Caleb was pretty much just a fat pud who'd never been in a fight in his life and whose idea of violence was maybe swatting a skeeter—she simply didn't want to lose the gravy train. Caleb had his own 24' by 52' trailer at Pelican Park that his parents bought him, and the trailer was fixed up real nice: window unit in every room, big Japanese TV and a VCR and a DVD, and one of those satellite dishes. He never had to work a job because he had some weird bone disease, made him walk a little funny, so he got $795 a month from S.S.I., plus a couple grand a month from his parents. See, Caleb was *upper-crust* white trash, the kind of man all women of Kari Ann's breed wanted to settle down with. He didn't smoke ice, he just drank beer and chewed tobacco, but he was sure happy to fork over a good helping of that monthly cash to his loving "girlfriend." Caleb kept Kari Ann in crystal meth, and Kari Ann kept Caleb in a falsified state of self-esteem.

A perfect relationship.

Caleb was Kari Ann's "gig," and she sure as shit wasn't going to lose it by being careless. Sure, she cheated on him at every reasonable opportunity, but she knew she'd have to be *real* careful with Jory. They were third cousins or something like that, and when Jory got out of jail the last time, he started sucking up to Caleb. Caleb, in all his insecurities, liked to be seen in public with a big tough redneck buddy like Jory. It made him feel good. So Jory had his game to play, too. And just as much to lose.

Her sweat soaked the crinkly forest bed beneath her. Jory pounded on. If her feminine real estate were a flower bed, Jory was digging it up from the roots, weeds and all. Her ecstasy was devouring her, and her first orgasm exploded. Jory's sexual capabilities reduced her to a small, warm, wet *thing* whose only purpose in the world was to squirm in the dirt and feel pleasure.

As much as she hated the suggestion, she whispered up between thrusts: "Honey, you're gonna have to hurry! Caleb's gonna come looking for us—"

Jory, ever the romantic, immediately pressed his palm across her mouth. Hard. "Quiet, bitch. I'm tryin' ta get it."

Now Kari Ann could only breathe through her nostrils. The rough and rude treatment offended her . . . for about five seconds, and then her pleasures seemed to only be heightened by this gesture of abusive disregard. Her eyes bulged upward into the night. Through the sprawling heads of palms trees overhead, she could see the moon, and the moon seemed to look back at her just as intently, as if monitoring her, a silent voyeur that was content to witness her pleasures.

She just writhed and writhed as further climaxes burst deep up inside of her.

In her bliss, she managed to think, *Poor fat little Caleb. I hope he's having fun with his fishing rod.*

Caleb winced at the slight twinge in his back whenever he cast. He tried to adjust his fat on the lake's sharp ebb, but that just brought more spider webs of pain. The osteopenia was a bitch, but aside from that, he couldn't complain. He was so fortunate to have cracker-rich folks and a nice double-wide. *And thank the Lord for my wonderful, loving girlfriend,* he thought. *Plus my great new best friend, Jory.* See, Caleb was a humble guy, and he didn't take anything for granted. Then again . . .

I wonder what's taking 'em so long . . .

All he'd done was send them back to the boat for

some more jiggers and bigger weights. Turned out the lake had a lot more chop than he'd expected; Caleb was gunning for some of the famed Crackjaw Eel, and this lake supposedly had them, but he needed a deeper sinker. He'd had his fill of saltwater fishing—he could catch grouper and sheepshead in his sleep—and he'd fished most every pissant lake in the whole bay area. Caleb needed some new digs, and that's why he decided to chance it and come here, here being Lake Stephanie, Lake Stephanie being a *protected* lake on a federal fish and game reserve.

Jory had helped him with his gear; he'd also made short work of the fence with the boltcutters. This form of trespassing was a federal offense, sure, and it was perfectly likely that anything Caleb might catch would be a protected species.

But Caleb was a big *ballsy* redneck, see? A tough guy who wouldn't be thwarted by any No Trespassing sign. He was a *man's* man, and by God if he wanted to fish this lake, he was damn well gonna fish this lake. In fact, Caleb was sure that his masculinity and lack of respect for the law was what turned Kari Ann on about him. Oh, and his sturdy good looks too. There was a lot of muscle under that beer gut.

Kari Ann and Jory were good sports to go along with him; they weren't into fishing much, and Caleb understood that. Fishing was like bowling, an *intricate* sport, a hobby for a man with brains. It was really nice the way they were always so eager to help him out in his disability. They were true friends. Caleb knew he'd ask Kari Ann to marry him soon, and of course Jory would be the best man.

Ain't nothing out there more valuable than a good woman and a good friend.

Moonlight floated on the ripples in the water. It lulled Caleb, made him drowsy. The eight cans of Keystone Light were helping out a bit, too, but that didn't matter. *Damn it,* he thought, and looked around. *They still ain't back? If I didn't know better, I might suspect 'em of . . .*

No need to even finish a perverse thought like that. Caleb knew there was about as much chance of Kari Ann cheating on him as there was the sun forgetting to rise tomorrow.

But his lures just weren't getting down there; they weren't holding. Crackjaw Eel, Graysby Catfish, Scamp Trout—they were all waiting for him in this lake, and he sure as hell hadn't come all this way to leave with an empty cooler. *I need heavier rigs in this chop!*

Guess I'll have to pick my big ass up and go back to the boat myself, he resolved. *Kari Ann and Jory must'a got lost.*

Caleb was about to get up when—something hit.

He set his hook, began to reel 'er in—

Pound and a half, two, maybe, he judged by the pull. Trout? Didn't feel like it. There was barely any fight at all. He reeled it in, and—

"Well, ain't that the screwiest thing . . ."

What hung off his rod, alive and kicking, was a lobster.

Caleb loved lobster, and this was a good sized one at that. But there was a big problem. Lobsters were saltwater decapods, and Lake Stephanie was a freshwater lake as sure as Florida oranges were orange.

"Hmm. Don't that beat all."

Not a man for much deep thinking, Caleb dismissed the fluke and put the frisky, tail-clapping creature in the cooler. It would never occur to him that what he'd caught wasn't really a lobster but a crawfish—twenty to thirty times larger than normal.

"Dang!"

Another hit, a hard one right after he'd recast. When he set the hook—

"*Double* dang!"

—his rod bowed like he was hauling in a brick. *Got me a big one! It's about dang time!* Eight beers and osteopenia notwithstanding, he stood up now to reel in his prize.

Then his "prize" bucked back so hard, his fishing rod was jerked right out of his hands.

Caleb couldn't believe it.

The rod flew back and landed in the water. *What the hell could THAT have been?* Caleb wanted to know real bad, and he also wanted his rod back. He could see it floating there, several yards out, by the float on the handle.

With difficulty, then, he waded out into the water, knee-deep, then hip-deep. *That rod'n works cost a good two-fifty. Ain't gonna give it to the drink.* And what kind of fish could that have been? In freshwater?

"Had to be something real big—"

Caleb suddenly stopped in the water.

Something *real big* brushed against him.

Don't panic.

He stood stock-still, hands poised.

Behind him, again, something big—something six or eight feet long—swam against him.

Fuck the rod'n reel. I'm gettin' OUT of here—

He turned very slowly, so not to agitate the water, raised one foot to take the first step forward back to the shore, and—

WHAP!

The water surged. Foot-wide jaws hit Caleb right in the crotch and clamped down. He fell over, screaming, splashing, reeling a frantic circle in the water as his predator reeled with him: an eel—yes—ten feet long and a foot in girth. The great jaws locked down harder; Caleb was paralyzed in agony, incapable of responsive action, incapable of even heaving out one last scream before the creature's sheer weight and crude animal strength hauled him beneath the water, into—

Silence. Blackness. Terror.

Caleb's brain impulses were still firing away, though all human reason was gone now. He would simply drown in this cold frenetic horror, with this thing gnawing on his groin. He would never fish again. He would never slug another Keystone. He would never make love to Kari Ann again, and he had slapped his last high-five with his good friend Jory.

Then, just as he would die—

A hand grabbed his collar and pulled him out of the water.

"Jory, thank God! Get this fuckin' thing off me!"

Eventually the eel let go, the gnawing gristly pain abated, and Caleb heaved breaths in a nearly mindless relief.

I've been saved! I've been saved!

Back on shore he collapsed in exhaustion, looked up at Jory, and . . .

It wasn't Jory.

Caleb wished he was back in the water again, with the eel, when he got a look at the face of the thing that had pulled him out.

Kari Ann lay naked and blissfully exhausted on the forest's soft carpet of fallen palm leaves and moss. She was the little love-sprite of the woods, a tropical Venus lounging in her plush domain. Her hair tousled, her skin shellacked in sweat, she breathed in the warm night air, gazing up dreamy-eyed to the stars. So peaceful, so natural, so beautiful . . .

Jory urinated loudy a few feet away, and during the same process he also belched, cleared his throat and hocked, and cut a long fart.

To seal the romantic moment, Kari Ann bid: "Sweetheart, I'm going apeshit I'm stringing out so fuckin' bad. Get the pipe; let's get all fucked up."

"I'm peein', girl!" he griped back to her. By the sound of it, he was starting a new estuary. She could see him aside, between the palm trees, hands on hips and back arched—whizzing away. *What a man . . . So handsome . . . It's too bad Caleb has so much money, 'cos I'd—*

The thought squashed her. *Shit! How could I forget?* "We were supposed to get those thingies out of the boat, Jory! Caleb's gonna be here any minute!"

Jory pulled his jeans on, then seemed to fiddle with something. "That fat puddin'? He's fishin'. Fuck him."

"But, Jory—"

Faint orange light briefly turned Jory's rugged face into a flittering mask. He was firing up his pipe!

"Jory! You're gonna share that with me, right?"

Jory made a sharp huff. "What do I look like, Santa Claus? You want dope, fuck a dealer." He inhaled briskly, in hot hitches. "Get some from your fat lover boy."

Kari Ann's frown was as deep as the night. Men. What a bunch of bastards. *After you give 'em what they want, they crap all over ya.* It was a sad resignation, but one she was quite used to. She lay back again, her fingers laced behind her head. Staring up at the sky. Even

Jory's rudeness couldn't destroy this moment of beauty for her—

thwup . . .

It was the tiniest sound, but . . . strange. Something had hit the ground. A coconut or something? No, Jory had probably just thrown her clothes at her, the rude prick.

She sat up, looked down—

And screamed so loud her lungs burned.

Cross-eyed and tongue sticking out, Caleb stared right back at her—Caleb's severed head, that is.

The head had been dropped in the area of leafy space between Kari Ann's spread legs.

Locked in horror, she pumped out quite a few more screams, so high and loud that birds lifted from the trees and lizards skittered for cover. Jory was walking toward her, and in her mostly paralyzed mind she reasoned that he was coming to help her.

But he was walking kind of funny, dragging his feet, and it looked like he was bringing something over, carrying something in his arms, and now he was standing right in front of her, and that's when he dropped what he was carrying.

He dropped it right into Kari Ann's lap.

An armful of his own innards.

The hot entrails slapped right into her, splattering her, and Kari Ann's response to the gesture was reasonable: she screamed higher and louder.

Jory fell over, the slit in his belly yawning as more of his lower g.i. tract spilled out.

Kari Ann kicked and screamed as the large unseen hand dragged her by the hair slowly and steadily into the woods.

But the evening still had much in store for her.

(III)

"You didn't wash, did you?" the huffy overweight woman asked in a rather insulant tone.

"No, ma'am," Clare replied.

The *ma'am* seemed to calm the panel leader down at once. It was actually three overweight women who sat before her at the table, and Clare was incredulous when she noted the little plaque that read OFFICIAL SNIFFING PANEL.

"The reason I ask is that—and don't take offense, dear—but people like you have a tendency to disregard instructions."

Another fat woman kind of chuckled. "Then again, people like you don't wash all that much anyway, right?"

People like me, Clare realized. *Homeless people, people on the skids. Bums.*

"Don't listen to her, dear. We understand your plight; that's why we allow a few of you to take advantage of the opportunity to take part in our tests. You know, to help you out a little."

Clare ground her teeth and took it. "I appreciate it very much, ma'am."

"Good. Now please remove your shirt and raise your right arm."

Clare did so, self-conscious that her poor diet had actually shrunk her breasts to the point that her bra sagged.

Each woman walked by and sniffed her armpit, then sat back down.

I can't believe I'm doing this. I'm letting fat ladies sniff my armpit for money.

"Very good, dear. Now put your shirt back on."

"That's it?"

"For now, yes." The leader's triple chin jiggled a bit when she took a fast glance at her watch. "It's ten o'clock now. Your next sniffing is at noon, then you'll have another at two."

"What should I do in the meantime, ma'am? Stay in the lobby?"

"No, no, dear. Go walk around in the sun."

"And don't wash!" another woman added.

"After the two o'clock sniffing, you'll get your twenty dollars."

"Yes, ma'am. Thank you, ma'am." Clare paused in thought. *I just thanked a woman . . . for sniffing me. Jesus.*

"You're a fine, respectful young girl, and since your blood tests are negative for alcohol and narcotics—unlike most of your kind—I'll sign you up as a regular tester. It'll mainly be soap, deodorant, and shampoo. If you keep your appointments, you'll make sixty dollars per week."

"I'm very grateful to you, ma'am."

"Good. Run along now. We have to begin our write-up."

Clare left the office, left the women to—evidently—write down descriptions of the smell of Clare's armpit. She didn't know whether to laugh or cry. To her, sixty dollars a week was *a lot* of money. They tested these new products for skin rashes, allergenic reactions, etc., but she would gladly take the minor risk. And once she started getting more food, she could get her protein-count back up and start selling her plasma too. Then she'd really be rolling.

Outside, back in the blaze of morning sun, she actually smiled. Unconsciously her hand slipped into her pocket, felt the tiny fortune from the cookie she'd found in the trash.

It had promised good things for her, hadn't it? Strange as it seemed, it was coming true.

Don't take anything for granted, she warned herself and headed across the parking lot. *Sure, it's going to be hot as hell today, but I'm gonna walk around in it and LIKE it*. It should be nothing anyway. In the service, she always maxed out every PT test. She'd do twenty-mile field marches with a full pack and barely break out in a sweat. Today she was actually going to get paid for something.

Yes, it was a good start, and who knew? Maybe it would even get better.

"Clare Prentiss?"

The man had seemed to appear from nowhere, out of the glare of sun bouncing off car roofs. Tall, thirties, sharp-looking in a light well-cut suit. He seemed to have walked away from a shiny Mercedes convertible, a new one.

Immediately, she thought: *Cop. Narc, probably*. In Florida, they all drove high-priced unmarkeds; they were drug-seizure cars.

"No," Clare said, and tried to walk by. She had nothing to hide but she just didn't like this.

"Social Security number 220-75-2516?"

Damn it! Who is this guy?

"Who I am is my business. Have a good day."

She walked on.

"We simply ran your SS number in the county database; that's how we knew you'd be here, Ms. Prentiss," he nearly jabbered, trying to keep up. His Guccis clapped the hot asphalt. "It's perfectly legal. Oh, my name's Dellin."

"What do you want, *Dellin?*" she asked without stopping.

"Well, like I said, I want to know if you are Clare P. Prentiss, formerly first lieutenant with the Air Force Security Service, 31st Bomb Wing, 1st Security Detachment, MacDill Air Force Base."

Clare stopped, fists at her sides, infuriated. "Yes!"

This Dellin person took a long look at her, exchanging a glance at her face with what must be a personnel photo on the clipboard he held.

"Wow, I guess . . . you've fallen on some hard times, huh?"

"No, I always dress like this!" She started walking again, fast. This whole thing stunk; she needed to get out of there. There were still vagrancy laws in Florida. Cops down here were well known for trucking stray derelicts to the Georgia border and dumping them off, and there was only one place worse than Florida for a bum to be, and that was Georgia.

"Wait!"

"I haven't done anything wrong! No, I don't have an address, I don't have a job, I don't have any visible means of support, but I'm not a criminal so leave me alone, officer!"

Then he started laughing. "You think *I'm* a cop? Do I look like a *cop?*"

She didn't answer, just kept walking. Fast.

"Jesus, I'm not a cop, I'm a cortical mitoectonologist!"

Even Clare, in her urgency and anger, had to stop at that one. She frowned, squinting at him. "A *what?*"

"I'm a—" He waved a hand aside. "Long story. I'm a scientist, that's all."

"What the hell do you want with me!"

"Relax, will you, Ms. Prentiss?" The short jog after her left him winded. "All I want to do is offer you a job."

Chapter Two

(I)

The island was V-shaped, the last of a string of barrier keys that began just off of Clearwater, Florida, and stretched down some twenty-five miles along the Gulf of Mexico. In fact, it was the southernmost island in this region, connected to the remaining line of islands by a single two-lane cantilever bridge, its only access to any areas of population. The base of the "V" pointed at the mouth of Tampa Bay—hence its original purpose as a naval garrison.

Fort Alachua Park was constructed in 1898, to safeguard the bay from the United States' latest enemy: Spain. But the Spanish "empire" never summoned the audacity to launch a credible attack; if it had, the fort's hefty 12-inch seacoast mortars and rapid-fire anti-ship rifles would have promptly relocated any offensive vessels to the bottom of the pristine waters, where most of the Spanish navy wound up anyway. The construction of the fort, ultimately, was criticized by some members of Congress as a colossal waste of the U.S. war department's money because it went virtually unused thereafter, until 1942, when the Army Air Corp developed it into a practice range for aerial bombing runs.

So perhaps it wasn't such a waste after all; a couple of fellas by the names of Tibbets and Ferebee learned to drop bombs at Fort Alachua. Though these two men only dropped one bomb together in combat, they proved a formidable team. Tibbets was the pilot and Ferebee the bombardier of a plane called the Enola Gay.

In 1960, the fort became an official listing on the National Register of Historic Places, not only for its past as a military post but for its existence as a complete subtropical habitat. Within the long, angular confines of its 900 acres, there was a spring-fed lake, a mangrove, a bayou, a hardwood forest, and seven miles of untouched white-sand beach. Today, the impressive artillery remained, as did the original stone barracks, observation posts, and the Tudor-arched headquarters bastion which now functioned as a museum—in all, a terrific draw for tourists. It was an even better draw, however, for nature-enthusiasts; the most unique of Florida's flora and fauna could all be found at Fort Alachua Park, and its additionally unique geography made it one of the very best Gulf-side parks for camping, boating, fishing, and nature-trailing.

In the mid-'90s, the park's entire eastern wing was closed to the public.

(II)

What choice did she have? Well, a more pragmatic choice might have been to walk away rather than get into a car with a perfect stranger. Clare's instincts told her that this handsome, well-dressed man named Dellin was probably not a murderer or serial-rapist but then Theodore Bundy was handsome and well-dressed too. Desperation, here, overrode basic common sense. She'd been homeless for almost a year, and all of a sudden here was this sharp, amiable guy in a fancy car offering her what she needed more than anything else in the world—a job. Clare knew that she had only one true choice.

She got into the car with this perfect stranger and let him drive her away.

It was little consolation but she still remembered all her hand-to-hand combat techniques. *If he tries anything freaky*, she reasoned, *I'll kick his ass*.

Simple.

He'd said he was some kind of scientist, and after they got on the road, he was forthright enough to show some identification without having to be asked. DANIELS, DELLIN, THE NATIONAL INSTITUTES OF HEALTH: TRANSFECTION AND MOLECULAR TARGETING. Clare didn't know what in the Sam Hill any of that meant but the ID was clearly official.

"So . . . what about this job?" she asked.

"Same sort of thing you were doing before. Security work."

Clare liked to think of her work as a military-police platoon leader in the Air Force Security Service as something a bit more significant than "security work." She wasn't guarding a candy store; she was in charge of perimeter protection of highly classified database facilities for the Air Force Clinical Research Corp. Still, she was in no position to complain. *Minimum wage, probably*, she guessed, *but it sure beats twenty dollars for sticking my armpit in a fat lady's face*.

"You've heard of Fort Alachua Park?" Dellin asked

next. He'd gotten off the highway and was now turning off in front of the Don Cesar—like a pink castle—the most famous hotel on the coast. Moments later, he was heading south on one of the barrier keys. *We're going to the beach?* Clare wondered. "Fort . . . what?" she said.

"Fort Alachua Park. That's where we're going."

She gave it some thought. "I was born and raised in Maryland. I spent four years in Florida, at MacDill, but to tell you the truth I was always so busy with my platoon, I never got much of a chance to see anything beyond downtown Tampa. Never even went to the beach. So I don't know much about the area. I've heard of Alachua Park but never been there. It's a big campground or something, right?"

"All that and a lot more." Dellin kept driving down the main drag. The posh beachfront hotels had thinned out to a quieter residential district. "During the winter it's a big tourist spot, great for nature hikes, canoeing, fishing. It's probably the most diverse campground in Florida, because it's got a little bit of everything. There's a spring lake, palm groves, a real glade and a real bayou. The nature freaks love it—during the winter, that is. During the summer, it's so insufferably hot and humid and mosquito-infested that no one comes anywhere near the place."

"Sounds like paradise," Clare said. "Can't wait.

"Don't worry, the clinic's air-conditioned."

"Clinic?"

Dellin shook his head. "Sorry, I'm getting ahead of myself. The bottom line? We want you to run our security operation at our cancer clinic."

"A *cancer* clinic?" Clare couldn't help but sound startled. "You built a cancer clinic in a tropical campground?"

"I know, it sounds strange, but it's all because of budget cuts. Fort Alachua is technically owned by the U.S. Park Service—in other words, an arm of the federal government. The federal government can't afford to buy new land for new projects, so they simply cut Fort Alachua Park in half. The west half is still a public park. The east half is now the private property of the Department of the Interior, and the Department of the Interior, in a manner of speaking, lets the Air Force use it."

"Oh, fantastic. You want me to work for the Air Force again," Clare sputtered over her confusion.

"No, you'll be just like me," Dellin said. "I'm on loan for the project from the National Institutes of Health. I don't work *for* the Air Force, I've simply been subcontracted out. Same thing with you; you'll be a civilian sub-contractor. I know you're not too cool with the Air Force, you know, after what happened to you, but don't worry. It's all civilian-run. No Air Force personnel on the property, ever. The Air Force funds the project, because they own the patent on the drugs."

Clare shrugged in exasperation. "What drugs?"

Dellin tapped himself on the head. "Jeez, sorry. It just occurred to me that you don't even know what happened. Your last duty station, the Clinical Research Corp, found a cure to one the absolute worst forms of cancer."

Clare's brow rose high. "*Really?*"

"Yeah. It was about a year ago, right around the time you got discharged. They invented a drug that targets tumor cells and destroys them in a type of cancer called stromatic carcinoma. It's always been untreatable because it spreads so fast; it's the fastest-growing cancer that exists. The Air Force found an immune agent that stops it cold, cures it, sometimes in as little as a month. It's quite a breakthrough."

"Yeah, it sounds like a *huge* breakthough," Clare agreed, but couldn't quite quell her cynicism. "So how come I haven't heard about it in the news?"

"Because it's not FDA approved yet. That's why they built the clinic—FDA-approved human testing began a couple weeks ago."

It sounded thrilling but . . .

The Air Force? Clinics? Land annexations?

I don't get ANY of this, Clare thought.

"Look, I know the details are confusing," Dellin continued. "The reason that it was legal for the military to annex half of the park is because they agreed to officially re-categorize the east sector as a Natural Habitat Reserve. That way none of the new environmental laws would be broken. Typically when *military* research happens to lead to a discovery that would improve public health, the research is then picked up by the U.S. Health Department. The reason that didn't happen in *this* case is purely political. If significant cancer treatment is derived from *Air Force* research, the Air Force gets a larger budgetary allotment for *future* research. Ordinarily, the military cuts stuff like this loose as fast as they can 'cos they don't want to bother with it. Let's face it, military research is supposed to lead to better ways to kill people, not save them."

"But because this is so significant," Clare deduced, "a major *cancer* treatment, the Air Force doesn't want to give the credit to civilians and lose a potential cash cow."

"You got it," Dellin said. "Security isn't a big issue at a cancer clinic, of course, but then you've got to consider the military mind-set. The spooks in the Air Force don't want any other parties stealing their research."

"Industrial spies," Clare remarked.

"Right. You and I both know nothing like that is going to happen, but the Air Force is anal-retentive about it. And there is a reasonable threat of theft simply because—"

"Cancer clinics use all kinds of painkillers, mostly morphine derivatives," Clare figured. "You need security to keep the local dopeheads from busting into the place and running off with their next high."

"You nailed it on the head."

She felt better about the whole thing now that she had more details. One part still didn't fit, though.

Why me?

"You seem to have gone to a lot of trouble to find me," she observed. "You do know that I'm damaged goods as far as the Air Force is concerned, don't you?"

"Oh, your discharge status? Sure. Don't worry about that."

His nonchalance on the matter was encouraging—which made her suspicious. "For a job like this, regular security work, why not just run an ad in the paper?"

After a short laugh, Dellin explained, "We can't just hire someone off the street for this job. What you said before is quite right; there's a *lot* of morphine in a cancer clinic. Same reason we can't hire people from a bonded security contractor. We need people with federal-level background clearances. Do you know how much it costs to have one of those done on someone new? More than a couple of these cars. But you've already been cleared. The other security staffers are ex-military too, MPs. Already cleared and already trained."

"Yeah, but my case is a little different. I have a *dis*honorable discharge—for perjury," she reminded him.

"They say I lied in a military court, that I—"

"Made up a story about being raped. I know. Don't worry about it."

Clare sat back with a soft frown. *Still sounds kind of fishy*, she admitted. "This is a minimum-wage job, I presume?"

Dellin shot her a shocked glance. "Oh, no, don't misunderstand. You're going to be *chief* of security at the clinic, not some guard punching a clock. I'm authorized to offer you a starting salary of $52,000 a year, plus free health and dental. In this day and age, I realize that's not a whole lot of money for someone with your experience but—"

Clare was incredulous. "Fifty-two *grand?*"

Suddenly Dellin seemed nervous. "Uh, er, plus a yearly COLA raise, ten-percent bonus if you stay twelve months, yearly contract after that, that you can negotiate. Wow, I'm really sorry if you're insulted by the offer."

He's serious! "I'll take it," Clare said. "When do I start?"

"Well, immediately."

Clare knew she could do it but now, all at once, other problems began to occur to her. *Shit. I'm homeless. I have to get clothes, I have to get a place to live. Is this damn park even on a bus line?* Embarrassed, she admitted, "I have some things I need to take care of, you know? Do you think it would be possible to get a small advance from my first paycheck?"

"Oh, I forgot—sorry." Dellin handed her an envelope.

A curiously *fat* envelope.

"We're not *total* skinflints," he said. "Here's some cash to cover moving expenses."

Clare's mouth hung open as she counted out $7,500

in $100 bills. "This is—*Jesus!* This is a lot of money."

"It's just the standard relocation allotment."

She couldn't remember being so excited. "I can buy clothes, get a used car, and still have enough leftover for a down-payment on an apartment!"

"Buy all the clothes you want," he said, "but you won't need a car. The employment contract provides the security chief with a new SUV free of charge. We pay for the gas, the insurance, everything. Oh, and you get a free apartment, too."

Clare almost collapsed in her seat.

"It's a nice one-bedroom cottage, right on the bayside beach, and it's brand-new too, not some dive. We built a small complex of cottages close to the clinic, for convenience. I live there, and so do the other members of the security staff. You can live in town if you want but rents are sky-high."

A cottage. On the beach. Free. "I think it'll do," Clare said, still astonished.

"And you'll love the area. Sure, it's hot as hell this time of year, but once you see the park, you'll understand what I'm talking about. It really is a tropical paradise."

Ahead of them, a long straight road bisected the barrier island. Sand dunes swept by on either side, backed up by lone stands of spiring palm trees, then came the beach. Through the trees, the water looked brilliant lime-green. The sky was cloudless, flawless blue. In her last year of destitution, she'd forgotten just how beautiful the Florida coast was. *And now I live here*, she thought.

Or so she hoped.

"I guess you'll want me to take an aptitude test of some kind, right? And what about my interview?"

"You just had your interview," Dellin said, and

winked at her. "You passed. I'm the admin director; I do all the hiring. Your Air Force commendations and that distinguished service award cover the aptitude test. You're hired."

Suddenly, a short burst of chuckling overcame her. "Looks like I don't have to make my noon sniffing."

"Huh?"

"Nothing. So you're my boss?"

"Nope. We're going to meet the boss now."

NO TRESPASSING
PARK CLOSED BEYOND THIS POINT
EAST BEACH CLOSED
EAST PIER CLOSED
ALL CAMPGROUNDS, HIKING TRAILS
AND NATURE HABITATS ARE
CLOSED!

The sign at the end of the main road was large as a garage door. Bright-blue with white letters. "Gee, I guess the place is closed," Clare remarked. It was quite a contrast to the previous, more cheery WELCOME TO FT. ALACHUA PARK signs that had marked the last two miles.

"That way—" Dellin pointed right. "That's the main leg of the park. That's where all the campgrounds and hiking trails are. And, as you can see—"

They idled around a sharp turn, the joining-point of the island's distinct "V" shape. Here, overlooking the mouth of Tampa Bay, stood the actual cut-stone edifices of the fort. Many of the ramparts looked as if they'd been built recently, the cannons at the ready, barrels up. Several tourists meandered into the rotunda-roofed visitor's center.

Then Dellin pointed left. "This is us."

Another hundred yards of perfectly straight roadway brought them to an unmanned gate post.

"Talk about a punch in the eye," Clare commented.

"Yeah, ugly isn't it?"

The high double-layered fence shined like tinsel with its rolls of brand-new stainless steel razor wire. More traditional barbed wire filled the gap between the two fence layers. The last two miles of the ride had shown Clare a nearly inconceivable range of natural beauty—to all be abruptly severed by this unsightly gate post.

"Only employees and patients have gate access, and at this early stage we don't even have a lot of patients coming in. All told, it's less than twenty people. The gate's all bark, though, not a whole lot of bite," Dellin said. A remote in the car opened the gate. "The fences don't span out very far into the woods."

"Appearance is ninety percent of effective security . . . and that gate makes *quite* an appearance," Clare commented. "A lot of wahoos would take one look at that security fence and turn right around, go somewhere else. That fencing wire is 460 steel; most boltcutters won't go through it, and even if they could manage to cut a hole, they'd never get through all that barbed wire."

"We certainly *hope* it projects that kind of deterrent effect." They drove through; the gate hummed as it quickly closed behind them. Clare easily noted the video cameras too, staring at them from high brackets in the trees. "And if that doesn't, maybe this will."

The next sign couldn't have been more clear.

RESTRICTED AREA
USE OF DEADLY FORCE AUTHORIZED BY SECTION 21, INTERNAL SECURITY ACT OF 1950- 50 U.S.C. 797
ALL TRESPASSERS WILL BE FIRED UPON.

"Wow. This looks serious. You have armed sentries here?"

"Yeah. You. And two others. Like I said, mostly bark—the budget won't provide for any additional guards. There's one ranger from the U.S. Park Service, but his jurisdiction stops at the gate."

"Why? It's all federal land, isn't it?"

"Yeah, but it's not open for public use anymore. Legally, there's a difference between U.S. parkland and a habitat reserve. Security of a reserve is the responsibility of the 'endorsing entity'—in this case, the Air Force. The Florida department of natural resources has no authority, either. As for the park-service guy, he only comes by our end once a week for potential violation reports, or, every once in a while you might see him staking out one of the favorite poaching spots. Any violation against the land itself, we report to him, but it's always just minor stuff."

"Can you give me some examples?"

"Some redneck carves his girlfriend's initials in an endangered species of palm tree, or tears up a replanted tropical hillock with his dirt bike, stuff like that. Oh, and fishing. You'll get your bearings soon enough, but the east end of the island is made up of three spurs that branch off the main stretch. On the middle spur there's a pretty big freshwater lake that's stocked with endangered fish. So every now and then the rednecks from south St. Pete sneak out and try to rip us off. The lake's one of the off-compound areas you'll have to keep an eye on."

So far, sounds good, Clare thought. But she wouldn't be presumptuous; Dellin clearly wanted her for the job, but she still had to meet the manager of the clinic, and regardless of Dellin's influence, she knew that a bad impression could jeopardize the whole thing. She looked down at herself and realized quite bluntly, *I look like a pile of crap. My clothes are dirty and crumpled, and I stink. If the boss of the place sees me like this, he'll boot my butt right back out the door, probably with a clothespin on his nose.*

"I really need to get cleaned up before I meet the boss," she peeped. "I want you to know that I don't always look like this."

"Don't worry about it," Dellin said for the third or fourth time. "There's a shower and locker room at the clinic. You can get cleaned up and put on a security uniform. You'll look fine."

She sighed in relief. She still had a multitude of questions but now the scenery was sideswiping her focus. The island's main stretch seemed to exist in perfect symmetry: the perfectly straight road, the perfectly straight run-off gullies, then perfectly straight rows of palm trees. "Now, check this out," Dellin said and smiled at her. He turned left, onto a well-leveled dirt road, and stopped.

Clare caught her breath. The road—again, a perfect straight line—seemed to *bore* into the forest, a virtual tunnel through a dense tropical woodland of hundred-foot-tall palm trees and Australian pines. The two trees marking the entrance were joined at the very tops by sprawling leafy vines and Spanish moss, like a natural archway. One moment the sun was beating down on them hard, but the next . . . the car moved slowly into a cool quiet dimness, a scape of unblemished nature unlike anything Clare had ever seen.

"Some sight, huh?"

"Yeah," Clare agreed. "Just a little bit prettier than Bum Row in downtown St. Petersburg."

"In this park there's a little slice of every natural geographical example in the state of Florida, and almost every example of fauna and flora. Working here is almost like being on vacation seven days a week."

"I see what you mean," she said, "but—"

She couldn't quell the sudden shot of pessimism. All those months in the shelter or sleeping under bridges and waiting for the handout truck had imbued her like a stain that wouldn't come out. "I have to tell you, Dellin. I'm not one to look a gift horse in the mouth but this is all too good to be true."

Dellin glanced at her, smiling. "Or maybe you just deserve something good for a change."

Clare sat back in the breeze. *Yeah. Maybe I really do. . . .*

Chapter Three

(I)

Essentially, Kari Ann no longer possessed the mind of a human being. All she was running on now were her nerves, adrenaline, and basic aboriginal instinct. Pockets of memory flashed every once in a while but only for seconds, replaying the horror of last night: Caleb's decapitation, Jory's disembowelment, and . . . what came afterward. Something else haunted her too, just as intermittently—a high, wheeling noise like a cat on fire, but then Kari Ann realized she was simply remembering her own screams.

Sixteen hours later, naked and mauled, she lay completely buried in the forest's detritus, only her nose and one eye exposed. Last night, the man who'd killed Caleb and Jory had dragged her through the woods for what seemed hours, but every fifteen minutes or so, he seemed to take a break—to rape her.

That's how the night had gone—*all* night.

She'd never seen her attacker—he preferred her on her belly, in the dirt—she'd only felt him, the grueling and almost perfunctory violation of her body. He'd never said a word. Resistance was useless, though, even unwise, as she learned fairly quickly. His arms felt firm as dried cement, and his grip—like a vise. Once she'd kicked him, aiming for the groin, but she'd missed. He'd responded to the action by merely grabbing her wrist, which he squeezed until—

crack!

—her wrist broke.

Later, she'd started screaming again, and evidently it was beginning to annoy him. He'd yanked her up by her hair, slapped the palm of one hand against her lips and sealed her mouth closed. With his other hand, then, he pinched her nostrils together. He let her smother slowly, shuddering, and at just a moment or two before she would die, he released her nostrils—only to pinch them shut a second later after she'd had time to wheeze in one breath. He did that for a while, pinch and release, pinch and release, until she got the message: Don't Scream. She got the chance to test her resolve right then and there; the action of alternately bringing her to near-death via asphyxiation caused him to grow aroused again, and then she was slammed back down on her belly in the mud and taken once more.

This time Kari Ann didn't scream.

She'd done some bad things in her life, and in the brief snatches of cognition now, she actually realized that. Cheating on Caleb, sure, and ripping him off every chance she could, but that was nothing. There was that drive-by, though, a couple, three years ago. This was long before she'd hooked up with Caleb. Her boyfriend at the time had bought some bad flake, turned out to be oregano with no PCP on it at all! They'd driven right back to the same street corner in southside; her man had opened up with a Taurus 9-mill, fourteen shots.

Killed the player who'd ripped them off, peeled his cap bigtime.

Killed a little boy, too, riding his bike on the next block.

But Kari hadn't done the shooting, she'd only been driving, so it wasn't really her fault, was it?

What else had she done that was really bad? She'd turned plenty of tricks in her time, and when her herpes was active, she didn't bother telling the john. But that was the john's problem. She'd dealt her share of crank and crystal meth too, but, hey, that was the life. Back when she'd been dealing, she had no reservations about turning on kids at the schoolyard. Kids were easiest, one or two tokes and they'd be hooked. First thing they'd do is run right home, steal all the money out of mommy's purse and come back for more. Easy money.

She had plenty more sins, in fact, but reflecting on them now wouldn't really do her any good. Yes, it was true. She'd done some pretty bad things in her life.

But were they bad enough to warrant a death like *this?*

Last night, she'd lost track of how many times her assailant had violated her. She was insensible, half-paralyzed from shock. She didn't even feel the pain anymore; each time he grasped her by the hair to drag her on, like someone pulling a duffel bag.

Had she actually died and gone to hell?

Was this it?

Was this her punishment for all those bad things she'd done in her life: to be raped by this faceless man *ad infinitum?* To be dragged naked through swamps and creek-muck and sawgrass beds and thickets? *Forever?*

No.

Because long into the wee hours, she'd escaped.

She didn't know how she'd gotten so lucky. He'd been dragging her further through the woods but suddenly there was a great thrashing sound and he dropped her. She'd been in and out of consciousness for the last hour, and her brain was only half-firing now, but when he dropped her, it jogged her senses enough to realize that something had happened. She rolled over in muck—they'd just entered a salt marsh at low tide—and she opened her eyes.

The clouds had broken and a great full moon beamed down on the marsh. There was more of the thrashing, then a loud snapping, followed by louder *thwacks!* and that's when Kari Ann's eyes were able to register what was going on. Her attacker was wielding a long stout branch like a weapon, slamming it into the ground, trying to hit—

Kari Ann's heart seemed to freeze in her chest.

—a ten-foot alligator.

The animal surged forward, the monstrous jaws snapping down.

"Eat him!" Kari Ann yelled to the alligator, her voice raw and whistling. "Bite the motherfucker's head off!" and then she was running blindly away into the woods, fast as an animal herself. Her attacker's back had been to her the whole time; she hadn't seen his face nor any other details, just that he was naked and muscular. But Kari Ann didn't *care* what he looked like. She just ran.

By then almost every square inch of her skin had been creamed in creek mud and swamp scum—perfect camouflage. Her best hope was that the alligator made mincemeat of her assailant but she knew she better not count on that. If he survived, and came after her, it wouldn't take him long to find her. Her sprint through the woods sounded like an avalanche, and the more deeply she progressed, the more the trees shut out the moonlight. She had no idea where she was going, no clue as to the best way to get off the accursed island.

So, instead—she buried herself.

She dove onto the ground and completely covered herself with leaves and forest mulch. *I'll lay here and not move a muscle till daybreak. If I hide all night, maybe he'll go away, figure he lost me. And even if the motherfucker doesn't, I'll stand a much better chance of finding one of the camp trails when the sun's up . . .*

And there she lay, all night long.

It was, in fact, the smartest move for anyone in such a predicament. What she didn't count on, however, was the extent of her exhaustion and shock. She fell asleep at once . . . and slept well beyond daybreak.

By the time she woke up, she was baking in her cocoon of detritus. The sun through the treetops seemed high in the sky—past noon. When she wakened, a normal mental function still alluded her; she was dehydrated now, and an empty stomach since yesterday along with the amphetamine withdrawal didn't help. At least she had a few senses together—enough to realize that last night was no dream.

Caleb, no head, she thought in chops. *Jory. Gutted. By that guy. Gotta get the fuck. Outa. Here.*

She had to find a main road, either that or—

Boat!

They'd come here on Caleb's boat!

Now if she could only figure out where it was . . .

But then another thought occurred to her, a crucial one.

Guy. Raped me all night.

Where was the guy? Had he given up on finding her? Had the alligator gotten him?

Even in her reduced mental state, she luxuriated in the fantasy: the alligator taking her assailant apart piece by piece. The head would be saved for last, of course; those huge jaws would crack it apart like a styrofoam ball, let the brains loll awhile on the mammoth tongue . . .

But there was no time for fantasy now.

As more awareness returned, she sat upright with a start, her cover of leaves bursting around her. *YECH!*

There were bugs all over her.

Panicked, she brushed several off her breasts at once, then quickly reached around and picked one out of the cleft of her buttocks—

—and nearly screamed aloud when she saw the size of it.

It was one of those wood roaches, as long and wide as a shot glass, and nearly as round. She could feel more down there, crawling lower, but then—

crunch-crunch-crunch—

Footsteps.

The reactive horror caused the blood vessels in her brain to swell, till they were fit to burst.

Him!

She slithered back down beneath the pile of leaves, covered herself over as fast as she could but as delicately too, so not to make an excess of noise. In just a few seconds, Kari Ann was buried again.

The slow, steady progression of footsteps crunched closer, louder. Kari Ann listened for voices, for talking—any indication that it might be campers or hikers coming through. But there was nothing, and it was clearly just one person.

It had to be him.

She lay still as a corpse, well realizing that that's what

she would be—a *corpse*—if she breathed too loud, coughed, flinched, or made even the most minuscule sound or movement.

Still, the footsteps crunched closer.

The humid muck from the forest bed lay on her body like a hot, damp heavy-pile carpet, but through the tiniest gap between some of the leaves on her face, she could see a little. She could see an area of space to her right, and judging by the sound of the footsteps, her attacker would be walking right by her.

crunch-crunch-crunch-crunch—

Louder. Closer.

Then Kari Ann stifled the sharpest urge to flinch, to even squeal. She'd forgotten about something, hadn't she?

The wood-roaches.

They were still there, of course—more of them now—massing on her skin mostly around her buttocks, inner thighs, and pubic region. It was reverse torture: the urge to pick them off but knowing that if she did, she'd be right back in the clutches of a rapist and cold-blooded murderer. The effort to resist moving felt like slow electrocution beneath her heavy cover. And the wood-roaches . . .

The wood-roaches were roving through her pubic hair now, heading lower, heading for the nearest source of moisture.

The current of her revulsion was peaking now . . . just as her assailant—

crunch—

—stopped.

He stopped cold, right next to her.

Could she hearing him sniffing? And what was the

sound that came next, something like a low, guttural grunt?

Through those tiny gaps in the leaves on her face, she could see legs, from ankle to thigh-level. His skin was mottled and seemed grayish in the dappled sunlight, and like hers, it was flecked with all manner of filth from the bayou and woods. And—

What was that, swinging at his side?

A bucket?

Yes, she could see it quite clearly. He was carrying a long, foot-wide plastic bucket.

This would've seemed quite a bizarre fact to contemplate save for a couple of *other* facts that were present at the time.

One, Kari Ann, by now, was half-insane, and—

Two, the wood-roaches had now found their way into her vagina.

Her heart-rate had surely trebled. Could he hear it? Was she whimpering beneath the muck and just not aware of it?

Could he *smell* her fear?

Just as her drug-wrecked, torture-and-rape-traumatized mind became convinced that he was reaching down now to slap the muck off her face, haul her out, and break her neck while he raped her a final time . . .

He stalked away.

Kari Ann waited a full twenty minutes, lying buried as if dead, before she unearthed herself, and scurried off in the opposite direction.

Her lungs wheezed in the new freedom, her soiled feet and filth-smeared legs hurtling her through the forest. She picked out the disgusting roaches while she ran, not knowing where she was running to but running just the same, away from *him*.

The woods seemed to darken, the palms and pines overhead so dense they were tenting out almost all sunlight; nevertheless, to her left, she could see light that was blindingly intense, and then it finally registered:

The water!

Was it Lake Stephanie? Was it one of the passes between the spurs of the island, or perhaps the Gulf itself?

She slowed down, glancing over her shoulder, then thrashed to the trees just before the shore and stared.

For the first time in her life, perhaps, luck was with Kari Ann Wells.

The body of water shimmered in the high sunlight, a mile-long stretch between two of the island's densely wooded spurs. It was the pass off of the bay.

And just a hundred yards or so down the nearest spur, she could see Caleb's boat, exactly where they'd left it last night.

(II)

As they'd neared, the arrowed signs read, simply, CLINIC. There was no sign on the building itself, and, like that first gate-access they'd had to come through, the clinic couldn't have appeared an uglier edifice. Sitting here, in the middle of this beautiful park? Clare would've expected something more appropriate, a log-cabin motif, perhaps, or something Isba-like with stained-wood plankwork and cedar shingling.

Nope, she thought, taking her first glance at the place through the Mercedes's windshield. *Typical Air Force. They can spend $800 on toilet seats and twenty-five bucks apiece for five-cent rivets, but they can't buy a decent architectural blueprint.*

The pitched roof had been built at an unsightly high angle, for hurricanes, she guessed, and the rest of it stretched on as a long one-story building with drab, oddly narrow windows and an overall structure of what looked like enameled cinderblock. The color scheme? Pale gray.

"The word 'institutional' comes to mind," Clare said when they were getting out of the car in the small asphalt lot.

"It's a sore thumb, all right, considering the surroundings," Dellin commented. "But you know the military: all function, no style. The Air Force could care less about what things look like as long as they get the job done . . . and speaking of getting the job done, see that old guy there?"

A thin, elderly man with a cane was slowly crossing the parking lot to a waiting car. Balding, stoop-shouldered, and what little hair he did have was snow white. He paused to wave at Dellin, then hobbled on.

Dellin waved back. "That's Mr. Hanklin. He should've been dead a month ago. Cancer of the intestinal stroma spreads so fast you wouldn't believe it."

"I've never heard of that kind of cancer," Clare told him.

"The stroma is a kind of connective tissue around the organs of the lower abdominal cavity. It's not even that rare anymore, but the reason your average person isn't familiar with it is because it's not in the top ten. Lung, liver, prostate, breast, and ovarian cancers are the leading killers. Stromatic cancer isn't too far behind. It's unique because it's virtually untreatable. Chemo, radiation, surgery—none of that works because it moves too fast. By the time it's diagnosed, it's already spread all over the place, and when it spreads, it accelerates the malignancy wherever it goes. In other words, when it spreads to the lungs, the cancer *there* becomes untreatable too. It makes the cancer of any place it spreads to just as unique because it mutates the growth markers in the cancer cells. We're talking about the mother of all carcinomas."

Clare followed him across the well-shaded parking lot. "But now you can treat it, because of some drug the Air Force invented?"

"Right. It's a monoclonal antibody, similar to older cancer treatments, only this one was genetically engineered. We call it Interthiolate. It was Air Force research that identified the exact gene-marker that initiates the growth of each cancer cell. By identifying that gene-marker, we were able to genetically manufacture an antibody that molecularly targets the marker itself, destroys it. It stops the cancer cold. Then the immune cells come in and wipe out all traces of it." Dellin chuckled as they approached the clinic entrance. "So far we've had eight patients participate in the trial, and eight cures. If we keep maintaining results like that for another six months, FDA will fast-track our drug and have it on the market in a year. We'll be saving a whole lot of people from one of the most painful kinds of cancer there is."

Clare was astounded, and she appreciated Dellin's effort to explain the highly intricate matter in layman's terms. It sounded to Clare that she would be working for a facility that might become very newsworthy very soon.

But what was happening to *her*, right now, overplayed the clinic's potential importance for the moment. Her life was about to change; someone had finally given her a second chance. She knew she couldn't blow an opportunity like this.

The inside of the clinic appeared as she might have expected. Sterile decor; light, solid tones; muzak. Anatomical diagrams hung on the walls instead of drowsy art prints, and accommodating little murals like HAVE YOU CHECKED YOUR BLOOD PRESSURE TODAY? DON'T FIND OUT WHY THEY CALL IT THE **SILENT KILLER!** and AFTER FIFTY, GET YOUR PROSTATE CHECKED EVERY YEAR! It was the kind of stuff that would always be found in a military medical facility: overt and styleless but efficiently to the point. They'd obviously decorated here by Air Force interior-design protocol, which didn't surprise Clare. "You'll love this, it's another great perk for employees," Dellin said and unlocked a door that read STAFF AUTOMAT/BREAK ROOM. "Only security and higher-level med staff get a key to this place. There's a public automat in the building but it's no big deal and you have to pay. But here it's free and it's really top quality stuff." There was a long couch, a knee-high table with some magazines, and a television. One small wall was fully taken over by a commercial-grade automatic coffee machine that offered a variety of types.

Clare immediately saw what he meant. "Maybe you don't know this but free coffee is every security guard's dream."

"And it's really top-notch gourmet coffee too, not the swill you'd usually find in machines." He pointed to the end of the unit. "There's the guards' favorite right there—it'll make all the iced coffee you want. The guards love it because they're out in the heat a lot when making rounds."

"It's an expensive perk," Clare noted, "but it actually makes great business sense. Security facilities in the Air Force do the same thing. When your guards are chugging free coffee all throughout their shift, they're not falling asleep at their post."

"Never thought of it from that point of view but, yeah, a great idea. Help yourself. I'm going to grab a water. Free bottled water and sodas too, in the fridge."

Clare took full advantage of the benefit, got a big cup of the iced coffee and loaded it up with cream and sugar, which would provide a great pick-me-up considering she'd consumed no calories today save for her lucky fortune cookie. *Good God, that's good!* she thought after the first sip. It was a test for her not to gulp it all down right away but she didn't want to appear gluttonous in front of Dellin.

"I'll give you your security key later," Dellin said, taking her back out. "It opens this, the security office, all the interior doors, and the monitor stations. Each key is individually coded—a provision mainly for you, as security chief."

"Coded?" Clare asked. "Oh, you mean with some kind of individual ID flag?"

"Yes. So the security computer can make a record of who goes where and when. For instance, when I unlocked the coffee room door, the computer logged it, so now it's been recorded in an entrance file that it was my key that opened the door."

"This is a great system," Clare enthused. "We used similar equipment in the Air Force. So all the doors in the building are wired?"

"Pretty much. Exterior doors and windows have active alarms, but just about every keyed door is connected to the computer."

"Well, that makes my job a lot easier."

"To tell you the truth, this alarm system is so intricate, even I don't know all of its functions," he said. "And I'm the one who ordered it."

"That's just another thing for you to *not* have to worry about. I can run systems like this with my eyes closed."

Dellin took her deeper into the building and showed her to the female side of the employees locker room. "My office is right down the hall," he said. "Just come by when you've gotten cleaned up. There are some uniforms in the supply room over there."

"Thanks. I won't be long."

Dellin left and suddenly Clare stood alone in the long, impeccably clean room. She stripped off her old clothes, grabbed a towel, and hurried into the shower—

"Oops! Sorry!"

As Clare was stepping into the shower room, she walked right into another woman who was just leaving.

"My mistake," Clare blundered. "Didn't think anyone else was here so I wasn't paying attention." She hoped the flash of embarrassment wasn't making her blush; as quickly as she could, she wrapped her towel around herself.

"It's so damn hot during these day shifts that I always take a quick shower during my break," the other woman said. She was naked, dripping wet, and didn't have a towel at the moment, yet she didn't seem the least bit uncomfortable standing in front of a perfect stranger without a stitch on. In her past life, Clare would never have been inhibited either—during her military service, she'd virtually lived with other women and had dressed and showered with them perpetually. But her embarrassment, at this precise moment, couldn't have been more plain.

The other woman was robust, heavily bosomed, glowing in good health, while Clare knew she looked terrible by comparison—bony, ribs showing, breasts tiny.

"I'm Joyce," the other woman introduced and shook Clare's hand.

"Clare."

"Don't mind me!" Joyce grabbed a towel, wrapped her long auburn hair up in it. She put one foot up on the bench and began to dry off with a second towel. As she bent over to dry one toned, tanned leg, a key swung before her, from around her neck. "I've got to get back to work."

A hint of jealousy now mixed with Clare's embarrassment. Joyce was beautiful, her short, compact frame accentuating her curves, waistline, and wide hips. The full, very deep tan made it clear that she sunbathed nude. "What do you do at the clinic?" Clare asked next. "Are you a doctor, a researcher or something?"

"Nope. Security guard." Now she was stepping into a pair of khaki slacks with a black stripe down the leg. "And I've got to really be on my toes today, because they're bringing in the new security chief."

"Uh, that would be me," Clare said.

"Oh, jeez! I'm sorry, I thought you were a, er . . . I had no idea!"

I'm so skinny, Clare thought, *she probably thought I was a patient*. "Yeah, Dellin's going to brief me in a few minutes. I was a SECMAT platoon leader in the Air Force for four years."

"Wow. Uh, I'll be out of your way in a minute." Suddenly Joyce was rushing; now that she knew that Clare was her boss, she seemed a little more modest, quickly buttoning her security shirt up over her ample breasts.

Along one wall, Clare noticed a Lexan gun locker

containing some shotguns, and another one containing bullet-proof vests. "Dellin was telling me earlier that there isn't much trouble on the site." She pointed to the lockers. "But those are police-grade vests and late-series Remington pumps. Do you ever really need that kind of gear?"

Joyce had hauled up her trousers and was tying up her work boots. "Not really, but we have it just in case—because of poachers. But if you were an SP in the Air Force, you already know the story on vevlar vests. I'll wear mine at night sometimes, but during day shifts? Forget it. It's way way too hot."

Clare knew exactly what she meant, especially in this environment. Ballistic vests and tropical heat didn't mix. "Yeah, at MacDill, my skin was always breaking out from the damn things, so I'd only wear it on critical security details."

"Same deal here," Joyce said. "We almost never wear them, and we never sign out the scatter guns, either. For a security site like this, they really are overkill."

Clare saw her point. But she couldn't stave off her curiosity about the perimeter and its potential. "Any homicides out here?"

Joyce chuckled. "Oh, nothing like that."

"What about arrests? You ever have to bust anyone?"

"We detain a trespasser on occasion but we turn them over to the police or the Park Service. But from what I've been told, that's another thing that almost never happens."

Dellin's tone had been similar, and that's what worried her. *They seem to be a little too confident that nothing really serious could ever happen out here . . .*

Joyce was dressed now. "I have to get back on my rounds. It was great meeting you!"

"Same here. You can show me around the site later."

"Great! Bye!"

Joyce was striding out when Clare interrupted her. "Wait, Joyce? Aren't you forgetting something?"

The younger woman turned, then blushed when she saw Clare pointing to her gunbelt hanging off an open locker. "Oh, great! What a terrific first impression! Sorry."

"That's all right."

Joyce grabbed the belt in haste. "See you later. I look forward to working with you."

Then she was gone.

Clare had to laugh to herself. *She's a little young but seems nice enough.* Clare had little doubt that, with proper training, Joyce could develop into a fine security guard. She seemed motivated, enthusiastic.

The cool shower felt sinfully indulgent; she wished she could spend an hour under the hard torrent, but there would be no such luxury today. She dried off and dressed quickly. Though even the smallest-sized uniform was big on her, she did her best with it, and thanked the fates for the hair-dryer on the wall. Her blond hair only came down to the mid-neckline but it was straggly, untrimmed for quite a while. If anything, it looked like she cut it herself—which was true, since hair salons didn't usually work into a homeless person's budget. But the blow-dry let her puff it out until she was reasonably happy with it. *There. Now I don't look QUITE so much like a wino that just crawled out of the gutter.* She left the locker room in a rush and went straight to Dellin's office. *First day on the job is no time to be late.*

"Sorry about the Afrika Korp-looking uniforms but we got the best deal on them," Dellin said. His small, cramped office was made even more cramped by two big computer screens and three walls of ceiling-high bookshelves.

"The color will reflect the heat pretty well," Clare offered. "It doesn't really matter how a uniform looks as long as it identifies the person wearing it as someone in a position of authority."

"Good point." He put away the patient charts he was reading. "I think I said before, we only have two other guards, Rick and—"

"Joyce," Clare finished. "I just met her."

"Ah, good. So I don't need to tell you that we have to cut corners on the scheduling. We won't get a budget increase till next fall, so we'll have to go with the three of you till then." He gave her a smile. "The schedule's your problem now. I've got Joyce doing eight a.m. to four p.m. and Rick four to midnight. Midnight to eight we go guardless and rely on the alarm system."

That was the worst possible schedule. Clare had learned well that alarm systems alone during peak crime times were never sufficient. "I'll take care of the schedule then. We'll go blank from noon to four, and I'll take midnight to noon."

Dellin looked at her. "We don't expect you to work shifts that long."

"It's a piece of cake and it's the best way," Clare said with little concern. "I'm used to it from the Air Force, and since I'm in charge of security, I don't mind losing a little sleep to prevent screwups. I don't want to *lose* my job the week after I'm hired. Whatever your security problems are, I'll take care of them."

"I love your attitude. I wish I could be as enthusiastic. You'll find out quickly—things get damn boring around here."

"Good, and it's my job to make sure they get *more* boring."

The statement amused him. "That's inconceivable but please feel free to prove me wrong. Anyway, since we were talking about scheduling, there's still some good news and bad news. The good news is, the clinic is closed on Saturdays and Sundays. Nobody needs to report, including security."

"Everyone gets the weekends off?"

"Yep." Dellin grinned mischievously. "Everyone *except* the security chief. You'll be on call all weekend. If an alarm goes off, you get beeped. If delivery comes in, you open the loading dock and sign in the delivery. If a motion-detector gets triggered at a punch station, you get beeped. That's the bad news. If you have a problem, you call the ranger, and if it's a serious problem, you call the police and then me. It sounds like a big hassle but it's really not that big a deal. Like I was just saying? Things are boring? Believe it. Not much happens out here, and just because you're on call doesn't mean you have to be on the site. For all we care you can go downtown, or sit in your cottage and watch tv all weekend—as long as you have your beeper. You can lay out on the beach in your bikini from sunup till sundown—but if your beeper goes off, you have to respond."

Clare shrugged. It wasn't really bad news at all, especially when she considered the pay and the benefits. "In the Air Force, I was on call for almost every weekend for four years. It won't be a problem."

"You'll get the hang of everything in no time." He led her out of the congested office and down the hall. "Now, let me give you the twenty-five-cent tour."

The facility proved unremarkable—essentially what Clare expected. Screening rooms, examination rooms, and a central treatment room equipped for surgery. There was a CAT scanner and an MRI machine, ultrasound, and typical other diagnostic coves.

"Check this out," he said next. "Perfect example of Air Force indulgence." He opened a door marked IRMT, which showed them a room containing a bank of computers, an examination table, and several large nozzle-like heads hanging from the ceiling from hinged braces. "Because this is a cancer clinic, the Air Force automatically supplied it with this machine. It's an intensified radiation modulator—a tumor killer, the very latest in cancer technology. Multiple matrixes of low-dose radioactive beams essentially put a cross hair on a malignant tumor. It can destroy a tumor the size of a BB without harming any surrounding healthy tissue."

"That sounds amazing."

"It is." Dellin laughed. "But we don't need it. This machine is useless against the kind of cancer we deal with. We told them we didn't need the machine but they sent it anyway; said that it was 'Air Force inventory protocol' that the machine be delivered. Ridiculous! This thing costs half a million bucks."

More waste and imprudent expenditure, but Clare had seen it all the time.

The clinic seemed larger inside than it appeared from the exterior. Next to the automat was a small cafeteria and dining area, staffed by two civilians. "Believe it or not, the food's pretty good here and it's dirt cheap," Dellin informed her. "Even though there's no Air Force personnel on the premise, the clinic is still considered a military karserne."

"So the food's discounted, like a PX," Clare supposed.

"Right. T-bone steak for two bucks. Fresh grilled fish, broasted chicken, all kinds of good stuff. Everybody who works in the clinic eats here every day. They even have all-you-can-eat ribs every Wednesday. Do yourself a favor and take advantage of the services. No offense, but . . . "

"I know," she admitted. "I'm pretty thin. A one-hundred-pounds-in-the-rain security chief doesn't make much of a visual presence of authority."

Clare smelled onions grilling, and steak. The succulent aromas reminded her how hungry she was, and how long it had been since she'd had a good meal.

First thing on the To-Do list, she thought. *Pig out.*

"Yeah, it's always best to look the part. How much confidence would my patients have in me if I weighed three hundred and chain-smoked? Same thing. And since we're sort of on the same subject," he said, pausing.

"Yes?"

Dellin seemed slightly uncomfortable now, his gaze moving about on the floor. "Uh, yeah. It's your business, of course, and I'm not implying that you have anything to be ashamed of; I realize that you got a bum rap in the Air Force and all. All I mean to suggest is that it would probably be to your advantage to keep all that to yourself, especially the lousy luck you've had since your discharge. It might—you know—"

A cruel truth. "It will decredulize me in the minds of the personnel I'm in charge of," she fully understood. "It'll be hard for anyone to take the security chief seriously if they know she's spent the last year standing in shelter lines."

"It's good that you can look at it that way."

"I'm not *ashamed* of what happened to me, because I didn't do anything wrong. But all that crap is behind me now—thanks to you. I'll do a great job for you."

"I'm sure you will," Dellin said.

Next he introduced her to some of the medical staff: tomographers, nurses, technicians, all of whom seemed competent and amiable. She found her eye wandering a bit, though, to Dellin himself. *Kind of a fox,* she thought, though she wasn't quite sure why she'd make an observation like that. She was trying to focus on her job. But with his jacket off now, tie loosened and sleeves rolled up, Dellin seemed even more attractive to her than before. Beneath the tailored shirt, he was clearly in shape, his arms strong and well-defined, broad shoulders. *Get your mind right off of that kind of stuff!* she yelled at herself. *Pay attention! Do your job!* But it definitely wasn't her style to be sizing a man up like that. *Get real. He's probably got a knockout for a wife and a bunch of kids.*

She got her mind back on business: site familiarization. "Here's your office," Dellin said, and showed her the small security cove. Pretty sterile. Desk, computer, file cabinet, key safe. A civilian-grade radio set sat in one corner, and a row of small black and white tv screens showed several areas of the clinic's interior and exterior.

"Great," she approved. "Closed circuit video cameras."

He showed her the console buttons. "There are ten cameras on the site, five inside, five outside. You've got six live monitors, A through F. You punch the buttons to pull up what you want. Probably an overkill expenditure."

"Sure, but it can't hurt."

"Here are your keys," he said next, and got a small key ring out of the desk. "You have a master key to every lock on the site—that's the personal security key that I mentioned earlier. Each of the other guards has a master too. Plus you've got this ring of duty keys, plus there's a second set for whichever guard is on duty."

Clare took her keys, then put her stringed master key around her neck and let it fall into her tunic. It tickled, cold, between her breasts. "Don't worry, we won't have any problems with key control."

"Same goes for this too, I'm afraid," and next he handed her a small beeper. "Like the key, you have to keep this with you all the time. But don't feel bad—" He pointed to an identical beeper on his belt. "I have to have one too."

"No problem," Clare said, and snapped hers on.

Next, Dellin led her down another hall. As they passed more coves and exam rooms, Clare's now-ingrained instinct for security caused her to take note of the locks on the doors: just typical house-grade key locks. "I hope your pharmacy doesn't have locks like these," she said right away.

Dellin seemed taken aback. "Well, yeah, it does. What's wrong with these locks?"

"They're inferior, that's what. I could open these with a bent fish hook and small flat-head screwdriver. If you've got heavy-duty painkillers in this place, you at least need a milspec-grade doorlock plus a deadbolt."

Right around the next corner, Dellin stopped. "Here it is."

The big sign on the door read PHARMACEUTICAL DEPOSITORY: NO ADMITTANCE!

Clare laughed. "You're kidding me, right?"

Dellin scratched his head. "What?"

"First thing we do is get rid of the sign. Otherwise, if someone *does* break in here, you're telling them exactly where the goodies are."

Dellin blinked. "Ah. Why didn't I think of that?"

They went inside so Clare could have a look around.

"Wow, you guys have got enough dope in here to drop Elvis," she said.

"Pretty much all morphine derivatives. All of our patients have to have it during the first stages of treatment."

Clare's eyes scanned the locked shelves. MS-CONTIN, DURA-MORPH, DILAUDID, and much more. Clare wasn't an expert on regional narcotics abuse but she did remember her several training blocks on the subject, and she knew that stolen prescription drugs were the biggest business on the gulf side of Florida, next to crystal methamphetamine. All the crack, cocaine, and heroin went to Miami and the east coast cities. "This is junkie paradise. The Dura-Morphs and any other time-released forms of morphine sulphate sell on the street for a hundred dollars per pill."

"Really?" Dellin sounded shocked. "We buy them wholesale for five bucks apiece."

"On the street, one of those pills gets cut ten times. I'd hate to think of the street value of all this stuff. Key control is very important for this room."

They walked back out, Dellin re-locking the door. "This door can only be opened by our personal security keys, and there are only five people in the facility who have them: you, the other two guards, me, and the director."

It sounded prudent but key control alone was never enough. Clare knew this well from her own professional experience. "Did you run everybody who works here for priors and drug histories?"

"Sure. Everyone's squeaky clean, even the janitors and the cooks."

"Contractors? The people who built the place? It's not

uncommon for a crooked contractor or workman to copy a key."

"The contractors who worked here were cleared first by the Defense Investigations Service."

"Good, that's what I need to hear." Clare was pleased that everything seemed to be falling into place; she wouldn't have to cover many bases herself. "So, first thing we do is take that sign down; I'll do it myself when you're done showing me around. Second thing—we really have to get a serious lock on that door, a lock like—" Then something caught her eye. She pointed. "A lock like that one," she finished.

At the furthest end of the corridor was another door. Here the sign read simply: B-WING, and on the door was not a key lock but a high-grade pass-buttoned deadbolt.

"What's B-Wing?"

"That's where we keep our patient records and our major treatment pharmaceutical, the stuff I was telling you about before—Interthiolate. Harry's the only one with access to B Wing."

"Harry?"

"The director of the clinic. From our standpoint, the Interthiolate is even more sensitive than all those painkillers in the pharmacy vault, and Harry's very paranoid about it, but I can't say that I blame him. If someone stole enough of our supply of Interthiolate to synthesize, the Air Force patent on it will be useless internationally. That's why Harry doesn't want anyone else in B Wing. He's kind of type-A sometimes but he's a nice guy. He's doing a symposium today in Sarasota but he should be back by five. Then you'll get to meet him."

At least that explained the off-limits wing, though Clare wasn't sure if it was such a good idea to deny access even to security. *It's their gig; they can run it the way they want.* "Fine, B-Wing's restricted. But we really do need a milspec lock on the pharmacy."

"I'll talk to Harry when he gets back. Getting him to send in a requisition request for a work order is like pulling teeth but I'm sure he'll listen to your reasoning." Dellin glanced at his watch, then muttered an inaudible curse. "I've got a patient coming in now, but I'll catch up with you later. Why don't you call Joyce on her radio and have her show you around the site."

"Will do. See you later."

Dellin smiled and walked off but as he did so, Clare caught herself again.

She was staring at him, wondering about the actual physique beneath the clothes.

Damn it, girl, there you go again! What the hell's wrong with you? You haven't even been on the job a full hour and you're already lusting after your boss! No, this wasn't like Clare at all and she had to wonder why. She didn't like mysteries, especially when they were about herself. But perhaps some of the more primordial aspects of her psyche were overcompensating now that she had suddenly been placed into a position of social normalcy. *I'm not sweating food and shelter anymore*, she hypothesized, *so now other instincts are kicking in, instincts that were deprioritized when I was homeless*. She'd been sexually dead since the rape, of course, and sexually inactive for several years before that, always placing her personal priorities on her job. She wanted her career well-established and rock-solid before she embarked on any serious relationship quests. It had always seemed the most sensible plan but now that she thought of it, maybe that had been a mistake all along. There was such a thing as being *too* serious, *too* sensible. She was almost twenty-nine years old now, and much of her romantic prime was behind her. *If I'd had a husband or a serious boyfriend during the rape and court-martial, at least someone would've been there for me, and I wouldn't have been homeless after the discharge.*

I played it all the wrong way, she realized now.

But *now* was clearly not the time for considerations like these. *Self-analyze yourself later*, she thought. *Now you've got a job to do. Don't ball it all up on the first day going ga-ga for your damn BOSS.*

She walked back to the security office, smiling at a patient or two along the way. The very first thing she did was grab a Phillips head screwdriver, then went immediately back to the pharmacy and removed the conspicuous sign from the door. *Now, call Joyce, have a look around the perimeter.*

But another sign rasped her eye just as she turned away from the pharmacy.

B-WING

And that's where they keep the top-secret cancer drug, she remembered. *Interthiolate*. Clare had to agree; the fewer people with access, the better, but she had to wonder if Dellin and the clinic director were being a little paranoid about the prospect of industrial spying and theft. Clare knew that the real theft target was the pharmacy vault. *I gotta find out about the alarm system, find out how many of these doors are wired*, she made a note to herself.

She took a last look at the B-Wing door, then returned to her office.

On the desk lay a clipboarded daily operating log; Clare could see that Joyce had already started it, listing her initial rounds. Clare signed in herself and noted her own primary site briefing with Dellin. Lockers on the other side of the office caught her eye. A plaque on one locker read SECURITY CHIEF.

That's me, so . . . Don't mind if I do.

She pulled up her personal security key from around her neck and—sure enough—it opened the locker.

All right! Now we're talkin'!

Hanging from a hook was a fully fitted leather gunbelt, complete with a thumb-snap holster and a six-inch Colt Trooper Mark III .357 magnum. "Works for me," she said under her breath. She had to take the belt in several notches to fit her waist, and that's when she noticed that the belt, though relatively new, had been used in the past. The belt holes were worn. At the bottom of the locker, a gold security badge shined. Clare picked it up and pinned it right on. But then—

Something else in there.

She leaned over and picked up a small brass plate. It was a nameplate.

FLETCHER, G.

SECURITY CHIEF

What the hell? I thought I was the security chief, but then it occurred to her that she must be looking at the nameplate of the person she was replacing.

Dellin hadn't actually mentioned that she was replacing anyone, but why would it matter anyway? Now she fished around in the desk drawers. It only took a few minutes of skimming some of the past operating logs to figure it out.

G. *Fletcher?* Now she saw the name on what appeared to be the very first logsheet. *Grace Fletcher. Security chief.* Dellin had told her that the clinic had only been open for about a month but Clare could see by the logs that even before the clinical trials had officially begun, there was a security operation here. *Of course.* Now it made sense. The actual security contract had begun almost a year ago, when the facility had gone under construction.

And this woman here—Grace Fletcher—was the security chief before me.

Clare sat still at the desk now, tapping a finger against the blotter. She couldn't resist the obvious curiosity.

I wonder what happened to her.

This seemed like a good time to find out.

I need to get Joyce to show me the site now anyway. I'll ask her.

She swivelled around in her chair, toward the radio set. It was a standard civilian model base station with a scanner, three multi-unit frequency bands, and a private channel. She was about to turn it on and call Joyce when—

What the hell is that?

The smallest movement caught her eye as she picked up the microphone.

Movement from one of the closed-circuit screens.

There were several screens but they weren't very large—only thirteen-inch displays. One showed the security gate on the main road, one showed the clinic entrance, and several more showed various points of the perimeter that were deeper outdoors.

On the last screen she saw something moving.

The camera showed an extended view of what seemed to be a back entrance to the clinic; she could see the building's loading dock on the screen, its single bay door pulled down, and the long dirt road leading away from it. The movement she detected was so distant, it was sheer luck she'd picked it up at all. What flagged her was the briefest wink, like a metallic flash, from a stand of palm trees and several squat palmetto bushes. And—

There it went again—the flash.

Clare stared at the screen but the detail was just too far away. "Where's the zoom on this thing?" she said aloud. "Ah, I'm in luck . . ." On the console she found the camera controls, each camera and its accommodating screen fixed with a letter. She hit the zoom arrow for Camera F, brought the frame in much closer.

"Don't tell me I've got an intruder on my first day on duty—"

The lens zoomed in remarkably tight, then she panned over to center her "intruder" in the frame.

It was a person, all right, two people actually.

Aw, no, Clare groaned in her head. *Looks like my first official write-up is going to be on my own staff.*

The flash she'd seen was a badge, a *security* badge, and the person in the frame was Joyce. The badge had winked in the sunlight when she'd opened her shirt to expose her breasts.

Right now she was in a tight clinch with another guard, a tall, dark-haired male.

"Great. That's just great."

The male guard was obviously Rick, whom both Joyce and Dellin had mentioned earlier, and it was just as obvious that Joyce and Rick were not-very-discreet lovers. Clare was maddened, not so much that she'd caught them, but because she now had a responsibility to do something about it.

Damn it!

Should she cite them in writing? Report them to Dellin? Fire them on the spot? She sighed, rested her chin in her hand. "This I don't need. Not on my first day." Her eyes strayed back to the screen.

The pair of lovers were wrapped up in each other's arms, trading deep, ravenous kisses. Joyce had Rick pushed up against a tree, and as her bare breasts rubbed into his chest, her hand wasted no time sliding down into his security trousers. Their gestures seemed frantic, desperate, as they practically mauled each other in the little cove of brush. Joyce's head fell back; Rick's mouth licked a wet line from her lips down to her jutting breasts, then sucked tight onto a nipple. When his mouth moved off, the nipple stuck out a like pink stud, and Joyce's entire body flinched when he tweaked the nipple hard with his fingers. Then his mouth licked over to the other breast, repeated the ministrations, while his hand opened brazenly over the crotch of Joyce's pants and began to rub.

Man! Clare thought. *This is some show, and now I better think of a way to end it . . .* She reached again for the radio mike but couldn't get her concentration away from the small video screen. She'd never been voyeuristic but this . . .

This . . .

It was too tempting not to watch.

Now Joyce was on her knees, Rick breathing heavily as he stood against the tree. The camera angle spared Clare the fine details but she didn't need to be told what was taking place. Part of her felt embarrassed watching it, uncomfortable. But another part of her?

Next, Rick pulled Joyce roughly back to her feet, embraced her again with vigor, and turned her around. Now it was Joyce who was against the tree, her eyes closed in bliss as Rick kissed her deeply on the mouth, his tongue plunging. Joyce's bare, flat stomach seemed to be sucking in and out in the excitement, and her large breasts seemed even larger, the nipples standing out like pinpoints.

All right, Clare, enough! This is a security office, not an x-rated theater! and as she repeated her order to stop watching the shenanigans on the screen and take some kind of managerial action—

Oh, no way! They don't possibly have the audacity to—

She stared further.

No, please! Not in broad daylight!

Rick was still kissing Joyce hard, but now his large hands were busy at her waistline. He unbuckled her belt, unfastened the front of her pants in a few steady, indelicate movements. Then he pulled her pants down right there against the tree.

I can't believe this! Clare thought.

The look on Joyce's face was like wanton rapture, her eyes radiant slits. Rick's hand roamed urgently beneath her panties, then he began to slide the panties off—

Clare could only shake her own head in disbelief but just as it appeared that Rick and Joyce were going to take their actions to the furthest limit—

Oh, thank God, Clare thought.

All at once, simple common sense swept over Joyce's expression, and she was grinning, pushing him away and shaking her head. Clare could see her lips silently saying *No no no no no!* as she pulled her security slacks back up and refastened them. Then she ran out of the frame with a silent teasing giggle on her lips. Rick slumped in an understandable frustration and walked off after her.

They must have thought the security camera was too far away to pick them up, Clare guessed. But catching them didn't making her feel particularly clever or observant either. *And they probably wouldn't have guessed in a million years that the new chief would be cranking the zoom in to the max and watching them.*

What should she do?

Of course, Rick and Joyce would need to keep their

torrid romance secret; otherwise they'd lose their jobs. It was easy enough for Clare to condemn their irresponsibility on purely objective grounds. Any way you looked at it, physical displays of affection while on duty could not be tolerated. And outright sexual activity? *It's a fireable offense, plain and simple.* No, they hadn't actually had intercourse right there in the woods but that hardly mattered. They got awfully close, and their intent couldn't be denied.

I should report them to Dellin and recommend that they be fired.

But then she remembered her own little weakness today: how many times had she caught herself dreamily staring at Dellin? *I guess I'm not exactly one to talk about moral malfeasance while in the workplace.*

She turned the microphone on, keyed it. "Joyce? This is Clare. What's your twenty?"

The radio crackled back at once. "I'm at PS-6."

Clare had no idea what that meant but a quick glance up to a site map explained: DETEX PUNCH STATIONS, followed by numbers going up to twenty-four. *PS*, she presumed. *Punch Stations*. "Okay. I need you to show me around the site now. Meet me at the front parking lot."

"Will do. I'm on my way."

You're on your way, all right—probably to the unemployment line, Clare thought, locking up the office and heading out. In the parking lot, even in spite of the sufficient shade from the high trees overhead, the heat had grown absolutely oppressive. *Get used to it*, she told herself. While she waited, a few more outpatients pulled into the lot and entered the clinic. They were all elderly and all smiling even with their grim diagnoses of cancer. *Of course they're smiling. They're being cured when a month ago their private doctors were probably telling them they were terminal*. Even though she was just a security guard, Clare found it extraordinarily exciting to be associated with a facility that had found a cancer cure. When the trials were over—and hopefully successful—Clare couldn't wait to see the news break in the headlines.

At the far corner of the lot, she noticed two parking spaces where bright yolk-yellow paint on new asphalt read SECURITY PARKING ONLY. One space was empty but in the other a shining new white Chevy Blazer sat parked. Clare walked slowly around the big fully-equipped four-wheel drive, thinking, *Could this be . . .*

Yes!

Dellin had said she would be provided with a vehicle free of charge; Clare saw at once that this must be it. Black stenciled letters on the doors read SECURITY CHIEF. Keys on her shift ring opened it; she couldn't help but take a closer look. The inside still smelled relatively new, and the upholstery looked immaculate. Air, power windows, a CD player, plus a scanner and radio unit that must be an auxiliary to the base station radio in the office.

"This will definitely do," she said to herself.

A motor roar rose up, then a smaller four-by-four rolled into the lot, with similar security markings. Joyce smiled and waved from the open driver's window.

Gee, Joyce, Clare thought in some witty cynicism, *is it my imagination or do you look a wee bit flushed?*

"Checking our your new wheels, huh?" Joyce said when she pulled up. "This is the shift truck, but that one's yours. It's great, isn't it?"

"Loaded. I like it."

"Yeah, so did the first security boss—"

"Grace Fletcher," Clare stated. She got into the passenger side of Joyce's truck. "Did you know her very well?"

"No, not really—actually it was only one day. She broke me in on the site, showed me where the punch stations were, and then that was it. Quit the next day. But she was pretty nice."

"Why did she quit?"

"She couldn't hack the climate is what she told me, but then one of the other guards told me they felt the grounds were too dangerous." Joyce drove back out of the parking lot and headed down the main road leading into the clinic. "I'll show you the eastern spur of the island first—that's the site's furthest limit—then the middle spur so you can see the bayou and quicksand."

The reference half-jolted Clare. "Quicksand? You're kidding me."

"Nope. Swamps, sinkholes, quicksand pits—we've got it all, along with snakes, sharks off the point, and even alligators."

"So Grace Fletcher wasn't exaggerating: the grounds *are* fairly dangerous."

Joyce laughed. "Walking around downtown Tampa at night—*that's* dangerous. None of the snakes are poisonous, the sharks only come into the middle inlet during the peak of summer, the alligators are more afraid of you than you are of them, and the quicksand field is completely fenced. Unless you're *really* careless, the site isn't dangerous at all."

Clare decided to save her own judgments for later. The road narrowed when they traversed the eastern spur of the island; suddenly the dense tunnel of trees opened to a completely untended beach and a stunning view of the bay. "That's some scenery," Clare commented. "And what a beautiful, isolated beach."

"Nobody goes there because, for some reason, the stingrays like this point for their breeding ground."

Fantastic, Clare thought. *Snakes, sharks, alligators, and now stingrays.*

"Oh, yeah, and the jellyfish too," Joyce added. "Certain times of the year, thousands of them float out to this point. Some of them have these stinger tentacles that are three and four feet long. Get one of those wrapped around your leg, you'll be feeling it for a week."

Clare was mildly flabbergasted. "Well, looks like I won't be going in the water. Ever."

"Oh, no, that would be a mistake. There's none of that in the middle inlet, where the cottages are. You'll be living on the island, right?"

"Yes. Dellin said I could if I wanted to."

"Well, believe me, you *want* to. It's the most beautiful place you've ever seen—and there's *no rent!* Right on the beach, too. A bunch of employees live out there, and it's less than a mile from work. I've noticed Mrs. Grable in the end unit, cleaning it up, so I guess that's the one you get."

"Mrs. Grable?"

"She's, like, the resident manager, lives out there too with her husband. She does all the maintenance, groundskeeping, and if anything breaks down in your unit, she's the one to call."

"I can't wait to see the place."

Joyce drove through the island's middle spur next: marshes, swamps, and, indeed, an overgrown, fenced perimeter marked DANGER! QUICKSAND! So far, everything Clare had seen was, literally, a tropical jungle.

"So, the east and middle spurs—they're so overgrown and dense. I can't believe you have any trouble with vandals and trespassers in those areas."

"We don't," Joyce confirmed. "And now you can see why they chose this half of the park to close to the public; the land spurs are much more narrow and much harder to maintain. But the center spur—where the clinic and the lake are—that's where we get our trouble."

"Poachers, right?"

Joyce nodded. "It's illegal to hunt alligators now, but every now and then we'll get some boneheads out here doing it. They sell the meat to restaurants. And Lake Stephanie is full of protected and endangered species of freshwater fish, so the crackers go out there at night with their fishing poles. We've caught several of them. It's a $1500 fine for each fish."

"Ouch!"

"Yeah. But the idiots keep on coming. Then, of course, there's good old Trojan Point. It's a little lagoon right at the end of the spur, surrounded by palm trees. It's considered the ultimate romantic nightspot for all the welfare rednecks in Tierra Rojo and south St. Pete. They'll go out there to drink beer and smoke dope. And I don't have to tell you why they call it 'Trojan' Point."

Clare thought about it a moment, then closed her eyes. "I take it we're *not* talking about Agamemnon and Achilles."

Joyce giggled. "I remember one morning I went out there to hit the punch station and I counted forty-six used condoms along the beach. It was just *so gross!*"

"Look at the bright side. They're practicing safe sex."

"Good for them. At least there'll be fewer meth-babies. The criminal element west of the mainland is one hundred percent poverty-level cracker. White trailer trash. Sorry if that sounds politically incorrect, but why beat around the bush? These people exist to fuck and smoke ice, and to a security guard, they're nothing but a pain in the ass."

Joyce's sudden rough-edged social observation gave Clare a quick surprise. Her own views on such things were a bit more considerate, or so she hoped: people weren't bad by choice, they were bad though the obliviousness of discrimination, subjugation, and the negative environments that they were forced to be raised in. Having been raised in an orphanage herself, not to mention a year of homelessness due to discrimination, she knew a little bit about the subject.

On the other hand, she'd always maintained her sense of morality, all on her own.

"Relax," Joyce went on. "I'm not turning racist on you. It just really ticks me off to see what these people do to themselves. I was raised in a New Hampshire ghetto, and when I was sixteen the tenement burned down, and killed my whole family."

"Wow. I'm sorry to hear that."

Joyce's airy tone indicated that she was not looking for pity. She just gave a toss of her shoulder. "I was abused by some creep teacher in second grade, I grew up eating surplus cheese, and I watched the Nashua fire department put what was left of my parents and little brother in body bags. Shitty things happen sometimes—that's life. But with all the crap that I've been through, I've never stolen anything and I've never taken or sold drugs. I had plenty of opportunities, and there were times when it was real tempting. But I never did it."

Clare listened hard to what her employee was relating, not just the words but what was between them. *She's had it even worse than me but she still kept it togther.*

Now that Clare knew these things, she felt different about her initial impressions. *I guess a little hanky-panky in the woods isn't that terrible an offense*. Clare felt morose after hearing about the young woman's awful tribulations.

Joyce laughed airily. "Sorry! I didn't mean to get so high and mighty."

"That's quite all right. You're a strong woman."

"Getting back to my point. When the rednecks aren't toking on their meth pipes, they're shooting themselves to Palookaville with—"

"Prescription painkillers," Clare picked up, "which the clinic happens to be stuffed to the gills with."

"Yeah. So that's our biggest concern. We can't have the 'necks breaking in and getting their hands on all of that."

Clare almost laughed at Joyce's casual parlance. *'Necks. Jesus. This girl's a hoot.*

"It's kind of funny, though," Joyce went on. "Dellin and Harry are more torqued up about the Interthiolate inventory than all that morphine. They're really worried that someone might break into the facility and steal some."

Clare raised a brow. "It does sound a little overly paranoid, and pretty greedy and corporate, too. But look at it from their perspective. Interthiolate is their baby. Sure, curing cancer shouldn't be about who gets the credit but let's face facts. If I'd helped invent this stuff, I'd want the credit too, and the money. And I'd do everything I could to make sure some other company didn't rip me off."

"Yeah, I guess you're right."

"They're paying us to guard B-Wing like it's Fort Knox, so that's what we do." Along their trek, Joyce pointed out additional swamps and marshes through the more desolate areas of the site; then she was driving back toward the clinic.

"Now that I think of it, the other spurs *are* kind of creepy."

"It's almost like a rain forest back there," Clare noted. She also noted the heat and humidity. It seemed to press her uniform blouse against her skin and suck moisture out. Suddenly the idea of someone leaving this job because of the climate didn't seem terribly far removed. "Getting back to what we were talking about earlier. Grace Fletcher told you she was leaving because of the climate but another guard told you it was because of potential hazards? Was it Rick who told you that?"

"Oh, no. This was before Rick was even hired," Joyce explained. Beads of sweat trickled down her cheeks and her neck but she didn't seem uncomfortable in the least. Her expression, however, seemed skeptical. "There were a lot of different rumors floating around from the staff. Grace had your job, and she had two other guards: Rob and Donna. The three of them made up the site's first security crew. Things were going along fine until all of a sudden—about a month ago—the three of them put in their two week notice. Dellin wasn't too happy because it forced him to take time away from his patients to hire a new crew. I was the first new hire. Grace breaks me in and tells me the reason they're all leaving is because it's too hot. Fine. I don't think anything of it and I'm happy as hell anyway 'cos I get the job. That night, though, I run into the guy, Rob Thomas, up at the bar, and he tells me they all put in their notice because they had a few run-ins with gators and snakes and they just felt the job was too dangerous. Sounded kind of overreactive to me but, again, what do I care? They don't like the job, that's their business. Follow me so far?"

Yeah," Clare replied, her arm crooked out the window. "There's more?"

Joyce paused for an odd moment. "A little, and it is kind of weird. I come in the next morning to start my shift, and Grace isn't here. Neither are Rob and Donna, and all their lockers are empty."

"Their two-week notice was up, you mean?"

"No, that's just it. They still had ten more days to go, but they all left the night before, all three of them, at the same time. That's why it strikes me as a bit weird. By not honoring their two-week notice, they lose their severance pay. I mean—damn—they must've *really hated this job* to leave that fast and say to hell with the severance. Don't you think that's a little weird?"

"Yeah," Clare admitted. "And it just sounds . . . fishy."

"Um-hmm, and no one'll ever find out the real reason. After they left, there was one rumor after another, to the point that it got ridiculous. Chick in the cafeteria tells me they skipped town 'cos they were really wanted fugitives. Janitor tells me he heard Dellin fired them 'cos they were stealing dope from the pharmacy vault. People at the bar say they were all a bunch of drunks, and the pest-control guy tells me it was a three-way love triangle that went bad." Joyce shook her head, amused. "Who knows? And if you ask me, who cares?"

"It is pretty unimportant when you get right down to it," Clare offered, though she had to admit, her curiosity was piqued. "You've been here a month and you still like the job, right?"

"It's a *great* job. Good pay, a health plan, and a free beach house? Are you kidding? It's the best job I've ever had. Whenever I see an alligator, I yell boo and it runs away."

"I'm encouraged already," Clare said.

They were back on the main road, Joyce's long auburn hair blowing in the breeze. "Believe me, Fort Alachua is as safe a park as you'll ever find."

(III)

She was being strangled. The hands twisted expertly around her neck, wringing her out like a dish rag. Her nude body convulsed beneath the crystal-clear water; bubbles burst from her mouth.

Poor Kari Ann.

How could God do this to her? And after being *so close* to getting away?

She'd been raped in the woods for hours last night, dragged through brambles and sawgrass and bug-infested swamps, and even with all that, she'd managed to escape this fiend, to hide out till daybreak and find the boat. It was a miraculous achievement by any account but especially so for a woman of Kari Ann's frame and constitution: thin, dehydrated by the bayou's sucking heat, starved. Yet in her sheer will to survive, she'd evaded this horrific rapist and abductor. She'd survived all that terror and pain and hardship—and for what?

To be caught and have it start all over again.

She remembered her manic, blubbering exuberance when she'd tramped her way out of the woodline to the gently lapping shore. Caleb's boat was still right there where they'd left it last night. She giggled like an imp, eyes wide open in lunatic glee, as she fumbled to untie the bowline from the shore roots they'd moored to, then pulled the boat out till she was waist-deep. The clean water of the inlet felt like the caress of heaven against her filthy, insect-bitten skin. She flipped herself into the boat and began to row at once. *I'm free! I'm out!* her tortured mind exclaimed.

I made it!

She rowed, literally, like mad, because she *was* mad by now, a stark-raving little madwoman who'd just been released from the clutches of an unfathomable death. She'd been jibbering some languageless exaltation, and then even more elation overcame her when she saw, little more than a mile in the distance, a sailboat moving lazily across the mouth of Tampa Bay. The safe, normal world was so close to her now, and she rowed and rowed and rowed till her heart was fit to burst.

And she thought again: *I made it! I made it!*

That's when she noticed that the boat wasn't moving forward.

She rowed harder, more furiously, the oar digging out plumes of water and shooting them yards behind her. But—

The boat still wasn't moving.

Was she aground? That couldn't be possible! She was at least fifty feet off shore now! She plunged the oar straight down, all the way down to the very end of the handle, for more proof.

If the boat wasn't aground, then why wasn't it moving?

Then her elation disintegrated.

Very slowly, her attacker, her nemesis of the previous night, rose dripping out of the water at the boat's bow. He'd been there all along, holding the boat with his hands.

He looked at her over the bow and smiled.

Kari Ann screamed so hard her lungs were nearly

ejected in hot chunks, so loud, the whites of her eyes hemorrhaged to bright red, and so high egrets and lorikeets lifted off the beach in terrified droves.

There was no safety in daylight—not here. She could scream all she liked, but the people on the sailboat would never hear her. No one would. In a split-second swipe, her rapist's hands were around her throat, and she was hauled into the water. The strangulation was slow, deliberate, the hands holding her down, then bringing her back up for just enough time to snatch a single breath before plunging her face right back down. Had she been more sentient at the time—and more sane—she would easily have sensed the glee, the sheer sadistic delight, on the part of her attacker. He was going to kill her slowly—

For the fun of it.

Submerged, her face bloated, her hair opened around her head like a tragic flowing aura. Her hands tried to break the grip on her throat but it was useless; her feet kicked out into cool water, striking nothing. Each time she was dragged up, she could feel the raging erection sliding against her belly and thighs.

By now Kari Ann just wanted to die.

Her hands fell off his thick wrists.

Just die . . .

Was she giving up?

Easier to die . . .

Her limbs fell limp in the water now. He was holding her down, watching her face beneath the rippling water. Kari Ann stared back, her tongue a fat cork in her mouth, sticking out between her lips. Though her brain was no longer capable of normal thought processing, something did register now, the starkest cognizance that shook her dying psyche like an eruption.

In all of the awful things that had happened, and with all that he'd done to her—last night and now—this was the first and only moment that Kari Ann had had a chance to really see his face.

And suddenly, that image—that face—buckled her. The basest instinct seized her like a breeze against the last lit cinder in a campfire, and her sheer horror was rekindled.

An instant later, her attacker was howling, his hands releasing Kari Ann's throat. The howl blared like a low horn, exploding around them—a howl of agony.

Kari Ann, without conscious thought, had reached down, grabbed one of his testicles, and began to twist. Her nails ripped into the scrotum. She planted both feet against his hips and *pulled*.

And tore the testicle off.

More bellows of agony exploded. Wheezing, Kari Ann thrashed to the shore and ran off back into the woods. The bellows followed her, loud as cannon shots, but her attacker did not.

It was well into the afternoon now, the sun high, the daylight raging, and in that daylight Kari Ann had finally seen her attacker's face, and now she ran, ran, ran, back into the tropical forest, praying to escape yet again because now she knew something beyond all doubt:

This madman rapist was no *man* at all.

Not a man, a *thing*.

Part Two

Federal Land Grid S27-0078
Central Florida
June 1995

Yes, the demon was reaching for Professor Fredrick now as he stood with both feet firmly planted on the bottom of the ancient cavern.

Fredrick's mouth fell open but all that came out was a parched rasp. His old heart seemed to stop mid-beat in his chest.

Then he noticed that the demon was eating Gummy Bears.

"Dales! My God!" Fredrick gasped. "You scared the—"

"Shit out of you?" Dales nodded, smiling. "You should've turned your torch on when you were coming down, then I would've seen it, would've called out so you knew I was down here."

Fredrick was still reeling in the afterfright. He was so mad he wanted to shout out loud into his assistant's face but then . . .

A larger part of him was relieved that it hadn't really been a demon waiting for him down here.

"You nodded off topside," Dales went on, chewing. "After chow I checked the air-probe and it was holding at green. I didn't want to interrupt your beauty sleep so I came down first-to make sure the props were secure." Dales winked in the torchlight. "Don't worry, I won't tell anyone that *I* was actually the first person to set foot down here in 10,000 years. You can have the credit."

"You know, Dales, I know I'm an old man, but I'll bet I could still kick your young, smart, sarcastic ass."

Dales smiled. "In your dreams, Uncle Joe, and speaking of ass-kicking, you were right. There was some *serious* ass-kicking going on down here."

"You saw them?"

"Yup, and they're not ossifications or fossils. They're bodies." Dales held his flashlight up under his chin. "*Dismembered* bodies."

"And beheaded, right?"

"Roger that, Prof. For a minute I thought those Mr. Magoo glasses of yours were making you see things, but then my own eagle-sharp sense of vision quickly verified your outlandish claim." Dales popped both brows at Fredrick. "Somebody pulled their motherfuckin' *heads* off."

"You speak with the eloquence of kings," Fredrick said. "In fact, I think I'll let you ghost-write my upcoming bestselling autobiography. Now get out of my way so I can take a look at *my* discovery."

The levity didn't last long after that. Even Dales, a natural-born jokester, looked utterly solemn when they turned their beams into the widest portion of the cenote.

The blood—some of it in elongated pools, some of it in gushes—had dried to a coffee-brown, but the rare mix of trapped methane and nitrogen made it appear to be still wet. It wasn't, of course, but the effect was chilling.

"Man," Dales muttered. "That's *a lot* of blood."

The shale floor appeared spotless, even polished in spite of its one hundred centuries of disuse. The limbs of the four Ponoye priests—warlocks by any other name—had been flung this way and that, while the heads had been twisted off and then placed right-side up against the cenote's wall. Again, the effect was chilling: the shriveled heads were looking at them.

"Creepin' me out," Dales observed. "If one of them starts talking . . . can we leave?"

Armlets and wristlets on the arms remained shining in their pure gold platework—no tarnish, no oxidation whatever, as though the fineries had been polished hours rather than ten millennia ago. Unseemly pagoda-sleeved tunics still adorned the torsos, fashioned from hide and intricately patterned with hand-inked markings that still looked crisp and sharp. The inevitable process of karyolysis, retarded by the cenote's protective environment, caused the insides of these ritual garments to fuse with the skin, producing fascinating ripples, while beaded necklaces and feathered fringes around the collarettes remained virtually unaffected. Fredrick had never seen anything like it. The headdresses too, strewn aside in whatever fray had taken place down here, remained absolutely intact, and odder still in their miter-like shape, nothing at all like typical feathered headdresses that were generally thought of as Native-American ceremonial vestment. So much of this, he knew, would begin to disintegrate now that it was being exposed to normal air (he'd have to get a photographic crew down here as soon as possible) but he also knew that very likely the organic remnants—the limbs, torsos, and heads—would experience no such disintegration if handled properly, the natural mummification essentially curing the skin.

Then he thought: *The skin. God.*

"Careful," Dales warned. "If you crack it, it might be toxic."

Fredrick didn't hear his assistant. He was kneeling before one of the arms, examining it under his torch light. The fingernails, not surprisingly, had continued to grow post-extremis, and the hand hadn't clawed up as he would've expected. Time and the air down here had preserved it so well that he could even see the whorls and bifurcations of the fingerprints still intact. Even more uniquely, where the arm had been disconnected from the shoulder, Fredrick could see the clean white ball of the humerus bone, and desiccated arteries hanging in frozen stasis. But he actually marveled at the appearance of the skin in the flashlight beam, which looked transparent as fine Depression glass and gave off a shiny hue of yellowed beige.

Incredible.

"These bodies are better preserved than Tatshenshini Park Iceman," he said aloud. "Better than the Peat Bog Children and the Nevada Spirit Cave mummy."

Dales's voice bounced back from the dark, an ominous echo. "Yeah, Prof. And *this* body too."

Fredrick glanced up, alarmed. He could see Dales's light play in the distance. "You've found another body?"

"Yeah. You gotta see this . . ."

Fredrick's old knees crackled when he jumped up and shuffled forward. The cenote was much longer than he'd imagined, much more spacious. Dales looked thirty yards away in the echoic dark.

"It's *horrible* . . . and beautiful at the same time," Dales said more to himself.

Fredrick's shuffling footsteps slowed as his light began to reveal his assistant's discovery.

It was a woman—

Good God . . .

—a woman so uniquely and perfectly mummified that Fredrick grew light-headed at the sight.

From small, finely-cut bricks of black shale, a dolmen had been erected in the center of the cenote—the sacrificial altar. And atop the dolmen lay the woman—more probably a girl well into puberty—petite, nude, and pristine in her 10,000-year-old death.

She lay serene, the velvety straight black hair still intact and arranged about her shoulders. The desiccation of time tightened the skin but in this cool, high-nitrogen/carbon-dioxide environment, it remained flawlessly smooth, no signs of shrivels, sags, ripples. The small breasts were still more than apparent, dark overlarge nipples still crisply defined, still distended from the fearful rush of murder. The eyes were gone, of course (they always were), but the beatific visage left the appearance of an endless gaze rather than gruesome sockets. Everything about her was fine, fragile, even angelic in the ancient beauty. Fredrick nearly felt ashamed when he looked between her slightly parted legs to the young pubis. *Fourteen, fifteen years old, probably*, he estimated. *And a virgin, no doubt*. Even her sex seemed delicately beautiful, the gentle cleft in once undefiled, dough-soft flesh. The scant pubic hair looked like a dark mist.

"Call me a pervert, boss, but this gal damn near looks good enough to take to the prom," Dales jested. "Christ, she's better looking than that cheerleader I was dating last semester, and the cheerleader *wasn't* 10,000 years old."

Fredrick didn't hear the foolish remarks; he was too enraptured with the find. Every archaeologist's greatest dream was right here, lying before him . . . shimmering in its strange, dead splendor and nearly smiling at his awe.

Most amazing to see, though, was simply the girl's skin. Poreless, smooth, perfect. The naturally dark pigmentation of her race had been leached away by time and absolute darkness, leaving a sheen like rice paper with an eerie off-white tint that reminded Fredrick of the stains in a spent tea bag. Faint chocolate traceries of veins could be seen through the skin's remarkable translucence, fine and thin as individual thread fibers. Fredrick reckoned that in all of history, death had never looked so alive.

"The state of preservation is astonishing," he said.

"It's not astonishing, Prof, it's *unequaled* in the annals of human preservation. This chick makes the Andean 'Pretty Sue' mummy look like a dried-up dog turd. You're gonna be famous, all right. A week from now, this floozie's gonna be permanently on display at the Smithsonian, with a neat little photo of you on the plaque next to it. And all those guys out there who thought you were full of b.s. can start eating crow now. After we get some pictures of this in the journals, nobody will ever again refute your claim that the Ponoyes were sacrificial."

"And, look! She isn't even cut," Fredrick reveled. Now more and more of his translations of the Ponoye entablatures were proving correct. Unlike the Toltecs, the Eleusinians, and other ancient civilizations that practiced human sacrifice, the Ponoyes did not cut out the sacrifant's heart—the archetypal offering. Instead, the virgin would be offered whole and unblemished to the dark devils that the Ponoye worshiped. It was with the most macabre enthusiasm that Fredrick further remarked: "She was garroted in place. You can still see the ligature mark on her throat."

"That you can."

"She must have died in sheer terror . . . yet she seems so peaceful, so serene."

"She probably believed in the same stuff the priests believed in, probably thought she'd go to some ecstatic afterlife as a reward for allowing herself to be sacrificed."

Maybe, Fredrick pondered. The thought seemed dreamlike. *Maybe she's there now . . . watching us*.

"But that's not the $64,000 question, is it?" Dales went on.

No, it wasn't. The cold hard facts of reality buffeted back into the old professor's sentience. What an absolutely arcane mystery. It gnawed at him.

Who killed these four priests?

Dales put it into his own terms. "First the priests punch the chick's ticket, then someone comes down here and goes totally caveman on all four of them, pulls them apart like a bunch of Ken dolls. Who could've done that, Prof? I mean, even if you forget about the motive for a minute, who could've done that? By the looks of their bodies, they were *manually* dismembered. No ax-marks, no cutting tools were used to do this. They were *pulled* apart. Almost like they were drawn by horses or yanked apart on a medieval rack. Now, correct me if I'm wrong, but I'm not seeing any horses or racks down here."

"I know," Fredrick confessed, science and logic not lost on him. "It doesn't make much sense. The answer is somewhere—we're just not seeing it."

"Members of a warring tribe? The Seminoles, maybe?

"The Seminoles hadn't even arrived here 10,000 years ago," Fredrick said. "They hadn't even migrated as far as Alabama. And neither had any of the Muskhogean peoples. And those who did live in the area were terrified of the Ponoyes; they ran from them, never fought—there weren't enough numbers. No, Dales, it's not logical that another tribe came down here during the sacrifice ritual and murdered the priests."

Dales had to chuckle. "Well, when you consider what the priests were actually doing down here . . . maybe no one else came down at all."

The ludicrous comment was difficult for Fredrick to ignore altogether. He felt anxious, queasy now in this darkness with all these bodies.

When you consider what the priests were actually doing down here . . .

Yes, the priests performed a human sacrifice in an attempt to incarnate one of the nameless underworld deities that they worshiped.

The silence seemed to hang around him like a pitch-black sheet. "Fine, Dales," he finally responded. "I'd be willing to consider the possibility of a successful demonic incarnation."

"You would?"

"Of course. After you find a genuine demon corpse, that is."

He expected a typical smart-aleck remark but now he noticed that Dales hadn't heard his sarcastic statement at all.

"Dales?"

Dales was standing perfectly still, flashlight poised, staring out. It seemed that he too was hanging there, with the silence and the dark.

"Dales?"

The younger man took several fast steps forward, then abruptly stopped.

"Enough of this, son. You're scaring me. Now what the hell are you looking at?"

Dales turned quickly around, standing stiffly as he re-faced Fredrick. His eyes seemed strained open they were so wide, and his face looked pinched as if tense from some briefly glimpsed dread. He said, very softly:

"About ten yards ahead of us, there's another hole."

"What!" Fredrick exclaimed. The prospect didn't scare him in the least; it electrified him. "An opening to another cenote? That's amazing! Show me!" and then he lurched forward.

Dales grabbed Fredrick's arm. "Wait. Listen."

"Stop acting like a fool! What's wrong with you?"

Dales's eyes remained frozen wide open. "The other cenote—the other hole . . ."

"What about it!"

"There's a clawed hand sticking out of it."

Chapter Four

(I)

By the time Joyce had finished showing Clare the rest of the property, it was four p.m. shiftchange; the heat had now compounded to a soupy haze. Joyce was off and the next guard, Rick, was on. Clare couldn't resist the tiny smile on her lips when she was introduced, remembering her sneak peek on the security camera. He seemed competent and bright, and he cited some military police experience of his own. *He's qualified, has brains, and as long as he lays off the hanky-panky on the job site, I don't think he'll be a problem.* She arranged to meet him back at the security office to relieve him when his own shift ended, at midnight.

As Rick departed in the truck for his first rounds, Dellin exited the clinic entrance, his jacket flung over his shoulder. He locked the front glass doors, then smiled as he approached Clare and Joyce in the parking lot.

"Joyce, did you show your new boss the ropes yet?"

"The whole site, yes sir," Joyce replied.

"And I'm happy to say," Clare added, "we didn't run into a single snake or alligator."

"Like the old saying goes, they won't bother you if you don't bother them."

"That's what I was telling her," Joyce said.

"Believe me, Clare, the only thing you have to fear out here is boredom." He pointed to the other security vehicle. "I didn't make it clear that that's yours now, at least for as long as you work for us."

"Yes, thanks," Clare said. " It's really nice. I'll take good care of it." But now she noticed that Dellin had his car keys out; it appeared he was leaving the clinic for the day. "So the clinic's closed now?"

"Yeah, we usually close down around four and most of the med staff goes home. The janitors stay till eight and the kitchen ladies stay on till six, so don't forget to grab some dinner."

Clare felt confused. "So I take it I won't be meeting the clinic director today?"

Dellin closed his eyes in the memory lapse. "Harry! That's right. I'm sorry, I should've beeped you when he called. His conference in Sarasota ran late so he's not going to bother coming back to the clinic when it's over. You'll meet him sometime tomorrow."

"Okay."

"Have you gotten your shifts all worked out?"

"I'll be relieving Rick at midnight, then working till noon."

"Sounds good." Then Dellin got caught in another memory lapse. "Damn, how thoughtless of me! You haven't even seen your cottage yet, have you?"

"No, not yet."

"I'd take you down myself, but I'm meeting some

friends in the city for dinner. Joyce, would you mind taking Clare to the cottages and introducing her to Mrs. Grable?"

"I'd be happy to," Joyce said. "I'm on my way home now anyway."

Dellin started for his Mercedes. "Great. See you two tomorrow. And, Clare, it's great to have you aboard."

"Thanks."

Dellin drove off in the sun.

"Dellin's cool but he's definitely a mystery around here," Joyce remarked after he'd gone.

"What do you mean?"

"Oh, you know. Good-looking but shy, intense yet remote. One minute he'll be joking around with you, the next minute he doesn't know you exist 'cos he's so wrapped up in his work."

"Well, it is important work, right?"

"Sure it is, but sometimes it seems like he's got other things on his mind at the same time. Nobody really knows anything about him. No ring, so I guess he's not married, but who knows if he's got a girlfriend, an ex-wife, kids? He has a beach cottage too but he's also got a condo in town."

"You mean Tampa, or St. Pete?"

"No one knows. He's never even mentioned if he's dating anyone, involved with anyone."

"That's his business," Clare stated outright. "And since he's *our boss*, it's probably a good idea not worry about his private life."

"Oh, I know that, but come on." Joyce's subdued smile seemed sly. "How is any natural woman *not* going to wonder a little? Christ, he's so damn *handsome!*"

Clare felt tempted to make this her first exercise of supervisor-to-employee discipline and remind Joyce that remarks like that were wholly inappropriate. She didn't bother, though; it would make her feel like a hypocrite. After her own wandering eye today?

"He's probably gay anyway," Joyce said, laughing. "The really good-looking ones around here usually are."

Clare decided to toy with her a little. "Hmm, well. Rick's a pretty attractive man. You think he's gay?" *Do you, Joyce?* she continued in thought. *Probably not, huh, 'cos that sure didn't look like a* GAY *man you were practically wrapping your legs around earlier.*

The comment put Joyce instantly on guard—and she did a poor job hiding it. "Don't get me wrong. Rick's a nice guy but I'd never date him, of course. We work together! It's against company policy to date someone you work with."

"Um-hmm."

Joyce was clearly not comfortable with the subject now. "Before we go to the cottages, can we go back inside for a minute?"

"Uh, sure."

"I'm roasting. These day shifts in the summer are killers."

Joyce unlocked the front doors with the key around her neck, and Clare followed her back in. The sudden gush of air-conditioning gave Clare a pleasing chill. But she felt a pang when they passed the cafeteria; about a dozen of the technical staff were sitting down to large meals. The aromas were delectable. "I'm skipping dinner tonight, trying to watch my weight," Joyce offered. "But I don't mind waiting if you'd like to go in and get something. The cooks are fantastic, and the discount we get is unbelievable."

Clare almost cringed against the knot of hunger twisting in her stomach. But she didn't want to look gluttonous, stuffing her previously homeless face in front of one of her employees. *I'll just have to get something later*, she willed herself. *Be strong. Stuff your pie-hole later*. "No, I'm fine."

"Okay." Joyce trod on, as if in a hurry, until she got to the staff coffee room.

"Oh, so this is where you're rushing to," Clare remarked.

"Have you had the iced coffee? It's just *so good*."

"Yeah, I had one earlier."

"I'll bet I drink a gallon of it per shift." Joyce pulled out her master key but before she could unlock the door—

click

—the door opened.

"What are—" Joyce frowned. "You're not supposed to be in here!"

A lean, thirtyish man with longish blond hair was stepping out of the room, a cold bottle of soda in his hand. Tall, tanned, an outdoorsy presence. *The guy from the U.S. Park Service*, Clare realized, noticing the obvious boots, slate-blue shorts, and white short-sleeve shirt. Federal patches and a badge adorned the shirt, and a pair of binoculars hung around his neck.

"Whoa, hold your horses there, hon," he said. "I'm just grabbing a Coke, not knocking the place over. I stopped by to talk to Dellin, see if you had any trespasser or dumping incidents to report. I *am* allowed in the building, you know."

Joyce seemed peeved by the man. "Not when it's closed, and *not* in the guards' break room!"

"Dellin unlocked the room for me before he left, told me to help myself." The man shook his head, gave a shucksy grin to Clare. "I'm sorry, since Ms. Friendly over here isn't going to introduce us—" He extended his hand. "I'm Adam Corey, the park ranger. And you must be the new security chief."

Clare shook his hand. It felt strong, firm. "Yes, Clare Prentiss. Dellin briefed me that any reports of vandalism or habitat destruction should be made to you. Is that correct?"

"It sure is," Adam replied, brushing some blond curls back off his forehead. "I usually drop by once or twice a week to check in. But if you need me, any time—" He gave her a card. "Give a holler on my cell. I'm on call round the clock."

"Thanks—"

Joyce had already brushed past him; she crankily called back: "Clare, don't you want an iced coffee or soda or something?"

Adam rolled his eyes at her tone. Clare didn't get it. "Yeah, I'll be right there," she said, then to the ranger, "Nice meeting you, Adam."

"A pleasure. I been working out here for years, know the site better than most. Any time you have a question or concern, feel free to—"

"I already showed her the site, Adam!" Joyce continued her mysterious bitching. "Now why don't you go count palm trees or something. Clare and I are *busy!*"

Another roll of the eyes from Adam. "Have a good day." Then he left.

Joyce was clattering things in the break room, filling a large insulated cup with iced coffee. When she was done, she snapped the lid on with a vengeance. She spun around and faced Clare, gritting her teeth.

"You've practically got steam coming out of your ears, Joyce."

"He just pisses me off *so much!*"

Clare filled a large cup of her own with iced coffee, then loaded it up with sugar. "What's your beef with him? Dellin's already told me that he's allowed here."

"Well, let's just say that one night I made a big error in judgment, and now I'll never hear the end of it. I went out with him once and he wound up pawing all over me like some animal. Told him I never wanted to see him again, but he just kept hounding me—for weeks."

"Really?"

"And I think he's peeping on me."

The whole thing was so trite but Clare couldn't rein her curiosity. "That's serious. If you're sure, you should report him to the police."

Joyce sputtered. "Well, I'm not *sure*. Not one hundred percent. But there have been a lot of times—you know. I'll be taking a shower or getting dressed, and I just *know* that someone's looking in the window. I'm also pretty sure he peeps on me when I'm sunbathing on the beach. Why else would he have those binoculars?"

"He's a *park ranger*, Joyce. They routinely carry binoculars. There's a pair of binoculars in each of the security trucks but that doesn't mean we're peeping toms. Adam seems like a perfectly normal guy to me."

Joyce was still talking but not *to* Clare. "Yeah, well, that's just his way, a real smoothie at first. Take my advice—keep an eye on him."

Clare smiled to herself, thinking it best to drop the issue. She knew there were two sides to every story, and given the sudden burst of hostility on Joyce's part, why bother pursuing it?

"Calm down and forget about him," Clare said. "And let's get out of here. I'm dying to see my cottage."

Moments later, Clare was behind the wheel of her Blazer, Joyce directing her to the easternmost spur of the island. The younger woman did simmer down in time, sipping her giant iced coffee. Soon she was back to harmless chatter. "Thanks for driving me. I usually walk back home—I'm trying to keep my weight down. It's only a mile when you cut through, but today it's just too damn hot."

"Yeah, it would be a pretty grueling hike." Clare was beginning to see some insecurities leak through Joyce's veneer. *She goes ballistic over the ranger, and that's the second time she's complained about her weight.* Clare wished she had a figure like Joyce—robust, hardy, but not a trace of excess fat. The sudden faltering self-esteem didn't match with the rest of her vigorous personality. *It didn't look to me like Rick had any complaints with your weight,* part of her wanted to say. But now she had to question herself for even thinking that. It was almost a snipe. *I guess I've got some self-esteem problems of my own,* she admitted to herself as she steered the Blazer down the narrow gravel road. She couldn't forget the look in Rick's eyes when she saw the two together on the video screen, the sheer ardent blaze. When was the last time a man had desired Clare with the same passion? *Admit it, Clare. You're jealous of Joyce.*

She willed herself to change subjects. "Tell me about this Mrs. Grable. She's a handywoman or something?"

"Think of her as the resident manager," Joyce said. She'd unbuttoned her tunic a few notches and was billowing it up and down to cool herself off. "She maintains the cottages, the grounds, fixes things that break. It's too bad—she's such a nice woman."

Clare blinked in a sudden confoundment. "*What's* too bad?"

"Her husband smacks her around. Every now and then you'll see her with a fat lip or a black eye."

Clare instantly fumed. "Is that so? The first time I see anything like that, I'll report him to the police."

"Won't do any good. She never presses charges, says she fell down the stairs or slipped in the shower."

"That's outrageous. Wife-beaters are like rapists—scum of the earth. What's the husband like?"

"Don't know, never met him, never even seen him outside of the house. She said he works midnight shifts at the desalination plant. For a while I was beginning to think she didn't even *have* a husband, like she was some delusional widow living in denial, but then one time I saw him standing in front of the kitchen window, looking around outside. Normal-looking guy from what I could see."

"Yeah, Joyce, but the freaks—the real criminals and sociopaths in our society—are always the *normal-looking* ones."

"Weird, though. The window was opened and he was just kind of leaning out, looking around. So I called up to him and said hi, but he completely ignored me. Ducked back in and walked away like he didn't even hear me."

"Yeah, that is weird."

"And there was one time . . . I'm pretty sure I saw choke marks on her throat. It really bothers me. She's so nice but she feels she has to put up with stuff like that."

"Well, if *I* ever see him beating her? I'll swear out a felony warrant myself," Clare vowed. Suddenly, she felt depressed, irritated. It really wasn't that long ago when she'd been the victim of a man's violence herself. She was relieved, then, when Joyce brought the topic to a close:

"Here we are. Aren't they great?"

Gravel popped under the Blazer's big tires when Clare pulled around within a neat, well-shrubbed cul-de-sac. Short, stout palm trees seemed to bloom overhead, and through them, the cottages stood. They were actually pile houses of dark, treated planking, built on a structure of four-foot-high stilts for occasions of high water. At least ten units ran along in a curving row with liberal stands of palm trees and brush between each. Less than a hundred yards distant, gentle waves broke on a spotless white-sand beach.

"Oh my God!" Clare exclaimed. "This is too good to be true. I don't really live here, do I?"

"You sure do. In the biggest one, right there."

In her excitement, Clare didn't even feel the stifling heat when she got out of the air-conditioned Blazer.

Joyce smiled after her. "I live two down. Come by any time if you need anything. You're gonna love it."

"Thanks, Joyce."

"Just go on in. Mrs. Grable's already there."

Clare nearly skipped up the short wooden steps. *This'd be a thousand-dollar-per-week rental property from a vacation realtor*, she guessed. It looked like a bungalow on a tropical resort. A long wood balcony stretched from end to end on the beach side, with ceiling-high plate glass facing out. One of the sliding doors stood open, light drapes billowing.

Inside she met Mrs. Grable, who was folding fresh bed linens. "Oh, it's so nice to meet you, Clare," she greeted more like a long lost aunt. She wore a simple sleeveless pullover jumper, its floral pattern gently faded, had dark hair, only traceably graying, pulled back in a bun. She had to be in her fifties but remained amazingly shapely and fit. "Dellin told me you'd be moving in at once, so I've been getting everything ready."

"It's just beautiful, Mrs. Grable."

A vast selection of potted and hanging plants gave the appearance that the tropical forest outside was subtly insinuating itself into the interior. A quick tour showed her a spacious bedroom with wide skylights, a small but efficient kitchen, and the living room looking out to the beach. The central air-conditioning hummed quietly, filling the bright sunlit rooms with shivery air. Blond hardwood floor shined under coats of shimmering sealant, with an occasion light throw rug here and there. TV, stereo, and VCR in the corner. *This is too much!* she thought. *Jesus! About the only thing missing is a Jacuzzi!* but then, to her near-shock, Mrs. Grable pulled open a sliding door along the next wall.

No! NO! Clare thought in disbelief.

A cool blue Jacuzzi bubbled before her, built into a stained-wood sundeck that ran the entire lateral length of the cottage. A six-foot redwood fence surrounded the entire deck—total luxury in total privacy.

"Mrs. Grable, I'm at a loss for words."

"In Florida we don't have hot tubs. The water's cooled. Yours is the only cottage that has this—it's a perk, for being security chief."

Clare was practically reeling. "Unbelievable."

Mrs. Grable took her back inside. "Oh, and I guess you already know how to use all of this," she was saying next. A small cove off the living room contained what was essentially a duplication of the security equipment back at her office in the clinic: a radio set and a row of video screens that were no doubt connected to the array of security cameras spread over the site.

"Yes, it's identical to the radio and display screens at the clinic. This stuff will really come in handy on weekends when I'm on call."

"I think you'll really like it here."

"I'm sure I will."

"And if there are any problems, I'm right next door."

"Thanks."

Only now did Clare realize an oddity; she hadn't noticed it at first because she was too overwhelmed by the gorgeous apartment, but now it occurred to her that Mrs. Grable seemed to be going out of her way to stand with the right side of her face *away* from Clare. In a wide wall mirror, though, Clare caught a glimpse of what the woman was trying to hide.

The side of her lip was swollen, like—

Like someone hit her in the mouth, Clare realized, instantly recalling Joyce's suspicions. *Damn it. That's horrible.*

She wanted to say something but knew it wasn't really her place. It would put the woman on the spot, embarrass her. But in the next instant—

Oh, no—oh Jesus no . . .

"And here's your key," Mrs. Grable said. It was when she bent over to pick the house key off the glass-topped coffee table: the top rim of her jumper drooped open, almost fully revealing the tops of her breasts. In the briefest glimpse, Clare noticed the ugly oval welt that completely surrounded the nipple.

It was a bite mark.

The glimpse of it only lasted a moment, and then Mrs. Grable had risen and was happily handing Clare the house key. But the glimpse of it—the mark—hurt just to see. *That was no love bite, either*, Clare knew. Mrs. Grable had been bitten so hard that the action had left a raised weal, damage well past the bruising stage. *The bastard almost bit her nipple off*. Clare's rapist had treated her similarly, biting down so hard that at several points his upper incisors made contact with the lower—through her flesh. The pain had been horrendous, and the mark had remained there for a week.

She felt awful at once. The sight of the perverted injury polluted the excitement of seeing her wonderful new home. *The poor woman . . .* Now wasn't the time, Clare knew, but she promised herself that, after she got to know Mrs. Grable better, she would talk to her about this problem, maybe get her and her husband into counseling or something.

"The sunsets are like nothing you've ever seen," Mrs. Grable went on as though nothing were amiss. "And, look. You've got two levels of curtains."

More and more the cottage was seeming like the weekend getaway of a rich Hollywood producer. Mrs. Grable pushed a switch on the wall: first set of long tulle-like curtains was pulled across the walls of beachside plate-glass windows. She could see through them to a soft, unfocused clarity.

Mrs. Grable made a precocious giggle that defied her age. "It's very tempting to just walk around naked; you get all the sunlight but no one can actually see you. And when the sun gets *too* bright—" The next button drew heavy blackout drapes across the glass.

"Wow," was all Clare could say. "This place is just fantastic."

"Well, I'll leave you to get settled."

Clare began a question. "My—" But then she stopped awkwardly, to think. What could she say? *Uh, up until a few hours ago I was homeless. I don't have any possessions, including clothes. Where's the nearest store?* Clare didn't like to lie but she thought a mere fib, in this case, would be appropriate. "Most of my belongings are in storage but there are some things I need to get right away. Are there any stores nearby?"

"Oh, yes, lots of shopping on the other side of the bridge. The Wal-Mart on Tyrone is huge. But if you don't want to go that far, just go back out on Gulf. There are lots of little shops. You can't miss them."

"Back out on Gulf. Thanks."

"I suppose you'll be working a lot at night. The previous security chief worked late shifts mainly."

"Yes, I'll be midnight to noon during the week, and on call on the weekends." A pause. Clare's curiosity kept scratching at her. "The previous chief—Grace Fletcher, right?"

"Yes."

"And she lived in this same unit?"

"Yes, she did. The other two guards each had a cottage out here too."

Clare rubbed her chin; the mystery wouldn't let go. "I just can't understand why they quit. The pay's great, the duty can't be *that* hard, and a rent-free cottage on the beach? I don't get it."

Mrs. Grable put her arm about Clare's shoulder, as a mother might when giving advice. "I don't like to speak ill of people, dear, but Grace and the other two? Well, they certainly took advantage of things. Dellin had no choice but to let them go."

"So they were fired. I heard they all quit at the same time."

"That's not quite the case, I'm afraid. There was quite a bit of drinking going on. Oh, you should have seen the empty bottles and cans that were lying around here after they left. And the parties? Everyone needs to have some fun, but it was just absolutely shameful what they were doing out here."

"What . . . *were* they doing?"

"Donna and Rob—the other two guards? They would always come here in the wee hours—because of the Jacuzzi, of course. And the three of them would party so loud—it sounded like a Roman orgy, I tell you. I can't imagine young people could be that naive; just because there's a fence around that sundeck doesn't mean the people can't hear what's going on. And it wasn't just on the weekends, either. They'd be getting together like that during the week, too—during their shifts. I'd see them, *sneaking* back here through the woods, for goodness sake! Who did they think they were fooling?" Mrs. Grable stopped for a moment. "I'll say no more. I never gossip."

Well then . . . thanks for the gossip.

The elder woman's arm tightened around Clare's shoulder, more motherly gestures. "Rick and Joyce are wonderful tenants, though, and I can tell just by looking at you—you're a smart, responsible woman."

"I'd like to think so." Clare chuckled. "And don't worry, there won't be any wild Jacuzzi parties going on, either."

"I'm sure there won't be, and I'm sure you'll be just fine here." But now came something like a stern expression. "And, dear, if you don't mind my saying so—you're awfully thin. So do get some meat on your bones. Honestly, working out there in this heat? You'll shrivel right up!"

"Don't worry, Mrs. Grable, I don't plan on shriveling up anytime soon. First thing I'm going to do after I get to the store is have a big meal."

"Make sure that you do—and if you ever need anything, I'm just next door."

"Thanks very much."

"'Bye!"

Clare smiled after the woman left. *A bit nattering, but I like her. She's sweet.* And she knew she was right about being too thin. She took another look around the apartment and remained astounded. *Couldn't have asked for anything better in a million years . . .* The next impulse was irresistible: with all the things that she knew she needed to do now, she *had* to look around one more time.

The living room, the bedroom, the sundeck. *Wow,* was all she could think. She motored the drapes back and forth several times, just for fun, watching the beach beyond appear and then disappear. Back in the bedroom, she caught herself staring at the big king-sized bed. *What a luxury . . .* After so many months of shelter cots and, worse, the ground under a bridge? She knew she would never take things for granted again—even simple things like beds and showers. Another quick glance at the Jacuzzi left her sorely tempted to just take all her clothes off right there and get in but the more responsible part of her nixed the idea. *I still have to go to the store, get clothes, food, then work tonight!*

Working, yes. Another thing she'd never take for granted. She had a job now. She had a home.

Now she was looking at herself in the bedroom mirror, and that's when it fully dawned on her.

I have a life again.

An impulse, then. She wasn't fully aware of it when her fingers slipped into her pocket and withdrew the crumpled fortune from the cookie this morning. She flattened it back out and stuck it on the mirror, sliding one edge under the frame so it would stay.

SOMETHING VERY GOOD WILL HAPPEN TO YOU TODAY

"It sure as hell did," she said to herself.

Yes, she had a life again, and she was determined not to disappoint the people who had given it to her. *Dellin, and this Harry guy, the director. I'm going to be the best security chief those guys have ever seen.*

She was about to leave when she noticed the box at the end of the dresser. It was just a little vanity box but beautifully fashioned in different tones of inlaid woods. When she raised the lid, she found the top tray empty, but when she lifted out the top tray—

Hmmm.

A stack of snapshots lay inside, and the one on the very top of the stack. . . .

Grace Fletcher, I presume, Clare thought.

The bright color picture was a shot from the waist up of an attractive woman in her thirties. Brunet hair pulled back, no makeup. The faintest smile suggested someone serious, smart, and competent. All business, no nonsense. And the nameplate on the uniform could easily be read: FLETCHER, G.

But it wasn't a security uniform she wore, it was an Air Force uniform, showing captain's bars on the shoulders. Clare found this odd but only for a moment. That Clare herself was ex-Air Force, replacing a previous security chief who was also ex-Air Force didn't seem like much of a coincidence after a second's thought. Dellin's explanation made perfect sense: the clinic was technically Air Force property. Why pay extra money for background checks on civilian trainees when they could hire ex-Air Force personnel who've already been cleared and trained? Rick and Joyce were ex-Air Force—

So it's no big surprise that Grace Fletcher was ex-Air Force too.

Curious as she was, Clare didn't have time to look at the other photos, and she supposed it was only fitting that she make some attempt to find out where Grace Fletcher had relocated to, to return the pictures. But . . . *No time to worry about it now*, and then, on a lark, she stuck the picture on the mirror, next to the lucky fortune cookie.

"Thanks for the great job, Grace Fletcher," Clare said to the snapshot. "I hope you're doing well . . . wherever you are . . ."

She rushed out, excited to get on with her tasks and officially begin her new job. When she was locking the front door, though, she noticed the door knocker. It hadn't caught her eye earlier because the door had been open when she first entered.

Strange, she thought.

The door knocker couldn't have been more inappropriate for such a living quarter: it was just a small oval of dull, old brass in the shape of a face. But the face was bereft of features, save for two, wide empty eyes. There was no mouth, no nose, no jawline really—just the eyes.

The eyes, at first, bothered her. They seemed ominous. But then as she looked at the knocker for a few more moments those same ominous blank eyes seemed to change. They seemed to somehow to welcome her.

(II)

Help.

Oh.

What's . . . wrong.

With.

Me.

Can't—

—can't—

Think.

Something's.

Wrong—

—with my—

Brain.

Yes. Something was *quite* wrong, due to the series of short-wave para-orbital lobotomies. The brain damage was resolute. She couldn't think anymore, not really. Just pieces of thoughts seemed to appear, like blobs of words she could barely understand. Even if someone had sat down right next to her and explained right to her face what had been done to her, she wouldn't be able to comprehend.

It wasn't her brain they were interested in.

She still had motor function, but it was uncontrolled now. The thick canvas straps kept her held down fast to the table. She could see the letters on the canvas straps, their manufacturer's name—POSEY—but she didn't really remember what letters were. At least she was fortunate in one respect: enough synaptic connections in her brain had been destroyed that, by now, the discomfort and the pain didn't register.

Lights came on and then went off. She heard voices but usually couldn't understand them because she'd pretty much forgotten what talking was. She felt things but didn't feel them: things going into her, parts of her being opened and prodded. At one point she turned her head when the lights were on and saw an intravenous line going into her arm . . . but she didn't know what it was.

She really didn't even know what her arm was either.

Once she looked up and saw faces peering back at her.

But couldn't comprehend it.

Something.

Wrong.

My brain.

"You're doing wonderfully," a voice said once.

Sometimes she convulsed. Her head whipped up and down for a few moments, spit flying off her lips. In her eyes an image registered. Her belly was swollen, the skin stretched pin-prick tight.

But she didn't know that the belly was hers. Didn't know that she was pregnant, didn't even know anymore what that meant. The only thing she really knew was that something had happened to her that wasn't right.

Who.

Did this.

To me?

The lights went off again.

She liked it better when the lights were off.

Her name was Grace Fletcher. But of course, by now, she didn't even know what a name was.

Chapter Five

(I)

Clare didn't want to use time unnecessarily. Making the longer drive to a department store back on the peninsula would've saved her some money but she wanted to get back to the clinic perimeter as fast as she could; she still had a lot to learn about the site, and even though her shift didn't technically begin until midnight, she saw it as her responsibility to get back promptly, get another look at the grounds before sundown. She also wanted to go back and read some of Grace Fletcher's shift reports, get an idea how she ran things. So instead, Clare had her shopping spree at the first beach store she saw and concentrated on sensible essentials—several pairs of summer-weight shorts; some light, airy blouses, sneakers, sandals, and—*What the hell?* she decided—a couple of swimsuits. But even the overly high prices scarcely put a dent in the cash Dellin had given her as a relocation allowance. Then she made a quick stop at the Publix supermarket for some groceries and toiletries and was back on the park grounds well before seven p.m.

First, back to the cottage to put the groceries in the fridge, then back to the clinic. The Blazer rode well, even over the rougher interior roads of the park which were mostly either gravel or grooved dirt. By seven it was cooling down, and when she'd progressed deeper into the property she found herself distracted again by the site's sheer natural beauty. Palmetto bushes and banks of widgeon grass grew wild between the endless palm trees. Petite green parrots squawked at her from nests of Spanish moss. Tiny lizards seemed flash-frozen against tree trunks, and at one point she saw a four-foot-high egret watching her as she drove by. When she stopped, the magnificent thing stared her down and spread its great white wings, as if to challenge her. *Don't worry, bird, I'm not messing with your turf.* She suspected the bird must be harmless; nevertheless, the sharp foot-long lance for a beak looked threatening enough.

"Oh, damn it . . . Don't tell me—"

Around the next bend, the small sign rose:

LAKE STEPHANIE 0.5 MILES
NO FISHING, NO BOATING, NO TRESPASSING
THIS IS A PROTECTED FEDERAL NATURE HABITAT

But the sign verified Clare's fear. "Airhead. I'm on the wrong spur." She must've missed her turn off the main road back to the park. *Careful,* she warned herself. She didn't want to drive all the way to the lake to turn around so she gingerly attempted a three-point reversal.

The road was little more than a service road, very narrow. *With my luck I'll back up over some rare endangered fern bush or something*, but when she was halfway finished with the maneuver—

CRUNCH!

Oh, no!

She stopped, got out quickly with her flashlight, and rushed to the rear of the vehicle. She couldn't imagine what she'd backed up over but the sound left no doubt that she'd hit *something*. She looked around, but . . .

Nothing.

Just mounds of dead leaves, palms fronds, vines and weeds. It didn't matter that it would still be light out for another hour and a half; this deep in the woods it was dark as early evening. She roved her flashlight back and forth, squinting, but still couldn't see that she'd hit anything.

What was the crunch?

She squinted harder, noticed a strange dip in the terrain, then finally she figured it out. It was a gully lining the road, but she couldn't see it because it was full of leaves. When she reached down, she felt something.

Sheet metal?

She brushed the leaves back and soon uncovered a small rowboat.

She shook her head, complaining to herself. "Why on earth is there a rowboat sitting in a ravine a half a mile *away* from the lake and even further from the bay?" Obviously someone had put it here, had deliberately hidden it under all the brush.

What for?

She scooped out some leaves, felt around inside the

hull. She didn't expect to find anything but after only a few seconds she hauled up a tackle box.

All right, not that big a deal. It was a poacher's boat. *They go after the fish stocked in the lake*. But that still didn't explain why they'd *hide* the boat here.

I guess I better get this back to the clinic.

It was a small boat, made of lightweight aluminum, and it would easily fit in the back of the Blazer. At first she thought of calling Rick for some assistance but then dismissed the idea. *Best to bring it in myself, show these people I can take care of things on my own*. Clare wasn't one to call on men whenever there was some dirty work to be done. She idled the Blazer forward, till the rear tire came off the boat, then got back out. Part of the bow was crushed by the tire. She flipped open the Blazer's back door, then walked right down into the ravine.

Her aim was to simply grab the edge of the boat, lift it up, and then slide the whole thing into the back of the Blazer. But there was one problem.

The instant she stepped into the ravine, she couldn't move her feet.

Yuck. Mud.

But she realized it wasn't exactly mud when she began to sink.

Quicksand.

The acknowledgment jolted her but she didn't panic. She willed herself not to move quickly, and for the moment, it worked; she could feel nothing solid beneath her feet but she wasn't sinking anymore. Was it an old wives' tale: the more you struggle, the faster you sink? She found out a second later when she carefully leaned to her side and reached up for the Blazer's rear bumper.

In only a few seconds, she sank from mid-calf to mid-thigh. With the flashlight, she scanned the edge of the road for vines, branches, anything she could grab, but there was nothing, and those few movements sank her a few more inches.

"Don't panic," she whispered to herself.

But now she was getting scared.

Even the rim of the boat was too far for her to reach; she stretched her hand out, grasping the flashlight, tried to hook its widened head against the boat's rim but—

clack!

The flashlight slipped out of her hand and fell in the boat.

Clare wasn't quite to the panic stage, even though now, she was waist deep and sinking further. Calling out would do no good, and she couldn't get to the radio or the horn.

But I can still make some noise.

Very slowly, she unholstered her gun, shook off the oatmeal-like quicksand that clung to it, and raised it in the air.

Someone will hear, she resolved, still fairly calm given the predicament. *Someone will come.*

At least that's what she was telling herself as she sank another inch. She cocked her pistol—

"Now don't you go and do that, Clare. Your muzzle-flash could start a fire. All this fallen brush out here—it's like tinder."

Clare looked up at the voice in a shocked relief. It was Adam Corey, the park ranger.

"Thank God!" she exclaimed. "I'm in quicksand!"

"Yeah, you sure are, just like the sign says." Adam stood grinning, a hip cocked as he lazily pointed his own flashlight to a sign posted a few feet in from the road.

DANGER! QUICKSAND!

Jesus, Clare thought. Some Spanish moss from a low tamarind branch obscured part of the sign. *But I should've seen it anyway,* she reprimanded herself. *I should've been more observant. If I had been, then I wouldn't be waist-deep in QUICKSAND looking like a perfect IDIOT!*

"Yeah, I obviously missed it," she said. "Had my mind on that damn boat. Help me out of this now, will you?"

"Sure, Clare," Adam said a bit too casually, still grinning.

Clare reached out, expecting Adam to do the same, but instead . . .

snap!

He lit a cigarette.

Clare was mortified. For the first time now, she truly *was* scared. "This is serious, Adam! I'm sinking! I'm about to drown in this stuff!"

He spewed smoke. "Naw. Fit gal like you? Ex-Air Force and all that? You'll be able to get yourself out."

Clare used all her might, churned her hips and legs was able to move aside slightly, but the effort only sank her another inch with each churn.

"You heard that old wives' tale? The more you struggle, the faster you sink?" Adam held the grin. "It's true."

Now Clare was up to the middle of her abdomen. *To hell with it. He's crazy or something—* She raised her revolver again. *Four shots in the air. And if that psychopath doesn't help me—two shots in him.*

The gesture wiped the grin off his face and suddenly he was rushing forward. "Whoa! Hold up there! Don't fire! It's a joke!"

"A JOKE?" Clare bellowed back.

"I'm sorry—it's a bad joke," he was saying now, reaching down. "It's only a little more than a yard deep."

Clare gaped at him. When she extended her feet in the quicksand, she felt something solid against her tiptoes.

"The ravine's brick-lined," Adam explained, trying to resist laughter. "It overflows with quicksand in the summer."

"You ASSHOLE!" Clare bellowed. The gun still heavy in her hand, she didn't actually contemplate shooting him but . . . the idea sounded kind of sweet.

A great, wet sucking sound ensued when Adam pulled her out. At one moment, her grimace lengthened when the viscid friction came close to pulling her pants down. Wouldn't *that* have been great! When her wrist began to slip from his grasp, Adam was left with no choice but to slip his other hand behind her thigh so that he wouldn't lose her. She didn't fall back in but the action left his hand clenching one side of her buttocks and a few fingers pressed against her pubis.

"Get your hand off of my ASS!"

"Sorry, I—"

Back out on the road, Clare stomped up and down, flops of the quicksand peeling off of her. She looked ridiculous.

"Look, Clare, I'm really sorry. It was just a joke. There was no way you could've been hurt."

Clare rarely exhibited outbursts that could be called explosive but in this instance . . . she exploded. "Shut UP, you unbelievable PRICK! You BASTARD! You SON OF A BITCH!"

"I said I was sorry, Clare. Jeez. And, come on, what were you doing in that stuff anyway?"

All she could do was continue to rage at him. "I was

trying to get that damn boat into the back of my damn truck 'cos it was hidden in the damn ravine! Then I sank in the damn QUICKSAND and then YOU come along and aren't any damn help AT ALL! DAMN you!"

He stammered more apologies as Clare used the edges of her hands to scrape the quicksand off her legs. "Here, let me help you," he offered, but she yelled, "Don't you even come NEAR me!" She bulled right past him, deliberately bumping his shoulder, heading back to the ravine. "I'm gonna get this damn boat back to the office, then I'm going to call the U.S. Park Service and file a complaint!"

"Aw, come on. That's a little excessive, isn't it?"

"No!"

"I could get transferred or even fired."

"You should've thought of that before you fucked with me!"

"Look, I'll make it up to ya. I'll—"

Something snapped the sentence off in Adam's mouth. When Clare's gaze jerked around, Adam's had too.

Something—a noise, a thrashing—seemed to be approaching them.

"You hear that?" he asked.

"Yeah. It's coming from the woods, isn't it?"

Yes, something thrashing rapidly, a large animal running through the woods. But Clare didn't think it was an animal. With the thrashing came a thin wheezing noise that sounded—

Human, she realized.

"Don't know what that is, but it sure doesn't sound right," Adam said, clearly disturbed. He shined his light into the woods, and drew his gun. Their row over the quicksand escapade was long dead. Something about that sound was very wrong.

Then the sound stopped.

"Hate to say this, but I could've sworn I saw someone looking back at us," Adam said.

The scarier part was, Clare thought she had too.

They both stood there for at least a minute, staring out. But it was just too dark.

"I'm going to bring the truck around, get the high-beams out there."

"Good idea . . ."

Clare went back to the Blazer, opened the door, and in less time than it took for her to even *think* about screaming, two long bony hands shot out of the Blazer and grabbed her throat.

(II)

After dinner, Mrs. Grable's husband, Derrick, fell asleep on the couch. She smiled at him, leaned over and kissed him on the cheek. She didn't have the heart to wake him and get him into bed. He just looked so peaceful there.

At least I still have him, she thought with some contentment. *We still have each other*.

That fact, the wonderful proof of love, made the other things tolerable.

Yes.

The other things.

She left the television on for him. It was the medications that made him sleepy at odd times. She wanted his favorite station on for when he woke up, the Travel Channel, with all those beach shows. She knew how he dreamed of going to the beach, going into the water, into the waves . . . He had his dreams but what of Mrs. Grable?

Day by day, that's all. That's all I can ask.

It had been Harry who'd gotten her into rehab all those years ago. He gave her this wonderful place to live, a job, a way to take care of her husband. Oh, sure, sometimes she hated him, because there was a price to pay. But it was only two or three times a week that she had to pay it.

And it was better than being dead.

She'd be dead for sure by now, if it hadn't been for Harry. It was ten years ago, before Derrick's accident, and it had been the fourth time that the black tar heroin had taken over her soul and forced her to abandon her marriage. Derrick had spent weeks trying to find her, and when he did, he called Harry. Harry had pulled some strings, got an investigative team out there. They found her in Seattle, in the 3rd-and-James District, turning bum-tricks and back up to slamming six quarter-gram hits a day right into her arm. The things she'd done, sometimes for as little as five dollars, didn't even revolt her at the time. She just needed to cop, anything to cop a quarter gram of tar. She'd lived like an animal, scrounging in dumpsters and doing repugnant things with abominable people.

Yes, she'd be dead for sure by now if it hadn't been for Harry. He just kept forgiving her and forgiving her—and so had Derrick. As it turned out, the last rehab had worked, and she had a life again.

So. Looking at it that way, that thing she had to do, two or three times a week, when the buzzer went off?

It's a small price to pay.

It would probably be tonight so she knew she should get ready. She downed two stiff shots of whiskey from the bottle she kept hidden in the laundry room. The blossom of heat they left in her belly always helped her cope, and they numbed her a little. The swelling on her lip had gone down to next to nothing; she guessed that he'd been told not to hit her much in the face. The tenants would wonder, ask questions. Sometimes it was quite a task hiding the bruises and swellings. The marks on the other parts of her body could be hidden with clothing, but her face?

God, I hope he doesn't hit me in the face tonight . . .

Her private area was another story. Sometimes she'd limp for a full day afterward, from what he did to her there, and then there was always the biting and choking. She didn't even dare think about it, couldn't.

When she got mad, when those inner rages began to grow and she began to hate Harry again, all it took was a stray image of her past life to flit back—shooting up under the Aurora Bridge or fellating winos in Pioneer Square—and the hatred and rage blew away like a wisp of steam.

Things could be *a lot* worse.

At least her return to normalcy had been kind to her body. Not just for her age but considering the rigors of heroin addiction, she looked quite good. Exercise and a good diet kept her toned. No cellulite yet, and no sagging breasts, thank God. She still had pleasures to offer Derrick, even in spite of his condition. She knew he loved her high, ample breasts. That's why she hated it all the more when she had to make love to him with her bra on. She cupped her breast now in the bathroom mirror and winced at the ache from that last bite. It still looked awful, that ragged bite mark puffed out around her tender nipple.

Sick bastard . . .

But there was no use in that, no use in hating. She'd learned that long ago. This was her lot. It was an odd way to help Harry but she owed Harry her life.

So don't complain about a few little bites.

She stood there looking at herself in the mirror as dusk began to claim the brilliant sky. The inside of the house turned blue, then orange, then darker and darker. Mrs. Grable watched herself turn into a shadow.

Sometime later, just as she'd predicted, the buzzer went off. Her body jolted as if she'd just suffered an electric shock. The house seemed to rattle.

It's time, she thought.

Mrs. Grable took off her clothes, turned in the dusk-tinted darkness, and padded softly for the steps that would take her down to the basement.

(III)

It saw them.

It saw the lights so then it hid.

It was upset, it was mad and sad at the same time.

It had been just about to get its hands back on the little skinny dirty girl but then those lights came on.

The little skinny dirty girl.

It liked playing with her. It liked hearing her scream when it was doing it to her. It was supposed to take her back to the place—it knew that—and it also knew that taking her back to the place was very important.

But it knew now that it had done bad.

It shouldn't have played with her so much; it should've taken her back to the place right away.

Now there was a big problem, and it knew that it was its fault.

Now there was this man and this other woman. They had the little skinny dirty girl now. Its first impulse was to go out to them. First it would claw out the man's throat and watch all his blood come out, and then it would rip open his stomach and pull out all those warm wet things that were inside. It liked doing that. And the woman? It would drag her down and do it to her hard. It would do it to her a lot. But this time it would be smart. This time the first thing it would do was break her legs. So she couldn't run away like the little skinny dirty girl. It would break the little skinny dirty girl's legs too, which it should have done in the first place. And then it would do it to her again too and probably just kill her this time because it was mad at the little skinny dirty girl.

Yes, it wanted to go out when it had first seen this man and woman but then it had seen that the man and the woman both had those gun-things.

It knew that the gun-things could hurt it.

It sat huddled behind a tree now; it was very upset. How could everything have gone so wrong?

Soon there were more people, more lights, funny flashing red and white lights, and then some men were putting the little skinny dirty girl on this long thing and then they put her in the thing with the flashing red and white lights and were going away, taking the little dirty skinny girl with them. Then the man and woman with the gun-things went away too. Now all it could do was sit by itself in the dark woods.

It had let the little skinny dirty girl get away.

They would not be happy.

(IV)

"Jesus." Clare sat at the table, and for a moment she covered her face with her hands.

"Yeah, that was sure something," Adam said.

After the ambulance had left, Clare and Adam had driven back to the security office, Clare's rage over the quicksand "joke" long forgotten. The first thing she'd done was brief Rick on what had happened, ordered him to suspend normal rounds and spend the rest of his shift patrolling the lake spur.

Maybe someone else was out there too.

It had been almost an hour ago, but she still felt rattled, and the caffeine from several iced coffees only made her feel more wired up. The whole thing had been terrifying.

"You okay?"

"Yes," she said. "I just can't get that image out of my head. That poor girl."

Clare and Adam had heard the thrashing sounds from the woods, had even thought they'd seen something. That's when Clare had gone back to her Blazer to turn on the highbeams and—

God! she thought, thinking back.

Those long thin arms had shot out of the Blazer, the grimy hands pawing at Clare's throat, not to hurt her but to grab on to her.

"Help holy Jesus please help me he's still out there trying to kill me I'm begging you please to help me!" the inhumanly high voice had erupted.

The girl in the truck—naked, delirious, and insect-bitten—passed out only minutes after she latched onto Clare. Long hair hung in slimy strings, her skin scratched, abraded, and smeared in muck. She'd obviously been mauled by an attacker, had spent a considerable amount of time fleeing through the forest and salt marshes.

Running from someone, Clare thought. *From someone who's still out there.*

The safety, now, of the security office seemed counterfeit. Clare looked up to Adam. "I guess the state police will seal off the island and dragnet the area. We better get back out there and help them."

Adam sat down, laxed back in the chair and without much class plopped his boots up on the table. There was an air about him now: that what Clare had said was naive and he was trying to find an inoffensive way of telling her that. "Well, see, I hate to tell you this, but there won't be any dragnet and there's no way the state police will do anything about this."

"A girl was raped!"

"Pardon my French but she was probably gang-banged by her friends—of her own free will—then got lost in the swamps 'cos she was all screwed up on drugs. That's Kari Ann Wells we're talking about, not Martha Stewart. That girl is infamous on the local crime blotter."

Clare held back on her next objection. Back out on the road, Adam had been able to identify the girl at once, claiming to have seen her around town many times. "Local tramp, bigtime drugger. Kari Ann Wells is her name. Ask any beach cop from here to Clearwater—that girl is *well*-known."

"I can understand your concern, Clare," he was saying now in the office, "but all that wild stuff she was talking? It's bullshit. She wasn't raped, she wasn't attacked or held against her will by anyone. She's a meth-head, that's all. All the white trash around here are into that stuff. They come out here to the island at night to poach, they smoke their meth, and get all screwed up. Long-time users get their brains fried, and believe me, Kari Ann Wells is a long-time user. The stuff makes you delirious, makes you hallucinate, makes you crazy. It can even make you see monsters."

Clare did have to consider that her own emotions might be clouding her judgment here, from the moment she'd heard the word *rape*. When they'd been on the road, the EMTs had put Kari Ann on a stretcher and covered her up, and that's when she'd regained consciousness for a few moments. Clare had time to ask a few questions:

"Kari Ann? You're going to be all right now, so don't worry. But we need to know about the man who did this do you. Do you know his name? Do you remember what he looked like?"

The girl's expression looked absolutely skeletal, and her voice was a grating rasp. "It raped me all night long . . ." Her face shriveled up like a white prune at the recollection. "It just kept doing it . . ."

The mere mention of rape only caused Clare to feel worse for the girl. She wanted to continue questioning her but—*I better leave well enough alone*, she determined. *She's in shock, she's incoherent.* "Just get some rest, Kari Ann."

Clare was about to leave, but the girl's bony hand grabbed her shirt. Somehow she grinned, even though the girl looked insane. "I hurt it, though. I hurt it bad."

"What, Kari?"

She extended her other hand, whose fingers seemed wrapped around something—

Something bloody.

Clare took it. *Yuck. What is*— She thought of a large skinned tomato. It was wet, hot in her hand. Was it really blood covering it, or just swamp muck?

"Ripped one of the bastard's balls right off . . ."

Yeah, she's out of her mind right now, which is understandable. She doesn't know what she's saying. Clare knew that the slimy thing in her hand couldn't possibly be a testicle. It was much too large.

But knowing what it wasn't only heightened the mystery.

What IS this thing?

Kari Ann hadn't let go of Clare's shirt. Rivulets of tears cleaned lines of mud off her face. "It wasn't a man. It was a monster."

The hand slipped off; the woman lapsed back into unconsciousness. Then the EMT's drove her away, the ambulance lights flooding the woods with red and white light.

Now that Clare thought of it, Adam's explanation made the most sense. *Drug-induced delirium and hallucinations.* But then there was always—

"I agree with you, Adam. But answer me one question. What's that thing I put in the fridge?"

Indeed, when they'd come back to the office, Clare had put the "testicle" in a plastic bag and stuck it in the refrigerator to preserve it as evidence. Initially, she thought the police might want it properly analyzed.

Adam chuckled, and retrieved the plastic bag. He held it out. "Again, pardon my French, but this sure as hell isn't some fella's *ball.* Jesus, it's as big as a fuckin' mango. I told you, the rednecks come out here to poach fish from Lake Stephanie. It's probably a carp belly or just a handful of fish guts. That crystal meth crap'll make you think anything." More chuckling, more shaking his head. "I'd like to meet the man with a pair of nuts *this* big." He dropped the laden bag into the garbage.

Crude as he was, the explanation seemed reasonable. "And the boat you found, back when you went for your little swim in the quicksand?"

Clare gave him the finger.

"It's obviously been there a long time. Poachers don't drive over here 'cos they know they can't get past the main security gate—so they come over here on a motor boat but they'll bring a smaller rowboat along with them, for the lake. They probably stashed it there under the brush so they don't have to bother bringing it back and forth each time they come out."

Again, another solid explanation. *No mysteries after all.*

"I'm off duty now so I'm gonna scoot," Adam said. Then he smiled. "Unless you want me to stick around, help you *dragnet* the woods for *monsters*. You know, I'll bet that monster's still out there looking for his nut!"

Clare's glare couldn't have been harsher. "Hey, Adam? Do me a favor and get the fuck out of here."

He paused at the door. "Come on, I said I was sorry about the quicksand. You'll cool off, women always do."

"Get out!"

He shuffled off, leaving Clare to stew. *What a jerk.*

It was nine-thirty now; her official shift still wouldn't begin for another two and a half hours. She spent some time writing the entire incident up; Dellin would want a full report in the morning. Over the radio, she instructed Rick to resume normal rounds. As much as she now detested Adam Corey, he was correct about what had happened. Given the girl's drug history? *No, there're no rapists in the woods.*

At least Clare had been able to assess her own flaws as a result. Kari Ann Wells's hysterical claim of being raped had instantly triggered Clare's worst conceptions, having been raped herself not that long ago. Her outrage had been instantaneous; she hadn't even paused to consider other more reasonable possibilities.

"Well, everything's okay now," she muttered to herself. She took some time to flip through the file cabinet in the corner, dig up some old operating logs. She wanted to get an idea how Grace Fletcher had run things, and after a half hour of perusing the log sheets, she was happy to see that her own protocols were similar. On one sheet, however, there was a yellow Post-It sticker, on which Grace had scribbled a note to herself:

ASK DELLIN IN A.M.: STEAM FROM B-WING VENT?

Steam? From B-Wing? Clare scanned the log sheet to more detail. Just below the Post-It was an entry.

0357 hrs: Returned from vehicular punch station rounds. No incidents, but I did notice what appeared to be steam venting from a roof duct on the B-Wing side of the clinic.

Hmm, Clare thought. *B-Wing's just a storage area. Why would steam be venting there?*

It was a good question. But then another one popped up a few moments later; Clare noticed another Post-It on a more recent log sheet.

FIND OUT WHAT A "MAGNA-FERRIC CARBON ELEMENT" IS, DO WEB SEARCH ON HODDER-TECH INDUSTRIES.

Grace Fletcher was an inquisitive woman; she was asking herself questions about the site, via reminder notes. Clare searched the logsheet, and sure enough:

2315 hrs.: Opened main gate for delivery from H.R. Trucking, Florida commercial tag 041601. Signed for one large box marked "Magna-ferric-

carbon element assembly," Hodder-Tech Ind. Secured the delivery in the loading dock hold.

Clare had never heard of a magna-ferric carbon element assembly, but her curiosity just kept ticking. *Some sort of medical or diagnostic equipment?* she guessed. It must be, but that and the report of steam from B-Wing?

Very interesting.

So interesting that she found herself leaving the building, walking around with her flashlight and inspecting the part of the structure that comprised B-Wing.

Her flashlight beam edged along the roof. A small metal out-flow vent poured forth steam to the extent that she was surprised she hadn't noticed it before. The steady gaseous plume unwound up into tree tops and twilight.

Why is steam coming out of B-Wing? The building's empty. Something's running in there.

She was so curious she went right back inside and, moments later, was pressing her ear against the wing's main security door.

But heard nothing.

Forget about it. It's probably a dehumidifier or something . . .

Back at the office, though, she turned on the computer but was instantly disappointed to discover that there was no modem in it, no way to access a web server. No way to do an Internet search and find out about this element gizmo. She supposed she could go into Dellin's office, see if his computer had any online capabilities, but that didn't seem justifiable. *Forget it,* she thought again.

Then the radio squawked. It was Rick.

"Hey, Clare, I just wanted to let you know, I'm opening the main gate for a delivery."

"Okay," Clare answered into the mike. On the surveillance screen, she could see Rick getting out of his security vehicle, approaching the fortress-like main gate. A large truck idled on the other side. "I'll meet them at the loading dock. Who's the delivery from?"

"Hodder-Tech Industries."

Chapter Six

(I)

"I don't like this place, Harley Mack," Cinny complained. "It's creepy."

"Shut your hole. You want 'em to hear ya?"

Don't you tell me to shut my hole! Cinny Bock thought. Of course she would never actually *say* that; she didn't have the guts. Harley Mack had a bad enough disposition, and it was only that much worse when he hadn't gotten high for a couple of days. Cinny knew that if she sassed him he'd just punch her up again.

But it was no exaggeration. This end of the park *was* creepy.

"Where's the bottle? Jesus Christ, Cin, if you chugged that whole bottle, you'll be seein' stars for a week."

Cinny didn't doubt it; frowning, she passed him the Wild Turkey. When they were stringing out, it took the edge off a little. Problem was Cinny never held her liquor very well. She was getting fidgety, woozy; her vision was getting fuzzy. *Oh, well. At least I have a buzz.* It was better than nothing, she supposed, and if Harley Mack starting smacking on her later, she wouldn't have to feel it all.

Cinny Bock was thirty but the cruel Florida sun and half a lifetime of "tweaking" had worn her out to at least a look of forty-five. The reed-thin physique and hair the color of a sink full of dishwater didn't help. If it were any consolation, permanent tan lines seemed to make the pancake-flat breasts look not quite that flat, and she'd never had any kids so her stomach was still pretty tight. And Harley Mack was essentially on his way to becoming a male version of the same social species. Together, they were pretty much the status quo of their heritage, two peas in an interminable pod, and what they were doing here was merely fulfilling a post-Darwinian providence. Their existence essentially revolved around two things: robbery and drugs—plus a third thing in between: sex. Harley Mack had already done two stints for burglary and he definitely didn't want to get a third strike. That's why he'd been staking out the clinic, to get a close look at the place before he knocked it over. Harley Mack was no dumb redneck. He was going to do this job right.

This, in fact, was the third time he'd come out to the park at night. From what he could tell, the guards were only on duty during the week, no security coverage on the weekends, and this meant that the clinic must have a pretty good alarm system. Harley Mack was a damn good lock-pick but with doors that were wired? He could forget it. But he'd already decided he was wasn't going to go through any doors.

He was going to go *up*—through the floor.

And he knew there was a whole bunch of dope inside, waiting for him to snatch. The money he got for a haul like that would keep him and Cinny in ice for a long time. "Looks like that damn park ranger's not coming back," he said. They were hiding behind a hillock of shoal grass, looking at the clinic. Now two security guards seemed to be signing in a shipment of some sort; lights blazed down over the loading dock, and a long box was being wheeled off of a rumbling delivery truck.

"Hope I don't have to take care of those guards."

Cinny immediately complained: "You said you weren't doing the actual job till this weekend 'cos the guards aren't on duty then!"

"Shut your hole. I said I *think* the guards aren't on duty then, can't be sure."

"Harley Mack! You promised you weren't gonna hurt no one!"

Harley Mack sputtered, gave the bottle back to her. They'd only been out here an hour and she was already being a pain in the ass. "Just have another slug and pipe down. I ain't gonna hurt no one."

"You promise?"

"I promise, baby."

No, I won't hurt no one, he amended, *but I'll sure as shit KILL them if I get seen. No witnesses this time. Can't go back to the joint.*

No, the state pen was no fun, and with his slim, wiry frame and long hair, he drove most of those long-timers nuts. Harley Mack doubted that anyone had even called him by his real name during the entirety of his last stint; he was "Baby," he was "Honey," he was "White Bitch." Harley Mack was about as tough a street redneck as you'd find, but in the pen? He found out fast—like in one day—that he didn't know what tough was. First time a con had patted his crotch, Harley Mack fought, all right—and was promptly beaten to within an inch of his life and sodomized right there on the floor while the detention officers pretended not to see. It didn't matter how tough you were on the outside. On the *inside* guys like Harley were *property*. His "Boy Cherry" had gone fast, and just as fast he'd become an integral part of a world that most people couldn't really conceive of, a world where men were traded to other men for a mere pack of cigarettes, and where "tossing salad" had nothing to do with lettuce. In stir, Harley Mack had done things that he could *never* tell Cinny about. One night, just after he'd gotten out, she'd asked him: "Did they, you know, did they ever like, hold you down, and try to-to—" "Oh, yeah, they tried," Harley lied to her face, "but I just beat the shit out of all of 'em. I got to be the cellblock hero on account of I'd beat the shit out of any'a them fellas who tried any of that queer stuff."

Cellblock hero, indeed. In truth, Harley Mack had been the Cellblock Bitch. But his little white lie had sufficiently allayed Cinny. He would always be a hero to her . . . even when he was smacking her in the face.

Now she was looking over the hillock herself. "That one guard there, Harley Mack—he looks pretty tough."

Harley gaped. "Sheee-it, girl. That big pussy? I'll have him hollerin' for his mommy with one hand behind my back." His squint narrowed; he noticed the other guard now, the woman. "Wouldn't mind a roll in the hay with the chick, though. That little thing? Bet she squeaks when she's gettin' in."

"You better not!" Cinny exclaimed, enraged. "You better not even be *thinkin'* stuff like that!"

Cinny was easy to rile up, especially when she was drunk—and Harley Mack's cruel streak never passed up an opportunity. "Yeah, I'll pull her little security pants down and give her the ballin' of her life. I'll fuck her from one end of this park to the other, then I'll flip her over and start again. Yes, sir, that blond bitch'll be walkin' like a cowboy for the rest of her life."

This time Cinny hit him in the back so hard her hand hurt. "Oh, yeah, you big prick! Well, you go right ahead! Why don't I just call her over here right now and—"

The rest of Cinny's inebriated objections were reduced to a smothered mewling sound when her boyfriend grabbed her lips and pinched them shut. Her arms and legs flailed in the pain.

"I done told you, keep your voice down, ya drunk ninny! I was just jokin' fer Christ's sake."

When he released her, she sidled back, hands to her mouth. "Damn you, Harley Mack," she whispered through her fingers. "That hurt!"

"Was supposed ta. Done told ya to keep your hole shut. See what happens when you don't do what I tell ya?"

She sure did. *Damn him. Treat me like that.* She sat behind him now, glaring as he continued to peer over the hillock at the clinic. *I just won't talk to him, see how he likes that, and later on when we're in bed and he wants some lovin', he ain't gettin' none.* Yes, she'd show him, all right. Actually, by the time that instance occurred, Cinny would be totally passed out from the sheer volume of alcohol and would have no say in the matter whatsoever. When Harley Mack wanted "lovin'," he took it; Cinny's state of consciousness hardly mattered.

Something hopped beside her.

What's that?

It hopped again, something about the size of a bar of soap.

Oh, look! A toad!

Cinny had always been an animal lover, and toads

had always been her favorite. Most women dismissed them as bumpy, disgusting things but not Cinny. To her they were cute. She remembered back when she was little (back before her father had introduced her to the act of sexual intercourse at the age of thirteen, and before she'd started smoking crystal meth in her tenth-grade locker room), she'd kept pet toads in an aquarium with dirt on the bottom. She fed them worms and crickets and put in jar lids with water. She loved the way they chirped and looked at her with those big black marble-like eyes. They were adorable and fun and she loved them more than any other pets she'd ever had. One day her brothers had used them to play baseball with but that was another story.

Here, though, behind the hillock, the sight of the toad overjoyed her. She picked it right up. "Hi, there, Mr. Toad," she whispered. "Harley Mack, look what I found. He's cute, ain't he?"

Harley Mack did not share her enthusiasm. "Ya got tits for brains? It'll pee in your hand and give ya warts, ya dumb ass."

Cinny just smirked. *He* was the dumb ass; everybody knew that toads didn't really give you warts. It did, however, pee in her hand, quite liberally, but Cinny didn't mind. It couldn't help it, it was just a harmless little animal.

Then the harmless little animal bit her right on the thumb.

It all happened so fast. Harley Mack had silenced her shriek in a half second, pinching her lips together again. "What the *hail* is wrong with you!" came his own enraged whisper.

Mewling, Cinny tried to fling the toad away . . . but couldn't. In the light filtering over from the loading dock, she could see the amphibian's jaw closed over her thumb.

And she could even see two thin, half-inch-long fangs puncturing her skin.

The pain was intense enough to occlude her memory to the fact that toads didn't have fangs. Harley Mack twisted the toad off and threw it away, then let go of his shuddering girlfriend's lips.

"It *bit* me, it had fangs!" she whispered.

"A *toad?*" He was tempted to bust her one in the mouth right there. "Toads don't bite people, you little jizz-head! And they don't have *fangs!*"

"Yeah? Look!" She held up her bleeding thumb, the two puncture marks obvious.

"You just scraped it against some saw-grass, a-hole. And it's a damn good thing that truck motor's running, otherwise them security guards would'a heard you. I'm trying to stake this place out so's we can make a good haul and you're back there playin' grab-ass with a toad. Now go back and wait in the boat."

Wait in the boat? Like, alone? "Screw that. I ain't walkin' around this creepy place by myself. There might be more'a them fanged toads out there."

Harley Mack just shook his head. "All right, then you keep quiet if you're gonna stay. One more peep out'a you and I'll crowbar your head."

The whiskey toned the pain down some, but there were still tears in Cinny's eyes when she looked at the wound. That toad *had* bitten her. It *did* have fangs. She could see the blood still dribbling from the pair of tooth-marks. Now she was getting depressed. *I wanna go back to the trailer . . .* At least the trailer park was safe (save for the drive-bys and the bathtub meth labs blowing up). *There ain't no toads with fangs!* she rationalized. Yes, this part of the park was creepy, it simply *wasn't right*. And as the alcohol dulled her senses further she became convinced that it was even more than that.

This damn park is evil . . .

She tugged on her man's MOTORHEAD shirt and in the quietest voice possible, she pleaded, "Harley Mack, let's just go. This place is scarin' me. Forget about that stupid clinic."

"We need the dope that's in there—"

"I'll-I'll get a job. We can buy all the ice we want with my paycheck."

"Don't make me laugh. You ain't kept a job more than a day in your whole life; ya can't even add two and two. I'm bustin' into this place and takin' their stash."

Cinny remembered the one-second glimpse of the toad: jaws clamped over her thumb, fangs digging in. The big black eyes were looking right at her, and she could swear she could feel its sticky tongue licking up her blood. She began to cry like a child. "Please, please, I wanna go home—"

Then:

Two spears of pain lanced into her lower leg; it felt like she was being knifed. In the split moment before she screamed, she looked down and saw that it wasn't a toad this time, it was a long coiling snake, drilling her with its fangs.

"A snake's bitin' me—"

WHACK!

Harley Mack didn't fool around this time. One quick impact of his big fist into Cinny's head silenced her shriek instantly and knocked her right out. He peered fretfully over the hillock and saw to his relief that the two security guards still had not heard her outburst thanks to the engine noise from the delivery truck. *Damn lucky*. He decided to throw in the towel for tonight; how could he possibly get a good stakeout of the place with this noisy drunk bitch screamin' every five minutes? *Fuck it, I'll just come back out here Saturday night and do the job, and I'll leave this pain in the ass home . . . if I don't kill her first . . .* He'd have to carry her back to the boat but that was no big deal; the meth kept her good and skinny. Before he reached to pick her up, he thought: *What the hell was she squawkin' about this time? A snake?*

Then he looked closer.

The little pinhead wasn't lyin'.

A snake indeed had bitten her—or, in fact, was *still* biting her, vigorously on the leg just above her ankle. It was just a green snake not even two feet long, and not poisonous.

Harley Mack grabbed the snake, yanked it off her, and flung it away, but as he did so a sudden nauseousness dropped down into the pit of his belly. He flung Cinny over his shoulder and tromped back toward his boat as quickly as possible.

Yes, there was something fucked up about this park, and Harley Mack wanted to get out of there fast.

Why?

Because when he'd pulled that snake off of Cinny's leg, he couldn't help but notice something.

The snake had two heads.

(II)

The wooden packing crate was eight feet long and a foot high and wide. Within the two-by-four beams that formed its structure, plywood sheets extended. Clare could easily read the black stenciled letters:

FRAGILE
ONE (1) MAGNA-FERRIC CARBON ELEMENT ASSEMBLY INCLUDING
ONE (1) CONDUCTION HARNESS
AND FOUR (4) MAGNA-FERRIC CARBON ELEMENTS.
DO NOT DROP!

After the driver and Rick had hand-trucked the crate into the loading dock hold, Clare signed for the delivery from Hodder-Tech Industries Inc.

"What exactly is it?" she asked the driver.

His eyes looked bloodshot from too much caffeine. "Got no idea," he replied, adjusting his backward Devil Rays ball cap. "I just make the drive and the drop. But we do make a lot of regular runs for Hodder-Tech."

"Where to? Hospitals? Clinics like this?"

"Yeah, but also lots of factories."

Factories? "Then I guess it must be some kind of an illumination element."

"Got no idea." He grinned at her with bad teeth. "Have a good 'un!"

He got back in his truck and left. Clare just shook her head.

"I think it's some kind of heating element," Rick offered after locking up the hold.

"Heaters? In Florida?" It sounded absurd to Clare. "If that's true, it's a damn long heater. That crate was eight feet. You mean like baseboard heating?"

"No, like a water heater or something, I think. I asked Dellin about it once. For some medical equipment. Oh, now I remember. He said they needed them for sterilization."

Clare's brow ridged. She didn't see how something that heavy and long could be needed for sterilization but then again, it wasn't her field. *Oh, well. Sterilization.* At least she had her answer, odd and rather boring as it was.

"Any word on how the girl's doing?" Rick asked.

"I called the hospital a little while ago. She's dehydrated and in shock but in stable condition. They're also treating her with a lot of antibiotics to ward off infections; she had a lot of insect bites."

"It's really too bad how these people get mixed up with drugs and then things like this happen. She could've died out here." He glanced at the red taillights of the delivery truck. "I'm going to go lock the main gate up after the truck leaves, then I'll come back and show you around. I've still got a half hour to go on my shift."

"Forget it," Clare dismissed him. "I'll sign you out on your log. Just go home after you lock the gate."

This news gladdened Rick. "You sure?"

"Yeah, Joyce did a good job of showing me around earlier. Actually I'm kind of anxious to make my first solo rounds. Just take off. There's no point in both of us sweating our butts off out here."

"Thanks, Clare! Have a good shift."

Clare waved as he drove away. When she walked down the loading dock ramp, back to her truck, the high-watt floodlights clicked off via motion sensor. For some reason, she felt listless now, bored—even after all the commotion of the day. She was eager to begin her first official round of the site's punch stations, to get a feel of the property on her own. The main gate, the lake, the beaches, several points on the clinic grounds, and a number of other areas of the site were fitted with punch stations that verified exactly what time the guard had been at the station. Long gone were the days of punch clocks that guards had to lug around with them; now all they needed was their master key, which logged the punch time in on the security computer. Clare had made many a round in her career but never on a site so beautiful. Even in the stifling midnight heat, the look of the place in its edges of moonlight seemed paradisial. The evening throbbed from the dense waves of cricket trills. Night birds frolicked. *This sure beats looking at Air Force security warrens and hearing F-16s taking off every two minutes.*

The exotic animal sounds faded when she approached the shore, and she smiled to herself when she recalled exactly where she was now, what Joyce had called "Trojan Point." The small lagoon lay still as black glass. *No lovers tonight*, she thought when she roved the Blazer's spotlight across the area. She drove around the lagoon's rim, then found herself on the beach. She turned off the engine, turned off the headlights. This late and this dark, the beach suddenly became a tiny domain of the surreal, a secret place only for her. The gentle surf lapped ashore. The moonlight lay long rippling lines, like foxfire, across the water, and all at once, Clare felt as though she were the only person in the world.

Eyes wide open on the water, she thanked God, or the universe, or the fates for what had happened to her . . .

Thank you so much for letting this happen to me. Finally—something good. Thank you.

It wasn't quite a prayer but it may as well have been. She was happy now, for the first time in over a year. But she was grateful too.

She wanted to just sit here for a few more moments, relishing the peace and quiet. It was so tranquil, so serene. But soon distractions began to intrude. Not thoughts as much as images—images of men.

Dellin and that attractive, preoccupied manner of his, doctorish but sexy. Then Rick, rugged, tough but smart, and the hard muscles she remembered when she'd secretly watched him and Joyce in their erotic clinch. *God*, she thought, a little short of breath. She was getting hot, and it wasn't from the evening heat. It bewildered her, this sudden rush of hormones; it had haunted her all day. She'd worked with attractive men for years but it never had such an effect. Hard as she tried to push out the images, they continued to sneak into her mind: now she was remembering more of what she'd seen of Rick and Joyce on the video screen: Joyce's bare breasts thrust out, Rick's hands all over her as if molding a voluptuous statue, his mouth sucking wet trails along her skin . . .

Stop it.

Something else, then—not an image from memory but a fantasy. She gave into it, she couldn't help it. It was not Joyce on the screen now, it was her. Suddenly Rick's hands were on *her*, Rick's mouth was laving *her* nipples. Clare was the sultry statue now. Her breath gusted as the image changed and got darker, hotter. It was no longer Rick who tended to her, it was Dellin, stolid, intent, his dark eyes hard on her. She cringed and rose to her tiptoes against the tree as *Dellin's* hands gripped her waist and began to slowly slide upward over her sweat-damp skin. The hands cupped her breasts and squeezed, tweezering her nipples in the V's of their fingers.

Ssssstop . . .

Even more inexplicably, the muse amplified. Yes, she was being touched now, as she would love to be touched, the slow deliberate hand sliding back around her buttocks. When her thoughts pleaded for the fingers to slide up further, they obliged, less than gingerly running up the furrow of her sex. But the hand wasn't Dellin's anymore, it was Adam's.

Here was the inexplicable part: as much as she deplored the impertinent park ranger, the effects of the fantasy sharpened. She knew where it came from. From earlier, when he'd lifted her out of the waist-deep sinkhole; he'd put his hand between her legs in the pretense of helping her out. It probably hadn't even been necessary, just a rude man copping a cheap feel—

But she didn't care now, and she didn't bother telling herself to stop anymore. She just sat there in the Blazer, in the moonlit dark, and gave in to it. The hand pressed harder, the fingers probing. His tongue slid up the side of her neck, and then he began to whisper to her:

Duh-duh-don't worry, Clare. I wuh-wuh-won't hurt you till I'm done.

The fantasy collapsed; her mind betraying her in the most treacherous fashion. Though it only lasted for a second longer, it seemed like hours, as every detail of her rape replayed in her mind. The dark, warm woods were gone. Now she lay flat on her back on a cold stainless steel autopsy platform. The examination lights nearly blinded her in their perfect white glare. It was Stuart Winster's hands that were running over the contours of her nude body. She'd always regarded him as harmless; he was a civilian who worked on the base, a janitor, and the only significant thing about him was his being the son of one *Colonel* Winster—the commander of the Air Force Clinical Research Corp, who obviously used his pull to get him the job. Clare found out quickly that *harmless* was not the word to describe the retarded twenty-two-year-old.

His left hand was normal, and this was the hand that held the sharpened awl. He traced the needlelike point slowly up and down the skin of her belly, not enough to break the skin, just enough to leave a caustic tingle. It was his right hand that roved lower—the deformed hand. A birth defect made the hand look clawlike, with only two fingers—thumb and forefinger.

It was the hand that maximized her terror. Not her abduction and rape, not the fear of death. Not the image of his face, nor the slightly warped forehead. It was that plier-like hand . . .

She'd been on a midnight shift, making foot rounds along the admin perimeter. He'd knocked her out from behind with a club and then injected her with some kind of paralytic agent. She'd come to in the autopsy suite. Ankle and wrist ties weren't necessary; what he'd injected her with effected total paralysis of the major voluntary muscle groups. She could open and close her eyes, move her lips a bit, but that was all, and the agent had no anesthetic properties.

She could feel everything. She just couldn't move.

Clare, Clare . . . You're real pretty.

Drooling, he licked all around her face while the two hideous fingers fished in her sex. A surge of agony like a cigarette to her skin ripped through her when he abruptly bit one of her nipples. Her reflexes told her to scream, to cringe and bolt at the pain but again there was the drug he'd injected her with. Not a single fiber of muscle moved in reaction, and not a peep escaped her lips. The teeth bit down so hard, she heard them click together.

It steepled her horror. What would he bite next? Her heart raced with that dreaded question when his mouth moved lower, below her waist where it was soon down there along with the hand, working in tandem. Clare just wished she could die. It was clear what he wanted to do, and without the extra breadth of three more fingers, it was rather easy.

I wanna play with you . . . inside.

Clare felt as though she were being operated on, if only non-surgically. Something alive and awful was inside of her but thankfully it didn't last long. The pervert's more dire needs took command, and that's when he climbed on top of her and just did it. Clare felt no longer human, no longer really alive herself; she was just a pile of hamburger meat, being plied and prodded on a cold countertop.

Whether he actually would've killed her was something she'd never know. He'd climaxed fast, leaving the physical fact like hot glue between her legs. *Now we play some more, Clare,* he slurred, but he wasn't off of her a minute before the SOD guard walked in. It was over just as quickly, Clare recovering in the hospital, expecting to see justice done.

Which never happened.

It had all been an exquisite setup. In only weeks, they had it looking like Clare was a pathological liar trying to manufacture a fake rape case to make herself famous.

Jesus God, was all she thought now.

At last, she was able to shut it all out of her head.

The nightmarish memory drifted away, as did the previous fantasies. Sitting in the truck now, she felt exhausted, icky with sweat, and partly nauseated. *So much for the idyllic vision of the beach . . .* She rolled up the Blazer's windows, cranked on the a/c, and drove off.

At least she got her mind off it quickly. The cooler air made her feel better. She drove around to the punch stations on the island's first spur and soon found herself on a road running along another beach. When she looked to her left—

Are those the beach cottages?

A narrow channel of water separated the spurs, and when she looked harder she could see the cluster of beach cottages on the other side. It was only a few hundred yards away. She could see lights on in some of them.

She thought about it a moment, then concluded, *What's the harm?* She was done with that hour's rounds, and it wasn't like she'd be deliberately invading someone's privacy. She just wanted to see what her cottage looked like from this distance.

She removed the pair of field glasses from the glove box and raised them to her eyes . . .

That's some view. She was surprised by the strength and clarity of the binoculars, and even more surprised when she rolled up the zoom. The ripples on the water looked just feet away, and when she nudged the binoculars up just a little, she was looking at her own cottage in superb detail. She'd left the long motorized drapes open behind the sliding-glass doors, and a kitchen light had inadvertently been left on but it was enough illumination to see just about everything inside. *Keep those drapes closed at night,* she reminded herself. If she could see into the place this well, so could anyone else, especially Adam Corey whom Joyce already suspected of being a peeper.

A brief movement caught her eye in the next cottage—Mrs. Grable's cottage. It was the only cottage that hadn't been built on stilts. More movement shifted in a window.

All right, I know I shouldn't be doing this but I've GOT *to get a look at this husband of hers.*

In one window she saw Mrs. Grable, quite naked. In spite of the woman's age, it was easy to tell that she'd worked hard over the years to keep fit; she looked even better naked than in the simple dress Clare had seen her in earlier when they'd met. *Good lord, she's got a body like a South Beach sun bunny.* Heavy breasts with dark, prominent areolae didn't sag in the least, and there was no trace of cellulite on the buttocks or thighs. Regrettably, though, even at this considerable distance, Clare could make out the awful bite mark she'd glimpsed when being shown around, an oval ring around the nipple like a branding mark, and now she noticed several similar marks on her back. Without the brutal marks, though, Mrs. Grable's hourglass figure and womanly lines would make most twenty-year-olds envious. *And some twenty-eight-year-olds too*, Clare admitted. The woman looked just as sexy after she'd slipped the tight maroon nightgown over her head, robust breasts jutting when she walked out of the room.

But where's the damn husband?

The crisp field of Clare's binoculars roved to the next block of light, the living room window, she supposed. The lights were dim here, though, and she could see the television on. *There's a man in there, all right*, Clare determined, *and he's just like all men—a slavering sexist pig*. It was obviously some travel channel on the tv screen, bouncy blondes in string bikinis frolicking on some exotic, faraway beach.

Then she saw the husband.

From the position, she could only see his head. A good-looking man, longish dark hair with only a few touches of gray, nice facial angles. *Just when I was starting to believe she didn't really have a husband, here he is,* Clare thought. *And Joyce was right, he's normal looking, handsome even.*

She could see him smiling warmly as his wife entered the room. Clare's eyes widened a bit behind the binoculars.

Mrs. Grable was now grinning, and there was something clearly wanton in the grin, a hot dirty passion. She stood in front of the television, blocking the screen—

And began to dance.

Not the jig, either. A slow, fluid, erotic dance, like a dancer in a strip joint.

Her hands opened against her trim waist, then began to slither upward until they were caressing her breasts. One hand lingered there, fingers tweaking a nipple, and then the other hand lowered again, smoothing over the sheer fabric that stretched across her pubis.

All right, she's doing a striptease for her husband. Nothing wrong with that—until he starts beating her . . .

But now something clashed with her motives. This didn't look like a dysfunctional marriage at all; it looked like a happy, lively one. The expressions on their faces were those of two people vivaciously in love.

But this man was really a wife-beater?

I don't know, Clare thought. *He just doesn't look the part. Christ, maybe Mrs. Grable is just a klutz; maybe she really IS falling down the stairs and slipping on the soap.*

Maybe those bite marks were really rashes from some skin disorder.

Clare knew she had trespassed on their privacy enough. Just as Mrs. Grable was slowly inching the hem of her nightgown up over her bare hips and crotch, Clare turned the binoculars away from the window, leaving them to their play.

But as she did so, the viewing field fell immediately on another window, just as dimly lit, only this time it wasn't light from a television, it was light from a few candles.

And it was a window in *Joyce's* cottage.

Here we go again. A little secret moral malfeasance amongst my employees. Then she frowned at herself. *And who am I to talk about moral malfeasance? I'm the one peeping in windows.*

Clare knew it was wrong but she watched for a few minutes, fairly fascinated by the physical dexterity of her two guards. Joyce and Rick were both naked, of course, and they were using Joyce's high poster bed for a sexual gymnasium, actively investigating every conceivable position—and some not so conceivable—through which their genitals might be joined. Joyce's pretty face seemed wide open in the most intent bliss, her nipples gorged, her sweat-slick breasts heaving. Rick's muscular arms and chest tensed to razor-sharp contours as he turned his lover every which way. *Jesus Christ, everybody's makin' bacon tonight!* Clare thought. It was almost a jealous complaint. *This is one happy friggin' island . . .*

She lowered the binoculars, thought about it a moment, then put them away. *I've been a bad girl long enough. Joyce really needs to close her blinds.* She knew that on-the-job romances always had a big potential for trouble, but she liked Rick and Joyce too much to report them. Besides, they were good guards, and Clare also hoped they could all become friends too.

She couldn't deny her own little crush on Dellin, but he was too distant, too wrapped up in his profession to regard Clare as anything more than an employee. Anything beyond a solid professional relationship was out of the question, and Clare felt absurd for even pondering a romance. In truth, she hadn't had any real friends in a long time—for most of her college years and her entire stint in the Air Force—to the extent now that *not* having any social life seemed normal. In college, she'd made grades her utmost priority, and in the Air Force, it was her job performance. Now, so many years later, she was beginning to realize what she'd missed out on.

Well, I'll work things out. It's only my first day! She would just have to find a roundabout way of suggesting that Rick and Joyce be more discreet. *And close their damn blinds when they make whoopie!*

She decided to get back to work. She started the Blazer back up and headed off. A door-check at the clinic sounded like a good idea, and it wouldn't hurt double-checking the main gate. The Blazer disappeared down the narrow road.

In a way, it was too bad she hadn't stayed here a few more minutes—with the binoculars—for if she had, she would've seen the darkled figure lurking about the cottages, looking into windows.

(III)

The hand, almost tenderly, rubbed the bloated belly. Her navel had popped inside-out by now, a little knot of flesh protruding.

Machines hummed.

Something beeped rapidly along with her heart.

"Push now. Push."

The name of the woman on Table 2 was Donna Kramer. She was fairly young, and could even be called attractive in her pregnancy. Prenatal lactation filled her breasts, glazed her nipples. The steel stirrups spread her legs wide.

She couldn't scream; she'd been gagged with an oral breather, a simple slab of rubber with an airway in it.

She couldn't feel much either, and she could scarcely think, because, like Grace Fletcher—the woman on Table 1—she'd been radioactively lobotomized. Technically her condition would be called a PVS—Persistent Vegetative State. Less than technically, one could say that her brain had been messed with to the extent that it didn't really work anymore.

"Twenty-eight days—it's amazing," the voice fluttered above her.

There were actually two figures standing in the room—two men—but that's all Donna's reduced mental functions would allow her to know. She didn't even know she was about to give birth, at least not really. The concept was lost to her now.

"Push, push. Don't worry. You're going to be a fine, fine mother—a mother of miracles . . ."

It didn't hurt. Between the spinal injections and the lobotomization of the prefrontal pain centers, all she felt was a great pressure. Perhaps it was instinct, then, or phantom memory, that enabled her to tighten her abdominal muscles whenever the man said "Push."

She pushed and pushed.

"I can see the head! Push!"

She pushed and pushed some more.

"Yes, yes!"

The great pressure left her, as though it were being pulled from her. Her head lolled on the table and her plump, milk-filled breasts wobbled. Though she couldn't understand what she was seeing, her sense of vision *did* still register.

She saw her tight shining distended belly collapse as quickly as a knife though a basketball.

Whatever had been inside was now out.

Some synaptic activity caused another phantom inkling of thought: Was she supposed to hear something now? A baby crying?

She heard nothing.

"Damn it. She didn't take."

"That's too bad."

"Don't just stand there with it. Take it away. It makes me sick to look at."

"Sorry."

Donna Kramer had seen the small thing they'd taken out of her. Some man was holding it aloft in the bright light, like a sack of onions. The pink umbilicus dangled as though it were a loop of intestine.

Donna's head turned involuntarily to one side now. Her eyes met someone else's eyes. It was Grace, the woman on Table 1, whose eyes looked right into hers. The eyes were dead but somehow still alive.

A long sigh.

"Clean this up now."

"What about—"

"Her? Leave her for now. We'll continue with the intravenal feeding. And clean her up. I'm not sure what we'll do with her yet."

"Can I—"

"Just do as I say. I'll let you know when I decide. Damn. We're still getting those teratologic syndromes. I don't understand it; we did a full screen."

A pause stretched over the white room.

Then the same voice said: "Try, try again, I guess . . ."

Donna could decipher none of the discourse, so it didn't really matter what was going on.

He'd said she'd be a mother of miracles.

Some miracle.

As close to clinically brain-dead as she was, even Donna knew it was no miracle that had come out of her.

It was a monstrosity.

Chapter Seven

(I)

"That's quite a first day," Dellin said. Steam from his coffee drifted upward. Clare sat opposite him in the clinic cafeteria where he'd kindly bought her breakfast, paying a princely $4.00 for both of their heaping plates of bacon, eggs, hash browns, and buttermilk pancakes the size of frisbees. Clare was briefing him on her shift.

"An abandoned rowboat that seems to have been hidden deliberately and a hysterical naked girl in acute refractory shock," he said. "You had more action in one day than we usually get in six months."

"Well then I sure hope that covers the *next* six months," Clare tried to joke. But none of it was a joke; the woman from last night could just as easily have died.

To be thorough, she'd faxed a report on Kari Ann Wells to the local police, and got a case number in the event that she wanted any follow-up information. The boat she'd simply stowed in a storage shed on the property. As for the girl, though, Dellin wasn't that surprised, citing much of what Adam had said about the local "meth-heads."

"I"m off shift at noon," Clare went on, trying only to nibble at her breakfast. It was so delicious, she would've liked to scarf it all down at once. *Don't make yourself look like a pig in front of Dellin!* she thought. "Unless you object, we'll go blank noon to four. Since it's Friday, I want to double up the guards from four to midnight, in case any more of the locals decide to wander over."

"Fine, fine. Whatever you think is best. Your judgment is part of what we're paying you for."

"Do you know when the clinic director is coming in? I'd really like to meet him today."

"Harry? Oh, yeah. It'll be Monday, for sure. Today he's doing rounds with the oncologists at Tampa General. We actually need more patients because the first series are all cured."

"That's wonderful."

"It sure is. In fact, I've only got two aftercare appointments today, then I'm out of here. I think I'm actually going to hit the beach today, if the UV index isn't too high."

Clare smiled at the thought. "Yeah, I guess cancer specialists aren't too keen on lounging in the sun."

"Just enough for a little color, that's all. Care to join me?"

The sudden question seemed to ram Clare's thought processes into a brick wall. *Damn! He's asking me to go to the beach with him? Should I-I-I—*

"Oh, sorry. Dumb suggestion on my part," he said before she could answer. "You just finished a twelve-hour shift—of course you're going to be going straight home and going to bed. Especially after all the commotion last night, you must be exhausted."

Crap . . . The only appropriate response was to agree. "Yeah, I am pretty tired. But thanks for asking."

"Some other time, then. I mean, if you feel like it."

Trust me, I feel like it. A tiny despair seemed to pat her shoulder. "That would be great." She struggled to keep the conversation from stumbling. "I think Joyce told me that you have an apartment somewhere but you also stay at one of the cottages on occasion?"

"I have a condo downtown, that's where I stay most of the time. But sometimes on weekends I stay at my cottage. I'm the one on the very end."

It just made her wonder more about him. *He's got a condo downtown. Does he have a wife to go with it? Kids?* Perhaps not, not if he just invited her to the beach. *Does he have a serious girlfriend, is he a casual dater? Jeez, Joyce is probably right. With my luck, he's gay.*

"Oh, and I signed in a delivery last night," she said, "from Hodder-Tech Industries."

Dellin merely nodded, mopping syrup with a forkful of pancakes.

"A magna-ferric carbon element assembly."

Dellin nodded.

"Rick said it was for sterilization or something?"

Another nod.

"Would that account for the steam venting from the roof over B-Wing?"

"Yep."

Jesus, help me out here. Just when she was starting to think that Dellin expressly didn't want to talk about it, he finished his plate, gulping. "It's called an industrial-grade dry-heat desiccator a bit more complex than sterilization The system is a lot more expensive but it keeps the EPA from harping at us. Most medical facilities get rid of their waste with an on-site incinerator. But these days? Burning that sort of stuff makes a lot of smoke and soot. Chimneys on a federal habitat reserve is a big no-no."

"Oh," Clare said. She still didn't quite get it. *No big deal*. But she felt anxious now—he was done with his breakfast, and she had nothing else to report. She desperately wanted something more to talk about . . . because she didn't want him to leave. But it made her feel totally unprofessional, like a little school girl with a crush on the teacher.

Dellin looked at his watch, then pushed his plate away. "Well, time for me to go."

Figures, Clare thought glumly. "'Bye . . ." *Yeah, I've definitely got a thing for this guy*. Hand in chin, she watched him exit the cafeteria, back to his office.

When the cafeteria had nearly emptied, she finished her meal and felt fit to burst as a result. She knew that it was the sudden melancholy that urged her to eat it all. Later, she moped around the clinic, logged tag numbers in the parking lot, finished her operating report. *Just making busywork for myself*. What she needed to beat the doldrums was a good solid block of sleep. *Ten more minutes and I'm out of here*, she thought when she looked at the wall clock.

Her attention snapped back when the fax machine suddenly sprang to noisy life. *Hmmm* . . . One sheet hung out of the roller like a tongue. She took it out.

DELIVERY VERIFICATION

HODDER-TECH INDUSTRIES, INC.

"OUR HEAT CAN'T BE BEAT!"

"You've got to be kidding me. . . ." She read the full fax, which informed her to expect a delivery on Monday afternoon.

ONE (1) MAGNA-FERRIC CARBON ELEMENT ASSEMBLY INCLUDING:

ONE (1) CONDUCTION HARNESS
AND FOUR (4) MAGNA-FERRIC CARBON ELEMENTS.

We just got this last night. Confused, she push-pinned it to the cork board as a reminder. *I'm just a security guard. Nobody tells me anything.* Dellin had just explained what this assembly was for—a desiccator for sterile-waste disposal. *Seems kind of off-the-wall that we'd need another assembly this soon,* the thought occurred to her. She knew that Dellin was in his office now; she could go and ask him about it. *I better wait on that; I'll ask him about it Monday. I just had breakfast with him a little while ago, I'd just be pestering him.*

Nine minutes later, she was about to lock up the office and leave, when the phone rang.

"Clinic security."

"Hi, Clare, it's me," a voice responded.

Clare's smirk twisted her lips. "Me *who?*"

"Adam, you know, the big bad insensitive park ranger."

Not that jackass again . . . "What do you want, Adam? I'm off-shift."

"I'm sorry to disturb ya, honey—"

"*Don't* . . . call me honey—"

"—but you might want to get down here to Lake Stephanie and check this out because—and I hope you'll pardon my French—there's something here that is one hundred-percent surefire fucked up."

(II)

"What . . . what IS that?" was all she could say.

"A frog the size of a bag of fuckin' groceries is what it looks like to me."

Adam's assessment was overstated . . . but not by much. Clare had never seen a frog so large or oddly colored. Tan skin with black dots. And it had a tail.

The thing was dead, squashed along the shore. Its eight-inch-wide jaws were parted slightly, through which most of its innards had been squeezed.

She looked quizzically to Adam. "Did you run it over?"

"Yeah, an accident, of course. I just thought it was a pile of mud sittin' there when I was drivin' along the shoreline. Then I felt a bump, and heard a big splat." He actually looked a little queasy now, gazing down at it. "Heard another sound too, almost like a *bark*."

"A bark? You mean like a dog?"

"Yeah, sort of." His eyes thinned in the confusion, then he attempted to mimic: "*Rrrruff!*"

Clare was baffled. She'd never seen anything like this. "It must weight ten pounds."

"Fifteen, I'd say."

"Well, I've never heard of frogs getting this big, but you're the nature guy, so . . . Do they?"

"Yeah, in fuckin' Madagascar—pardon my French. And even the ones that *do* get this big . . . don't have tails."

Disgust pulled at Clare's face when she peered closer. "They don't have fangs, either, do they?"

"That they don't," Adam said, standing cross-armed with one foot up on an old felled tree. "All frogs and toads got teeth, but usually just two up front and they're tiny. But fangs like that? I never heard of it."

The rim of the creature's jaw looked like a strange saw-blade, with overlapping fangs up front. Clare's stomach hitched when she got a full view, and realized that if the animal chose to bite a human, it could do serious damage. Its brow seemed very un-froglike, though, angling outward over the eyes as if emerging to points, and the feet at the ends of its pronated forearms were the size of a baby's hand.

"It's either some very rare species that I don't know about, or it's a mutation," Adam said.

"A mutation? You can't be serious."

"Why not? Happens all the time. Long time ago I did a field stint at the reserve off of Lake Crotalus. Turned out that a solvent factory was dumping their dregs in the lake every night. It fucked everything up—er, pardon—"

"I know, Adam, pardon your French," she said crankily. "Why bother even saying that if you're gonna cuss? And are you telling me that industrial dumping could cause mutations like *this?*"

"I don't see why not. The stuff they were dumping at Crotalus made salamanders grow six legs. All the pickerel and sunfish developed carcinogenic tumors, and the tumors were shaped like fish heads. Egrets and gulls would feed on the shore worms and then they'd lay conjoined eggs. The hatchlings were worms with beaks. All kinds of mutations can occur from something like that. It's not uncommon at all."

Clare knew nothing about it. She walked toward the woodline, looking around.

"Careful," Adam said. "There might be quicksand." Then he let out the faintest chuckle.

I wish I had some rope 'cos I would LOVE to hang him. Beyond the trees, she noted nothing out of the ordinary, but what did she expect to see? *Another giant frog hopping around?* Next she walked back to the shoreline, peering into the nearly motionless water. Her stomach hitched again when she thought she saw a snakelike shape—ten feet long—slip along beneath the surface. *No, no,* she thought. *That was just a shadow or something. A ripple in the current . . .*

Adam lived up to everything that Clare might believe of him now when he thumbed a ball of chewing tobacco into his cheek and began to spit. "You're the security chief. What are your conclusions?"

It was a pertinent question. "I guess someone's dumping something toxic into the lake."

"Yeah. Like who?"

"How do I know?" She leaned over, hands on knees, to look again at the immense frog. *This is just what I need to see after that huge breakfast. A mutated frog with its guts hanging out its mouth.* The sight distracted her; Adam's own gaze abruptly jerked away when she stood up and turned around. *The pervert was staring right up my butt!* "Get a good look?"

"Huh?" He spat a line of brown juice into the water. "Well, do I need to point out that there ain't any solvent factories around here? But what *is* around here?"

"The clinic, Adam. What are you saying? That the clinic is dumping toxic by-products into the lake? That's ridiculous. There are no toxic substances being produced there. They treat elderly outpatients."

Now Adam lit a cigarette.

He chews AND smokes, Clare observed. *This guy is the prize. I'll bet he's never put a toilet seat down in his life.*

"I'm just thinking about past associations. When something fishy's going on, you look around and see if there are any fishy *people* in the immediate vicinity."

"You mean you, right?"

Adam smiled through the comment. "I mean maybe the guy you work for."

Clare blinked. "The clinic director? Harry?"

"Naw. Let's face it. It's pretty obvious you got some eyes for Dellin Daniels—"

Clare was outraged. "It is NOT! That's preposterous!" she blared back at him, all the while, thinking, *How did he know!* "And there's nothing *fishy* about him!"

Adam moped back to his truck. "Yeah, well, maybe you're right."

"What? What's fishy about Dellin?"

He pulled a large sack out of his truck. "Let's just drop it. Forget I said anything. You're the real authority out here anyway. It's your job to do the investigating, ain't it?"

He's just a total crackpot! Clare decided she wouldn't even acknowledge his arcane accusation by responding to it any further.

"What are you doing now!" she asked, annoyed.

"Wow, you must really be on the rag today." He flapped the bag open, leaned over. "You may be the authority on the property, but this is still a government-owned reserve. I gotta take *this* to *my* authorities. Want to give me a hand?"

He meant the frog! He was trying to shove the disgusting thing into the bag.

"Uh, no," she assured him

She headed back to her own truck, too angry to say anything more.

"Aw, there ya go, stompin' away all flustered. Just like a woman." He'd managed to flop the dead frog all the way in the bag now, it drooped off his arm like a sack of potatoes. "But when you're out of your tizzy-fit . . . think about what I said. You hear me?"

"Go away! Take your frog and get out of here!"

Adam shrugged. "Watch your back 'round *that* guy."

Clare slammed her door and drove off.

(III)

"I'm not losing my old Air Force starch, am I?" she asked herself in the mirror. She was absolutely frazzled and so infuriated she could feel her temples beating. Could it all be blamed on Adam Corey? If so, she'd let her professional edge become considerably worn down. Sexism in the working environment—in particular—and crummy people in general were aspects of life she'd learned to deal with. She'd never let it affect her to this degree. It wasn't in her makeup to let an incident, or an obnoxious person, get her this angry.

Calm down, Clare. Jesus, it's no big deal. There are a lot of jerks in the world—you can't let them piss you off.

She knew right away that it was foolish to deliberate the cause of her aggravation. It had nothing to do with her shift last night, and it had nothing to do with the hideous frog. It wasn't even Adam Corey's complete lack of couth when he constantly undressed her with his eyes.

Dellin.

That's what it was. First, there was the ranger's cocky statement about Clare having "eyes" for Dellin. But even that wasn't what got her going. Adam had implied that Dellin had less than a pristine past; in not so many words, the lowbrow ranger hinted that there might even be something criminal in Dellin's background. She gave that some hard thought, then just shook her head at herself. *Consider the source. He's just jealous of Dellin, doesn't like him for some reason, so he's making up a bunch of crap. Sure, I have "eyes" for Dellin, but that jackass Adam Corey's definitely got eyes for me.* In Clare's view, there was a time and place for everything, and there was a big difference between being admired by men and being stared at as a sex object. Stuart Winster had been one to stare at her a lot too, and she'd wound up being molested and raped by him. *The last thing I need is another pervert gaping at me behind my back.*

But these observations seemed confusing right now. *Adam Corey's lusting after me? That's a mystery . . .* She stood nude in front of the mirror over the long dresser . . . and didn't like what she saw. It had been a long time since she'd felt anything close to attractive, and the image in the mirror didn't help at all. *I've never looked WORSE in my life.* Her ribs were showing, her hipbones stuck out. The huge breakfast made her abdomen stick out, yet her breasts were tiny from the last year of eating from handout trucks, often just one meal a day.

She beat her hand on the dresser, then smiled at her reflection.

She refused to let herself become insecure; she wasn't going to mope and boo-hoo to herself. That was not Clare, and had never been.

Yeah, I'm skinny as a pipe cleaner and I've had a bad year. But all that changes today. I'm going to gain weight and get back in shape. I'm going to excel at my job and go forward. And I'm NOT going to let morons like Adam Corey bother me.

Simple.

A final attention made her feel even better: *And, besides, Dellin invited me to go to the beach with him, so I must not look all THAT bad . . .*

Even better.

First thing she'd done upon returning to her cottage was take a long cool shower. For bed clothes she wore a simple extra-large t-shirt that she'd picked up at the store; it came down nearly to her knees, and blared LIFE'S A BEACH on the front. She was about to fall into bed that very moment, but the snapshot of Grace Fletcher on the mirror caught her eye, and it reminded her . . .

That's right, there were more pictures.

She reopened the wooden vanity box and removed the remaining photos.

A few more of Grace Fletcher, a few of the cottage, the beach, the lake—typical photos anyone would take.

The last photo was a group shot.

"I don't believe it," Clare murmured. "That's not—"

Three people looked back at her from the photo, all smiling and all dressed in security uniforms. One was Grace Fletcher, one was a man with a dark buzzcut and mustache, and the third was . . .

Donna Kramer, Clare thought. They'd gone to basic training and MP school together; they'd been friends. *Now there's a coincidence.* Clare remembered Donna Kramer as a bright spunky woman, a quality recruit and great person. They'd hung out together quite a bit during their training months, had even corresponded a bit after they'd moved on to their separate permanent duty stations. After a while, though, they'd grown out of touch with each other, which Clare regretted now. Seeing this picture of Donna was a happy reminder of some of the *good* times she'd had in the Air Force.

She'd never seen the man in the photo. *Ex-military too.* The haircut told all. Clare couldn't quite remember but she thought Mrs. Grable had said his name was Rob or Bob. Clare's eyes narrowed, though—something else immediately came to mind now.

Mrs. *Grable said Grace Fletcher and the other guards were fired for partying on duty*. Hot tub parties at night. Excessive drinking. A *Roman orgy*, the woman had inferred. Clare had no way of knowing how much of that owed to exaggeration but she certainly didn't remember Donna Kramer like that.

Then again, who knows? People change.

Her drowsiness seduced her; the large soft bed and cool air couldn't have felt more comfortable. *Please, no nightmares, no rape dream today*, came the hopeful thought. Sometimes she had the dream several times a week, a cruel ploy of her own psyche. Why would some mental part of her make her relive the rape in her dreams? She felt so good now, though, she was sure she wouldn't have it this time. She drifted off quickly, one arm slung over her head. She had the habit of sleeping on her belly, and her forearm dangled in the gap between the edge of the bed and the wall. *Yes, sleep*, she thought. *This is just . . . so . . . nice . . .*

Just as she would fall fully to sleep, her fingers touched something.

Her eyes slid back open. With her forearm dangling in the gap, the tips of her fingers landed on something flat. *Damn it*. There was a box of some sort under the bed, and she knew her curiosity wouldn't let her sleep until she found out what it was.

All too often, her curiosity was her curse. Next she was on her knees, sliding what she'd touched out from under the bed.

A shoebox.

But there weren't shoes in it.

Clare sighed through a smile when she lifted the lid.

The first thing she saw in the box was a vibrator crafted of green transparent rubber. *Grace Fletcher, you naughty girl . . .* The device was shameful in the detail with which it duplicated the contour of a penis; if anything it was a caricature, *too* large, *too* veiny, *too* stout. Clare nearly squealed when she picked it up. The clear kiwi-green rubber that surrounded the battery housing was warm and jelly-soft. It looked beastly, alien. Clare couldn't imagine using one like this on herself yet she giggled just the same.

But there was something else in the shoebox too.

MAXELL, she read. GX-SILVER 3-PACK

Videotapes.

Two VHS tapes were stacked in the slip-box they'd been purchased in. Clare slid them out but discovered nothing written on them, no dates, no topics. The box was for a three-pack, though, and there was no sign of the third tape. *Maybe it's still in the VCR,* she thought, *but . . . I'm exhausted. Do I really want to bother with this now?*

She frowned at the answer, trudging out to the living room and the more-than-adequate entertainment center arranged in the corner.

There was no tape currently in the VCR.

Still got the first two, she thought. *And I guess it's show-time.*

She popped in the first tape, lounging back on the long couch. *Probably vacation videos or something like that,* she supposed.

But she was wrong.

Quite wrong.

(IV)

He had her all to himself now but probably not for long, so . . .

Have a little fun while I can.

Her head whipped back and forth when he licked between her breasts. It tasted really salty; he liked it. Then he gripped her face with his hands—"Hold still"—and licked both of her eyes.

Her head shuddered in his grip.

"I'm just licking you—stop it!"

He didn't know why—he just liked to lick pretty girls.

"There's worse things I could be doing so just stop. Be nice and you won't get hurt. Now . . . stick out your tongue."

He tightened his grip on her face; her face was getting red. Her eyes were squeezed shut and she was keeping her mouth closed.

No tongue today.

He ran his tongue across her lips, but she had her lips closed so tight it wasn't any fun. When he started sucking—

"Whoa!"

tick, tick, tick!

He yanked his face back just in time. In an instant, she'd jerked her head forward, teeth exposed. She'd tried to bite him!

He was mad now. "I can bite too."

She actually shrieked this time. They never shrieked, even when he *really* worked them over. The machine with the nozzles was supposed to stop that, it did something to their brains so they couldn't make noise and move much.

But the nozzle-machine must not have worked right with this one.

The shriek sputtered down.

He chuckled. "Aw, come on. I didn't bite you *that* hard."

This time he bit hard, high up on the inside of her thigh. Her shriek exploded into a loud, ugly scream, and her whole body lurched up. If her ankles and wrists hadn't been lashed down, she would have been able to grab him!

This was no fun.

He guessed he shouldn't be playing with her anyway; no one had told him for sure it they were done with her yet. Sometimes he was allowed to play with them afterward, if they didn't take, or if there was some problem. Most of the first ones had been like that, hitchhikers, prostitutes—the experiments, and when they were done, he got to play with them and kill them.

He wished he could kill this one.

He walked over to the shorter haired one, the one on Table 1. She was older but he liked her more. She looked like she would be nice to him if she got to know him. He rubbed her breasts; they felt big and wobbly, like water balloons. Her eyes were open and she was blinking but she didn't move at all when he'd touched her.

"You're pretty," he said. "Even with your stomach like that."

He touched her pregnant abdomen and rubbed it. When he tickled the pushed-out bellybutton, she didn't react. When he licked it and sucked it, she didn't react.

Yes, he liked her.

"I'm-I'm-I'm gonna bite you but just a little and not

that hard," he told her all at once in a long verbal stumble.

He bit her on the side, over her ribs, not too hard at first but—well, harder a few seconds later. He couldn't help it. He liked to bite them.

She tremored a little; he could see her knees shaking in the stirrup braces. But she didn't make any noise at all, she hadn't even turned her head to the other side.

"I like that."

He rubbed his finger over the mark. It was a crisp purple oval.

Wow, that looks neat.

He wanted to make another one.

He turned her head over on the table. Her eyes seemed to dart around wildly.

"I'm-I'm gonna bite your face now but just a little teeny bit and I promise it won't be hard—"

He leaned forward.

He was going to bite her on the cheek, right at the cheekbone part, right under the eye—

"No, no," another voice came in.

The door clicked shut.

"You mustn't torment her, not that one. The prenatal environment is just as important as the formative, as any developmental stage for that matter."

He didn't know what that meant. "S-sorry."

Footsteps ticked across the tile flooring, an arm came around his back.

"It's all right, you needn't worry. Use the other one for your play—the one that didn't take."

He was led back to Table 2.

"She's no fun. She tried to bite me."

"Hmm."

"She made noise too, and tried to grab me. But-but she couldn't 'cos she—"

"Because of the restraints, of course." A pause. Then he went over to where the screens were and he turned one on and pushed a blue button on a box.

"My fault entirely. I should've taken a bit more care during the first treatment." On one of the screens an x-ray of the girl's head appeared.

Neat!

It showed veins and stuff, and when she moved her head, the x-ray head moved too.

Two of the nozzle-things were pulled over, pointed at her head.

"These short-wave nuclear lobotomies have never been that precise. She's a strong girl, though, I must say. But if she's still got motor function . . . that's simply unacceptable. It's for their own good, after all."

He adjusted the nozzles, while looking back and forth at the screen.

"Might as well use her for practice now. Brush up on my technique. Something trans-orbital this time, yes. Let's just irradiate the entire motor sulcus . . . and . . . well—the hypophysis too. Why not?"

Not too much longer, then:

"There. That should simmer her down."

He walked up, looked down at her.

He wasn't sure.

"Well, if you're still *that* concerned about her biting you . . ."

A scalpel with a blade shaped like a lemon-wedge flashed in the light. Through the cheek, at the area where the upper and lower back molars met, the blade was inserted, then shoved down.

It made a slight grisly sound, like cutting through the

joint of a raw chicken leg. Surprisingly little blood came out. Then the process was repeated on the other side of her face.

"Ah. Right through the lateral and medial pterygoid groups. She won't be biting anyone now."

Her mouth just *hung* open now. Inside, the tongue seemed to be jumping around.

"Wuh—wow!"

"Go on, have your fun." Footsteps began to tick back toward the door. "We won't be needing her anymore, so . . . when you're done?"

The finger pointed to the large round hatch on the wall.

"Oh, wow! Thanks!"

A pause. A gentle smile.

The footsteps left.

The door clicked shut behind them.

His bright eyes gazed down at the girl with the unhinged jaw.

I can have all kinds of fun now!

Indeed.

And he would.

Chapter Eight

(I)

Holy smokes! Clare thought when the video was done.

In her entire life, she'd only seen sexually explicit videos maybe once or twice, way back in college during the weekend keggers. And she'd never watched more than a few minutes. All that moaning and groaning, naked people manipulating themselves into asinine positions, every detail of genitalia zoomed in on. It just seemed dumb to her, not erotic at all.

But the tapes she'd found under the bed?

They were quite a bit different.

These were not typical commercial offerings from the adult video industry; there were no foolish titles like *Backside to the Future* or *The Bare Witch Project*. These tapes had no titles at all, and no "porn" stars.

The stars of *these* movies were Grace Fletcher, Donna Kramer, and Rob Thomas, the previous security staff for the clinic.

All of a sudden, Mrs. Grable's analogy of a "Roman orgy" was proven all too accurate. Clare was absolutely shocked by what she saw. A threesome to the maximum, and every imaginable sexual act pursued. Amid laughter, giggling, and harsh lights, they'd taken turns taping each other during the revelry. The Jacuzzi, the couch, the living room floor, all provided stages for the lewd action. In most of the scenes, the antics seemed desperate; in several fleshy vignettes, they still had their boots on when they were going at it. In one portion of footage, Grace and Donna were manically making out on the foyer floor, so caught up in each other, they'd forgotten to close the front door. In another scene, Rob and Grace were having sex on the couch with such ferocity, the couch actually tipped over.

This is outrageous! They're like dogs in heat!

The busiest scenes, though, were the ones in which all three participated at once; Rob would adjust the camera from a stable position and join in. He lounged back, laughing—"Am I the luckiest man in the world or *what?*"—as Grace and Donna fellated him at the same time. Both tapes were a kaleidoscope of earthy sexual frolic: hips thumping, breasts bouncing, heads whipping back and forth. Buttocks were groped, legs were thrust apart, nipples were plucked, tweaked, and sucked. It was carnal pandemonium. In many of the scenes, Rob climaxed first but this was not a problem for Grace and Donna. They'd finish each other off with the translucent green vibrator.

"That was a *bit* much," Clare muttered aloud when the tapes played out. She couldn't imagine people being so out of control, and she was particularly surprised by Donna Kramer's conduct. Clare remembered Donna as being fairly straitlaced, conservative even, but the last video image of her had shown the polar opposite: sprawled out nude on the floor—*this* floor—with her legs wrapped around a man's head and a woman using her face for a place to sit.

So much for straitlaced.

A bunch of sex maniacs . . . and the place I'm living in used to be their love shack. They'd obviously filmed their exploits as an erotic curio, they same way regular couples sometimes did—something arousing to watch in the future, a passionate remnant of their three-way affair. Clare wondered how she'd react if she ever ran into Donna Kramer again, how she might compose herself if she ever met Grace Fletcher. The prospect—now that she thought of it—wasn't even that remote. *They'll have a friggin' cow when they realize they left these tapes here*. It made sense that someone would come back for them. Who would leave tapes like these with a stranger?

Now that she'd seen the tapes, her curiosities were slaked. There was still one question, however: *Where's the third tape?* The set came in a three-pack, but there were only two. Was the third tape at the cottage? *Who cares!* she yelled at herself. *Forget about it! It's not important!* She put the tapes back in the shoebox, was about to take it all back to the bedroom, but she just slid over, limp. Her fatigue ambushed her; suddenly sleep was dragging her down right there on the couch. *At least drag your butt back to bed*, she thought, but, no, that wasn't going to happen. The long soft couch was too comfortable. Ordinarily it might have bothered her—did she want to *sleep* on something that people were having group sex on not so long ago? *Too tired to care . . .* The soft hum of the air-conditioning lulled her to sleep in moments.

She didn't dream of her rape, thank God. Instead, she dreamt of the videos, of Grace, Donna, and Rob, a replay of what she'd just watched, only the dream version was silent. No lewd giggles, no waves of moans or climactic shrieks. Just silence and movement, all that sweat-shiny skin converging, loins splayed, tongues roving. It was the orgy all over again. Did they come here and do this every night? The three of them seemed *addicted* to each other, their ecstasy desperate.

What was that like?

Grace was on hands and knees, while Rob took her hard and steady from behind. Donna lay beneath them, inverted, her toes curling in the carpet. Her gleaming thighs vised against Grace's head, which was buried between her legs. When Donna orgasmed, she writhed on the floor, shuddering, and moments later, in the aftermath, Grace's head lolled aside. She looked right up into the camera and grinned.

And it wasn't Grace anymore. It was Clare.

At once, the faces didn't matter anymore—just the bodies, the naked, tensing, hypersensitive bodies that converged in this overflow of lust, that cringed for more. Clare was one of those bodies now, naked and wanton as the rest. It was *Clare's* buttocks being splayed, *Clare's* breasts being pressed together and squeezed, *Clare's* tongue gliding over clitoris and penis alike. Everything that had been done in the videos was now being done to her.

She came repeatedly, from a multitude of operandi. From behind, she felt skewered by a rising spike of pleasure, the V of two fingers sliding hotly back and forth over the outer folds of her sex, while the inner folds were plowed into. When the buzzing vibrator tip squashed the nub of her clitoris, it might as well have been a button that was pushed, and there she went again, the string of climaxes breaking like a wall that had finally fallen against a great, opposing weight. The orgasm felt devilish, the pleasure so rich it could've been inhuman. Her loins bolted and quaked. Her nerves seemed to pulse like arteries, but the blood that filled them was raw selfish primitive pleasure.

She rolled over and collapsed on her back; for a moment she was too exhausted to move. She could feel herself purring deep in her throat, and all she could think was *more, I want more* . . . Her companions descended, just as selfish. Now that Clare had been done to, it was time for her to do . . .

And that was just the beginning, the *beginning* of the dream that would go on for hours . . .

(II)

"Jesus," Joyce sighed.

"I know," Rick agreed.

Spent now, totally exhausted, they lay propped up against each other in the security truck, both bare from the waist down, their shirts hanging open and their boots kicked into the back. They'd just made love ferociously, and this was the "afterglow" part: bugs buzzing and inferno-like heat. It was an hour past sundown but the heat and humidity seemed to flow into the truck like broth . . . along with mosquitoes. They'd parked on one of the old logging roads that had been closed since the '40s; Joyce didn't want to take any chances of being seen by Clare.

Can't let her know about me and Rick.

Maintaining that concealment was getting harder and harder lately.

Lately, their passions for each other seemed insanely

intense. An hour wouldn't go by without Joyce thinking about him, craving him.

We'll just have to be careful. REAL *careful.*

She loved this job and she needed it, and with the job market the way it was she needed it a lot more than she needed all this fooling around with Rick. But the Air Force hadn't set her up for much in the civilian world. Police work was out; these days most good departments practically required a masters in criminology just to get into the academy. This security job was a blessing.

Don't blow it.

But she just couldn't figure the craze of feelings for Rick. Did she love him? *I definitely don't think so,* she answered herself. She'd been a tomboy for as long as she could remember; she wanted to discover her world and her life with herself, not with someone else tagging along. In other words she was not a lovey-dovey touchy-feely kind of girl, and those tomboy sensibilities prevailed, which was just the way she wanted it. *In the future, sure. I might live with a guy, I might get married, I might want to get involved like that.* She shook her head. *But not till I'm real old, like thirty-five at least.*

Her thing with Rick was purely physical—it was just the way that she craved him sometimes that sort of bothered her. *He's just so . . .* GOOD! And as for being an inveterate tomboy: *I guess I'm a tomboy who's also a sex maniac.* Joyce knew where *she* stood but did *he? God, I hope so. I'd never want to hurt him . . .*

They both half-sat and half-lay across the truck's bench seat, Rick with his arm around her, her head against his slick, muscle-ridged chest.

"I-I've never felt like this before," he whispered. His hand tightened over hers.

Oh, no, she dreaded.

His hand squeezed tighter. "I . . ."

Don't . . .

His fingers lovingly strayed through her hair. "I'm pretty sure I—"

Joyce gritted her teeth. *Don't say it!*

"To hell with it," he resigned. "I'm just going to say it. Joyce, I love—"

"Rick, please! I'm not ready for all that! Please don't say that!"

Rick leaned up abruptly, lit a cigarette. "What are you getting all bent out of shape about? I was just going to say that I *love* living down here in Florida. Don't you?" Then he grinned and started laughing.

She slapped her open palm hard against his chest. "That's why I like you, Rick. You're an asshole and you don't mind proving that fact often."

"Damn straight."

Joyce chuckled herself now. *Yeah, I've got nothing to worry about. He knows the score, and he's just like all men. All he wants is sex.*

"I guess we can lie here all night and whisper sweet nothings," Rick pointed out, "or we can put our clothes back on and get back to work. Clare'll be relieving us before long. And last night she came on duty early. With our luck she'll do the same thing tonight and see us."

"Don't worry. I drove by her cottage before I picked you up. Her lights weren't even on."

"Yeah, but that was two hours ago," Rick pointed out.

Joyce quickly sat upright. "What? You're kidding!"

"Nope."

It seemed impossible. It seemed like only ten minutes. "You mean we've been—"

"Fucking for two hours," Rick finished.

Shit! Joyce was suddenly frantic. "We've go to get dressed, get back on rounds. Knowing her she *will* come out early. Our gooses are cooked if we get caught!" She was on her knees now, leaning over into the back. When Rick turned his head, all he could see was her beautiful bare bottom jutting out.

"Oh, honey, you can't be showin' me that right now. I'm tapped out—"

"Get dressed!" she yelled back.

He got back into his trousers. "Hey, my boots are back there too. Could you get 'em?"

flump!

She fired his boots into the front seat, missing his face by an inch. Rick pulled them on but couldn't take his eyes off the naked rump that was still bent over right before his eyes. "Hey, Joyce? I hope this doesn't sound too romantic, but your ass would start a riot in a monastery." He couldn't resist; he ran his hand up the flawless curve of flesh. "Hell, it should hang in the fucking National Gallery of Art." Then he brought his hand around the inside of her thigh . . .

"No! We don't have time!"

Rick couldn't believe it. He was already aroused again. "Aw, come on. Just a quick one? It wouldn't take long."

"No! And where's my—*damn* it!"

Joyce plopped herself back in the front seat, only one boot in hand.

"Where's your other—"

"It's not back there! I must've kicked it out the window by accident. Be a sweetheart and go get it."

Rick made a face. "What am I, your personal manservant?"

Joyce looked right back at him. "Yeah." Her beautiful bare breasts seemed to look right back at him too.

"Ah, well. Just so we have that fact properly established," Rick replied, and got out of the truck. He tromped around behind it, looking down for the boot but all he could think about was—

Joyce. Christ. So beautiful . . . The moonlit image of her body was like a tiny vertigo behind his eyes. Her sleek bare butt sticking out, those big perfect breasts beseeching him through the open blouse. It didn't matter that their lovemaking had exhausted him; suddenly he wanted more of her, needed *more.*

Rick was from South Dakota, arid cattle land and a pretty low notch on the social scale. The cows were more attractive than most of the local women. After his discharge, he'd come here just to check it out, and now he just shook his head at the incredible quirk of fate that had dropped Joyce into his lap.

I am one lucky son of a bitch to be rolling around with her.

"Rick, hurry! We've got to go!"

Her boot, he had to remind himself. He'd been too caught up just thinking about her. He really did love her, though, but he knew it would be a giant mistake telling her that. He could read her gauges pretty well; she wanted no big attachments, so that's how Rick would play it, act like it was just casual. And if she wanted to date other guys, that was fine with Rick too, because if she did—

I'll just have to give it to her better than them . . .

He was pretty confident about his ability to do that. She'd come right back to him after her one-night thing with Adam Corey, hadn't she? It was all Rick's fault; he'd taken her out to the bar and they'd both had a few too many and got into a big argument. It had been Rick who'd said: "Hey, if you don't like it, it's not like you're tied to that bar stool. You're the one who's always saying how we're just friends and you don't want commitments. That's fine with me. You can walk any time you want."

Yeah, BIG mistake that night. Have another drink, Rick.

Joyce had walked, all right. She'd walked right out of the bar and right *into* the bar across the street, a big redneck place called the Slappy Beaver, a pick-up joint for locals who were paralyzed from the neck up. And about an hour later, he'd seen her leave with that park service schmuck Adam Corey.

Rick hadn't pitched a fit over it; that wasn't his style. Of course, it wasn't his style to peep in windows either, but in this case he felt he had no choice. On a scale from one to ten, Joyce scored in the negatives when it came to first impressions. She could be pretty naive—especially with a few Killians in her. On the other hand, though, Rick could tell just from one look at the guy's face that Adam Corey was a walking whack-job. Rick could see right through that shucksy smile and the bronze blond nature-guy look—behind all that, there was something *disturbed* bubbling like a pot of water on full boil. The guy was a perv.

That's why he'd followed them. It was one thing he could never tell Joyce, of course—not *ever*. Then *Rick* would look like the perv. But he'd done it for her own protection. In case Corey tried to pull something demented, Rick needed to be there to save her dumb behind.

It never got to that but it probably would have if Joyce hadn't had the common sense to leave when she did. Rick had snuck around to the back of Corey's saltbox bungalow on Sunset Beach, but he didn't have to peep through that back window for long before his suspicions were proven in spades. Corey and Joyce were making out on the bed, pretty normal stuff at first. Then Corey stood up and dropped his pants. "Thought ya might want to check out my rig. Chicks dig it."

Joyce *didn't* dig it. In fact, she took one look at it, screamed, and ran out of the place. She was in her car and gone in thirty seconds.

Rick had nearly shouted aloud himself, half in revulsion and half in hilarity. *He's got more stuff in his dick than I've got in my tackle box!*

Adam Corey could've been the poster boy for genital piercing. Rings, studs, and pins of various sizes adorned his private parts to the extent that they shimmered. It was all chrome, and the intricacy with which these things had been fixed into his flesh was astounding. Some of the studs looked like small rivets, and from them tiny silver chains seemed to hang. Chrome bb's ringed the foreskin, while the scrotum dangled pendulum-like from all the weight of the trinkets that pierced it. The glans was the worst thing of all to view, though:

I don't believe it! The guy's got a fuckin RING *hanging out of his peehole!*

Rick didn't tarry; he was out of there nearly as fast as Joyce, and the vision of Adam Corey's armored genitals was not a vision he'd soon forget. *Yeah, Joyce sure learned a lesson that night*, he thought now, still searching for her lost boot. She'd come back to him the next day, in tears and begging his forgiveness. And though he'd never told her that he'd been watching, she eventually told him everything that had happened, and included detail about the ranger's "rig." From that point on, Rick often referred to Adam as "Ranger Jingles" and "Lightning Rod."

"Rick! Are you waiting for the Devil Rays to win a game?" Joyce complained. "Come on! Find my boot so we can get out of here!"

Here's the damn thing. The boot lay further out than he thought, the sock next to it. He scooted them up, was about to go back to the truck—

Then he saw something behind a palm tree.

I've seen these at the clinic, he thought at once. What sat behind the tree was a large white-plastic bucket. Floor wax for the janitorial staff came in this kind of bucket; he'd signed in the deliveries himself.

But it wasn't floor wax inside.

Rick didn't have a flashlight but he could see well enough. The bucket was filled with something light-colored and granular in texture. It was not quite as fine as sand, and it felt gritty when he touched it. *Soap or something?* he considered. *Detergent?*

But what was it doing out here?

Looks like someone just left it here.

"Jesus CHRIST! Where ARE you?" Joyce yelled.

Rick jogged back to the passenger window. "There's a bucket full of soap or something, right over there behind a tree."

"So what! We're in a hurry, remember?"

Rick scratched his head. "Well, I don't know what it is, and it shouldn't be there. Should I bring it?"

Joyce gaped at him. "Why?"

"You know, to report it."

"Did you put your brains in the kleenex the last time you blew your nose? This road is *closed.* No one's supposed to be on it because it's a sinkhole hazard. What are you gonna tell Clare, Einstein? Oh, Clare, we were out on that closed logging road, you know, the one that no one's supposed to drive, because we needed a place to hide so we could FUCK for two hours, and we found this bucket full of soap—"

"Got'cha," Rick said. "Didn't think of that. So I'll just leave the bucket?"

"Forget about the damn bucket." She reached out, grabbed her boot out of his hand.

"Don't forget your little sockie," he said, and handed her the sock.

"I'll sock *you!*" She snatched the sock away.

Rick grinned. "Wow, you're feisty tonight. I like that in a woman."

Joyce simply glared at him. "Just shut up and get in the truck! You putz around worse than a ninety-year-old woman!"

Rick laughed to himself. *Yeah, she's a piece of work, all right. Too bad I love her*. He got back in the truck, was about to start it, but—

Joyce screamed.

The abruptness of the scream left Rick very close to wetting his pants. Suddenly, Joyce was kicking away at something, and she jumped over right into Rick's lap.

"What the hell's wrong?"

"That!" Joyce replied and kept squealing. She was pointing down into the footwell where she'd dropped her boot. "There was something in it! Something alive!

"What, in your boot?"

"Yes yes yes! Something crawled inside my boot! It's a rat I think!" She was hugging him now, grossed out and terrified.

Rick kind of . . . liked it.

"Relax, baby. There's nothing in the world gonna hurt you while I'm here."

Her hysterics continued. "Please please please, Rick, kill it! I'm so scared of rats!"

Rick grinned. *Looks like all I gotta do to be a hero tonight is squash a rodent.* Out here, with all the marsh rats? He'd stepped on plenty. "Calm down, honey, I'm here." He turned on the dome light. But he didn't see any signs of a rat in the footwell, didn't hear anything either.

"Are you sure? If there was a rat in here, we'd hear it scuttling around."

"I'm SURE!" she barked. "When I put my foot in the boot, I could feel it with my toes—it was *moving*, Rick! And I could hear it too, a little clicking sound like its teeth clicking together!"

Rick looked around, then stroked his nightstick under the seat. "Honey, I don't think it's—"

She tugged desperately on his sleeve. "Maybe," she whispered, "maybe . . . it's still in the boot."

Rick picked up the boot.

Feels . . . kind of heavy . . .

And something was moving inside.

He raised his nightstick, ready to ram its butt-end down on the rat. But when he upended the boot, it was not a rat that fell out and began skittering around on the truck floor.

It was a cockroach.

The *size* of a rat.

(III)

"Clare? Clare? Are you all right?"

Clare felt dead in the dream now, but she couldn't

be dead—she was still thinking, she was still feeling.

It was the nightmare but . . . *different*.

She'd been in the middle of the most sexual dream of her life—and *liking it*—but then it all changed. The frantic orgy seemed to last for hours and hours, and in it Clare had done things she would never do in real life—the most lascivious things. It was just like the videos she'd watched: desperate sexual abandon, a bacchanal. In the dream, her two suitors were faceless, bereft of identities. But they didn't need names, they didn't need faces—they were merely players from Clare's subconscious; to serve their purpose, they didn't need to *be* anyone, they only needed to do, because by doing they fulfilled their function: to uncover something that Clare's psyche was trying to reveal about her. The dream was so liberating . . .

But then it changed.

No no no, she thought.

It changed around her, her lovers melting away, the scene dissolving and then reforming into—

no . . .

—the blaring white lights of the Air Force autopsy suite, the chill of the stainless steel table on the skin of her bare back.

And the warped face of Stuart Winster grinning down at her.

It was the same at first: her total paralysis, the scratch awl tracing thread-thin lines on her belly, and the words she'd never forget . . .

"Duh-duh-don't worry, Clare. I wuh-wuh-won't hurt you till I'm done."

What a cruel thing for her subconscious mind to do to her: titillate her with the deliciously erotic dream and then drop it right into the middle of the most appalling memory of her life.

He was molesting her now with that hideous birth-deformed hand, and all Clare could do was feel the hatred raging inside of the quivering, immobile container that was her body. Eventually the hand withdrew, in grueling slowness, but the nightmare's cruelty amplified; it felt like something ten feet long was being pulled out of her. And then—

SPLAT!

"Huh-huh-here's a present, Clare. I got it just for you."

Something weighty and wet had been dropped on her lower abdomen. It was hot. She couldn't imagine what it was and she couldn't see it because her paralysis prevented her from raising her head. It felt like a pile of hot, slimy meat.

Then the meat began to move.

It floundered there for a moment, drenching her pubis and inner thighs with its slime. Wet slopping sounds could be heard as whatever it was began to seek purchase, to climb . . .

It was crawling up her belly now.

Stuart Winster drooled through a witless grin. He came around to the front of the table and raised her head so she could see.

It was the frog, the mutated thing she'd seen at the lake today. Only it wasn't dead now, and its innards weren't hanging out of its mouth. The grape-sized eyes were *looking* at her, *seeing* her. And on its forepaws the size of baby hands, it was scuttling forward, climbing ahead, its enslimed, spotted body sliding slowly over Clare's belly. She could see its awful rimmed mouth partly opened, and its fangs—like white nails. The aberration of nature seemed to be smiling. Then it hitched up a few more inches, its forepaws flat on her breasts.

"Froggie's gonna give Clare a great big kiss!"

As the thing crawled closer, its jaws opened impossibly wide and then they began to close over Clare's face . . .

"Clare! Wake up!"

She felt motion, terror, and when her eyes sprang open, she thought she'd been thrown out a high window and had just landed. She opened her mouth to scream as someone grabbed her but then she recognized who it was—

Joyce.

"Calm down, it's me!"

Clare sucked in a breath as if she'd just emerged from deep underwater. It was dark around her, only the foyer and kitchen lights were on. She jerked upright not on her bed but on the couch. *That's right, I fell asleep here . . . after watching those videos . . .*

She brought a hand to her chest, and then remembered the awful dream. First, the orgy, then the rape, then—

She winced. *That DISGUSTING frog!*

"Rick, everything's okay so go wait in the truck."

"Huh?"

"Just do as I say!" Joyce yelled. "Go wait in the truck!"

Rick's here too? Clare thought groggily. And why was Joyce yelling at him? And—

What are either of them doing here in the first place?

"Clare, get this down," Joyce was saying and pulling at her nightshirt.

"What?" But now she was fully waking up, and that's when she realized she was practically naked. When she'd brought her hand to her chest, her chest was bare; during her sleep, her nightshirt had somehow gotten pulled all the way up over her breasts. *I must have pulled it up myself!* she realized with an inner shock, and suddenly she was coruscating with embarrassment. She quickly pulled the long shirt the rest of the way down.

Joyce smiled in the dim light. "Don't worry. Rick's a big dumb animal. He didn't see anything."

"I—" *Jesus.* Only now were Clare's mental bearings resurfacing. "Why are you and Rick here?"

"Well, we were getting worried. Your lights haven't been on all night, and when you didn't come in at midnight—"

"What time is it?"

"It's going on one a.m."

I'm an hour late for work! The fact infuriated her; one thing she'd always prided herself on was punctuality. *I've never been late for work in MY LIFE! What's wrong with me?*

"I'm really sorry, Joyce," she bumbled. "You and Rick will get double-time for the hour. I don't know what happened. I'm *never* late for work."

"Clare, it's no big deal. We're just glad you're okay. You were probably just really tired and you overslept."

Clare put her hand to her forehead, remembering. *That damn frog!* It was enough that she'd dreamed again of Stuart Winster; the inclusion of the freakish ten-pound frog only heightened the dream's disgust. *And it all started out so differently*, she recalled now. Watching the videos had clearly been the impetus; her dreams had begun erotically—there'd been nothing horrific about them at all. In fact, they'd excited her.

Then it was all ruined by the rest.

"I had the *worst* dream," was all she could say and finally got up off the couch. The first thing she noticed was Joyce: one foot was bare, the other booted.

"How come you're only wearing one boot?"

"We'll show you when we get back to the office," Joyce said, a sudden edge to her voice. Had something happened on the site? "You won't believe what we found."

Before Clare could question further, the front door clicked open; Rick stuck his head in. "Everything all right?"

"Yes!" Joyce cracked. "Wait in the truck!"

Rick nodded sheepishly and went back outside.

"And you really should lock your door when you're asleep, Clare," Joyce said next. "We just walked right in."

Clare was dismayed. There was another thing she never did. "I left my door unlocked?"

Joyce nodded.

"I must be getting absentminded, either that or just plain irresponsible. I'm really setting a terrific example as the new security manager—I leave my front door open and I'm late for my second shift."

Joyce laughed. "Forget about it. Go get ready, I'll wait for you here." She paused, then came closer to Clare and pulled something out of her pocket.

What's that she's got? Clare wondered.

Now Joyce was whispering. "And don't worry, Rick didn't see this either."

What was placed into Clare's hand was the creepy green vibrator. Clare's tongue seemed to sink into her stomach.

"I took it out of your hand before he could see."

Clare's embarrassment rooted her to the floor. Her mouth opened but her voice froze.

"Oh, you're priceless! You should see your face!" Joyce

said. "Don't worry, I'm not gonna tell anyone."

God, I hope not, Clare thought. She looked at the vibrator and its eerie clear-green rubber. The veins fashioned into its shaft were repulsive. "You mean I was . . . *using* it, on the . . ."

"On the couch, in your sleep. I've heard of sleep-walking but I don't even want to *think* what this would be called. That's a nice one, though."

The comment confused Clare. "Huh?"

Joyce rolled her eyes. "Clare, you act like you're the only woman in the world who owns a vibrator."

"It's not mine," Clare was quick to say.

Joyce was just as quick to frown. "All women have vibrators, Clare. Show me a woman who says she's never used a vibrator and I'll show you a liar."

What could she say, especially as she stood there with one in her hand? She felt inclined to explain everything, that the vibrator was Grace Fletcher's and that she'd been watching the sexual videotapes, etc., but—*Why bother? It doesn't matter anyway*. Explaining it all would be too complicated.

"Let's be real," Joyce went on. "Sometimes men can't quite do the trick, that's why we've got mama's little helper. I don't know what you're acting all embarrassed about; I must have over a dozen different kinds by now. And I've got one just like that too, only it's red." A mischievous grin tinted her face. "Those veins are wild, huh?"

The simple reference to them made her stomach flip. The thing looked ghastly to her, *particularly* the veins. "I don't know if I'd call them 'wild,' Joyce. I can't believe I was . . . using this and don't remember. How can you—" Clare couldn't quite form the words. "—in your sleep?"

"You'll learn quick, the sun down here can do weird things to you; it takes a while to get adjusted. You can get a minor case of heat exhaustion without even knowing it. You get dehydrated, sodium-depleted, and it screws up your sleep cycle. Add all that to the fact that you were a little rundown already, plus you had the incident last night with the crazy girl in the woods—it all jumps up at once and kicks you in the butt. Gives ya weird dreams, makes you do funny things. Just drink a lot of water tonight and you'll be fine. I'll even work your shift for you if you're not feeling well."

It was a generous offer but one Clare couldn't accept. She had an example to set and so far she was doing less than a bang-up job. All the while, Joyce was proving herself to be a quality person and friend. *I WILL make it up to her*, Clare vowed. Besides, she actually felt pretty good now.

"Thanks, Joyce, you're a gem. But I'll be fine. Give me two minutes to take a shower and get dressed."

"Sure, I'll wait out here."

Clare was in the shower a few seconds later, the incriminating vibrator tossed aside. *What a screw-up I am*, she scolded herself. But at least everything was all right. The cool shower revived her further, washing away the perspiration of the nightmare. The afterimage of the mutant frog crawling up her stomach made her shiver; she sudsed herself up a second time, as if to clean off its slime.

Just a dream, just a dream, she told herself. An absolutely awful dream, yes, but it was over now. She didn't even want to ponder the psychology of it all. *I was masturbating in my sleep, I was sexually excited . . . but why would I be doing this during a nightmare that was totally disgusting?* The initial part of the dream—the orgy—had been very stimulating, but then it all collapsed into the nightmare of Stuart Winster's rape, and then that monstrous frog molesting her. Even now, wide awake and energized by the shower, aspects of the nightmare haunted her, like lingering images of a car wreck or a death. Was there something in her subconscious mind that found such horrors stimulating?

No, it couldn't be. That would make no sense at all. *My metabolism was out of joint*, she deduced, squeaking off the shower spray. She dried off fast, pulled on her uniform and strapped on her gunbelt. *It's like Joyce said, a combination of fatigue, too much sun, and too much commotion. I'll be fine now.*

Joyce was waiting for her out in the living room. They left the cottage and this time Clare made a point to lock her door. Then she got in her Blazer and followed Joyce and Rick back to the clinic.

Clare had no idea that while she'd been showering, she was being watched through a crack in the bathroom window.

Chapter Nine

(I)

Voices.

Through the wall.

He put his ear to the wall and listened.

The one's mad . . .

"I'm just saying that we've got to be more careful. You don't seem too concerned."

"What's to be concerned about?"

"The fuck? There's people here now, there's a full security staff. And you've got that freak walkin' around at night."

That freak, he thought.

Does he mean me?

"He's only exposed for a very short period of time. The drainage pipes provide excellent cover. They're five feet high, for God's sake. No one's going to see him down there."

"Yeah, well he's not *down there* all the time."

"Of course not, we need him for procurements and disposal, things like that."

"Procurements? Yeah, he did a great job with that girl

who went psycho in the woods, and don't tell me about disposal. He's supposed to be dumping that crap, not leaving it in the woods. I've found two buckets of the stuff already."

"The purpose is to assign him a schedule of tasks—it's a training endeavor. It's beside the point that he occasionally forgets where he leaves things after he sets them down for a moment."

"Yeah? Well what if he does that with a body?"

He wasn't quite sure what they were talking about. All he knew was that something sounded wrong.

"Get rid of the freak. We're risking too much keeping it around . . ."

Freak.

He thought he knew what *that* meant.

Is he talking about me?

He was getting upset now. He could feel his heart beating faster. Suddenly he was anxious, pacing around.

I'm not a freak.

He would have to take the tunnel back to the basement now, and he'd have to get Mrs. Grable. He'd already gotten rid of the pretty girl on Table 2—and he needed someone to . . . to do something to. He wasn't allowed to hurt Mrs. Grable much—even though he'd like to hurt her a lot, really bite her and punch her a lot. But that wasn't allowed, not with her.

He was allowed to do it to her, though.

And he was going to do it to her real hard tonight.

It was the only way to calm him down, the only way to make him not upset anymore.

I'm not a freak, damn it!

There was nothing wrong with him, and he didn't like it when people said there was. He was just as smart as anyone.

And it's not my fault my hand's like this . . .

(II)

The mystery of Joyce's missing boot was solved . . . when Rick turned it upside-down over the small sink in the break room.

"Un . . . believable," Clare droned.

"You ever seen anything like that?" Rick asked.

"Thank God—no."

Fortunately the cockroach was dead. *Un*fortunately it was eight or nine inches long and must've weighed a full pound.

"I flipped it back into the boot after I butted it to death with my billy club," Rick recounted. "Brought it back here 'cos we thought you'd want to see it. Bet I hit it four times, full force, before its shell even cracked, and it took ten more whacks to kill it."

His voice sounded diffuse through Clare's astonishment. The insect was impossibly large; she'd never heard of cockroaches getting that big.

"And look," Joyce said, holding up her boot. "Before it died, it was eating through the boot leather."

More astonishment, when Clare squinted at the boot. Its tip looked like it had been gouged at with a sharp knife. "If it can do that to leather, think what it can do to human skin."

"Yeah, and I put my *foot* on that thing."

"You're lucky you still got all your toes," Rick said.

"Well, one thing's for sure," Joyce added. "I need a new pair of boots 'cos there's no way in hell I'm ever putting this one back on." She dropped the boot in the garbage can with a thunk.

It didn't occur to Clare to ask how the repugnant insect had come to find its way into Joyce's boot; she was too busy just looking at it and wondering if she could believe what her own eyes were showing her.

"That's the grossest thing I've ever seen," Clare spoke up. Then— "Correction, the *second* grossest thing."

Joyce and Rick both looked at her. "What could be grosser than a cockroach that big?"

"Try a ten-pound frog," Clare said. "Eviscerated. With teeth like a dog." Then she went to explain the details of what Adam had found at the lake that afternoon.

"Well that's pretty bizarre, isn't it?" Joyce posed. "I'm no zoologist but I can tell you roaches and frogs don't get that big. It's got to be some kind of mutation."

"That's what Adam said. He even said it's not that uncommon around here. Some toxic compound gets into an isolated ecosystem and causes defects and mutations."

"Adam's the biggest asshole on the island," Joyce offered, "but he does know his field. And he's right, there has been a fair share of toxin-based mutations in the state—"

Rick cut in, "Yeah, I remember that bit on the news a while back, alligators with two tails."

"Right, 'cos someone was dumping industrial waste water into a bunch of lakes in Polk county." Joyce looked quizzically down at the crushed insect. "And all of a sudden we've got two different kinds of mutations right here at Fort Alachua Park. What did Adam do with the frog?"

"He took it, said he had to report it. Evidently there's some authority in the U.S. Park Service that he has to turn things like this in to." Clare looked at the mammoth insect, then smiled at Rick. "Rick, be a trooper and wrap that thing up in foil and put it in the fridge, will you?"

Rick though nothing of it, and as he was wrapping

the thing up, he said, "I wonder what the hell Ranger Jingles was doing out at the lake in the first place. He never goes out there unless *we* report something to him."

Clare caught the reference. "Ranger . . . *Jingles?* Why do you call him that?"

Joyce shot a repressed glare at Rick.

"What, he walks around with a lot of change in his pocket?" Clare prodded.

"He walks around with a lot of *something* in his—" Rick began—

—but Joyce cut him off: "Rick, just put the thing in the foil!" And to Clare, "It's nothing, it's a long story."

"And a pretty funny one, too," Rick goaded, placing the package in the refrigerator. "Want to know why he's more afraid of lightning than anyone else?"

Joyce grinned through grit teeth. "Thank you, Rick. You really should be leaving now, right? 'Bye!" She turned him around by the shoulders and pushed him out the door.

When he was gone, Clare said, "I won't even ask."

"Thanks. Now, are you sure you're feeling all right? If you're not, I'll still work your shift for you."

"No, I'm fine. But thanks." But Clare couldn't help being aware of the giant roach in the fridge. "Adam doesn't work at night, does he? I want him to take that bug away ASAP."

"No, he just works day shifts. Call him in the morning, he'll probably be around, and believe me, he'll be happy for any excuse to come over here."

Clare thought of the mishap at the shallow quicksand. "I got to know him a little better today, and you're right. He's a dick."

"That's putting it mildly. I'm telling you, don't trust

that guy as far as you can throw him." Joyce signed out on her logsheet. "Thank God for the weekend. You'll just be on call, right?"

"Saturday and Sunday? Yeah. But I'll probably make some rounds anyway," Clare said.

"Give me a call if you want to do anything tomorrow. See ya!"

"'Bye. And thanks for helping me out tonight. Sorry about the screw-up."

"No problem."

Joyce left, and Clare smiled after her. *Yeah, she's cool, and so is Rick. And they're good sports too.* Clare still couldn't believe that'd she'd overslept and missed shiftchange. *I have to make sure that DOESN'T happen again.* She felt confident that it wouldn't, and even more confident about the job in general now that she was getting to know the site and the people. Every workplace had its good points and bad points; identifying them quickly was the key to succeeding, and from there she could adjust to the bad points and use the good points to her advantage.

So far the only real bad point was Adam Corey.

I can handle him, she knew. But what of this roach, and the frog?

All I can do is report it to the proper channels, and Adam just happens to be that channel. From there, she supposed, it would be the job of some arm of the Department of the Natural Resources to investigate the possibility of pollutants in the area.

She couldn't help but wonder, though . . .

I think I'll drive out to Lake Stephanie. See if there's anything else out there that's bigger than it should be . . .

She checked the alarm system, locked up the office, and made for the exit. But on her way, she noticed a door open a few inches, in the treatment wing.

The door marked IRMT.

She remembered Dellin telling her about the system—Intensified Radiation Modulation Therapy—something about crosshairs of low-dose radioactive beams killing tiny tumors with exceptional precision. But he'd also said that the half-million-dollar system wasn't needed for the stromatic carcinomas that were treated here. *Whatever*, Clare thought. *But that door shouldn't be unlocked.*

She remembered when she'd looked in the other day: the room contained an elaborate bank of computers and viewing screens, plus the large nozzle-like discharge heads hanging off the ceiling. Someone could easily come in here and steal a monitor or a CPU.

When Clare looked in the room, it was empty.

(III)

KEEP OFF!
THIS REGISTERED SEA TURTLE NEST
IS PROTECTED BY THE U.S. ENDANGERED
SPECIES ACT OF 1973
DO NOT TAKE SEA TURTLES OR THEIR
EGGS!
VIOLATORS WILL BE FINED AND
IMPRISONED!

With a bleak chuckle, Bill-Boy noted the last line of the yellow sign; it didn't say that violators *may* be fined and imprisoned, it said they *will* be. Down here, they took that shit serious. One time Bill-Boy himself had been fined $1500 for possessing one female stone crab. Just one. And they took his boat too! It was any poacher's risk, especially in Florida. You could bust your wife's jaw with a two-by-four and you wouldn't do as much time as you'd get for digging up sea turtle eggs. Florida police hardly gave a flying shit if you drove drunk, but don't you dare mess with those palm trees and sea oats. He remembered once reading in the paper about how the DNR cops opened fire on some yahoos for taking shots at a dolphin.

That's fuckin' Florida for ya, Bill-Boy thought. *You get a suspended sentence for dick-spankin' your daughter, but if I get caught pinchin' a few sea turtle eggs, I go to the joint for a year.*

Just a day in the life of someone in Bill-Boy's profession.

Bill-Boy wasn't a meth-head or synthetic smack addict like most of the low-scale area rednecks. He was just a good old fashioned chronic alcoholic. He had the look: bone-skinny, MOTHER tattoos, long hair and a Fu-Manchu. Didn't want a job—not that he could keep one if he did—it was easier to poach gator, stone crab out of season, and the ultimate prize: *Chelonia mydas* a.k.a the Green Sea Turtle. Bill-Boy had the gig where others in his trade simply didn't. Unless you had a line on a middleman for private collectors, selling Green Sea Turtles was like selling the Hope Diamond. But Bill-Boy knew this dealer in Tampa Chinatown—the fuckin' guy paid a c-note for every egg that hatched. Paid *twice* that too, if you had anything a week before Chinese New Year. Was Bill-Boy game for that kind of action?

Bill-Boy was game.

One good nest could keep him in Milwaukee's Best Ice for a year.

You had to be careful digging was all, as careful as he was being right this very minute: on his knees on the east beach of Fort Alachua Park at two in the morning. The nests were cordoned off by yellow tape and stakes—he could hardly fuckin' believe *that. Thanks for TELLING ME where the eggs are!* You'd see the cordons all over the place, even on the tourist beaches—*way* too risky to hit. But Fort Alachua Park, at this hour? The endangered eggs were begging to be pinched.

He teased his fingers into the damp sand; it was a delicate process. Break the egg and the turtle inside croaked—and there goes a hundred bucks out the window. Of course, Bill-Boy wasn't too keen on what the Chinamen did with the baby turtles once they hatched—they cut the shells off the little critters and deep-fried them alive. It was some Oriental delicacy or some shit. Sounded kind of cruel to Bill-Boy—frying baby turtles on an endangered species list—but—

Fuck, it man. Business is business. If I don't get 'em the eggs, they'll find some other swingin' dick who will.

Bill-Boy was what you'd call a "functional" alcoholic, in that he still was able to pay the rent and strive to be happy, cirrhotic liver and all. A couple poaching jobs per month paid for his dump motel room and he could even hang out at the Beach Saloon where they had dollar drafts and all the drunk tramps you could look at. These days, Bill-Boy just teased the gals; they were all nuts for him on account of he had the look. But he never picked them up anymore—it was best to keep them wanting, it preserved his mystery. Fact of the matter, though, there was no *reason* for him to pick up a woman. Thirty years of chronic alcoholism will have a tendency to take the lead out of the sexual pencil, so to speak.

Aw, the motherlode! he thought. One by one, his fingers gingerly lifted out the eggs. An older turtle would sometimes lay seventy-five, and the hatch rate was close to one hundred percent if you transported them carefully. Bill-Boy transferred each egg into the padded bucket he'd brought, using such care you would've thought they were pellets of nitroglycerin.

Half hour later he had sixty-six eggs in the bucket.

God is a'smilin' down on me tonight, yessir!

It was time to book; he'd made his haul. He could be greedy, of course, and look around for more nests, but in his business the longer you hung around, the more risk you exposed yourself to. There was a ranger who patrolled the park sometimes, and there was always a chance that the marine police might see his boat. He'd even heard there was security around here too. Why take the chance?

That's why, he thought.

Not a hundred feet away was another cordoned nest.

This is too easy.

He was back to digging right away. Wouldn't take too long to top off the bucket. But—

Man, it's hotter than a pizza oven out here.

That it was, even this late. And the mosquitoes were hitting on him too, drawn by his sweat. *I need to cool off for a sec . . .*

And he knew that just fifty yards or so inland there was a place he could do that. Lake Stephanie.

Bill-Boy stood up, brow dripping. The thought, in this heat, was tantalizing. *Yeah, I think I'll take me a quick dip*, and then a few minutes later he was wading right into the water. *Man, that's good!* When he was hip deep, he squatted down on his knees, cut-off jeans and HIGHWAY TO HELL t-shirt right along with the rest of him. The cool water caressed him. *Shit, alls I need now is a cold beer and I'm in heaven!*

Perhaps.

But heaven probably didn't have what swam up his shorts a moment later. Alcoholic or not, his reflexes were still hair-trigger quick. *What the motherfuckin' HELL?* and he was standing back upright in a flash.

Bill-Boy froze.

Had it just been a weird current?

He wasn't sure at first. But it had sure as hell felt like something long and thin had swum up his pants, through the leghole. He didn't want to move too abruptly, in case . . .

Well, in case it was a snake.

But whatever it was, it hadn't felt big enough to be a snake. It had felt extremely thin, no fatter than a pen, and he wasn't sure if he felt it at all now.

Had it swum right back out?

Or maybe it *was* just a weird subsurface current.

Bill-Boy wasn't quite sure what to do; it was merely some instinct that induced him to keep still. The moonlight was bright here, bright in his face and on the water, and when he looked down—

Holy lord God of all, what is THAT?

—he could see what at first appeared to be a yard-long length of yarn floating on the water but when he squinted he could see that it wasn't floating, it was swimming.

Very slowly, Bill-Boy reached down and, without moving the rest of his body, he snatched the thing out of the water.

Gotcha . . .

Then he started to feel real sick.

It was no yard-long length of yarn, it was a yard-long millipede, some kind of bizarre *aquatic* millipede that he didn't even know existed. He held it close at one end, the end the head was on, while the rest of it quickly curled around his arm. He could feel the thousands of tiny hairlike legs moving, but they didn't hurt, and then that sudden nausea began to subside when he remembered that millipedes were essentially harmless.

Owww! MotherFUCKer!

That's when the essentially harmless millipede began to bite him.

He flailed his arm, trying to shake it off—to no avail. Soon it wasn't just biting him, it was boring into his skin, on his forearm. He grabbed the body again, pulled, and was aghast when he saw that in only those few seconds it had bored six inches under his skin. When he was able to pull it out, he howled—it felt like a hot iron poker being drawn out of his flesh. When he retracted it all, he grabbed the thing just under its head this time, and he pinched it hard as he could between his thumb and the side of his index finger.

The nausea returned like a gut-punch.

The millipede's mouth, if you could call it that, existed as an expanding and contracting hole rimmed with the tiniest hook-like teeth.

He pinched down hard, harder, pressing, until the long repulsive thing fell limp. He flung it away as far as he could.

Good godDAMN that hurt like a son of a—

Sheer dread lopped off the rest of the thought. In his constant alcohol buzz, he'd momentarily forgotten one crucial possibility.

The thing that had swum up his pants . . .

Had that been it? The thing that he'd just killed and flung away?

Or—

Is there another one just like it . . . IN MY FUCKIN' SHORTS RIGHT THIS MOTHERFUCKIN' SECOND?

The latter, regrettably, proved to be the case. Suddenly his crotch came alive with an explosive tickling sensation, those thousands of tiny legs coiling around his scrotum and penis. The most primal intuition of horror gave him a solid idea as to exactly *where* the millipede intended to go, so Bill-Boy was just going to have to get the thing OUT OF THERE before it was able to succeed.

He yanked his shorts right off, grabbed his terror-shriveled genitals, began to uncoil the millipede, and—

—screamed high and loud as a truck horn when an eel with a head the size of a Doberman shot out of the water and took out most of his right bicep with one bite. A second later a similar-sized chunk of flesh was bitten out of his buttocks.

The pain, of course, could be described as cataclysmic. Bill-Boy's mental sentience took a quick exit, to be replaced by a sole impulse of self-preservation. Another millipede was now boring quicky into his sinus cavity via a nostril; another was boring into his ear, while his *other* ear was bitten off whole by a spectacularly striped fish whose head was mostly teeth.

The water around him seemed to percolate with activity, as a feeding frenzy commenced.

Hideous fish and more eels used him as a biting post; the millipedes were already laying eggs deep in his body. Yet with all that, Bill-Boy deserved at least some credit for his resiliency. In spite of losing roughly a chunk of flesh per second, his now mostly mindless instincts allowed him to eventually thrash himself out of the water, where he collapsed on the narrow shore. The beastly eels and fish were gone—along with thirty percent of his muscle mass.

And his heart was still beating.

I-I-I'm . . . still . . . alive..

But as some modicum of the mental process returned so did that reactivity of the central nervous system known as pain.

And Bill-Boy began to flop on the shore like a flounder on a hotplate.

That first millipede? The one that had swum up his shorts?

It was eating its way quite nicely up into Bill-Boy's lower gut, via the urethra.

Chapter Ten

(I)

Clare's shift had passed dully. At one point, while on patrol, she'd thought she heard someone shouting, or even screaming, but then it occurred to her that the sound must be vaulting across the inlet, from the trailer parks on the other side. The partying over there regularly carried over to the island.

As for the distressingly large cockroach in the refrigerator, she was actually miffed that Adam Corey wasn't at his office phone when she'd called at nine a.m. It wasn't that she wanted to see him—not by any means—she simply didn't want that dead, foil-wrapped *thing* in the fridge any longer than it had to be. Unfortunately its removal relied on Adam. *Damn it*, she thought. *Looks like it'll be sitting in there all weekend*. All she could do was leave a message on the ranger's answering machine. A morbid curiosity had pestered her all shift; at least once an hour she'd fearfully peeked into the refrigerator, half-expecting the silver package to be broken open, the cockroach gone.

Giant cockroaches, *giant frogs*. She wondered what

Dellin would say when she told him that Adam had all but accused him of dumping some toxic by-product into Lake Stephanie.

Maybe I should . . .

But she severed the idea. See if Dellin's at his cottage today? Go knock on his door and report these incidents to him now, on his day off? In the Air Force, it would've been her duty.

Yeah, but this isn't the Air Force anymore, this is Civvieland, and civvies don't like to be bugged on the weekend.

She admitted to herself what she was doing: manufacturing an excuse to see him, and verifying Adam's allegation that she had "eyes" for him.

Well—hell—I do.

But she also knew that bothering him on a day off was the wrong thing to do.

She spent the last half hour of her shift in the office, treating herself to a last glass of iced coffee and finishing off her logsheet and incident report. The clinic felt weird in its silence; no one was coming in today, not even the janitorial staff. Her footfalls echoed through the long, white hallways as she set the alarm system and left.

The noon heat hit her like walking into a curtain; the sun was high in a perfect blue sky. Even though she was technically on call for the entire weekend, she didn't have any shifts to fill, and suddenly it struck her that the day was too gorgeous to go home and sleep. She could drive around, see the town. If the alarms went off, the system would beep her. She could go have a little fun.

Then her more diligent half kicked in. *You can have a little fun some other time. I just started this job two days ago. The responsible thing to do is stick close to the site, just on the off chance that something DOES happen.*

The matter was settled, and she was pleased that her sense of discipline didn't waver—even with the pocket full of money she still had. She took the Blazer to the front gate, just to make a final security check, then headed back to her cottage.

I wonder who . . .

She squinted; fifty yards ahead, at the turn to the cottage road, a light-colored four-wheel drive with a revolving light on top had pulled out and turned away. When she made out the crest on the back, she realized it was Adam.

What the hell is that weirdo doing on my road?

She could pursue him, to find out, but—

Forget it. I've had enough of that pain in the ass. I'm not gonna let him wreck my weekend.

She kept on her way, and any ill feelings she might have had—about Adam Corey, about what her nightmares might mean, or the grotesque frog and cockroach, about *anything*—were whisked away when she pulled up in front of her cottage. The elation returned; she still couldn't believe she lived in this wonderful place, couldn't believe her sudden good fortune. She left her worries and confusions in the Blazer, and all she took up the front walk with her was her smile.

"Hey!"

Clare turned around at the front door, her keys jingling. Joyce smiled back at her from the end of the walk, in a beach robe, flip-flops, and sunglasses. "Hi, Joyce," Clare greeted. "Hitting the beach, I see?"

"Yeah. You want to go too?"

The offer sounded tempting. "Well, I really shouldn't. I should—"

"Go to the beach with Joyce," Joyce said, coming up

the walk. "Come on, the sun'll be peaking in an hour. It's perfect. And we'll probably have the whole beach to ourselves."

Clare stalled. Actually she wasn't tired at all, especially after oversleeping the day before. "I—"

"Great!" Joyce declared. "I'll wait for you while you get ready."

Clare smiled and opened the front door.

"Don't walk on your mail," Joyce remarked.

"Huh?" *Mail? Who'd be mailing* ME *anything?* But there was a letter slot in the door, and when they'd entered, Clare almost stepped on an envelope lying on the slate foyer.

"It's probably your apartment checklist from Mrs. Grable," Joyce told her and made straight for the kitchen. "Anything that doesn't work, just check it on the list and give it back to her. She'll make sure it gets fixed quick. Hey, can I have a banana?"

The question distracted her; she'd bought bananas and peaches yesterday at the store, put them in a bowl on the counter. "Oh, sure. Help yourself." Then she looked at the envelope that had been dropped in the slot. A *checklist* . . . It was just a blank envelope.

"It you don't have a swimsuit, it's no big deal," Joyce commented, peeling the banana.

Just then, Clare remembered—and a delayed embarrassment threatened to make her blush. *Last night, when she woke me up from the nightmare . . . She saw me holding that vibrator—good God!* But the fact that Joyce had thought nothing of it only reinforced Clare's growing self-awareness. *I guess I'm kind of a prude . . . I keep forgetting, it's the 21st century, people aren't uptight about sex. Most people, anyway.* Joyce had even casually admitted to owning several vibrators herself. She was a fully sexualized woman, and that realization made Clare feel inept. Joyce's lusty physique seemed to radiate through the beach robe. But it wasn't just her body that was attractive, it was her attitude, her casual confidence. Suddenly, Clare felt like the librarian sighing in secret envy of the cheerleader.

"Earth to Clare? Scotty beam you up?"

Distractions overwhelmed her. Why was that? Why was that happening so often now? *She must think I'm a total airhead!* "Oh, a swimsuit? Yes, I picked up a few yesterday at one of those beach shops. Got a big towel too." Then it occurred to her. "Oh, but—damn it. I forgot to get any suntan lotion."

"I've got plenty of that," Joyce dismissed. She dropped the banana peel in the wastebasket, then pointed to her bag. "Plus I got a big jug of sun-brewed iced tea. You'll love the beach we've got here. It's a private beach, so you know what that means, right?"

"What?"

"Swimwear is optional."

Clare could think of no response. *Does that mean she's going to sunbathe in the nude?* She didn't feel comfortable enough asking. Eventually she stammered, "That's probably not my style. And right now most of me is whiter than the sand."

"Oh, we'll fix that. Why don't you go get ready and then we'll get out there."

At once Clare figured out that she was politely being told that she was dawdling. She scurried into the bedroom, disrobed hurriedly. From the few swimsuits she'd bought, she slipped into a maillot-type Lycra one-piece, a soft mint-green. As she ran a quick comb through her hair, she wondered: *Should I tell Joyce that Dellin asked me to the beach yesterday?*

But immediately she frowned the idea off. *Why do that? Joyce might get the wrong idea.* In some catty, girlish way, it might sound like Clare was bragging. The thought occurred to her simply because Dellin's sudden offer had taken her by a pleasant surprise, and he'd even suggested that they might go to the beach together sometime in the future.

Then an even better thought popped up: *Maybe he'll even be out there today . . .*

"Hey, Clare? We're just going to the beach, not the prom!"

"Be right there!" *Towel, beach bag,* she reminded herself. *Am I forgetting anything?*

If she was, she'd find out when she got there. She donned her sunglasses, stepped into her flip-flops, and was about to head out—

Oh, the envelope . . .

She'd left it on the dresser. She was inclined to leave it, look at it later. *But what if it's not what Joyce thought? What if it's something else?*

She opened the envelope, extracted a single sheet of paper.

And stared.

The layout of the print was off-angle on the page, and the print quality was quite poor—obviously a multiple photocopy of a photocopy. But what snagged Clare's concern most of all was the item's nature.

Clare had seen things like this before.

It's a notification of criminal charges . . .

From: Office of the Judge Advocate General
The Pentagon, Washington, D.C.
To: MILPERS Detachment
Fort James K. Polk, Akron, Ohio

Re: NOTIFICATION OF INTENT TO PROSECUTE

1) JAG HQ posts this inter-branch FYI: Log and process the following ITP's with the MILPERS Registrar, via provisions of Army Regulation 201-173, Paragraph F, of the UCMJ.

So far, Clare knew what everything meant. MILPERS meant "military personnel," and UCMJ referred to the Uniform Code of Military Justice, the military code of law. This was a list of criminal arraignments being sent from the military's highest legal authority to be officially input into the U.S. Army's judicial database. It was a list of *people* the Army intended to try for crimes.

The rest was the actual alphabetized list, of Army personnel being slated for prosecution. About a third of the way down the sheet, a particular name hooked her eye:

-DANIELS, DELLIN, K.

Captain O-3/MOS: 45C20- Molecular-Targeting Technician

DUTY STATION: Fort Dietrich, Maryland, (BWS)

FORWARDING CHARGE(S):

a) Unauthorized redeposition of potentially hazardous/potentially classifiable materials.

Good God, was all Clare could think. But her next thought spiked her: *Adam!*

It couldn't have been anyone else but Adam who slipped this into Clare's mail slot. *Jesus Christ, I just saw the guy driving out of here fifteen minutes ago!* Her dislike for Adam sparked her first emotive reaction: *The son of a bitch is trashing Dellin 'cos he knows I've got a crush on him. He's trying to steer me AWAY from Dellin and TO-WARD him.*

But that was the least practical reaction and she knew that after another moment's thought. What it all meant was something much more important.

His motives don't matter. Adam was right. Dellin's got a crooked past. We've got something mutating the local animal wildlife, probably from toxic chemicals being illegally dumped . . . and now I'm looking at an official document charging Dellin with the exact same thing . . .

At once, she was depressed. She'd read Dellin all wrong, and this undisputable truth had just completely sabotaged her infatuation with him. She couldn't do anything about it, of course. Possessing the document itself represented a clear violation of Dellin's right to privacy, and even if the police investigated under the table, there'd be nothing they could take to court without genuine evidence. *I could even be charged myself, for having this document, and just because I know that Adam was the one who put it here, I've got no proof of that. With my OWN military record?*

Clare knew that even acknowledging this information would just get her fired from a great job and cause *more* trouble for her.

Damn . . . Whenever something good happens, something comes right along behind it to screw it up . . .

"Clare? I think I'm turning forty out here."

She grabbed her things, rushed out. She tried to seem unaffected but guessed it would show. "I'm ready. Sorry."

"Great!" Joyce's smile beamed. "You're gonna *love* this beach!"

They walked out the back, took a small path that worked through the palmetto bushes and thinning trees that lined the beach. Joyce was practically trotting in her enthusiasm; Clare only wished she could share in it now.

Of course, she couldn't tell Joyce about this either—she couldn't tell anyone. She had no idea how she would react the next time she saw Adam. She could only hope she *didn't* see him.

"Grab a chair. Isn't it gorgeous?"

Several folding lounge chairs were stacked at the beach's rim. Joyce grabbed one and was striding out ahead of her.

The beach *was* gorgeous. The sand was perfectly white, and the green-blue waves of the surf lapped serenely just ahead of her. Across the mile-wide bay inlet, she could see the island's first spur and the high sun radiating on the water. It might have been the most beautiful vision of her life.

But one she barely recognized now. Her crush on Dellin was demolished. It was hard to recall a deeper disappointment.

I sure know how to pick the guys to like. A military convict . . .

But there was something else too, an unpleasant concern that seemed to dig at her like an insect bite right in the middle of her back, one that couldn't be scratched.

Something about the list . . . the acronyms, maybe.

Her distraction was so complete she actually set out the lounge chair facing the wrong direction.

"First time at the beach?" Joyce said and started to laugh. "I guess you really want to soak up that stunning view of your back porch."

"I'm a real dunce today," Clare replied. "I just remembered what I forgot. My *brain*." She righted the chair, but her thoughts were still in a fog.

Yes. The acronyms. There was one . . .

She stretched out on the chair, staring out at but not

really seeing the gentle surf. That's when she remembered the acronym that bothered her. Just under the listing for Dellin's name on the document, it listed the location of the infraction. Suddenly she remembered precisely what it said:

Duty Station: Fort Dietrick, Maryland, (BWS)

The abbreviation at the end was the one that flagged her.

BWS, she thought in perplexion. *BWS* . . .

She knew that she'd heard that before. Whatever sort of department or technical specialty it was, she was sure the Air Force had one too.

Damn it! I HATE that! It's right on the tip of my tongue!

But in a few moments her aggravation turned into a pallid shock—when she finally remembered what those three letters stood for.

Biological Weapons Section . . .

(II)

They would be mad at it for being out here like this when it was the light part of the day. They didn't want regular people seeing it, so it was supposed to stay down in the pipe. But sometimes it came out anyway, because it liked to see what things looked like when the light was on them.

Yes, it liked the way things looked.

It liked just sitting here like this. It sat in some bushes, looking out. It knew that it should go back in the pipe soon but it didn't want to yet.

Last night was exciting. It watched the long-haired man flip-flop and howl on the lake shore.

The things in the lake had gotten him.

It was fun watching him die.

When the long-haired man had stopped moving and howling, it walked over and picked him up and then threw him back into the water. It liked the things in the lake, and it liked to feed them.

The long-haired man had come up on the beach side; that's when it had first seen him. He was digging in the beach sand, pulling things out and putting them in a bucket. It didn't know what the things were. They were whitish and sort of round. They were sort of the same shape as the part of it between its legs that the little skinny dirty girl had taken away from him the other day when she was trying to get away in the boat.

It hurt a lot when she did that, but it didn't matter.

The part of it that she'd taken off was already growing back.

Later the little skinny dirty girl got taken away in the truck with the funny popping lights. It wished she hadn't gotten taken away because it liked doing it to her.

They were mad at it because she got taken away.

It wasn't allowed to kill the girls, just the men. It knew they needed the girls to put in the special room. That's all it knew—that they liked to put the girls in that room.

They were also mad at it because of the buckets.

The stuff in the buckets.

It was supposed to empty the stuff in the buckets into the lake but a couple of times it had forgotten.

It would set the bucket down for a minute to pee, or catch a snake to eat, and then it would forget about the bucket.

They yelled at it when it did that.

It would forget where it left the bucket!

It knew that it would have to do better.

It sat there now, looking out. It felt full. Now that it was thinking of buckets, it remembered the bucket from last night, the one that the long-haired man was using. He was filling it up with the whitish round things he dug up in the sand.

After it had thrown his dead body back into the lake, it ate all the little white round things in the bucket.

They moved around in its mouth before it swallowed. They tasted good and filled it up. It liked snake better, though. It would bite the head off and suck out the guts. It ate lots of bugs too. It liked the way they crunched.

It was getting anxious now.

It needed a woman to do it to. It needed one soon.

It didn't know where the little skinny dirty girl was now but if it did it would go and get her and do it to her hard.

Yes, it needed a woman bad, and it hoped one would come soon. Sometimes they came at night with their men. It knew that it wasn't supposed to take the women in the tan clothes with the shiny plates. It wasn't allowed unless they said so. There were two of them, and they were real pretty. It was too bad that it wasn't allowed to take either of them.

It knew what they wanted. They wanted women from the outside.

It knew that if it got them a woman from the outside, they would be real happy with it.

It really hoped that one would come.

Maybe one would come tonight.

It started thinking about the two pretty women in the tan clothes. It liked the shorter one the best, the one with the hair that was the color of the sand on the beach.

Yes, it *really* liked her.

It wished it could kill her and do it to her while it was killing her.

It didn't know why it felt that way.

It just did.

(III)

"This cracker tan has got to go."

"What?"

"You have what we call a cracker tan, Clare. Your face and arms are great but the rest of you is white as a ghost."

So. I'm a cracker. "I definitely need to get out more."

"Well, we can start on that right now."

They'd lowered their lounge chairs, and Clare lay on her belly, eyes closed and chin resting on her wrists. Joyce was smoothing suntan oil up the backs of Clare's legs, and when that was done she moved up to her shoulders..

God, that feels good, she thought. *But I better not say that; she'll think I'm coming on to her.*

Joyce's hands firmly worked the shoulder muscles and back of the neck. "You sure you don't want to get out of that suit—a full tan is best. Don't worry, I'm not a dyke; I won't try to ravage you."

Clare chuckled. "No, I admit it, I'm a chicken." It wasn't her style, the idea just seemed too weird. She just wasn't confident about her body. *Too skinny, breasts too small.*

"Well at least pull the top of this damn one-piece down to your waist."

A long moment's thought, then, "Okay." When she sat up, Joyce helped her pull the top of the suit down.

She seemed very cognizant of Clare's unease, never letting her eyes fall on her breasts.

"There. This'll give you a good start on your back. Nothing looks more *wrong* in Florida than a girl with a tan line running across her middle of her back."

Joyce double-timed the application of lotion as an expert back massage, her fingers working stiffly up the spine. Clare felt herself slipping away in the hot, dreamy lassitude. This time it slipped out: "God, that feels good."

"It's supposed to."

As for Joyce herself, she'd verified her earlier implication the moment they'd unfolded their chairs. She'd slipped off the beach robe to reveal total nakedness, and didn't give it the slightest hesitation, her entire body bronze from the sun. Clare wished she could be that comfortable with herself.

Hard fingertips walked up the long strip of muscle on either side of her backbone. "Now I'm just saying this as a friend," Joyce commented as her hands continued their magic, "so don't get your feelings hurt, but you really need to gain some weight. You're a good-looking woman but you'd be so much better-looking if you'd put on ten pounds."

Clare wasn't offended; in fact she appreciated the remark. It was best, of course, not to explain her poor nutrition. Dellin's own insinuation on her first day was quite right: How credible a security manager could she be if her guards knew she'd come here straight from a homeless shelter? Instead, she just said, "I know. I've kind of let myself go since I got out of the Air Force. But all that changes now."

"Good."

It was all the last year—the worst year of her life. The remainder of her adulthood had kept her in great physical condition, especially her Air Force time. Even since puberty, she'd never had a bad self-image. She'd always thought of herself as average-looking, normal. What was wrong with that? It had been the stress of homelessness that had dragged her looks down. A vicious cycle. Even when there was food available—the sandwich truck, the soup kitchens—just the sheer stress of her situation killed her appetite. It was more than just eating properly now, she needed to manage her stress properly, and that meant not fretting over every little thing, not worrying about things past a practical point. She could already see it happening now; she could see it becoming a problem if she didn't keep a rein on her reactions. Atypically large animals and insects, toxins possibly being dumped in the lake, the clinic and Adam Corey and Dellin and everything else. It was all piling up. Should she be *worrying* about these things? Were her concerns over-reactive?

Probably, she answered herself. *Gotta keep a handle on it now. No choice*.

Her discovery today hardly helped. Dellin's military criminal record: the stiff Army lexicon—"Unauthorized redeposition of hazardous material"—meant the same thing that Adam suspected of happening here: dumping toxic waste. His assignment with the Biological Weapons Section only tripled the intensity of the implication.

But she also knew that she could be wrong about it all.

Worry about it later, she ordered herself, and what a luxurious order it was, lounging on a beautiful beach. But just as she'd vowed to put these concerns behind her, more popped up.

"Have you met the clinic director?" she asked. "I have yet to even catch a glimpse of the guy."

"Harry? Yeah, I've met him. Rick and I both met him when we in-processed. Nice man, fiftyish. Not exactly a ball of fire personally but what do you expect from these egghead types? We don't really see him much. From what I understand, he's the guy who discovered Interthiolate, Dellin's the guy who administers it to the patients. Harry's not a hard-ass, if that's what you're asking."

"Hmm. Dellin said I'll probably get to meet him next week. I was just wondering about him."

Now Joyce's fingertips were vigorously stippling up Clare's back. "I'll tell ya, the guy *I'm* still wondering about is Mrs. Grable's husband. She's always talking about him like he's the World's Greatest Man. Christ, he's beating her up every night."

"I saw the husband yesterday," Clare admitted, but of course she didn't admit *how* she'd seen him: through binoculars. "I know how deceiving appearances can be, and I might be dead wrong, but if you ask me, he just doesn't look like the kind of guy who'd abuse his spouse."

Joyce shrugged. "Well, somebody's beating the hell out of her. And it's real calculated too. It's almost like he leaves the marks where they can't be seen when she's dressed. Today, she was weed-whacking around the flowerbeds and I saw her back when she leaned over too far. It looked like it had *bite marks* on it." Now her thumbs teased around the nub of the tail bone. "But I guess there's always that option no one's considered yet?"

"What's that?"

"Who knows? Maybe Mrs. Grable's *into* that kind of thing. Masochism and stuff like that. Some women get off on being hit. Pain is part of the pleasure. The whole business sounds crazy to me but I've known several girls like that."

It sounded crazy to Clare too; some things she just couldn't figure. Of course, she'd heard of the phenomenon also but doubted that Mrs. Grable had such inclinations. "I don't know," was all she said. The sun on her back, along with Joyce's hands, made her so relaxed that she didn't really want to think about anything of import. *Worry about it all later*, she told herself, eyes barely open.

The tone of Joyce's voice softened. "If you don't like this, just say so."

Clare was confused by the remark. The back rub? "It's wonderful," she said.

"No. I mean *this* . . . "

Oh—Christ! Clare thought in a bolt of shock.

Joyce's soft hands slipped around; now they were on Clare's breasts. Clare's muscles tensed in reaction; she opened her mouth to object but—

The hands slipped around her breasts some more, fingertips tweezing the very ends of the nipples. Not *too* hard but hard enough.

Clare felt turmoil, then her spirit just deflated to surrender. *I should have known something like this might happen . . .*

She said nothing, did nothing to indicate she wasn't comfortable with this.

Joyce's warm breath brushed the back of her neck: "I didn't think you'd mind," and now she was lying flat out on Clare. The wet hands squeezed around the front of her hips, under the pulled-down swimsuit, fingers playing in the private hair. Clare could feel her friend's nipples hardening against the hot skin of her back. Her entire body went abuzz with clashing emotions and delicious sensations. The shock that locked her up . . . *snapped*. Then she just seemed to turn to fluid at Joyce's touch, floated away in a gush of complex pleasure.

Soon she was struggling with herself. The lewdest impulses swept her, she wanted to turn around, fling the swimsuit off, and just wrap her legs around Joyce, slither up right against her perfect bronze body and kiss and caress and touch.

"Stay like that, on your stomach."

Clare cringed; she wanted to see what Joyce was doing, she wanted to do something in return. She tried to turn around twice, but Joyce gently pushed her back.

"I think you'll like this . . ."

The soft humming sound was strange at first but then its familiarity grabbed her. Joyce was running a vibrator slowly up the inside of Clare's thigh. The exotic sensation stalked her; instantly she wanted more, she wanted it up high, right between her legs.

God, this is too much -

And just as she would moan out loud—

"Clare? Clare, you better turn over now."

Clare shook out of a vertigo. She felt a momentary disorientation, then she quickly raised herself up on her elbows. Her open eyes flinched over to Joyce, who was lying on her own lounge chair.

"Whuh-what?"

"You've been asleep for almost an hour," Joyce said without looking at her. Her face was turned up to the sun, eyes closed behind the sunglasses. "You better turn over now, or your back'll burn."

Clare sighed, astonished. *Jeez, another dream. Pretty soon I'm going to need to go to a sleep disorder clinic . . .*

She'd been railroaded again, by her subconscious. Nothing had happened but even so, she still felt an aftermath of excitement, all for naught now. Did the lesbian scene mean something Clare wasn't consciously aware of? *Where did THAT come from? What am I, a closet lesbian now?*

She turned around on her back, hoped she was acting normally. It was just another puzzle, just another aspect of herself that she couldn't control. The frustration crushed her.

I know I'm not a lesbian. I know I'm not sexually attracted to Joyce, or to any woman. What's wrong with me NOW?

At least there was one bright side—the dream hadn't been a nightmare. There'd been no images from her rape, no appearances of Stuart Winster and his twisted two-fingered hand.

All right, I had an erotic dream about Joyce, she resigned. *It's not that big a deal . . .*

"Don't forget the oil. The sun's really peaking now."

Clare unscrewed the bottle of suntan oil and spread it over the tops of her legs and feet, then her arms, throat and face. But she was still topless, her suit rolled down to her waist. Her nipples were impossibly erect, and she was sure Joyce had noticed them. *This is so embarrassing!* Her hands nearly trembled, as if she knew what would happen next. When she smoothed more oil over her stomach and breasts, the surge of excitement almost made her toes curl. Spreading the oil over her own breasts felt like someone else doing it, a lover.

Eventually she lay back, and even chuckled to herself. *I'm ALL messed up!*

"Why don't you come to the bar with me tonight?" Joyce asked. "It's a pretty cool place, we'd have fun."

"Thanks for the offer, but I really shouldn't. I'm on call all weekend; I really should stick close to the site.

And I'm not much of a bar person anyway, never been much of a drinker."

"So drink Coke. It's a ten-minute drive, right up Gulf Boulevard. If something happens at the clinic, the system will beep you, and we'll come back and check it out right away. But believe me, nothing's going to happen anyway. Come on, I don't want to go there by myself."

Clare didn't really want to; she'd never felt comfortable in bars, but then again, it might be a good idea to go somewhere to relax for a little while. "Sure, I'll go with you, but I'll just have one drink."

"Or two. Great! It'll be fun, you'll see."

Seeing new places and acquainting herself with the area would do her good, and maybe it *would* be fun. She hadn't been to a bar in ages.

The sea breeze and the sound of the surf had Clare drifting off again, in and out of sleep. No dreams this time, just the short waves folding over and the sun's warm caress. Fragments of thoughts threatened to take chips out of the wonderful cloud of peace and quiet—Dellin, roaches and frogs, Adam Corey, etc.—but she wouldn't let them get a foothold. It was such a luxury not being bothered.

"Howdy, girls. Whoa, Joyce! That's the best flesh-colored swimsuit I've ever seen."

"You ASShole!" Joyce bellowed, lurching off her chair and pulling on her beach robe. "Don't you have any respect at all? What are you doing here!"

Clare's peace and quiet shattered like a beer bottle on pavement. She knew before she even looked. Adam Corey, ever-present in his park service uniform, had walked right up behind them.

"Adam, that's low-down even for you," Clare said and quickly pulled up her top.

Joyce was steaming. "Get out of here, you pervert! What are you doing sneaking up on us?"

Adam made a long face. "I'm not sneaking up on anyone. How was I to know you'd be out here with nothin' on?"

"Adam, it's our day off," Clare complained. "There's no reason for you to be out here. That's really vulgar."

Adam frowned. "I don't know what you're talking about. You're the one who called *me*, remember? Some kooky message you left on my machine."

The cockroach? Clare thought. "It was just an FYI, Adam. The clinic's closed till Monday morning, you can come by and pick it up then."

"Why not now? I mean, some of us take our jobs seriously. When there's something to be done, we do it, we don't sluff it off till Monday because we'd rather sit around on the beach buck naked."

Clare sighed. "It'll *wait*, Adam. It's not that urgent."

Joyce was still glaring at him. "I can't believe you'd pull a pervert move like this. You just used that as an excuse to see us naked. I ought to report you."

The ranger cut a wide smile. "That's a hoot. Nude bathing on government land is a federal offense. Go ahead and *report* me. All my boss'll do is ask for your address so he can send you the summons and the fine for indecent exposure."

Joyce turned away from him, sat back down in her chair. "Oh shut up, Adam. Consider this your thrill for the day." Then she overdramatically pulled her robe collar tighter around her neck. "You got your eyeful, now hit the road. Peep-time is over."

Adam was ignoring her now, addressing Clare. "And

I just thought you might want to know, since you're the security boss—it looks like Kari Ann Wells ain't gonna make it."

Clare leaned up. "What?"

"I called to see how she was doing, but they said her heart started fibrillating a lot last night. She's in intensive care now, in critical condition." He began to stalk off. "Sorry to interrupt your important work out here."

The news, and the whole situation, made Clare feel crummy. "That's too bad about the girl," she said.

"Yeah. But what can anyone do? These drug addicts bring it on themselves. The human body can only take so much abuse."

Clare supposed this was true but it didn't make her feel any better. "And—I don't know. Maybe we overreacted a little to Adam. Maybe he really didn't come out here on purpose, just to see our boobs."

After a moment's thought, they both looked at each other.

Joyce said, "Yeah, and maybe the Pope shits in the woods."

Part Three

Federal Land Grid S27-0078
Central Florida
June 1995

Neither Fredrick nor Dales could deny what they were seeing with their own eyes. Their wide-lensed flashlights stared blankly as their faces. The westerly wall of the cenote stood far less even than the other walls, more like a pile of sedimentary rubble, but hard as slab shale nonetheless, fused together by eons and geothermic pressure. And what they'd first believed to be a second pit—or a simple hole at the edge of the wall—after closer examination proved to be something more like a crevice in the jumbled stone.

And from that crevice, a hand jutted.

Dales was the first to say it: "That's not a human hand." He looked beseechingly at Professor Fredrick. "Right?"

Fredrick's throat felt dry as the shale floor. "I would have to say that, mmm, it appears not to be—"

"No no no!" Dales insisted. "Just so I know I'm not crazy. If I *am* crazy, then that's fine. You tell me that

that—" he jabbed a finger violently at the frozen hand—"is a human hand. Go on. Just tell me, and I'll get out of here."

Fredrick understood his young colleague's anxiety—Fredrick, too, was anxious, and confused and excited and a little bit scared. But he remained composed in the grainy dark. "Dales, no, it doesn't look like a human hand. It's too large. But there are a few things that could account for its disproportionate size."

"Like what?"

"Well, the vagaries of the subterranean environment, for one thing."

Dales's frown cut like a knife. "Come on, boss. The four priests and the sacrifice victim pickled perfectly down here. Then why didn't *that?*"

Fredrick's mouth opened, closed.

"And don't tell me it's swelling from some disease or blood-born infection. You can see the contours of that hand as well as I can. There's no evidence of edema—it's morphologically consistent."

"Dales, we'd need thorough microscopy before we can positively rule out an edemic symptom."

"Bull-DICK, Prof!" Dales pointed back to the hand. "It's got claws!"

Well, Fredrick thought. *There is that.*

The hand was obsidian-black, fully open in its petrification. If he could equate the appearance of the skin with a word, it would have to be crocodilian: segments of varying size, scale-like, hundreds of them.

The claws were another thing.

Each finger came to a vicious point, and there was an excessive ugliness about them; they seemed more *part* of each fingertip, and less like something that had grown out like human fingernails.

If Fredrick had to equate a word to *this* feature, it would have to be . . .

Demonic, he thought.

"Can't see anything down here with these damn drugstore flashlights," Dales griped. "I called up for a goddamn light crew twenty minutes ago."

"Be patient, son."

"Hey, piss on patient, boss. Patient can kiss my hairy ass. You and I both know what that thing is. I want to see it *now*." Both of their harnesses lay on the floorwall right in the circle of light beneath the drop-hole. Dales put on his radio headset that was connected to the ascending hoist line.

"What the hell is wrong with you people up there! We need that light team down here *now!* Jesus Christ, the continental drift'll move Florida over to Texas by the time you numbskulls get your shit together! If that gear's not down here in five minutes, I'm gonna climb back up and start kicking some ass!"

Laughter could be heard coming from the drop-hole.

"Yeah, go ahead and laugh, assholes. See how hard you laugh on grade day when I flunk all your asses."

The lights and crew started coming down a minute later.

"Dales. Look."

Along the floor lay a long curved object. It was hardwood, and clearly it had been hand-carved. One end was the handle, and from there it extended, widening and flattening out, to form an edged blade.

"What's that?" Dales asked. "A Ponoye war hammer?"

"Close. It's a *kirri-manano*, the Ponoye "Gift-Blade." Remember, there was no metallurgy—the Ponoye were masters at affecting blade-sharp edges on hardwoods. There was never bloodletting in a Ponoye sacrifice—the sacrifants were always garroted—but the priests would always bring a kirri-manano to present as a gift. In the event that the incarnation, er, what I mean—"

"You mean if the incarnation worked, and they summoned a demon, they'd give the demon one of those kirri-things as a gift," Dales said. Then he spared a laugh. "Well, it looks like he didn't think much of the gift, boss. He pulled the arms, legs, and heads off of the guys who gave it to him!"

Frustrated, Fredrick pinched the bridge of his nose. "Dales. I know what you're considering, I really do, and any other time, I'd be surprised, even disappointed. But under these circumstances, I can understand how even men such as us—men of *science*—might give solid credence to the possibility—"

"Save it, boss," Dales interrupted. "Just answer yes or no." He turned his flashlight back to the stone dolmen on which the young woman lay. "The woman—the priests killed her on the dolmen?"

"On a typical sacrificial dolmen, yes. They choked her to death with a ligature, as was their custom."

"They *sacrificed* her in a clearly occult ritual."

"Yes."

"A ritual of incarnation."

"Yes."

"They were attempting—as did countless ancient tribes of mankind—to incarnate a devil."

"Yes."

"In a *cenote*. Which is what we're standing in right now."

"Yes."

Dales took deep, steady breaths through his following words. "Then . . . who killed these four priests?"

Fredrick could barely bring himself to answer. "I-I

suppose the only logical conclusion would be—"

"Bullshit. That *thing* killed the priests, that *thing* that is clearly not human." Dales's voice grated down. "Those priests were incarnating a demon—and they succeeded. What else could that thing be . . . but a demon's mummified corpse?"

Within an hour, the cenote was lit up as daylight; within two, every square foot was graded, gridded, cordoned, photographed, and digigraphed.

Within three, they were getting their first MMADS readings.

"You'd think the damn college would at least spring for one of the newer models," Dales complained, sitting at the display assembly. "This old hunk of shit takes goddamn forever just to process a prelim readout."

"Patience," Fredrick repeated the advice that had taken him decades to learn himself.

"I know this wall is a deadfall, it *has* to be."

"Probably, but not necessarily," the older man warned.

Dales acted as though he hadn't even heard his mentor. "Sure, a quake, a tremor? It brought down this end of the cenote, which means that once we excavate we'll see what *else* was in here ten thousand years ago."

Fredrick decided to toy with him. "You seem hopeful."

"Why shouldn't I be?"

"If this really is a fall instead of part of the original cenote, then the rest of your demon friend's body will have been pulverized beneath the rubble. If I were you, I'd be hoping that this isn't a fall. I'd be hoping that this crevice is intact, in which case the rest of your friend's *corpse* might be intact."

Dales didn't respond; he kept his face stolid on the MMADS screen. *I think he really believes that it's a demon,* Fredrick thought. He'd seen things similar to this happen to younger and more ebullient archeologists in the past: a serious discovery would sometimes corrupt their conceptions. It never lasted long, though. *Dales will come back to earth in a short while. I'm sure that a blood disease can explain the hand's excessive size. Perhaps an impact injury shortly before death. Perhaps the wall fell down on the fellow and didn't kill him instantly. The bruise-swelling and outpouring of excess creatinine in the blood could account for the size.* The explanation would come in time. Fredrick would make an effort not to rub Dale's embarrassment in his face.

At least not for too long.

What Fredrick didn't consider, though, was that his hypothesis *didn't* account for one thing: how their swollen rock-fall victim had managed to behead and dismember four strong men with his bare hands.

MMADS stood for magnetic mass-activated detection system, a relatively new technology in that it was invented in the '80s. From round, dinner-plate-sized sensors, low-wave sonar was emitted, taking an "x-ray" of whatever might be embedded, for instance, in solid stone, a block of concrete, a shale bed, a clay bed, or simple compacted earth. It would measure discrepancies in the consistency of the object's solidity. It would work on a pile of stone rubble, too, or in this case, what Fredrick believed was a rock fall from a partial cave-in.

"Wow," someone said behind them. "Her nipples almost look alive."

Fredrick frowned behind him. It was the photographers, bending over the sacrifant on the stone dolmen. "Don't get that close!" he yelled.

Immediately they stepped back.

Someone else: "Yeah, anyone who messes with the Professor's mummies'll get his ass kicked by Dales."

Laughter cackled, but Dales just smiled. "How about we put one of these MMADS sensors on *you*. Then we can count how many gerbils you got in your rectum today."

Louder laughter ensued. *Boys will be boys*, Fredrick thought.

"Hey, Prof? How're we gonna get these mummies up that drop-hole without damage?"

"With extreme difficulty." Even Fredrick knew the necessity of some levity on occasion. If you kept them laughing, and occasionally related to them on not-so-scholarly terms, then they'd respect you more, and work harder. "Anyone who so much as harms a single crystalline hair on any of my mummies—I'll decapitate him and engage in sexual congress with his esophagus."

Now they were honking. Good spirits would prove essential; there was a lot of hard labor ahead, not just the seemingly impossible removal of the mummified remains, but the entire site needed to be analyzed now, every square inch combed, sifted, and brushed. And then there was always—

Fredrick looked down at the hand. In the bright halogen light, it didn't look nearly so intimidating. *Maybe it's a glove of some sort. A ceremonial gauntlet? Hell, mold and oxidation could even account for the increased size. Why didn't I think of that before?* And the claw-like appearance of the fingers? *Of course, a ritual gauntlet with shark's teeth or animal claws sewn into the fingertips; mold grew over the tips to make them appear homogenized. There's your demon, Dales.*

But he didn't voice this most recent conclusion; it was best to just leave the overzealous teaching assistant to his current task at the MMADS dials. The vision of the hand, though, continued to highjack the professor's attentions. Yes, originally it looked like the hand was reaching out of a hole on the floor's base but that wasn't quite the case. *It's a fissure, above floor level.* More and more, it seemed that the subject must have been engulfed by a partial collapse of the cenote. Fredrick could only pray that at least *some* of the body connected to the hand was salvageable. The skull would likely be crushed but maybe the rest of the skeleton would be in good shape.

Poor Dales is probably wasting his time. I'll bet he gets maximum density readings . . .

"Unbelievable," Dales mouthed and looked up.

"Let me guess. Maximum density readings. Fallen stone rubble fifty feet deep."

Dales shook his head as he scrutinized the readout screen. "It's just the opposite, Prof. I'm getting a triple zero reading at a meter and a half."

"What!" Fredrick yelled in shock.

"This isn't a rockfall. There's another room behind this."

Fredrick's vision seemed to swim as he stared at the inclined wall of broken stone. "Another room," he muttered. "Another cenote . . ."

Chapter Eleven

(I)

Joyce drove in her personal vehicle, an old Plymouth convertible whose canvas roof was permanently locked down. This she called her "knocking around" car. She cranked up some hard rock band as she took them both up the coast road. Clare felt immediately awkward by the periodic honks, hoots, and whistles as they drove; the convertible put Joyce out for display. She wore a scoopnecked apricot tank that read GROW YOUR OWN DOPE, PLANT A MAN but it wasn't the amusing ditty that was nearly causing minor collisions during their drive. Joyce's buoyant bosom stretched the top's sheer material to its physical limit. Even the smaller details of the aureola could be discerned. *I'd be the happiest woman in the world if I had breasts HALF that size*, Clare thought. But Joyce *was* remarkably attractive. Clare dressed in simple beach shorts and a sleeveless tee. *I'll probably stick out like a sore thumb sitting next to her . . .*

Just another trifling insecurity; she let it pass with the breeze sifting through her golden hair. She also let pass the fairly inexcusable incident at the beach with Adam. *I guess if you're gong to lie around on the beach with no top, you have to expect a creep or two to crawl out of the woodwork every now and then.* It didn't really bother her; she doubted that Adam had cast anything but the briefest glance at her anyway, not with Joyce lounging next to her totally nude. It was too bad about Kari Ann Wells, though. *Maybe she'll pull through,* Clare hoped. *Maybe she'll get better.*

Soon they were off the coast road and following a waterfront avenue that seemed lined with beach bars. PARTY TILL YOU PUKE! one sign blared. Another: THE WORLD MIGHT END TONIGHT SO . . . DIE DRUNK. And another: DON'T MISS OUR HAPPY HOUR SH*TFACE SPECIALS!

Clare raised a brow. "That's what I call enthusiasm."

"It's a hard-drinking town," Joyce said. "The locals take their partying seriously. But these places are pretty redneck. We're going farther down."

"What's *that* mean?" Clare asked, pointing to a sign on another bar that read FREE T.G.I.G.M.F. SHOOTERS!

"Thank God it's goddamn motherfuckin' Friday," Joyce answered. "Since you asked. I know what you're thinking, that I'm dragging you to some dive, but relax. We're going to the only *sane* bar on the strip. The other places are either sanctuaries for alkies or pick-up joints for the brain-dead."

Further along, they pulled into a parking lot whose edge ran along a fishing inlet. The first thing Clare saw was a tow truck pulling a white sedan out of the water. *Not a good sign,* she thought. Next, she noticed several police cars stopped in the middle of the road; officers and several residents gathered round a man who'd passed out cold on the double-yellow line. And next? Someone hung out the window of a second story apartment; he was bent over at the waist, noisily vomiting in front of a life-size cutout of the Three Stooges. Lastly, a man fishing in the inlet fell into the water when he was reaching for his beer.

"Yeah, I can see, they *do* take their partying seriously," Clare said.

"Oh, this is nothing, it's still early," Joyce said.

Of the crush of taverns that were crammed along the street, they walked into one with the debatable name of DIABOLICAL DICK'S. Based on what she'd seen of the immediate surroundings, Clare's hopes were less than high, but she was relieved when they actually entered and she found herself standing in a non-pretentious but nicely appointed tavern full of casually dressed patrons who looked decidedly normal. *No one's throwing up or passed out on the floor*, Clare thought. *So far, so good.* Intelligent alternative rock, not heavy metal or Jimmy Buffet, eddied from the sound system, and Clare was instantly enticed by the aromas drifting from the kitchen. This was clearly several notches up from the typical beer and bar-food joints she expected. Preposterously attractive barmaids and waitresses milled through their tasks, while the Devil Rays were getting butchered on a huge projection tv.

"Damn, all the tables are full," Joyce noticed. "This place is always so packed. Do you mind sitting at the bar?"

"Fine with me."

They went around one end, and some guy with a goatee and glasses was citing to a friend, "For one half second—maybe even *three-quarters of a second*, you could see the side of Xev's left nipple. I *swear!* On Sci-Fi Channel!"

"You don't say?"

Someone else was making reference to Florida's governor with a term that began with the prefix mother and ended with the suffix hole, but in a perfect John Wayne imitation. Another guy, drunk, was exclaiming to all that John F. Kennedy was really assassinated by a Marseilles mobster hired by the South Vietnamese executive branch. No one was listening. But across the bar, three more guys argued over Florida's official state fish. One guy: "It's grouper." The next guy: "No, it's not, it's red snapper." Third guy: "I thought it was Floating Syringe."

Just ahead of them, a younger guy in a Devil Rays shirt edged up to the bar and asked for a beer. A bartender appraised him with narrowed eyes, and said, "Sorry, buddy, you look kind of young. I gotta see it." The guy stood flummoxed, then shrugged. He began to open his fly. "Not that!" yelled the bartender. "Your ID!"

"Oh, look," Joyce said, as if surprised. "There's Rick."

Clare could've laughed at the obvious setup. *Now isn't THAT a coincidence!*

"And there're two seats next to him . . ."

Of course.

"Hey, all. Fancy meeting you here," Rick greeted.

"Do you come here a lot?" Clare asked.

Joyce laughed. "Rick lives here. He's got a cot in the store room."

"Funny. You know what's funnier? Joyce keeps *her* cot out in the back alley. Ten bucks a ride. That's how she pays her tab."

Joyce poked him in the ribs. Hard. "Keep it up, Mr.

Laughs. How'd you like to try on a pitcher?"

The women sat on either side of Rick. A leggy, amply bosomed barmaid stepped up, size sixish, with honey-blond hair. "What would you like?"

"Shut up and fuck me," Rick replied.

Clare exploded. "Rick! What is wrong with you!"

But the barmaid tittered. "Sure. Three?"

"Yeah," Rick said. "And three light drafts, please."

"Don't fall off your stool," Joyce said to Clare. "It's a shooter."

Clare couldn't believe it. "You're telling me there's a drink called Shut Up And Fuck Me?"

"Oh, yeah," Rick affirmed. "This town's famous for its shooters. My favorites are the Red-Headed Slut, the Flaming Asshole, and the Leg Spreader. Maybe later we'll have a Frankenstein's Jism."

Clare looked aghast. "I hate to be a party pooper but I'll have to pass on the Frankenstein's Jism."

Joyce and Rick were obviously amused by Clare's naivete. "You act like you haven't been to a bar in ten years," Joyce said.

"Oh, not that long. More like seven or eight."

Rick feigned alarm. "Poor girl. Somebody—please—give this girl an Orgasm!"

"All right, I'm not *that* old. I do remember drinking a few of those in my college days."

Levity aside, some truth rubbed in. Clare began to fear that too much of her own persona had been damaged by her sense of dedication. It wasn't just the fact that she hadn't been to a bar for so many years, it was that in all that time she'd barely been *out* at all. Not everything in life was work—the relationships with the people close to you were what you worked *for*. Clare never really had people close to her, she figured that later would be better for all of that, and in the meantime she needed to progress herself as effectively as possible. And she'd been doing exactly that—until it all came to a tragic halt. The rape. The trial. The whitewash. All at once it became clear that living by a standard and a set of rules that anybody would consider commendable had been a mistake. It had left her with nothing, and when the time came that she sorely needed the support of the people close to her, there was no one there. *Damn. There I go feeling sorry for myself again. Joyce and Rick are my friends. Dellin's a friend or at least someone I have a positive working relationship with. Quit whining! You could always be back in the shelter. You're out with people who like you—don't be a mopey pud.*

She felt better in short order, and when the shooters came she proposed a toast—"to giant cockroaches and frogs"—and downed the shooter in one toss.

"Excellent style and form," Rick said. "Joyce, there's hope for her yet. She's a true party animal in training."

"Hear, hear."

"I'm relieved," Clare said.

In less than complimentary phraseology, Clare and Joyce briefed Rick on their beachside encounter with Adam. "Put a collar and chain on that oddball," Rick suggested. "Don't let him get out of the yard."

Clare sipped her beer. "So when are you going to tell me why you call him Ranger Jingles?"

"It's too gross," Joyce said.

"And Joyce should know," Rick blurted next. "She actually had the honor of—"

Joyce jabbed him in the ribs again, after which he chuckled and put his arm around her.

Joyce instantly bumped her knee against his, then

Rick took his arm off with a look on his face that said *Oops*.

Clare saw it all.

She wasn't surprised by the awkward silence that followed.

"Look it's not right for us to be dishonest," Joyce owned up. "Rick and I are . . . kind of . . . involved."

"Really? I never would've guessed," Clare said.

"But you have our guarantee that that all stays out of the workplace," Rick added.

Clare put on a cheery smile. "Good, 'cos if it doesn't I'll fire both your butts on the spot. Seriously, though. Any relationship between the two of you is your business." Maybe it was the shooter and the half a beer she'd drunk so far, or maybe it was just because she liked them, and felt that she needed to be honest too—but Clare couldn't resist. "Just do me a favor. Next time you decide to fool around in the woods, don't do it in front of the loading dock surveillance camera—like you did the other day."

Joyce turned beet-red. Rick buried his face in his hands.

Now it was Clare's turn to be amused. "Now *that's* what I call a reaction."

Now Rick put his arm back around Joyce. "Like they say, women—can't live with 'em, can't put big rubber corks in their mouths when they talk too much."

Joyce elbowed him in the ribs. Hard. "Yeah, and men—can't write 'em off on your taxes 'cos there's no deduction for life-support for a penis."

"Your secret's safe with me," Clare assured. "Just try to keep the public smooching to a minimum, and the same for when you're around Mrs. Grable. She's a sweetheart but she loves gossip."

It was far better for the air to be cleared on the matter, and Clare knew it would be a lot easier for her to deal with them on a day-to-day work basis as a result. For the next hour, they took turns talking a little bit about themselves, and Clare found it interesting as well as encouraging that they all had similar histories in that they'd all served as military police in the Air Force and were all raised in the Foster Care system.

"And it looks like we all turned out all right," Rick said. "I don't know about you and Joyce, but *I* haven't shot up any schoolyards lately. And I never even smoked pot. Yet all the time you're hearing on the news about how Foster Care fails."

"Funny we should be talking about it," Joyce added. "Grace Fletcher mentioned that she was an orphan too."

"And she was in the Air Force," Clare said, remembering the snapshot she'd seen. "She was a captain in the Air Force Security Service." More mental gears began to turn. "In my cottage I found some snapshots, and one was of Grace and the two previous guards all standing together."

"Donna and Rob?" Rick said.

"Yeah, and it turns out that Donna is someone I know—er, knew. Her name's Donna Kramer. I went to basic and primary AIT with her at Wright-Patterson."

"Yeah, but that's not really a coincidence that we all happen to have been MPs in the Air Force. Dellin even told me they save money on background checks."

"I know, but isn't it odd that we're all orphans?" Clare asked. "During training, I knew Donna Kramer pretty well, and guess what she told me once? Her parents abandoned her when she was little, and the state put her in the system."

Now Rick's eyebrows shot up. "Rob Thomas, the third guard—"

"No way," Joyce said. "You're not gonna tell us that *he* was an orphan, too."

"He was an orphan too. We were on permanent duty together, he and I were hanger guards at Holloman. We partied together at the EM club every weekend, and I'll be damned if he didn't mention that to me. Said his father died before he was born and his mother got killed in a car crash when he was a baby."

"Kind of weird," Clare said.

"So weird, in fact, that we need more beers." Rick ordered another round from the knockout barmaid. "And what's weirder is how they all vanished overnight."

"Oh, Rick," Joyce said wearily, "don't start with that malarkey again."

"Please," Clare said. "Let's hear some malarkey. Joyce, you said they all quit because they were afraid of alligators or quicksand or something."

"Grace told me she came from up north and she put in her notice because she couldn't stand the heat, which is kind of reasonable when you consider how damn hot it gets out here. Then that night I ran into Rob right here—"

"You never told me you dated him," Rick said with a bit too much haste.

"I didn't. He was just here." Joyce winced. "And shut up. But he said he and Donna put in their notice because they thought the site was too hazardous between the 'gators and the quicksand and all that. They were lightweights, that's all. And it's a good thing they were 'cos *we* got their jobs."

"Sure, but it's not a good thing if we *actually* got their jobs because they all died."

Clare instantly straightened on the bar stool. "Because they all *what?*"

"Hey, there were all kinds of rumors," Rick pointed out. "Everyone in the area had a different story. They were afraid of alligators, they were all drunks, they got caught in a love triangle, they were fugitives with warrants out on them. Hell, I even heard that Dellin caught them doing a three-way naked pretzel while they were on duty."

Well, Clare thought. *At least I can attest to that last one* . . . But it was too inappropriate to mention the videotapes. *And too embarrassing,* she caught herself. They'd probably ask to see the videotapes themselves, and— *There are a few scenes on those tapes where Grace and Donna were using the green vibrator on each other . . . the same vibrator Joyce saw ME using* . . . But the direction of the conversation was intriguing now; Clare wanted to hear more.

"I love a good mystery," she cajoled. "Keep going."

"Keep going," Joyce sniped. "That's what I tell him every night, but he just rolls over and starts snoring."

"No, no, you're confusing me with Ranger Jingles—"

Joyce elbowed him in the ribs. Hard.

"Come on, Rick. This is fascinating. What else did you hear?"

Rick leaned over on his elbows. "Then I'm sitting in here one night and an off-duty local cop comes in. He gets faced in a hurry and starts spouting off about how his chief is afraid the town'll lose a lot of their peak-season tourist business if the newspapers find out about all yahoos who've been disappearing."

"You mean, like—"

"Local rednecks and meth-heads, like that girl you found the other night," Rick went on. "This cop said that a *bunch* of 'em have been disappearing over the last year. Said they think they're getting hit by bull sharks that knock over their canoes and little row boats when they paddle out to—can you guess where?"

"Fort Alachua Park," Clare said.

"Right, *our* side of Fort Alachua Park. Why? Because it's a great poaching ground. Cop said they've been finding a fair share of boats capsized in the bay, and some of those boats have been registered to yokels who've been reported missing."

"Interesting," Clare said.

"But *that's* not all—"

"Give us a break, meathead!" Joyce complained. "You're boring the yeast out of all our beers."

Rick thumbed her way. "Wanna know the *real* reason she wants me to shut up?"

Clare smiled. "Why?"

"Because she's afraid, too—oww!"

Joyce elbowed him again.

Rick rubbed his ribs. "If you keep doing that, you might hit some stray nerve branch, might make me impotent."

"Don't I wish."

Clare tugged Rick's sleeve. "What were you saying? The boats they found were registered to people who turned up missing?"

"Some of them. Even the most irresponsible yokels register their boats so they can get their full saltwater fishing licenses. This cop said over a dozen of them have disappeared."

"Okay, the big scary story's over. That means Wicky Poo can shut up now."

Rick held up a finger. "But . . . there's more."

"Somehow I thought there would be," Clare said. "So out with it, please."

"I stop by here one night for a beer when Joyce is working, and one of the drop-dead gorgeous barmaids starts making some time with me because—" Rick shrugged "—let's face it, who can blame her? I'm a damn good-looking guy and she knows the total package when she sees it—"

"Somebody give me a barf bag!" Joyce howled.

"Anyway, she starts telling me about the last time she saw Donna; it was supposedly the night before she disappeared. Donna came in here to get some carryout—three orders—said she was on her way to meet Grace and Rob, and she specifically said that they all put in two weeks notice."

"Big deal, Bozo," Joyce offered. "So what if they decided to leave the next day? People balk out on their two-week notice all the time. They didn't feel like waiting so they left."

Rick kept talking as if Joyce hadn't spoken at all. "Aaaaaaand, while she was waiting for her food, she has a few drinks but, wouldn't you know it? She gets a little tipsy."

"How convenient," Joyce droned. "It's too bad the *total package* wasn't here. If she was that drunk, he might've gotten lucky."

"Hey. *She* would've been the lucky one. Anyway, she has one too many Johnny Blacks and she starts telling this barmaid about how they're all scared shitless because there's—"

"A monster prowling the park," a voice behind them cut in. "Not a man, a monster."

All three of them turned around at the same time.

Dellin was standing behind them, smiling with his arms crossed.

"Hi, Dellin," Joyce said.

"I guess we better buy the boss a drink," Rick added, "so he thinks we're cool."

For some reason, though, Clare was nearly choked up. She couldn't have been more delighted to see Dellin, but she sight of him left her tongue-tied.

"Thanks for the offer, Rick, but I'm just here for a carryout grouper sandwich." Dellin was wearing tennis shorts and a t-shirt that read UNIVERSITY OF SOUTH FLORIDA ONCOLOGISTS GROUP-CHARITY LEAGUE. He looked right at Clare. "How's it going, Clare?"

"Uh, fine. Great," she blurted. "Pull up a seat." *PLEASE!*

"Naw, I can't stay; I'm pooped. I'm in this charity softball league with the Florida Physicians Board. We did a double-header today."

"Did you hit any home runs?"

"No, we got crushed both games. I struck out grandly, though. Ten times, as a matter of fact."

Clare's heart was fluttering. She knew it was a foolish reaction but she couldn't help it.

"Well, I guess I'm not in that bad of a rush," he reconsidered. He took the stool right next to Clare. "I did stop into the clinic today," he went on, "before the game. And I saw your incident reports."

Clare had to drag herself out of her distraction. *He's going to think you're a complete airhead! Say something.* "Then I guess you also saw—"

"The cockroach in the refrigerator? I sure did. And the other report said something about a frog?"

"A *big* frog, near the lake. Adam accidentally ran it

over in his truck. It was enormous, just like the cockroach. Much bigger than it should've been."

Dellin didn't seem the least bit alarmed. "Mutagenic pollution is a lot more common than people think, especially in Florida, and I have an advantage understanding it simply because I'm a cancer physician with a background in genetics and organic transfection. Ultimately most cancer is the result of a process of mutation, often precipitated by foreign substances. Every cell in the human body has a mutagenic gene. Carcinogenic toxins will target that gene, and from there anything can happen because the entire DNA blueprint becomes misappropriated and, hence, adulterated."

"I left my doctorate at home, Dellin," Rick said. "Do you think you could put that in—"

"Less sophisticated technical terms, sure," Dellin caught himself. "There's a switch in every cell in your body. The switch regulates changes and growth. When pollutants get into a cell and throw that switch, anything can happen. One thing that happens most often is a highly accelerated growth rate. That's obviously what happened in this case."

"I've heard about stuff like that happening in the area, near lakes and reservoirs," Joyce said. "But have you ever seen cockroaches that big before?"

"Well, not that big, no. That really was enormous."

Clare felt stifled by her own shyness. It was Dellin, she knew, and her intense attraction to him.

"I have seen frogs, though, as large as the one Clare described in her report. It was at a transfection study I did some work for several years ago."

"What exactly does that mean—transfection?" Clare finally got a few more words out. "I've never heard of it."

"It's a genetic engineering term. Transfection is like gene splicing, only on an even smaller molecular scale. When you put genetic properties from one cell into another cell. A growth gene, for instance. If you saturate a growth gene with carbon in a high-oxygen environment, then put the compatible part of that gene in, say, a liver cell, the liver cell grows at an exponential rate. Controlling the nature of the growth is the key, though. The growing liver cell doesn't develop normally. It becomes tumorous, then malignant. Here's an example: An industrial pollutant that seeps into a lake or a pond can transfect mutagenic properties into a frog egg. The growth gene in the egg—the switch—is turned on in an abnormal way, then you've got your giant frog. What we're doing at the clinic is the opposite of that process. We're turning those growth genes *off*, which leaves the cancer helpless against the patient's own immune-system responses." Dellin suddenly frowned at himself. "Jeez, I'm sorry, I must be boring everyone to death. This isn't exactly bar talk."

"Oh, it's fascinating," Clare insisted, but then darker recollection began to spoil some of her infatuation. *Dellin was criminally charged in the Army, prosecuted . . .* The last thing Clare wanted to do was challenge Dellin, or put him on the spot, but her urge to feel him out on the subject was too irresistible.

I wonder what he'd say if . . .

"So what we're talking about," she continued, "is someone sneaking out to Lake Stephanie and dumping toxins into it?"

"Probably not *someone*, " Dellin replied with no hesitation. "After World War II, the Army Air Corps buried a lot of unexpended explosive propellents on this end of the park. Most aerial bombs of that era contained ammonia-based explosive compounds. Those same kinds of compounds are well-known chemical mutagens. During the war, Fort Alachua was an Army bomb center. They'd test different kinds of bombs here on obsolete ships they'd put out in the bay. It was also a practice range. But some of those propellents they buried are seeping into the inner-island water systems. Unfortunately, there weren't any dumping regulations back then. Their only concern was winning the war, not environmental protection."

The casual response to Clare's question relieved her. It didn't explain the criminal notice, and she couldn't very well call him on that. But suddenly Adam's allegations seemed much less probable.

Dellin smiled. "As for the far more interesting subject you all were talking about when I came in—"

"A monster in the swamps," Rick said though a grin.

"Yeah, that was one of the rumors, I'm afraid," Dellin admitted. "A psychopath or even a monster. Anything that Donna Kramer may have told anyone else was just founded in an overexcited imagination. Local poachers disappear on occasion, and yes, it's logical that some of them were eaten by alligators because that's what they poach in most cases. And some are likely eaten by sharks: they're drunk in the first place, their canoes tip over because they're careless—instant shark food. But the rumor mill turns anyway, and we're talking about a class of people who are largely uneducated and much more prone to alcohol- and drug-related delusions. Every locale will have its own version of the Jersey Devil, or Goat Man, or the Loch Ness Monster. This happens to be *our* version."

"Thank God for rednecks," Rick said. "Life would be so dull without them."

"That's pretty much what Kari Ann Wells said the other day," Clare offered, "before the ambulance took her. She said that something attacked her—not a man, a monster."

"Or a pink elephant," Joyce said. "That crystal meth junk makes you see anything."

"And from what I understand," Dellin said, "she was a long-term addict. All kinds of delusional disorders are the result, then outright schizophrenia. It's a terrible tragedy. Drugs cause people to flush their lives right down the toilet."

Dellin had sensible answers for everything, which further encouraged Clare to discount any implications of Adam's. There was one more question, though, and Joyce asked it before Clare could:

"But Dellin, our gullible minds need you to solve one more mystery. What exactly *did* happen to Grace, Donna, and Rob?"

Dellin shrugged. "I fired them."

"What for?" Rick asked. "We heard—"

Dellin nodded amusedly. "That they were convicts, dopeheads, thieves—I know. I heard all those stories too. In truth, they weren't any of those things, they were just irresponsible, low-quality employees. I mean, it wasn't just a little negligence here and there, it was an out and out abuse of their positions. They were having hot tub parties every other night at Grace's cottage while they were supposed to be on duty. One night I caught them, so I fired them. Had no choice. It was my bad judgment for hiring them in the first place, and Harry was pretty ticked off at me because we had a major therapy session starting up right at the same time. I had to take valuable time away from that to replace them. I definitely could've been a better judge of character; their military records were all quite good from what I could see." Another discreet smile, in Clare's direction. "But I like you all much better than them, and I'm sure that things will work out fine. In a strange way, it's a good thing I fired the previous crew."

Clare nearly wilted at the smile.

"Well," Joyce said. "We promise there won't be any hot tub parties."

Another comment, directed toward Clare: "I don't care if you do—just, *please*—not while you're on duty. Harry would skin me alive."

A delicious spicy aroma wafted around them when the busty barmaid reappeared with Dellin's carryout order. "Time for me to run. See you all on Monday."

Clare's spirits plummeted. She wished for anything to say to keep him there, if only for another minute. Then she remembered . . .

"Oh, Dellin? One last thing, since you're here anyway."

"Sure," he said.

"Remember when you were breaking me in the other day? You showed me that one room where they had that big machine with the nozzles? You were saying how it was a great example of wasted federal tax dollars because you didn't really have a use for it at the clinic but they installed it anyway?"

Dellin stood in a moment in silence, thinking. "No, I—"

"You said it was a tumor killer. Intensified radiation something or other."

"Oh, yeah, you mean the IRMT. It might as well be a half-million-dollar toilet seat, 'cos we don't need it. But what—"

"I read somewhere once that Michael Jackson has a

half-million-dollar toilet seat," Rick interrupted. "Solid gold."

Joyce winced at him. "Shut up."

"Anyway," Clare finished to Dellin. "It's gone."

Dellin gave her a baffled look. "*What's* gone? You don't mean the IRMT?"

"Yeah. I was doing a routine door search on my last shift, so I stuck my head in there, and the room was empty. The nozzles, the table, all the computers and monitors are all gone. It was no big deal to me that the stuff was gone—I'm sure you or Harry simply ordered it to be returned to the supplier. What I don't understand is how and when. Whoever came and took it back—somebody at the clinic would've had to open the main gate for them and sign them in and out. No one on security did, and the computer would've indexed the time the gate was opened and closed, but there's no record at all in the system."

Dellin finally spoke out of his confusion. "I never ordered it returned, and I can't believe that Harry did without telling me, and even if he had—"

"Like I said," Clare added, "the in and out times would've automatically been logged in the computer. But they weren't."

Rick looked at Joyce, shaking his head through his next sip of beer. "I don't even know what they're talking about."

"Rick, you *never* know what *anyone's* talking about," Joyce told him. "Ever. So for God's sake. Please. Just shut up."

"That is really weird," Dellin said. He seemed truly puzzled, even traceably angry. "I'm supposed to be in charge of all the clinic's logistics. Looks like I'm not doing a very good job. I can't imagine anyone *stealing* an intensified radiation modulation therapy system."

"I can't imagine anyone even saying it much less stealing it," Rick said. His next sip of beer dribbled when Joyce elbowed him in the ribs.

"Seriously," Dellin continued, more to Clare. "Something that big? It couldn't very well have been stolen, could it?"

"I don't think that's feasible at all," Clare said. "It's not like a crooked staffer could put that kind of stuff in their pocket and walk out with it. There's just no way that equipment could've been taken out of the building in that short a time period without somebody seeing, and no way to get it past the main gate without authorization. Only the four of us, plus Harry, have a key to the room anyway."

"I didn't take it, I swear!" Rick said. "I'll be honest, though, I *thought* about it, but when I asked my fence what he'd give me for a half-million-dollar intensified radiation modulation therapy system, he threw me out, told me to come back when I had some good watches."

"Dellin?" Joyce offered. "I'll kill him if you want. Just say the word and I'll do it. I'll cap him right here."

Dellin didn't even hear her; his annoyance wasn't at Rick's verbal antics, it clearly was the information. "I'm really stumped on this one."

"I'm sorry to bug you about work stuff on your day off," Clare said.

"Forget about that; it's your job to tell me. I just can't figure." Dellin ran a hand down the side of his cheek, thinking. "None of it makes sense."

Clare was eased that her report didn't pester him. "There was that, and the second delivery from Hodder-Tech. That kind of struck me as odd too, since we just got one the other night."

Now Dellin was rubbing his eyes, half-chuckling to himself in aggravation. "Hodder-Tech Industries. A second delivery. Not more magna-ferric elements?"

"Yes, exactly. So you *didn't* know about it?"

"No. I did not. And, yes. It's odd. It's *more* than odd. It's got to be a mistake. Those element assemblies last six months per unit, at least."

"How many units are installed at the clinic?"

"Just one."

All Clare could do was shrug at him. "Hodder-Tech must think we have two, then. They're delivering another order sometime on Monday."

"Want me to ask my fence what he'll give us for a magna-ferric element assembly?" Rick offered.

Joyce wagged her finger right in front of his face. "Cement-head, they're having a private *work* conversation. That means it's time for Wicky Poo to shut face-hole and stop making noise."

Dellin smiled at the whole mess. "Well, my fish is getting cold, and the last thing *any* of us need to worry about on the weekend is this kind of dreck. I'll . . . fix it on Monday. See ya all later."

They all bid their goodbyes as he left but just before he walked away, he winked at Clare.

Oh, what I wouldn't do . . .

"Hey, Clare," Rick said. "You can turn the pinball machine off now."

"Huh?"

"'Cos that's what your face was lit up like for the whole time he was here."

"It wasn't!"

Joyce raised her brows, nodding.

"Oh, well. Screw it," Clare resigned. She'd just have to work harder at being less obvious. A *lot* harder.

"He really is a good-looking guy," Joyce remarked.

"Just like me," Rick edged in.

"Yeah, Rick, but Dellin's got some things you don't."

"Name one."

"Smarts. Acumen. Sophistication."

"I said name *one*." Rick scoffed. "And who needs all that anyway, when you can be the total package?"

"What a lunkhead."

"Yeah, but I'm *your* lunkhead."

Joyce and Rick were kissing now, and these were no pecks on the cheek. Clare ordered another beer, and when she took a stray look around, several other couples at the bar were kissing too. Over one woman's shoulder, Clare saw Dellin's Mercedes through the window, driving away.

It had been fun to get out with Joyce and Rick, but Dellin's sudden appearance had sabotaged her mood. She'd been delighted to see him but now that he was gone, she felt dryly depressed. The romantic frolic around her seemed surreal, details and proportions warping. She could hear the wet, clicking kisses; she could see the moist shine on joined lips. When she glanced again at her companions, they were going at it, Joyce's breasts pressing against Rick's chest, her hand under the bar top slipping up the gap of Rick's shorts. Somehow, though, it wasn't lewd, it was passionate, their kisses joining them in their love, verifying their honest need for each other. Clare actually tensed up a bit watching them, not because the public display was too explicit but because it was arousing. It made her wish that she was doing the same thing—with Dellin.

Clare managed a smile in spite of her dejection. *At least someone's going to have a good time tonight.*

Chapter Twelve

(I)

"It's a pretty night, ain't it?"

"Quiet."

Cinny wouldn't let herself be discouraged—even after he'd hit her earlier at the trailer. She was a positivist. They were both itchy from withdrawal and flat broke, but Cinny was determined to make this work. He said she talked too much, and that it got on his nerves; Harley Mack was a good man but when he went too long without his ice, he got mean. Heavy drinking would take the edge off a little, like the other night when they'd come out here and Cinny had been bitten by that big fat toad and the snake. Harley Mack had only hit her a few times that night, and he'd said he was sorry later. But tonight they didn't even have enough money for a bottle of cheap whiskey.

Withdrawal with no alcohol made Harley Mack *really* mean.

He'd dropped her off for a couple of hours on 34th street, along the motel and strip joint corridor, but it was useless. Cinny didn't mind turning tricks if it meant money for their relationship—she would do anything for that. Some of the men who picked her up weren't very nice and smelled bad. *But who said life was easy?* she reasoned. Her mother had always told her—when she was turning tricks herself—*Hardship is good for the soul, honey. It's God's way of testing us. Moses suffered hardships, Jesus suffered hardships, and that's why we gotta suffer hardships too.* Cinny looked at life the same way—even though she doubted that Moses or Jesus ever had to turn tricks for meth money.

When Harley Mack picked her back up later, he'd punched her hard in the jaw when she confessed that she didn't get a single trick. She was dizzied for ten minutes and saw stars, and he'd said a lot of mean things, "Good godDAMN, girl! You can't even sell your skinny ass for ten bucks anymore!" and "Useless bitch! I ought'a cut your heart and kidneys out and sell 'em to people who need transplants 'cos you are not worth a PINCH OF SHIT!"

No, Harley Mack was no fun to be around when he got like this, but that didn't thwart Cinny's determination. *You have to take the bad times with the good.*

It was late now; they dragged the boat up shore and covered it with palm leaves at the edge of the woods, and now they were sneaking back to that clinic where all the drugs were. Most of it was morphine, Harley Mack had said, because it was a cancer clinic, and they were going to sell it for meth money. Cinny was impressed with her drug-addict ethics. *I would NEVER do morphine! It's the same as smack. The only people who do morphine are white trash!*

"Harley M—"

In about the same amount of time that it took for an eye to blink, Harley Mack had whipped around, slapped his big dirty hand to Cinny's mouth, and was squeezing her lips shut so hard she whined.

A finger pointed right into her face like a gun. "Not one word," he said, gritting his teeth against the withdrawal. "I ain't going back to the joint 'cos of your whiny motor mouth. If you say *one more word*, before we get into the clinic, I'll bite your lips off and glue your teeth together with Crazy Glue. Understand?"

Cinny nodded vigorously, a few tears of pain glittering in the corners of her eyes. *I HATE it when he does that!* she thought when his fingers let go of her lips. Sometimes he did it too hard, her lips would swell up so bad they looked like a big pink sucker. But she knew not to annoy him, not when he was jonesing this bad. *Look at the bright side—in an hour or two we'll have a whole bunch of junk to sell to the junkies, and we'll be in crystal for months!*

That was the great thing about Cinny. There was always a bright side to being a busted, skinny, poverty-stricken redneck living in a rusted trailer and going absolutely nowhere.

Harley Mack had brought his lock-picks—he was real good with them, he'd learned how to use them when he was in jail. He could open doors with them usually in the same amount of time that it took with the actual key, but he'd already said he wasn't going to use them to get inside the clinic. Those outside doors were alarmed. That's why he brought the cylinder jack, and the long crowbar. *We're going in through the floor*, he'd said.

Cinny had no idea how he planned to do that, but she didn't dare ask. Her biggest worry had haunted her all night, though.

That toad.

And that awful two-headed snake.

Both of the disgusting things had bitten her, and she still had the marks. And now her stomach squirmed because Harley Mack was kneeling down behind the clinic and unscrewing a ventilation screen that was set in the building's cement footing.

We're crawling under there, Cinny realized with no small amount of dread. *It'll be dark and slimy and gross, and I'll bet there's a bunch more of those fanged toads and two-headed snakes under there . . .*

Harley Mack got the screen off in less than a minute; it was impressive—he'd done it with only the moonlight to show him where the screws were.

But under there, Cinny knew, *there ain't gonna be no moonlight*.

He glared up at her, talking in a rough whisper. "We're goin' in now, and remember, not one word till we're inside. Now gimme the flashlight."

Another bolt of dread fired up her spine. *Did I bring the—*

"I told you to bring the flashlight," he said in the deadest tone. "If you forgot the flashlight, I'm gonna snap your skinny neck right here."

Cinny, regrettably, didn't have a great memory for details. She'd brought a bag with her, with cigarettes in it as well as several extra-large black plastic garbage bags for them to carry the drugs out in.

But she didn't recall ever putting the flashlight in there.

Her mouth dropped open.

Harley Mack stood up and looked down at her with the blankest face. "You stupid brainless bitch. You forgot the flashlight. Now I have to go all the way back to the trailer to get it. But you know what? I'll be going back to the trailer *alone* because I'm killin' your useless ass right here and now. I'm gonna get rid of you once and for all because you are the biggest fuckin' headache—"

Cinny reached into the bag, then handed Harley Mack the flashlight.

"That's my good girl," he said.

Thank you Jesus and Moses! Thank you for puttin' that flashlight in the fuckin' bag!

Cringing then, she followed Harley Mack in through the hole, crawling on her belly. She more or less had to follow his scuffling sounds because she could barely see the light ahead of her. It had been hot enough outside, but under here it felt like a hundred and twenty degrees. Sweat sopped her skin at once, and all the dust and dirt down here just stuck to her. Each movement forward left her praying that her hand or knee wouldn't land on one of those snakes, and soon it was worse because Harley Mack was moving much faster; he was way ahead of her now.

Just when she couldn't see any of the light anymore—

If I get lost down here and he has to come looking for me—

She heard the ratchet working.

That's two I owe ya, Moses and Jesus . . .

She followed the steady metal *clacks* until she found him again.

"Piece'a fuckin' cake, baby," he said, cranking the jack's handle. A flat brace-plate against the tip of the crowbar was pushing the floor up from underneath; Cinny could hear it crackling.

She was happy to see that *he* was happy. It took a while but his efforts eventually pushed up a big enough square of flooring for him to break all the way back like a trap door, and then he was climbing up.

A light came on overhead; the opening turned bright

white. Just seeing that light made Cinny feel better—down in the humid darkness, she felt on guard, nervous. Then:

"Jesus H. Christ in a hotdog stand . . ."

"What is it?" she whispered up.

Harley Mack's head appeared in the opening, grinning down. "Luck's on our side tonight, baby!"

"Huh?"

He reached down and hauled Cinny up through the hole by one wrist. Next thing she knew she was standing on her feet in a small brightly lit room full of shelves.

"Can ya believe it? The room we bust up into just happens to be the *drug locker!*"

Small boxes and bottles lined the shelves. Cinny saw weird words on them: DURA-MORPH, DILAUDID, MS-CONTIN. Lower, there were boxes of glassine vials that read MORPHINE SULPHATE. That pretty much said it all.

Harley Mack put his brawny arms around Cinny and gave her a great big kiss.

Cinny was shocked.

"Aw, baby, I'm sorry I treat ya like shit and slap ya around, but it's just 'cos I'm strung out. With this haul, we're set for a long time. I'm gonna buy you nice things like what you deserve—and lots of crystal." He hugged her tight. "Aw, baby, I love you so much!"

Cinny burst into joyous tears, bruised, puckered lips and all. Just as she would kiss him back, he thrust one of the black garbage bags at her.

"Here. Start fillin' 'er up."

It took all of five minutes to clear the shelves of their treasure trove of drugs. The street value would probably be in the five figures. But Cinny's exuberance wasn't just from the score, it was from her love. *Without havin' to worry about dope, we can have a normal loving relationship—the way it's supposed to be!*

"That was fast, huh?"

Cinny looked into a toothy grin. Then Harley Mack dropped both bags into the hole.

"Smartest thing to do is get out of here right now."

"Let's do that! Let's go back to the trailer'n cuddle!"

Harley Mack chewed the inside of his lip. "Fuck, we gotta at least take a quick look. Don't seem right coming all this way just to bust into one room."

Cinny didn't like it. "But we already got what we came for."

"Maybe there's more. Maybe there's a safe, or a petty cash box. Come on."

Damn!

Turning the knob latch was all it took to unlock the door. Now they were standing in a long lit hallway, and suddenly they were both looking at the same thing.

The door at the end of the hall.

"That looks different from the other doors," Cinny observed.

"That's 'cos it's a security door. It's got a keypad on the lock."

"What's that mean?"

"It means I can't pick it, and it means the door's probably wired." Harley Mack's eyes narrowed. "But that ain't all it means."

"What?"

"It means the people who run this place got something behind that door that's more valuable to 'em than that fuckin' shitload of smack we just bagged. Ain't no way in hell we're leavin' here without takin' a look see."

"You just said it's wired," Cinny whined. "It'll set off an alarm!"

"Yeah, it sure would, if we busted the door down. But not if we go around it."

Then Cinny knew.

They were back down the hole and into the hot darkness again. Cinny realized it would be a really bad idea to complain—it would spoil Harley Mack's good mood. Back on her belly and crawling through smelly dirt and dust, she followed her man's scuffling, dragging the bags with her. Ten minutes later, Harley Mack and his jack had cranked open another hole in the floor, and they were crawling up.

"Exam room. Big deal."

Now they stood in a typical examination room as one would find at a doctor's office. When Harley Mack opened a door, he found a similar room behind it. Cinny opened a second door—

"Here's a hallway."

"Let's make this quick. Just look for drugs or safes; meet me back here in five minutes. You go that way, I'll go this way.

Cinny's swollen lips parted to object—

"Don't start," he warned. He touched her lips with a pointing finger. "I'll make 'em fatter if ya start whinin'."

No way Cinny wanted that again. Her lips *already* looked like a pair of bratwursts pressed together, and they hurt like the dickens.

Just do what he says . . .

So far all of the doors were unlocked, and there was nothing of interest behind them. Another exam room, a records room, a room with a bunch of computers. Toward what must've been a far rear corner of the building, though, she opened a door and found a room that contained nothing but a round hole in the floor, like a manhole. *We went to all the trouble of breaking the floor with a jack when we could've used this?* But when she looked down she saw that that wasn't the case. A metal ladder descended down at least ten feet, well past the ground level below the clinic. *Looks like a big pipe*, she deduced, squinting harder. It looked like the ladder dropped down into a sewer pipe that was at least five feet in diameter.

All right. So what?

She just wanted to get the search done and get out.

"Shit, there ain't nothin' here," she muttered. A few more doors revealed offices, a conference room, a lab, a janitorial closet. Nothing of interest.

Cinny frowned when she opened the last door in the hall. Yet another examination room. Larger than the others, though, and against one wall were four separate exam areas that were curtained off. Metal cabinets mounted over a counter showed a variety of drugs through their glass panes but the cabinets were locked.

Should I break 'em? she asked herself. *Naw, I better go get Harley Mack, see what he wants*. But then a better idea occurred to her.

They'd had great luck so far. Why jinx the luck by being greedy?

This is dumb. We already got plenty of junk. I just won't tell Harley Mack about these cabinets. Damn it, I just wanna go home!

She was just about to leave when—

Her eyes widened. Did she hear something?

What was . . . that?

Maybe she hadn't heard anything at all. It was probably just her imagination . . .

Then she heard it again, the softest sound, almost like a sigh.

Very slowly, her wide-open eyes turned toward the row of curtained sections.

No! I ain't lookin' behind them curtains!

Thc sigh slithered out again, and as she concentrated, she thought she heard something else even softer: the faintest humming like a distant machine.

If there really was someone here, she needed to find out and tell Harley Mack. There might be a patient behind those curtains.

Twitching with fear, Cinny walked to the first curtain, peeked in through the gap.

Nothing!

Then she pulled the curtain all the way back. It was an empty convalescent bed, and that's all that was behind the second curtain too. Her heart slowed down a bit now, as her fear tapered off.

The third section was different. There was a long metal table with two grooves down the middle that reminded her of a rolling track of some kind, and at the head of the table was a wide hatch-like device with a round window in it.

A *fuckin' washer machine!* she laughed at herself. A large one like the kind at laundromats. This must be where they washed the clinic's gowns and linens. *What a scardycat I am!* Cinny thought. *Practically tinklin' myself 'cos of a washer! And it must be the dryer over here behind the last curtain. That's what the humming sound is.*

Unafraid now, she pulled back the curtain and—

There was no "dryer" behind it.

The scream ripped out of her chest like a bomb-burst. Spittle flew off her lips and her eyes bugged out. What lay before her on the padded table was a quivering naked woman who had to have been nine months pregnant. Straps secured her to the table and her legs were raised and wishboned from the gynecological stirrups that her ankles were belted to. Sweat glazed the woman's skin so profusely that she looked drenched in oil. The huge gravid belly was churning.

Horror pushed Cinny back a full yard; she hit the grooved table behind her and fell sideways.

"Harley MAAAAAAAAAAAAAAAAAAAAAAA-AAAACK!" her lungs exploded, and when she turned back upward to regain her balance and run, she found her face looking directly into the washer's circular window.

Harley Mack's face looked right back at her from the other side.

He's inside the washer!

None of this she could reckon, of course. The pregnant woman began to gibber at her, drooling. The humming was coming from the washer, and Cinny's first impulse was to open it, pull Harley Mack out, but when she yanked on the handle nothing happened.

Harley Mack was locked inside.

Frantic, she looked in the window again, and that's when she realized it wasn't a washer machine.

It wasn't revolving, and something bright and orange began to glow inside. Harley Mack's face was pressed right against the glass, and so were his hands. He was staring out at her, screaming. Cinny could only look back in the horrific confusion.

Harley Mack's face looked like it was *cooking*.

Each time his mouth opened to scream, smoke came out. He was flip-flopping in there now, more smoke sifting off his hair, steam pouring out of his ears, and then—

splat!

His eyes exploded against the glass, the humors boiling instantaneously.

Cinny's screams pinwheeled behind her as she flew out of the atrocious room. Escape was the only impulse now, and though there wasn't much space in her psyche for calculation, some baser part of her mind was able to recognize a few deductive points. Harley Mack hadn't gotten into the hatch-thing by himself—someone had *put him* in it, and they'd obviously done so within the past few minutes.

So whoever had done it was probably still here.

She raced down the hall, tore around the corner. She flattened herself against the wall, listening over the thud of her heart for the sound of footsteps following her, but she heard none.

She didn't consciously remember how to get back to the room they'd entered through; instinct took her instead. Jesus and Moses were coming through in spades—the first door she threw open was it, the section of flooring torn up and open, as if waiting for her. Cinny jumped in, thudded to her knees—

I'm out!

But—

She looked out from the small block of light she was kneeling in. The cloying, hot darkness looked back from all sides. Without the flashlight, how would she find her way back to the screen they'd removed? Her heart was thrumming, her breathing close to the point of hyperventilation. It never occurred to her that she was wasting precious time.

Just go! Crawl in a straight line till you get to the outer wall, then just follow it around till you get to the screen—

It was the only option, but one she would never get the chance to take.

In the split-second before she would begin to crawl out she was screaming again, a high, hard shriek more

like an animal being dragged down by a leopard's jaws.
A hand had reached down and grabbed her hair, and was pulling her back up into the building.

(II)

The cottage was hot when Clare returned; she'd forgotten to leave the a/c on, but after a second's thought she elected to leave it off and open the drapes and long sliding-glass doors instead. She kept all the lights off and stood for a while just looking out on the moonlit bay and feeling the breeze sift in through the screens. The sheer serenity relieved her.

An aimless glance to one side showed her a glimpse into the next cottage: Mrs. Grable's. *Not this again*, she thought. In candlelight, Mrs. Grable was doing another sultry dance for her husband, moving vamp-like in the shadows and dim slices of light. Clare looked away.

Yes. This again, she thought, for when she turned her gaze away from the Grables' cottage, it fell immediately on Joyce's. Rick and Joyce were brazenly making love right out on the back balcony, Joyce's sleek legs wrapped tight around Rick's back. It was the contours of their bodies that betrayed them, the moon highlighting lines of glimmer from the sweat on their skin. Clare nearly winced as she dragged her gaze away. She didn't want to watch this time.

Love was all around her tonight, but none for her.

She traipsed back into her living room, removing her top, shorts, and panties one at a time as she did so, then lay down on the long couch. By now her disgruntlement was no mystery to her at all; her crush on Dellin was so potent, and she knew now how useless it was to just keep ordering herself to get her mind off it. *Ain't gonna happen*, she thought, curled up on the couch in a fetal position. The night out at the bar had been a lot of fun; it let her feel like she was part of something for a change—and she *liked* that—but now it was all over and she was alone again, in the dark.

She decided to sleep on the couch again, suddenly too depressed to even walk the short distance to the bedroom. Inadvertently, her eyes fell on the large blank tv screen just ahead over her, then lower, to the storage shelf on the television stand. She could see the shoebox there that contained the lewd videotapes. A *three-pack*, she remembered, *but only two tapes in the pack*. The inkling wouldn't leave her: *Where's the third tape? What's on it?* Two tapes had been enough, though, the erotic revelations all too impressed in her memory. Yes, Grace Fletcher and her colleagues were a kinky bunch. It had been shocking just to see such things on a tv screen, but even more shocking to see her old friend Donna Kramer so eager in her participation. Donna had never seemed the promiscuous type, but . . . *Who am I kidding?* Clare thought, her eyes sliding closed. *I'm probably just jealous and not admitting it. The girl nobody wants is always the first to call someone else a slut.*

Next, just as inadvertently, she caught herself wondering if the lucent-green vibrator was still in the shoebox too. *Great* . . . Her inhibitions and deteriorating self-esteem clashed with her memory of the images from the tapes, and even with thoughts of Dellin now. She knew that the rising arousal was less genuine and more a reaction to her frustration. She didn't dare masturbate; it would be too unreal, it would make her even more depressed afterward.

The soft breeze continued to eddy in off the bay. She

knew she should lock the sliding doors and close the drapes, if only for security reasons. Then, a fleeting thought: A *monster in the woods* . . . She chuckled groggily. *And to hell with closing the drapes*. Sleeping nude on the couch right in front of the sliders would've been out of the question any other time, but: *I doubt that even a pervert like Adam would be up at this hour, and if he is— I don't care*.

Sleep was what she needed. The happenstance depression would be gone tomorrow, and she could start afresh. Yes. Just a nice, long sleep.

What seemed moments later, her eyes shot open to blinding white light. Her heart was racing at the ceaseless, bloodcurdling shriek, but as adrenaline and instinct urged her to lunge for her gun, the ruse of fitful sleep wore off. *Jesus Christ!* Nude, sweating and shuddering, she rolled off the couch, thudded to the floor. A nice, long sleep indeed. The night had passed in the cruelest haste; the wall clock read ten a.m.! That blinding white light proved to be the sun glaring from the porch, and the screaming?

It was just the phone, set a bit too loud for her liking.

It seemed to have been ringing so many times, she thought the caller would give up before she got to it.

"Hello?"

"Hi, Clare, this is Dellin. I'm really sorry to bother you."

Dellin! But her mind felt bogged down, sluggish. And his tone didn't sound right. "Is something wrong?"

"Well, I'm at the clinic right now." A pause. "Did your alarm beeper go off last night by any chance?"

Now she felt even more fuddled. She snatched up the beeper at once, saw that no messages had been sent.

"No, and it's been with me the whole time. Dellin, what's wrong?"

"I remembered what you'd mentioned last night at the bar, about the unnecessary second delivery from Hodder-Tech."

"Right. Those element things. The delivery confirmation said they'd be arriving Monday," Clare said, trying to shake out some cobwebs.

"I'd planned to call them today to cancel the order but it just now dawned on me that their offices are closed on weekends. So I came in to the clinic to send them a fax, but I can't figure out how to get the damn fax machine to work. Would you mind—"

"Give me ten minutes and I'll be there. It's easy." A sudden burst of enthusiasm rushed her; any excuse to see Dellin would make her day. But then she thought a second. "But, Dellin, why did you ask me if my beeper went off?"

"That's the other thing," he said with some uneasiness. "Something's not right here. I think someone's been in the building."

Chapter Thirteen

(I)

"All exterior doors and windows are sensored to the alarm system," she was explaining, showing Dellin the readouts on the monitor. "You ought to know, you're the one who ordered the system. And the entry/exit-record in the computer shows zilch for Saturday night. No authorized entrances, and no breaches. If anyone had broken in, not only would the alarm have been engaged, the location of the breach would've been flagged right here on the computer. But as you can see . . ."

"Nothing," Dellin acknowledged, examining the screen. "But, damn. I'm sure someone was in the pharmacy vault."

Clare shrugged. "The door's lock is wired. If someone had gone in there, the key code would tell us who it was and what time. And if someone had broken the lock, same thing. Time of the breach would've been recorded."

"Hmm."

"Let's go look at the room itself," she suggested. "Maybe it'll occur to you what's wrong."

Dellin followed her, quiet, preoccupied. She suspected he felt a bit foolish, with this "hunch" that something was wrong in the vault. After his strange phone call at the cottage, Clare had taken a fast shower, put on her uniform and gunbelt, and was at the clinic as quickly as possible. *Looks like it's all just a false alarm*, she realized now. In her business, it was always prudent for security guard to be paranoid, but not the client. *What the hell's bugging him?* she wondered.

"And you were right about this, too," Dellin mentioned off-handedly. On their way down the hall, he stopped and opened the door marked IRMT. The room was empty, as Clare already knew. "I just don't understand how all of this equipment could've vanished without me knowing about it."

"I'm sure there's a reasonable explanation," she tried to assure him. "One mystery at a time."

Down the hall, Clare unlocked the door to the pharmacy vault, turned on the light. Nothing appeared amiss, and all of the pharmaceutical inventory appeared to be intact. "The room looks normal to me," she said. "Just take your time, think. What is it about the room that doesn't seem right to you?"

Dellin shook his head, frustrated. "I don't know—you must think I'm an idiot. I'm not doing a very good job of putting it into words but—" He squinted around the small room. "The drugs are all here but . . . they don't look right. It just seems that some of them aren't in the right place."

Clare took down a small box of pills marked MS-CONTIN. She opened the box, took off the cap, but was satisfied by the safety seal. "I'll check every bottle, make sure the seals haven't been broken."

"No, that's not necessary. And it would take hours."

"It's my job, Dellin. If you think someone's been in here, I have to investigate every possibility. I'll call in Joyce and Rick to help."

He shook his head again. "No, it would be a waste of time. You've already established that no one came into the room."

"All right." But Clare didn't know what to do beyond that, and she definitely didn't want to suggest to her boss that he must be imagining things. "So you think that some of the boxes are in the wrong place? That someone's moved them?"

"Yeah, that's what it looks like to me. But why would someone do that?"

"Who does the inventory?"

"I do."

"How often?"

"Any time I sign out a prescription, I log it into the computer, and the computer says everything's here."

"Does somebody come in every now and then to double-check the stock, or check expiration dates?"

"No. That's all done in the computer too. And me, Harry, and security are the only people with the key. I'm really sorry to have brought you out here for nothing."

"It's no trouble, Dellin," she told him, but her own frustrations were starting to scratch at her. The professional wall she knew she must maintain just kept cracking in places. It had been since the day she met him. *God!* At one point, her nails were digging into her thigh in an effort to avert her eyes. She just couldn't help stealing glances at him through the cracks in that wall.

It relieved her when the awkward silence broke. "Wait, there's one more thing I can check. Didn't think of it till now."

"What's that?"

"The people-counter."

"Huh?"

She pointed to the tiny unit on the wall. "The motion-detector. They're part of the security system, and they're all over the building."

Dellin seemed fuddled. "I didn't even know we *had* motion-detectors."

She locked the room back up, led him back to the security office. It amused her, though, how little he knew about the clinic's system. "They're not alarmed, either, don't need to be since all exterior entrance points are. We call it a people-counter because it lets us know if the building's still occupied when we're getting ready to lock up."

"It's a good thing you know what you're doing, 'cos I sure as hell don't."

"Come on, I'll show you. I'll prove to you that no one was in that room."

Back in her office, Clare opened the proper program. "This'll only take a minute."

"Okay. I'm going to get some bottled water. You want anything?"

"Sure, an iced coffee if you don't mind."

"Be right back."

The motion-detectors merely registered human-sized movement, not so much as a security function but just a precaution. If an elderly patient became disoriented and got lost, the motion sensors would find him immediately. It was the best way to ensure that all of the medical and maintenance staff had left when it was time to close up. Clare typed in a time-margin and yesterday's date. *Maybe when he sees the evidence that no one entered the vault, he'll realize he was just being paranoid.*

But by the time the Dellin reentered with their drinks, Clare was staring astonished at the computer screen.

"I stand corrected," she said.

"What do you mean?"

Next she clicked on the building map. In the small square that represented the pharmaceutical depository, a red dot blinked. "This is *really strange*, Dellin."

"I'm not following you. What's the red dot?"

"The breach. Someone *was* in that room, last night, just after one a.m. For exactly seven minutes and eleven seconds."

"But I thought the exterior sensors indicated that no one—"

"Right. No one entered the building from any exterior window or door."

"But that doesn't make sense . . ."

Clare was already up and out. When she opened the vault door again, the first thing she did was look down. "Is it my imagination, or was that carpet not here when you first showed me this room the other day?"

Dellin stared down, acknowledgment blooming. "I— You're right! There's never been a carpet in here."

Clare pulled the carpet back. A very makeshift repair job had been discharged. A large chunk of the floor had been pried upward and cracked out. Then someone had come along, hammered it back into place, and covered it over with this carpet.

"Unbelievable," Dellin said.

Clare let out a long breath. "Makes perfect sense to me, Dellin," she said in all sarcasm. "Somebody broke into the clinic through the floor, right into the dope vault—and left without taking a thing."

"And then somebody else covered it up," Dellin said. "Somebody on the inside."

(II)

Further investigation of the motion-detection program showed that that part of the system had been turned off immediately after the breach. More cover-up. And Dellin was right; it all had to have been done by someone on the inside, someone deliberately making an effort to hide that fact from security. *This is just fan-friggin'-tastic*, Clare thought.

Dellin stood just behind her at the computer console. "As the security chief," he began in a depressed tone, "I suppose I know what you're thinking. You've already ruled out Joyce and Rick because they were at the bar with you when this happened. But who left the bar not an hour before the breach?"

Clare smiled in spite of the frustration. "All right, Dellin, I'll be honest. For about one second, I considered that it might be you. But then I thought about all the other factors and realized how ridiculous that would be. Why would you break into your own clinic—through the *floor*—and not steal anything? And why would you cover that up after the fact? And how could you possibly disable specific sections of the alarm program when it's more than obvious that you know less about this system than I know about open-heart surgery?"

He laughed to himself, and when he put his hand on her shoulder, Clare felt a deep flash of something totally unrealistic—a flash of desire, as if the touch were intimate. *But it's not intimate*, she told herself just as quickly. The touch was incidental—she only *wished* it were more.

Even more aggravating was the clash of perceptions that arose—her secret longing for this man impacting headlong into so many obstacles. Her feelings were keeping her from being objective, the ultimate sign of unprofessionalism. "So, Dellin, you were in the Army, right? The chemical corp or something?"

"I was in the Army, yes." His tone was already sounding like a confession. "Not the chemical corp, though. I was a research technician for the Biological Weapons Section at Fort Dietrich. And I guess the reason you asked is because you already know that I was criminally charged. It was Adam who told you that, right?"

"Yes," she said, guilty now.

"He's never liked me, and I don't know how he got a hold of that information."

"It's none of my business, Dellin. I just felt obliged to ask."

"But it is your business, because you think it may have a connection to some of the problems that've been occurring here. I wanted to tell you anyway, so you understood. I'd feel terrible if you thought I was some sort of criminal."

The awkwardness was growing thicker. Clare stared at the computer screen, pretending to be doing something.

"I authorized the disposal of an inert by-product from a synthesis experiment," he went on. "Some people there believed that the material was a hazardous, classified weapons component."

"What happened next?" She knew she had to ask.

His hand squeezed her shoulder—again, just an incidental contact, but to Clare it proved an arousing distraction.

Then he explained the rest: "I had my day in court,

proved that the material in question had been mistakenly labeled as hazardous, and then JAG dropped all charges. I'll bet Adam didn't tell you *that* part, did he?"

Clare turned in her chair, hard-pressed to restrain her delight. "Dellin, really, I never suspected you of any wrongdoing, it's just my job to assess all the facts," but without realizing it, she put her hand over his for a moment.

He didn't pull it away. "Adam's disapproval of me is too nonsensical to even bother explaining. Same exact thing happened when Grace Fletcher was here."

He didn't continue, which secretly addled her. *What's he mean by that? Adam had the hots for Grace but was jealous of Dellin's better looks?* The question was intriguing—and completely inappropriate. The soap opera stuff had no place in the middle of this dilemma. *I've got to get to the bottom of this security foul-up*, she reminded herself. *Somebody busted into this building and I've got to find out who and why*.

Her hand slid off the tops of his fingers as she tried to regain a professional posture. She couldn't guess as to the "why" just yet. But the "who?"

"Dellin, I hate to say this but right now, your boss isn't looking too good."

"I know," he admitted with surprising ease. His hand slid off her shoulder now. "Come on to my office with me. I better call him, get him out here."

Clare followed him back and now she was standing behind him as he opened the phone-number log on his own computer.

"I hate to sound so negative but I can't help it," she told him. "Harry's the boss, the director of the entire clinic, but I've never even seen him, and Rick and Joyce have barely seen him themselves. It strikes me as really weird."

"It is weird," Dellin said. "And in all honesty, a lot of weird things have been happening around here lately. The only way to get to the bottom of this is to get him out here. I'm sure that he'll be able to explain it all, but until he does . . . I'm as suspicious as you are."

Dellin dialed a number, then whispered "Damn!" under his breath. "It's his answering machine—Harry, this is Dellin. Someone broke into the clinic last night. Put up your golf clubs and get out here." He hung up, then sputtered his own frustrations.

Clare was looking down, behind him. The top of his shirt was unbuttoned several notches, and the angle at which she stood made it nearly impossible for her to not notice the tanned skin and well-toned chest. When she forced her gaze away, she noticed that his computer was also equipped to access the alarm and security indexes. "Excuse me a second," she said and leaned over. "Here's another thing I forgot to do."

"What?"

She grabbed his mouse and clicked on the icon for the security files, then reopened the motion-detector program as she had in her own office. "When I first checked the program, I only checked the map section that covers the main hall and the pharmacy vault." She typed in the same time-spread, and clicked the WHOLE MAP option.

"What the—" Dellin began.

"Yeah," Clare said to him. Red tracking dots set off by the motion detectors ran trails all over the back part of the building. "You definitely better get Harry out here. Maybe *he* can tell us who he's got running around in B-Wing at one in the morning."

(III)

"Thanks for coming out on your day off," Dellin was saying. "You'll both be paid double-time. As you can see, we've got a problem."

Joyce and Rick stood in the small room with them, both in their uniforms and both looking a bit confused. And what they all stood around was the large hole in the floor.

"Someone broke into the building last night, through here," Clare said, pointing to the hole. "It was the only way to circumvent the alarm."

"But nothing was stolen?" Joyce asked.

"No."

Rick eyed the shelves. "That's a lot of dope to leave sitting around. They busted into this room, then turned right back around and left without snitching anything? Why?"

"Possibly," Dellin began, "because this wasn't the part of the building they were trying to break into."

Clare again: "The only thing worth more than the pharmaceuticals in this room is the Interthiolate supply."

"But that's all stored in B-Wing," Joyce said.

"Yes, and the motion-detectors picked up activity there, too," Clare continued, "only a few minutes after the breach occurred here. In other words, they broke in here, saw they were in the wrong place, then broke into B-Wing. Through the floor."

"As you both know, only the clinic director had the pass code to open the B-Wing door," Dellin added. "I don't even have access to B-Wing."

Rick frowned. "This is four shades of fucked up." He looked right at Dellin. "And it's an inside job."

"That," Dellin said with reluctance, "would appear to be the case."

"So there's a hole in the floor over in B-Wing too?" Joyce asked.

"We can't know for sure until we check," Clare replied. "But there's no other way anyone could've gotten in there without leaving an entrance-time on the computer."

Joyce still didn't seem clear on what was going on. "So we're all going to stand around here like a bunch of dopes and wait for Harry to arrive? Rick's right, this is an inside job, and, well—"

"I'll say it if you won't," Rick cut in. "Harry's the only guy who could be behind this. He's ripping his own place off, and making it look like another party did it."

Dellin raised a finger. "Maybe. But let's wait until all the facts are in before we make a conclusion like that."

Rick raised a brow.

Clare addressed the other two guards. "What I need you two to do right now is check the immediate grounds, say within a quarter-mile radius of the building, starting with the building itself. Just a good old-fashioned grid search. Whoever did break in here got beneath the clinic through one of the ventilation screens in the footing. Start at those points and work out. Look for tire tracks, footprints, anything like that."

Rick frowned again. "What about B-Wing? That's the priority, isn't it? We've got to get over there and see if the Interthiolate has been ripped off."

"We can't open the door until Harry gets here," Dellin said.

Rick seemed close to losing his temper. "I hate to tell you this, Dellin, but Harry's probably not coming at all. He's probably on a plane halfway to Europe right now, gonna sell samples and the formula to the highest bidder. Don't you think there might be a few pharmaceutical companies out there who might be interested in the most important cancer breakthough in the last ten years?"

"I hear what you're saying, Rick," Dellin said, "but I think I know Harry a little better than that. I really don't think the problem here is that extreme. A better guess would be that an outside party broke in here last night and maybe Harry tried to cover it up so the sponsor and the insurance companies don't find out. I don't know. But let's at least give him the benefit of the doubt."

"Dellin's right," Clare said. "Let's do this the right way—search the crime scene for all possible evidence. Getting over to B-Wing right now isn't feasible. Someone would have to go down into that hole and crawl under the building until they found the breach over there."

"Yeah?" Rick said. "That doesn't exactly sound like brain surgery to me. *I'll* crawl under the damn floor and get over there."

"No, Rick," Clare ordered. "It's too hot."

"You're joking, right? Are we all little kiddies afraid of the heat?" he scoffed. "Get me a flashlight and I'm there."

"It's probably 140 degrees under there, Rick," Dellin warned. "Low oxygen, high humidity. I'm not questioning your courage, but even the toughest guy wouldn't last long down there. You'd lose consciousness after five or ten minutes and be dead from heatstroke in five more. Your electrolyte balance would fall apart and your heart would stop."

Joyce was pushing Rick toward the door. "Come on,

tough guy. Let's go do what we're told. How's that for an idea?"

Clare smiled after them as they left, but Dellin wasn't smiling at all.

"Maybe Rick's right," he said. "Maybe Harry's long gone, and I'm just a naive fool."

"If that's true, we'll all be looking foolish, Dellin, not just you. All we can do now is wait. If Harry's a no-show, then we can all go to the unemployment line together." Clare tried to maintain some spirit. "But you know what I'm going to do right now? I'm going to go have a little chat with the person I suspect even more than Harry."

"Who's that?"

"Adam."

(IV)

"I guess we should split up, cover more ground," Joyce suggested.

"Good idea." Rick followed her around to one side of the building, until they arrived at one of the footing screens. "You start at this one, I'll start at the screen on the other side." Then he smiled to himself. "But remember to keep an eye out for those big-ass cockroaches. Those things'll probably bite the shit out of ya."

Joyce stopped, looked back at him worriedly. "Well, on second thought, maybe—"

"We shouldn't split up? I thought you'd see it my way."

"Smart-ass."

When Joyce bent over to examine the ground leading

away from the screen, Rick ran his hand over her buttocks.

She jumped. "Stop it!"

Next he hugged her. "Come on, they're inside. How about a little afternoon delight?"

She jerked away from him. "Jesus, Rick! You're like a billy goat—all you want to do is eat and screw."

Rick opened his palms. "What are you talking about? I'm not the least bit hungry."

"Quit dicking around. We've got a job to do."

Rick looked around without much conviction. "We're not going to find anything out here, come on."

"We're going by the book, like Clare said."

"Fine, but I still don't think that'll do any good. And Clare's not exactly being very realistic, is she?"

Joyce smirked at him. "What's that supposed to mean? What's Sherlock trying to imply now?"

Rick leaned against a palm tree, lit a cigarette. "Come on, Joyce. Clare's cool but she's got such a jones for Dellin she's not seeing straight."

Joyce let out a frustrated sigh, snitched the cigarette from him, took a long drag, then exhaled in exasperation. "You're the one who said it was an inside job!"

"Of course it is, it has to be." But now Rick seemed reluctant to continue voicing whatever was on his mind. He walked a few more yards away from the building.

"Where are you going?" Joyce demanded.

"I'm looking for clues," he snapped back. "That's what we're supposed to be doing, isn't it? And *what* is it we're trying to find? Tiretracks? Footprints?"

"Yeah, shovel-head. And what were you about to say?"

"Forget it. You'd just give me a ton of shit for saying it."

She trotted after him, into the outskirts of the woods now. "What!"

"Hey, look at this, Joyce . . ."

"Don't change the subject. I hate it when you do that!"

Rick had turned around, was holding up a 5-gallon plastic bucket. "Another one of these. It was right over here behind this log, and it's full of that granular stuff."

She didn't know what he was talking about. She looked in the bucket and saw the material, ran a finger through it. "It feels like some kind of detergent or cleaning material."

"Yeah, but what's it doing here? It exactly like that bucket we found the other night."

"When?" Joyce asked.

"You know, the other night. When we were making love."

"Rick, that's every night of the week," she reminded him. "You think you could be a little more specific?"

"The night when we were in the truck, out on the old logging road. The night the cockroach crawled into your boot."

An instant expression of disgust flashed with the recollection. "Oh, that's right. You *did* mention something about a bucket, when you were looking for my boot."

"Right, and you told me to forget about it. But now I'm kind of curious. Come on," and he began to stalk off. "That road is only a couple of hundred yards away if we cut through here."

"But I don't *want* to go back there!" she exclaimed. "There might be more cockroaches!"

"It's broad daylight," he scoffed over his shoulder. "Cockroaches are nocturnal—and I want to see if that bucket is still there. You can stay here if you want, I'll only be a few minutes."

"Shit!" she muttered, then trotted after him. "Why don't we just take the bucket you just found and turn it in to Dellin?"

"No," Rick said, much more adamantly. "I'm not really thinking too highly of Dellin right now."

Joyce had to keep trotting to keep up. "And what does *that* mean?"

"I'm not gonna even go there, 'cos you'll get all pissed off like you always do."

"I'm already pissed off! So start talking . . . and stop walking so fast!"

"Ah, here's the logging road. Watch out for sinkholes."

He stepped over some brambles, then helped her over. The ground was very wet—poor drainage. They could still see the vaguest tiretracks from where they'd parked here a few nights ago.

Rick's boots clicked through the muddy ground when he loped across the road. "I knew it. That first bucket was right over here—and now it's gone."

But Joyce stood still, fuming. "Rick, stop jerking me around. What were you going to say?"

"Honey, look. The bucket's not here any—"

"I don't care about the goddamn bucket! What were you going to say?"

Now he stooped over, examining the ground. "You won't like it, same reason Clare wouldn't—'cos you're both girls."

"You should've noticed by now that I'm not a *girl*. I'm a woman. So what kind of sexist-moron crap are you about to lay on me?"

"I guess Clare knows what she's doing as the security chief, but she's just not seeing every angle," he began, still stooped over looking at something. "She's got the hots for Dellin so bad it's clouding her professional judgment. And you think he's the greatest thing since sliced bread too."

Her irritation was flirting with anger now. "Brainchild, I don't have the *hots* for Dellin. If I did I wouldn't be in bed with your dumb ass every night, would I?"

"I don't mean that you have the hots for him, but it's this thing with you chicks. Dellin's the handsome egghead. Every time the guy walks into the room, you and Clare both act like it's fuckin' Mickey Rourke who just walked in. Neither of you are seeing past your noses because of this chick thing you've got going on."

"If you say *chick thing* one more time, I'll twist your nuts off."

"Get serious, Joyce. You and Clare both think Dellin is oh-so-cool that he couldn't possibly have anything to do with this. Am I right?"

"I think you've got your head up your ass but that's beside the point. And do I think that Dellin staged a break-in to his own clinic? No. That's ludicrous."

Rick shrugged. "See? You just proved my point. Personally I've got nothing against Dellin, and until today I thought he was a perfectly cool guy. But after all the shit that's gone down? He stinks worse than Harry and Adam combined."

She opened her mouth to complain further, then just said, "It's too hot and muggy to even bother listening to an explanation."

"Think what you want," he said, still stooped over. "All I know is this: some inside jobs, the guy who calls the cops first is usually the guy behind it. If I was going to rip Interthiolate out of the clinic—as an *employee* of the clinic—I'd report it to security as fast as I could. Because the gesture makes me look more innocent than anyone else. And who called security on this?"

"Dellin. But we don't even know that any Interthiolate was stolen. There's no evidence that *anything* was stolen."

"Um-hmm, and we *won't* know until we get into B-Wing. And who won't *let* us into B-Wing? Dellin. Don't tell me you believed that jive about it being too *hot*. Jesus Christ, I did boot camp in Nellis, Nevada—in August. They were PT-ing our asses four hours a day in 120 degrees. We didn't fuckin' *die*. Nobody dies from heat stroke in ten minutes—except ninety-year-old geezers. I could've crawled over to B-Wing under the floor in a couple minutes, and Dellin knew that. That's why he wouldn't let me go."

Joyce was about to fire off another lambasting . . . until she began to consider his words.

Maybe he's right.

"What are you looking at?" she asked, her annoyance dispersing.

He glanced over. "You said we're supposed to search the site for footprints. Well, here's a whole line of fresh ones. And it looks like they lead right to the lake."

When she edged over, she saw that he was right, and suddenly her firecracker personality lost all of its kick.

"Come on," he said. "We're the security guards here, let's do our job."

"Why don't we just report it to Clare—"

Now he was having some fun. "Oh, big tough Joycie scared of the woods? Hmm?" Then he made chicken sounds.

She couldn't help but smile. "There could be poachers or something, more than a match for big tough Wicky-Poo."

Rick tapped his gunbelt with snide confidence. "Hey, be a man large or small in size, *Colonel Colt* will equalize."

"Poachers have guns too, shovel-head."

Rick shrugged. "Then we'll run away. Come on!"

She followed him, however reluctantly. Then he put his arm around her, for further assurance. *I guess I really am a chicken*, she admitted.

"Nothing's gonna happen," he told her. "It's broad daylight."

The line of footprints they followed were poorly formed; there was too much water on the ground for them to keep there outlines in any detail. At several points, when the ground got drier, the prints almost disappeared entirely, but Rick managed to keep the trail pieced together. In another twenty minutes, they'd arrived at the placid edge of Lake Stephanie.

"Can you believe it?" Rick said. "The footprints go right up to the lake, stop, and then branch off."

Joyce squinted down. "And there's more of that stuff . . ."

Some of the strange soapy granules hadn't washed away.

"So it's true," Rick said. "Somebody dumped that stuff right into the lake."

"Somebody from the clinic."

"Yeah."

"So, what? We don't tell Dellin we found the bucket and the tracks?"

"No friggin' way we tell Dellin." Now Rick was scanning the rest of the shoreline. "We tell Clare. Why don't you go do that right now? I want to see where the rest of those footprints lead."

Joyce's lower lip quivered. She grabbed his arm. "I'm

too scared to walk around in the woods by myself."

"These footprints branch off along the marsh. Marshes often have snakes. Snakes don't bother me, but—"

"I don't want to get anywhere *near* snakes!" she almost shrieked.

Rick gave her a hug. "I know. So that's why you should go back to the clinic and tell Clare about the buckets. I'll follow these tracks along the marsh. I'll meet you back at the clinic in an hour."

"Okay," she peeped. "You're my big brave stud, aren't you?"

"That's a fact."

She kissed him and let him go off. *Maybe I really do love that lame-brain*, she realized. Then she turned around, heading back to the clinic.

Crunching through the brambles, she had to keep reminding herself, though. *Nothing's going to happen*, Rick had assured her just a short while ago. *It's broad daylight . . .*

"Yeah," she murmured to herself. "Just—please! No snakes. And no giant cockroaches."

Broad daylight or not, however, Joyce didn't get very far. She didn't even have time to scream before the clammy, two-fingered hand grabbed her by the throat from behind.

And dragged her down.

Chapter Fourteen

(I)

"I'm sorry, miss, but he hasn't been in today," a cheerful older woman told Clare at the front desk of the Fort Alachua Park Information Center. But the woman paused, glanced at her watch. "And that's actually . . . kind of strange, because we'll be closing in an hour."

"What you mean is that Adam Corey usually comes in on Sundays?" Clare asked.

"Oh, yes. Even if it's only to check his messages, he'll stop in at least once."

Great. "Is it possible that he came in sometime today, checked his messages, and then left without you seeing him?"

"I suppose it's possible, but I don't think so."

It was five p.m. now. Thus far, the clinic director had never come on or called back, and now it looked like the same thing was happening with Adam. Back at the clinic she'd left messages at his work phone, his cell-phone's answering service, and his home number. It had been Dellin who suggested she come out here to the info center. But so far—

Wild goose chase.

"It just so happens that *I* left a message with Adam, on his office answering machine," Clare went on with the woman at the desk. "I really need to know if he got that message, and it's rather urgent."

The woman gave Clare an appraising look. "Well, I can tell you're official," she said, noting Clare's uniform, gunbelt, and badge. "Go right on in and check his machine yourself. His office is just down the hall."

"Thanks."

Clare hurried down the cool corridor, passing admin offices and portraits of famous Floridian historical figures. It was just some instinctive inkling that rose up in her sometimes, a professional hunch, and Clare couldn't shake it. She hoped that she wasn't being prejudiced, and that she was effectively keeping her personal dislike for Adam out of her total assessment of the situation. All she knew was this: *something's really screwed up at the clinic and I know damn well he's involved somehow. Maybe he's not completely behind it, but he's in on it some way.*

Of this, she felt certain.

No message lights blinked on the answering machine in his office. *Which means he already played the message back*, she thought. *Either he came in here without the lady at the desk seeing him, or he retrieved by phone.*

And that could only mean he was on his way to the clinic.

It was a lot of running around for nothing but at least it would work out in the long run. *Unless Adam decided to head for the hills after he got my message, he's* GOT *to be going straight to my office.* It was one or the other. If he'd left town, then they'd all know he was guilty, and if he hadn't, she'd get to confront him, and Clare was *very* interested in how the ranger would answer her questions. . . .

She was back in her Blazer and back on the road immediately. But just as she'd checked herself through the security gate—

beep beep beep

—her pager went off.

This whole day's becoming one big Chinese fire drill, she thought. She kept driving for the island's main spur, carefully slipping her pager off her belt as she did so. She thought sure it would be either Dellin calling to tell her Harry had arrived, Rick or Joyce to tell her they were done with their search, or Adam returning her call.

It was none of those.

It's an alarm code!

Clare was mystified. Another feature of the alarm system was the automatic dialer; if an alarm on the grounds was triggered, the mechanism would first call the security office, and if no one picked up, it would dial the on-call officer's pager and leave a code.

The little LCD strip on the pager read: ALERT! @ PS-13

PS-13, she thought now. *That's one of the punch stations out on the site*. She lead-footed the Blazer now. She'd only been on the job a few days—not enough time to commit all the station numbers to memory. One hand fumbled in the glove box as she drove, feeling around for the duty manual. *Probably just Joyce or Rick tripped one of the perimeter alarms by accident*, she deduced, but when she found the list of station numbers, she saw that number 13 was one of the stations at the lake.

Damn it. I guess I better go out there first, see what's going on before I go back to the clinic.

Everything darkened when she reentered the site, branches from myriad palms and pines joining overhead, blocking out most of the sun. When she arrived at the edge of Lake Stephanie, she saw no vehicles and no people.

The punch stations, she thought.

The punch stations worked by key—each guard's master key. When the key was turned clockwise, the time would be logged in the computer, proving that the guard had made his round. But if there was trouble, the key would be turned counterclockwise, which triggered the system. *Nothing here*, Clare thought when she drove by the first station post. *Who the hell activated the sensor?*

She stopped and stared at the second post. *Jesus, is that—*

When she got out and rushed to the punch station, someone's master key and chain was hanging out of the keyway. The key had been turned counterclockwise.

And there was blood all over it.

Blood dripped off the chain, too, and when Clare looked closer, she noticed something like dragmarks starting at the foot of the post and going all the way back to the lake shore. Almost as if—

Someone crawled to the punch station . . .

Her guts seemed to sink when she followed the dragmarks backward. Just at the edge of the shoreline—

The vision made her stomach clench. She knew exactly what she was looking at: a great wash of blood.

Two spent shotgun shells in the dirt answered the rest of her questions. *The key in the punch station has to belong to Joyce or Rick. And all we carry are pistols, not shotguns.*

Clare ran back to the Blazer, the rear tires blowing

plumes of mud when she floored it and cut a hard turn. *Somebody shotgunned Rick or Joyce—a poacher probably. Gotta call the police, gotta get an ambulance out here—*

She felt horrified and numb at the same time. Panic would only hinder her. When she called back to the clinic on the walkie-talkie there was no answer. *Phone*, she thought next. *Where's the nearest phone?*

The clinic itself was a mile away, while her own cottage was only half that distance. In no time she was skidding to a halt out front. But when she barged into her cottage and picked up the phone—

"Shit!"

The line was dead.

She was jogging back for the Blazer when she saw Dellin's Mercedes parked in front of his own cottage. She didn't ask herself what he might be doing back here; all she thought was *Maybe he's got a cell phone!* and was running over.

"Dellin!" she called out and strode right into the cottage. She'd found the door ajar, and wasn't surprised to discover that his phone was also out of order. "I need your cell phone! I think someone's been shot at the lake!"

Only silence answered her back.

Where the hell is he?

She quickly searched the entire cottage, but he wasn't there. She was about to leave—to run over and see if he was at Mrs. Grable's—but she stopped quite suddenly, noticing something.

The strangest sensation grabbed her gut, and the silence only amplified the unease. Around her, Dellin's cottage was tidy and well-organized, everything in its place.

Everything except the single videotape siting atop the television.

When she picked it up, she discovered that it wasn't actually a tape, it was the tape's empty box. The box read: MAXELL, GX-SILVER.

Then she looked down at the VCR, saw the tape in the loading slot.

Even before she turned on the TV and pushed the tape in, she knew that the tape was the third one from the three-pack at her own cottage.

More sex stuff, she felt sure, *of Grace Fletcher and her kinky security friends*. She'd already seen the first two tapes, and the evidence of this third one wasn't what put the knot in her stomach. It was the question: *What the hell is Dellin doing with this tape?*

She wondered if there was something special about this third tape, then doubted it when the screen fizzed on. Grace, Donna, and Rob all frolicked nude on the big bed—it was the same old thing. But in a moment Grace sat up on her elbows, wide eyed.

"What was that?"

"Hmm?" Donna replied, and that was about all she could say given her current activity.

The heavy erotic atmosphere was snapped when Rob got up from the orgiastic tangle. "I heard it too. Someone's outside."

Rob put on his jeans, then stepped offscreen, while Joyce and Donna got up and hurriedly pulled on their robes.

"I didn't hear anything," Donna fretted.

"I did," Grace said. "Like a twig snapping."

"Rob, where are you!" Donna asked a bit too excitedly.

"Calm down," Grace told her. "He's getting his gun."

Now it was Donna who hurried offscreen, running after Rob. This left Grace by herself in the room, the urgency of the moment making her forget the video camera was still running. She picked up her own pistol off the nightstand, then left the room, calling out, "Where did you two go?"

Unfortunately, the camera angle only afforded a view of the bed, and didn't go higher than waist-level. The only other thing she could see was the nightstand and the bottom third of the window.

Oh my God, Clare thought.

The window was opening.

Someone was sliding the window open from the outside, then climbing in.

Clare froze where she sat, eyes riveted to the TV. All she could see of the intruder were his boots stepping inside, and mangy denim overalls. In only a matter of seconds he was inside, and a second after that he was out of the frame. But in that last moment of movement, Clare was able to glimpse what he was carrying in with him:

A double-barreled shotgun.

Another few seconds ticked by with no movement on the screen at all, but then—

What's he doing?

She could see the end of the shotgun barrel slowly inching back into the frame, pushing against the lamp on the nightstand. Eventually the lamp tipped over and crashed to the floor.

"What the fuck was that!" Rob shouted from the other room.

The worst realization was that this had all taken place in what was now Clare's bedroom. She quickly recalled the room's layout and realized at once what the intruder was doing. *He's hiding in the closet, and he just tipped the lamp over to draw the others back into the room—*

"Rob! Wait!" Grace could be heard now. "Don't go in there!"

All Clare saw was Rob from the waist down traversing the bedroom, when—

"Holy sh—"

BAM!

—and everything after that was madness. A gut-shot blew Rob backward, dropped him on the bed where he howled for a few moments, trying to put his innards back into his abdomen. The large white bed turned red almost instantly. Rob convulsed briefly, then fell still. Loud footsteps, breaking glass, and screams could be heard from the other room, though, but it all broke off very quickly.

Clare edged closer to the TV screen, terrified. The scene fell dead silent now. She frantically grabbed the remote, upped the volume.

Footsteps came back into the room. A brief shadow fell across Rob's gut-shot body on the bed.

Next, a voice: "Cuh-cuh-camera. . . ."

The frame began to wobble. Obviously, the intruder had noticed the camera and was picking it up.

He turned the camera around and was now looking right into the lens, and suddenly it was the intruder's face that filled the television screen.

Clare's heart nearly stopped.

It was Stuart Winster's face.

The malformed face grinned, showing wet, drooly lips and crooked teeth. He was waving into the lens with his two-fingered hand.

* * *

The shock of what she'd seen on the tape left her unable to move for several minutes. She was nearly hyperventilating, her heart skipping beats.

Stuart Winster.

Her rapist.

Was *here*.

The demented deformee was responsible for everything amiss on the site. All the disappearances were clearly his doing.

Clare had to sit still a while longer before she could come to grips with the revelation and think intelligibly. But this incontestable truth rammed two questions into her head.

Why and how?

Both seemed impossible to calculate with so little information. But one answer, at least, came to her after just one stray glance across the room. How could this criminal retardate possibly have anything to do with the clinic?

A small writing desk sat on the other side of the room, and above it, on the wall, several of Dellin's framed medical degrees hung. One frame, though, wasn't a degree. Clare got up and walked over.

It was a framed newspaper article.

Just a short one, from the *St. Petersburg Times*. The headline read: **Air Force Retiree and N.I.H. Specialist to Head New Local Cancer Clinic.**

A small photo accompanied the article: two men standing in front of the clinic, both in white lab coats, both smiling.

One was Dellin, the other was Colonel Harold Winster.

"Harry," Clare croaked. "Is Harold Winster."

Her former Air Force commander, and the father of her rapist.

It was more like a fugue state that took over from there, logic taking a back seat to the coldest emotions. Going straight to the police was the smart thing to do, but Clare already knew in her heart that she was not going to do that.

She was going to find the Winsters, and, perhaps, she would even kill them.

There was no mistake in her mind. Winster and his son were involved in some inexplicable conspiracy that was killing people. That was her rationale, and she felt quite satisfied with it. It also occurred to her—as she checked the cylinder of her revolver—that the harrowing revelations of the last few minutes might well have afflicted her with a solid dose of temporary insanity, but of that possibility she just thought:

I don't care.

She was running back to the Blazer when she noticed the cottage on the other side—Mrs. Grable's. The front door was wide open, which seemed odd.

Then she heard something crash.

Through the open door, she thought she could see something moving on the floor.

Clare re-drew her gun and went over.

She could tell that the living room was a shambles even before she got on the porch. Clare ducked inside, covered each corner as she checked the room. Then she just stared.

A middle-aged man lay on the floor. It was Mrs. Grable's husband; Clare remembered seeing him in the window the other night. She leaned over, checked his pulse, and wasn't surprised to find none. The ugly angle of his neck left no doubt—it was broken. And she knew in an instant that he was not the one responsible for the bruises she'd noticed on Mrs. Grable.

He wasn't the one beating her, she realized.

The man had no arms.

The dismemberment wasn't new; he'd obviously suffered some catastrophic accident years ago. *If he wasn't the one beating her, then who was?* The answer hardly mattered, though. He'd been murdered.

And where was Mrs. Grable?

Another door stood open; she thought it must be another room until she saw the steps descending. This cottage had a basement.

Clare's heart was racing. She began to go down the steps.

Downstairs she discovered a makeshift bedroom: a cot, a table, a small television, an old couch, but much of this room, too, was a shambles. *Someone lives down here, and I think I know who . . .* A single bare bulb overhead provided the only light—Clare could barely see.

She edged forward, her gun out.

"Get down!" someone bellowed. Hands grabbed her from behind, pulled her down just as—

BAM!

The room flashed for a split-second. The shotgun blast from behind the couch tore up the wall, the area of space which Clare's head occupied only a moment ago. She'd been yanked out of the kill-zone—

—by Adam.

"Keep low," the ranger whispered. He'd dragged her aside, behind some storage crates. Clare could contemplate nothing of what had just happened—except that Adam had saved her life.

"I heard the woman screaming," he said. "So I came in. Found the husband dead upstairs." His voice cracked, his thumb gesturing toward the other end of the room. "That *thing* did it."

Thing, Clare thought. *He means Stuart*. But before she could try to figure out anything more—

She cringed when a scream tore through the room.

It was a woman's scream, high and blood-curdling and insane.

Mrs. Grable's back there. He's got her behind the couch.

"Cover me," she whispered to Adam. "He's killing her."

Adam gulped, nodding. He raised his own pistol. Clare was about to make a break to the corner but she never got the chance.

Another shotgun blast shook the room, severing Mrs. Grable's scream. *JESUS!* Clare pulled herself back behind the crate.

"We're pinned down," Adam said. "One of us has gotta get out of here and get some backup."

Easier said than done. Clare jerked her gaze over her shoulder. The only way out was back up the stairs, but that would bring her right into his firing lane. *Suicide*, she knew. "We're going to have to take our chances and rush him."

Adam's strained face didn't look very confident about the prospect.

But then—

What's that?

Adam heard it too. Rapid footfalls, fading off.

"Sounds like he left," Adam wheezed.

"But to where? The basement's tiny. Is there a door back there?"

"Shit, I don't know. But I guess we gotta do it? You ready?"

Clare nodded. "You take that side, I'll take this one."

Adam gulped again. Then he whispered "Go!"

They both dashed up. Clare fired a covering shot over the couch as Adam dove over the cot.

"He's gone," Clare announced. "He got away—through *that*."

"What the hell?" Adam's gun hand was still shaking from the aftershock. He peered closer along with Clare. The wall at the end of the basement wasn't really a wall—it was some sort of drainage conduit. And there was a hole in it.

Clare peeked in, gun in the lead. The foul-smelling passage was almost as high as she was tall. "He ran away, through here. It's like a tunnel."

Adam sat down on the edge of the bed as if exhausted. "It's the old underground runoff system, they put it in in the forties, for storm surges." He glanced down inadvertently, then groaned. "Aw, Jesus . . ."

His gaze fell on Mrs. Grable's body. Clare winced. The woman was naked and had been bitten all over. The massive shotgun wound to the chest had finished her off.

Clare grabbed a sheet off the bed and covered the corpse.

Then she looked at Adam, and felt another shock of adrenaline. "You've been shot!" she exclaimed.

"Tell me about it." He'd caught part of a shotgun blast in the shoulder. "It's not that bad I don't think," he said, pulling out a small first-aid kit off his belt.

Clare helped him apply the gauze. "Do you think you can drive?"

"Huh?"

"The phones are all out—they're all rooted through the clinic." She was about to hand him her keys to the Blazer. "You need to get to the hospital, but you're going to have to drive yourself." Then she looked at the hole on the side of the conduit. "I've got to after that guy, and I'm pretty damn sure that runoff pipe leads straight to the clinic—the B-Wing side."

Adam still looked shaken. "You don't understand. That was no *guy* that did this. It was something really fucked up. I saw its face, Clare—just for a second but that was enough, and then I saw its hand. All them stories are true." His lower lip quivered. "It's some kind of—"

"It's not a monster, Adam," she said stiffly. "It's a man named Stuart Winster. He's deformed and he's ugly as hell, but I assure you, he's a human being."

"Stuart Win—"

"That's right. Same last name as the clinic director. Stuart Winster is Harry's son. He and I go back a ways, and it's too involved to explain. I've got a big score to settle with those assholes, and I'm going to do it—now. Get yourself to the hospital."

Adam took a long breath, then got up. He popped a wad of chewing tobacco into his mouth and lit a cigarette on top of it.

Clare frowned. "Do you have any idea how disgusting that is?"

Adam just shrugged. He spat in the corner. "Right now I'm more shit-scared than I ever been in my fucking life . . . but there ain't no way I'm gonna let you go out there alone."

"Forget it. You're hurt."

"Still got my gun hand," he said, and waved his pistol. "Let's go do this."

"Thanks," Clare said.

She grabbed a flashlight off the table, stepped into the pipe. There wasn't much water in it but all manner of fungus grew up along the rounded sides. Their boots clicked through the muck.

"I really misjudged you, Adam," Clare said next. But she *did* owe him an apology. "I'm sorry. It turns out that you were right all along about Dellin. I'm not sure exactly what they're doing out here, but they're in on it together."

"In on what?"

"They're using the clinic as a cover for some kind of experiment, something genetic, I think. They're putting something in the lake that's causing those mutations. Dellin's medical background is in genetic engineering, and he worked for the Army's Biological Weapons Section. And Harold Winster used to be the commander of the Air Force Clinical Research Corp. I was part of the security force there, and all we ever heard was that most of the research involved genetic science. Beyond that, I don't know and I don't care. But I'm shutting them down tonight. Anyway, I'm sorry for the way I treated you. I thought *you* were behind whatever's going on out here."

"Apology accepted," Adam said. He shrugged again. "It's somethin', my fuckin' karma, I guess. Just something about me that makes every fuckin' woman I ever fuckin' met think I'm snake shit."

"You sure it's your karma and not your language?"

"Fuck. Did it again. Pardon my French."

The malodorous passageway continued. Foul condensation dripped down on them from the lichen and mold infestations overhead.

"Aw, shit!" Adam yelled.

Clare whirled, gun cocked. "What?"

Disgusted tweaked Adam's face. A cockroach the size of a shoe was skittering up his pants. He flicked it off and stomped down hard. The insect made a crunching sound, almost like someone stepping on a soda can. It squealed, ejecting black liquid from its head.

"Oh, great. Those things are down here," Clare said, just as disgusted. *They better not try crawling on* ME!

"Yeah," Adam said. "And I wonder what *else* they got down here."

Clare could not forget the preposterously enlarged frog they'd encountered. *With fangs*, she thought.

Next, they both froze where they stood.

A squeaking sound could be heard up ahead. It reminded her of a bad wheel bearing.

And it was getting closer very quickly, and soon another sound could be heard along with it: pattering.

"Oh, no," she muttered.

"Only one thing I'd expect to find more of in a sewer than cockroaches," Adam said.

Clare knew exactly what he was talking about, and the steady squeaking only made her more fearful.

She kept her light trained straight ahead and down, while both had their guns ready.

The squeaking stopped, as if whatever was coming down that pipe sensed their presence. After so much time passed, Clare stepped forward slightly. She and Adam squinted ahead but saw nothing.

"Where is it?" she said.

"If it turned around and ran away, we would've heard it."

The comment made sense, but— *Maybe not*, she thought.

Then she flicked the flashlight upward, taking its beam off the bottom of the passage and flashed it to the top.

And screamed.

"Holy motherfucking shit you gotta be shitting me!" Adam yelled, and he and Clare both fell backward at the same time, splattering in the muck and firing their guns simultaneously upward.

The rat had been walking upside-down, on the ceiling of the pipe, and when they'd finally seen it, its face had only been inches from theirs.

The thing made a sound more like a dog barking when the volley of bullets knocked it down. It twitched wildly when it hit the cement bottom, blood more black than red jetting from the wounds. But it didn't die. It started to get back up—

Clare and Adam emptied their cylinders into it, the concussion of the shots nearly deafening them. When the stinging smoke cleared, the thing indeed lay dead.

"Don't get near it!" Adam yelled.

Clare had *no intention* of getting near it, but she did need a closer look. She reloaded, then knelt a few yards back, roving her light over it.

A wave of nausea rose up.

"Adam, this is not good! That thing is huge!" she complained.

"Yeah, and we're in its home. There's probably more of 'em, lots more."

Clare couldn't contemplate that. She couldn't contemplate the thing itself but she had to try. It did possess overall features that were ratlike, only it was completely hairless, its foldy skin a whitish pink with dark veins vaguely visible beneath. But the skin's texture was loose, more like fresh-plucked chicken skin.

And its size?

"That thing's as big as a full-grown Husky," Adam groaned. "I think I'm gonna throw up."

"Join the club."

But as repulsive as the creature was, Clare couldn't take her eyes off it. The head was decidedly *un*-ratlike.

It was not elongated and it didn't have ears. A *monkey's head? A cat's?* She was trying to come up with a comparison. What chilled her most was the *symmetry*. "Look at how even the head is, Adam."

"Huh?"

"The lines are all even, and the head doesn't look like a rodent at all."

"It's a mutation!" he objected, still queasy. "It's fucked up, deformed!"

"Yeah, sure, but usually genetic defects cause mutations that are asymmetrical because the growth genes run amok."

"Who the hell cares? It's *fucked up!*"

It just bothered her. She held the light on the head. "And look at that there, look at the forehead."

"I'd rather not. Let's just *go*."

The creature's brow seemed ever-so-slightly angled. Upward.

Like it was trying to grow horns, she thought.

No more surprises met up with them during their journey through the pipeline. It took them another fifteen minutes to make it the rest of the way. A steel ladder awaited them, ascending up into a manhole.

"He'll be waiting for us," she whispered. "He's probably got his shotgun aimed at the top of that manhole right this second. Any suggestions on how we do this?"

"There's only one way I can think of," Adam said, "and as far as I'm concerned, the sooner we're out of this damned sewer, the better," and then he simply charged up the ladder, shouting at the top of his lungs and firing his pistol.

More concussion pounded Clare's ears as she looked up and watched Adam climb over the rim of the manhole. *Gotta hand it to him*, she thought. *He's got balls*.

"Come on up," he said. "The room's clear."

Clare emerged into a small room with nothing in it, but just beyond the door, she saw a long, brightly lit hallway.

"This is B-Wing," she said.

"Never been back here before," Adam added, peeking out.

"I think we're about to find out why Winster and Dellin keep this section off limits to everyone."

Clare was about to step out into the hall, but Adam held her back. "What do we about Winster's kid?"

"Find him and kill him," Clare said as bluntly as possible.

"Shit, and all this time I never knew Winster even *had* a kid."

"By now I'm sure that Harry has to keep him hidden."

"Why?"

"Because it's the only way to keep him out of prison or a psycho ward." Clare subconsciously checked to make sure she had sufficient ammunition. "But he's already killed Mrs. Grable and her husband, and he shot you and tried to kill me. I think that gives us the perfect right to blow his brains out. That's something I've been wanting to do for over a year."

"What exactly did Winster's kid—" Adam began, but then thought better of finishing the question.

"Thanks," Clare said.

They checked and cleared each room in the corridor, each either an office, a lab, or an exam room. Suddenly Stuart Winster and his shotgun weren't anywhere to be found. *Maybe he left the building, found his father and headed for the hills*, she considered, but she doubted that and she sorely hoped not. Those two had wrecked her life—she wouldn't rest until she had her final confrontation with them.

And it was just like Colonel Winster—Harry—to toy with her like this: having Dellin recruit her for this job, hand-picking guards from the Foster Care system—hence, no families to come looking for them after they "disappeared." She knew he had the same thing in store for her.

"Aw, fuck," Adam said when they walked into the next room. Walls of glass tanks made it clear: this was a specimen room of some kind, and Adam had been peering into one of the tanks when he'd made his remark.

"What's that, a big aquarium?"

Clare looked in too.

"Aw, fuck," she said.

The tank stretched half the length of the room. Bubbles roiled up from filters on either side, and its top was bolted down.

The tank contained things that resembled eels but these eels were yards long, and where their pectoral fins should be were growths that looked more like—

Hands, Clare realized. *Tiny hands*. . . .

The eels frenzied when they saw Adam and Clare looking in. Long jaws filled with wolf-like teeth tried to gnaw through the glass; Clare and Adam both stepped back out of reflex.

Then Clare took note of the heads. Like the rat-thing they'd seen in the sewer, these ferocious eels seemed to all possess similar protrusions above the eyes . . .

All the other tanks contained more and more mutations: snakes, insects, fish, an array of amphibians, shrews the size of guinea pigs, mosquitoes the size of bats, caterpillars the size of billy clubs, all fanged, all uniquely mutated, and all bearing the odd angular point-like protrusions over the brows.

"What the hell you think this is?" Adam asked. He was across the room, having opened a closet. Inside stood a container, about the same dimensions of a ten-gallon drum, but lined and topped with bolts. Small indicator lights glowed from some kind of a switch panel. On one side was a porthole-like window lit up from the inside, and when Clare looked in she saw a rack of strange narrow test tubes. A printed out label on the rack read:

11 JUNE 95
MASTER SAMPLE
GRID #: S27-0078

Some kind of genetic specimen sample? Clare guessed.

"Guess it's one of them big freezer things," Adam offered without much fluency.

"Cryolization," Clare said.

"Unless there's a bottle of Bud in that thing, let's get out of here," he suggested, rubbing his gut. "The things in all them tanks're making me sick."

Clare commiserated. They left the specimen room. Clare opened the next door, walked in—

"We've been waiting for you, Clare. Please, come in!"

Smiling at her from the other side of the room, wearing a clean white lab coat, was Colonel Harold T. Winster, and standing next to him was his overalled son, Stuart.

"Huh-huh-huh-hi, Clare!" Stuart stuttered, waving at her with his two-fingered hand.

Stuart wasn't holding the shotgun.

Not a whole lot went through Clare's mind when she raised her pistol and drew a bead on Stuart's warped face.

Chapter Fifteen

(I)

Could it be that easy?

Her pistol was cocked, her finger on the trigger.

I'm going to kill them both, aren't I? she asked herself, and it looked like the answer was *Yes*.

Self-defense and justifiable homicide would probably stand up in court—if she perjured herself a little. But the real law-enforcement officer in her knew that it was technically murder.

What I really should do is cuff them and take them in, let the authorities work it out.

But then it could all wind up as another whitewash.

A second later, though, it didn't matter.

Harold Winster's DeLoreanesque visage remained where he stood, smiling into her gunsight.

Then—

click

Adam cocked his own gun and put it to her temple. "Don't make me empty that pretty head of yours, honeybunch."

Clare was appalled. "You lying, backstabbing ASS-HOLE!"

Adam took her pistol and stuffed it in his belt. "It was kind of a pain in the ass fingering Dellin, but the look on your face just now? It was worth it. I guess women's intuition is all the same, huh? It *sucks*."

He spun her around and slammed her against the wall to cover her better.

"Good work, Adam," Winster said.

But it was Winster's son who giddily approached her, the warped face beaming at the sight of her. At once, his foul breath was in her face, his hands—one normal and one two-fingered—were on her. "Uh-uh-uh-I'm gonna bite her, okay, Daddy? Just once please, Daddy?"

"If you do," Clare began and was about to grab his throat.

Adam's gun was at her temple again. "If he does, you'll just get bit, sweetcakes, and I'd really like to see that."

"Uh-uh-uh-I like ta bite girls, 'specially Clare."

Clare's eyes squeezed shut: Stuart's drooly tongue was licking her face, crooked teeth on her cheek, about to bite down.

"Son, son, none of that now," Winster commanded. "You'll have your fun in due time, with Clare and our other pretty new friend." Stuart backed off, and Clare breathed a sigh of relief.

But she knew the relief would not last long.

Behind Winster were several curtained-off cubicles, like in a hospital room. "Come, come," he bid, waving her forward. "You must see the entirety of my operation."

Adam nudged her forward with the gun in her kidney. Winster drew back one curtain—

—and Clare wilted.

It was Joyce who lay on the exam table within, strapped to it. She lay either unconscious or dead.

"Don't worry, Lieutenant," Winster said. "She's still quite among the living, and quite vital to us. She's been well-conditioned for our needs—as have you."

Clare didn't know what he meant, didn't want to know.

"We're ready to actually begin in earnest now. Oh, yes, the initial trials were subject to many flaws, but we expected as much. We just fooled around, you might say—with subjects such as this, to perfect the proper dosages according to body-weight, blood-counts, etcetera."

He whipped back another curtain. A severely thin naked woman with stringy dark hair lay on a metal table. The table had wheels on its top, and some sort of track system. "The locals weren't much of a crop to pick from, I'm afraid," Winster was regretting. "Bad nutrition and the ravages of drug- and alcohol-abuse reduced their fertility. But they served their purposes well nonetheless."

Winster nodded to his deranged son, who pushed on the girl's thigh, whereupon her body slid slowly over the table's wheels. The girl rolled into a large round opening just behind the table, but as she rolled, Clare saw her fingers moving slightly, her head lolling back and forth.

Still alive, Clare thought.

Stuart closed a large windowed hatch over the chute. Instantly an orange glow could be seen in the window, and the girl began to thrash madly inside, mewling.

"Good God," Clare muttered.

"It's the very latest in organic waste-disposal, Clare,"

Winster went on in his coy tone. "An industrial dry-heat desiccator. Did you know that it takes six to twelve hours to cremate a body conventionally? And then there's all that smoke that goes along with the process. We can't have sooty smoke stacks visible on a federal habitat reserve. This process requires only thirty minutes to fully desiccate a human being, distilling *all moisture*, every molecule of water. A grinder reduces what's left to a small, manageable pile of granular desiccant, much like sand." He raised a finger, enthused with his awful explanations. "Lately we've taken to disposing of it in the local waterways—just to see what happens. And there have been some impressive results."

"We've seen those results, Winster," Clare spoke up. "It's mutating everything in the lake."

"Indeed."

"And it's scarin' the crap out of me," Adam confessed. "You should've seen the fuckin' rat that was down in the pipe tonight."

Now Winster was nodding. "Yes, we'll have to tone down to a more controlled setting from here on."

"And I just saw some of your 'specimens' in that room with all the glass tanks," Adam added. "I had no idea you were getting results like that already."

"Marvelous, isn't it?"

"Not when I gotta walk around in the same woods with all that shit!" the ranger complained. "This place is turning into a freak show, Harry. Sooner or later people from the outside are gonna get wind of what's going on here."

"No, no, Adam, you really must leave that to us."

"How the *hell*," Clare began, "can desiccated remains of a human being create the things I've already seen around here?"

"A perceptive question," Winster replied, "and the answer is this: We've desiccated more than just human beings here."

Clare stared at him.

Winster was enjoying this, walking about the room in his lab coat like a medical professor before a classroom full of students. "Unlike cremation, which oxidizes the material, desiccation leaves certain cellular attributes in the waste intact. Gene markers, for one. And we're talking about an *absolutely unique* gene marker."

The recollection clicked in her head: what she'd seen in the other room, the cryolizer.

"The master sample," she deduced.

Winster pointed, impressed. "Excellent, yes! The master sample. See, Clare, that sample is what this entire clinic really exists for. And it contains properties previously unknown to genetic science. Certain links of the master sample's chromosomal chain were spliced into the reproductive genes of a subject, anything we wanted—a rodent, an amphibian, any manner of insect—"

"Or a human," Clare blurted.

"Ultimately, yes," Winster said with pride. "But that was the easiest part. Achieving reproductive *success* was the hard part. And we did it."

Winster pulled back yet another curtain, unveiling a typical hospital bed, but there was nothing else typical about it at all. A nude woman lay on it, wrists and chest lashed to the rail, ankles bound to gynecological stirrups. Grotesquely pregnant, the woman's swollen belly shuddered. Her head turned to one side, eyes open and looking blankly at Clare, tongue hanging out.

Grace Fletcher, Clare knew at once.

Winster pointed to several large white nozzled devices that hung off hinged arms over Joyce's bed, the device that Clare now recognized as the missing IRMT machine. Then he patted Grace Fletcher on the head. "I lobotomize them all first, of course—it's the humane thing to do. It makes them more manageable. In fact, I'll be lobotomizing your friend Joyce in a few moments, and I'm delighted that you'll be here to watch."

Clare's knees were wobbling.

Now Winster was patting Grace Fletcher's gravid belly. "Everything we're doing out here revolves around one process, a process is called transfection."

Clare remembered the word; Dellin had explained it when they were at the bar. Gene-splicing on a molecular scale, splicing selective *parts* of genes into another cell, then the targeted cell takes on new properties.

"Grace, here, has done quite well for us, and so did Donna for a time," Winster went on. "The transfection worked *marvelously* with them. Donna birthed two near-perfect fetuses, and Grace birthed three."

Clare could only hope that she had misunderstood him. "You mean you—"

"We transfected a reproductive gene marker from the master sample into their eggs, fertilized them *in vitro*, then replanted them into their wombs. It's a terribly simple process these days. Since we're still in a preliminary stage here, we used Stuart's sperm for the fertilization."

"And they gave birth to—"

"Let's call them 'genetic prototypes,' shall we?"

"Where are they!" Clare yelled.

Winster's hand bid the desiccator, whose window was now filled with illumined steam. "We destroyed them, of course. As I just said, we're only in preliminary stages at this point. A full compliment of incubators won't be installed until next month. But by then, we'll be ready—for Stage Two."

"You put babies into that thing!" Clare screamed.

Winster cast back the darkest grin. "Believe me, Clare. These things weren't *babies*."

This was madness. She had to get out, but how could she do that with Adam's gun to her back? *I've got to make a move, got to try* SOMETHING . . .

"And you can believe this too, Clare: there are some compartmentalizations in the Defense Department that are very happy with my results so far, and will do anything to accommodate me, anything to protect me. All they care about are results."

Clare had no doubt about that. What good was justice when the authorities were as evil as the perpetrators?

Winster turned around to check Grace's vital signs, and during that moment, Adam brought the gun to her neck and grabbed her hand. "They're gonna use you for that, honeybunch," he whispered. "But before they do, I'm damn well gonna get a piece of you first, and it ain't gonna be no sloppy seconds after the freak kid of his, either." Then he rubbed her hand firmly against his crotch. Creases of revulsion webbed her face when she realized what she was feeling: what must've been a dozen metal piercings in his genitals.

Clare thought she would throw up.

Adam let go of her hand when Winster returned his attentions.

"Grace and Donna didn't go missing until just a few months ago," Clare challenged him. "They couldn't possibly have given birth to anything in that short time."

Winster seemed pleased by the question. "Under normal reproductive conditions, no, they couldn't. But here's where our success shines, Clare. We weren't just transfecting genetic components of the master sample into the host egg, we were also transfecting a growth marker at the same time, and for that we have only one man to thank, your love-interest, Dellin."

Now Clare smirked at his name. "Where is Dellin, by the way? I would think the evil prick would be here gloating right along with you."

Winster walked across the room, ran a finger through Clare's hair. "You'll be relieved to know that Dellin was kept ignorant of our real purpose here. He's a molecular-targeting scientist, and a brilliant one. It was his skills that enabled us to identify the particular genetic marker that causes stromatic cancer to spread so fast. It's the fastest-growing carcinoma that exists." He held up a finger. "If we could only be able to take that genetic property out of the cancer and transfect it into a human reproductive gene—*that* was our Holy Grail. And Dellin got it for us, without ever knowing what we were really doing. His techniques in the *front* of the building solved our most paramount problems here in the *back*."

The relief, however useless, swept through her. By now it was obvious to her: Adam had planted the videotape in Dellin's cottage, knowing full well that that's where she'd go after finding her phone out of order. *He was innocent all along. But—*

"Where is he?" she demanded. "You killed him, didn't you?"

Winster snidely stroked his chin. "To be honest, we're not quite sure. As you're aware, last night, we had some visitors break through the floor. I didn't really care that they broke into the pharmacy vault, but then they were rude enough to do the same thing back here in B-Wing. After you went on your rounds, Dellin crawled under the building himself and came up through the break in the floor. He discovered everything, of course, so we had to . . . subdue his distemper."

"Where is he!"

Winster cast a glance to his son, who for the entire time had his eyes on Clare. "Stuart, bring our good friend Dellin out here for all to see."

Stuart loped to the back of the room, to a door which read STORAGE. But while he was out of earshot, Adam spoke up: "Harry, Jesus Christ, you gotta do something about that kid of yours; I told you a million times, he's a loose cannon, he's got no sense. You should've seen the shit he pulled tonight."

"And what might that have been, Adam?"

Adam's whisper was fierce. "He went berserk! He killed your sister and her husband, trashed the house"—Adam raised his wounded arm—"and then the retarded little fuck damn near killed *me!*"

"You know how volatile he can be, Adam. Are you sure you didn't do something to incense him?"

"No!"

"Are you sure? Are you sure that he didn't come into the basement to find *you* raping my sister, Adam?"

"Is that what he told you? You're gonna believe him over me? He's fucked up in the head!"

"By now, Adam, I'm sure you know that I'm a very focused man," Winster went on. "I don't care about incidental mishaps or incidental *people* for that matter. My sister's use to me, as a sexual pacifier for Stuart, was slowly fading. The project is more important than any of that, and whatever mess you caused at the cottage, you'll simply have to clean up. Or I'll find someone else who will."

Caught in his own lie, Adam just gulped and nodded.

Stuart unlocked the storage closet and dragged Dellin

out. There was blood all down one side of his head. He wasn't moving, didn't seem to be breathing, either.

"You killed him!" Clare shrieked.

"The butt of my good son's shotgun put a quick end to Dellin's snooping around back here." Winster walked over, leaned down. "But how do you like that? He's still alive," he announced after feeling for a pulse. He stroked his chin again, more contemplative now, and looked at the desiccator. "I'm not sure what I want to do with him just yet. Ordinarily, the desiccator would do but . . ." He shook his head. "Lock him back up in the closet, Stuart. We may need his knowledge for the next stage." Then he smiled at Clare. "I'm sure that Dellin will continue to work for us—under the proper amount of duress."

Stuart dragged Dellin's unconscious body back into the closet and re-locked it. Winster walked toward the tables. "And I hate to be the spoiler, but you can forget about Rick barging in here at the last minute and saving you all—"

With all that had gone on, it hadn't even occurred to her. *Rick. Where is he?* She'd found the bloody key in the punch station at the lake but never found a body.

"It's a wonderful surveillance system we have here—the government spares no expense." Winster turned on a large security monitor. "You'll find this tape even more interesting than the one Adam planted in Dellin's cottage," Winster promised.

The lake, Clare thought when the picture formed. It was a long shot from a high camera mounted up in one of the palm trees. There was no sound but she could see all she needed.

Rick was frantically turning his key in the punch

station but a figure dragged him off. When he stood up straight, reaching for his sidearm—

No! Clare thought, gritting her teeth.

—Rick was literally picked up off the ground and blown backward as the other figure emptied both barrels of a twelve-gauge into Rick's belly.

The figure, of course, was Stuart, who then calmly flung Rick over his shoulder and carried him toward the shore. He didn't walk in very deep, not even to the knees, and then he let Rick's body splash into the water. Stuart trotted back to shore quickly, as if fearful of something in the water.

Then that *something* arrived.

Even on the monitor, Clare could see the swerving ripples approach. Long and serpent-like, the thing broke surface and quickly wrapped its body around Rick, then pulled him under the water. Even though she'd only caught a glimpse, Clare knew what it was.

One of those mutated eels, like in the tank in the other room . . .

Only this one was much bigger, and so were the crocodilian teeth sprouting from its jaw. Clare just closed her eyes. Rick wasn't able to even put up a fight as the creature carried him deep under the water.

"So much for him," Winster said.

"People like you shouldn't be allowed to exist," Clare muttered.

"Ah, but we are, Clare, and do you know why? The world doesn't evolve on its own, it evolves by the efforts of a rare few who dare to break the rules and challenge convention."

"You're just screwing around with genetics, Winster. You're not doing anything here that's going to change the world."

"Oh, but I will, Clare, and those certain, more obscure compartments of our federal government are all too confident of this. Rest assured, you will be helping in your own little way—"another smile"—while providing my good son with some healthy diversion in between gestations."

Stuart loped back over to her, ran his deformed hand along her face. "I mmmmmmm-issed you, Clare."

Winster looked on proudly. "I'm afraid Stuart has always been quite fond of you, and like many fathers, I can't help but get him whatever he wants. Of course, once we've fully entered Stage Two of the project, we won't use Stuart's sperm. Trust me, Clare, *your* ovums will be fertilized quite carefully, with the best-screened genetic material that science can produce. I'll be using you for your *womb*, Clare, and Stuart will be using you for his personal plaything. But it's not as grim as it sounds." Winster shrugged. "You'll be lobotomized, you'll never feel a thing—er, at least you *probably* won't."

Clare struggled just to maintain ordered thought. *These sick bastards are serious. I've got to take a chance . . .*

But what?

Stuart's plier-like hand slid down to her chest, blundering over her breasts, then slid down even lower.

"Get away from me, you freak," she hissed.

"Aw, he's just coppin' a feel," Adam said. "Better get used to it—he'll be doin' a lot more than that soon enough."

"You're so pruh-pruh-pretty, Clare. I'm gonna bite you a lot, and then fuh-fuh-fuh—"

"Son, enough," Winster called him back. "We haven't the time for that now. Be patient. But let's show Clare what's more presently in store for her." He stood at the side of Joyce's table. Joyce still lay unconscious, and Winster reached up and pulled one of the IRMT nozzles down. "Thread-thin beams of short-wave, high-amp radiation are manipulated through the necessary nerve centers of the brain." He flicked on a panel switch, adjusted some knobs. One button glowed red, and Clare could read the word DISCHARGE above it. "We're going to dumb her down a little, that's all. It's best that she go through her gestations without the ability to think. The resultant stress could make her less receptive to ovum replantation, even in spite of the fertility therapy."

"Fertility therapy?" Clare asked. "What are you talking about?"

"Oh, but you've been undergoing the same therapies yourself, Clare. That delicious iced coffee in the break room? It's loaded with Bromacripine, oxytocal stimulants, citrate-based nutrients—which all enhance uterine health and optimum ovulation. There are also some hormonal adjutants mixed in too, to make the twenty-three chromosomes in your ovums more susceptible to the new transfection factors from the master sample."

"You've been pumping that stuff into us, and we never even knew!" Clare yelled.

"Exactly, and it's a very successful regimen. The side effects can't be helped, and they're hardly debilitating anyway."

"What . . . side effects?" Clare asked.

Winster spread out his hands. "Hyperactive sexual response. Surely you've noticed it yourself. No?"

Then she knew. The flux of erotic thoughts and fantasies over the past few days? The lusty dreams and the sudden increase in her sex-drive? And all the while, the secret additives to the drinks in the break room were tuning up her reproductive potential—for this.

It just made her sicker and sicker.

But, still, she knew she had to buy time, she had to think of something to do, a ploy, some move to pull . . . But she just kept drawing blanks.

Winster had the nozzle to Joyce's forehead; his hand reached out to press the DISCHARGE button on the machine.

"Wait!" Clare said.

Winster paused, looked up at her.

"You knew your son raped me on the base that night, didn't you?"

"Of course. Stuart gets a little out of control sometimes, like any growing boy."

"So it really was you who rigged the trial. The phony polygraphs, the bought-off witnesses—you did it all."

"Yes, I did. I couldn't just sit back and let my only son be prosecuted, could I? Even considering his deficiencies, I couldn't let him be institutionalized. Stuart is my *son*, Clare. And you? You're just a little orphan girl, a little cog in my great wheel. You should feel privileged that I'm going to let you live."

"You call that living? A brain-dead piece of meat on a table? A womb to make fetuses for you?"

Winster pouted. "I'm hardly as evil as *that*, Clare. What do you take me as?" Then another of his wry smiles. "You won't be brain-dead, you'll be cerebrally modified."

Adam gave her buttocks a squeeze. "You and that other bitch'll be real lonely in here," he whispered. "But don't worry. I'll be sneaking back here every so often when they ain't around." He rubbed his groin against her hip. "*I'll* keep ya company."

Clare put her revulsion aside and shouted "Wait!"

again, just as Winster would hit the button.

Winster raised his brows.

"There's a witness!" Clare blurted out. "She'll have the police investigating in no time."

"She's a lyin' bitch, Harry," Adam said. "There ain't no witness."

"That girl from the other night, the one we found in the woods." Clare's mind struggled to recall the name. "Kari Ann Wells! She didn't die, Winster. She's getting better, and it won't be long before the police'll be interviewing her."

Winster stood up straight, his brow runneled in concern. Then he exclaimed, "Oh, *that* witness," after which he and Adam burst into laughter.

Now Adam's hand reached around and tweaked her breast. Clare flinched.

"Where do you think I was earlier today?" Another wet whisper gusted into her ear. "Had to stop by and visit the poor little gal, ya know? And I gave her a little present, from Harry."

"Digitalis in an i.v.-line?" Winster remarked. "Stops the heart every time. Adam comes in very handy around here."

Clare's spirits could not have descended any lower.

"I was actually beginning to believe it," she said, more to herself.

"What's that, Clare darling?"

"The rumor," she said, "that there were monsters out here. Even Kari Ann Wells said that it was a monster that attacked her. But there was no *monster*. It was just your kid, Winster, who might as well be a monster anyway."

Now Winster offered a pinched look, as if he'd just remembered an oversight. He took his hand yet again away from the discharge button. "I do apologize, Clare. You *don't* know, do you? It's only fitting that I explain the rest—before we divorce you from your capacity to think."

He extracted something from his pocket, brought it to his lips and seemed to blow.

A *dog whistle?* was all Clare could think.

Then Winster put his arm around Stuart's shoulder. "*This* is my son, Clare."

A large shadow fell on the floor.

"*That's* the monster," Winster finished

He pointed across the room.

Clare nearly passed out when she saw what stood in the doorway.

"You see," Winster gloated on, "Dellin's expertise in various genetic mitoectonologies, cellular particle-targeting, and overall transfection protocols proved to be the most valuable contributions to the project, yet all the while he never knew what we were really using his skills for. His techniques not only successfully integrate DNA segments—they also vastly accelerate what we in the field call carbon and oxygen saturation points. To a layman? It means that his techniques vastly amplify organic growth rates, and all this together—combined with what you're looking at now—will one day allow us to clone some very *special* kind of people."

It was at least seven feet tall, with a shoulder-span of close to a yard. Bizarre webworks of muscles and veins moved beneath skin that seemed covered in mucous. The color of the skin was the same purple-tinged white that she'd noticed on the huge hairless rat they'd killed in the pipeway. Two holes for a nose, two little fleshy nubs for ears. The eyes were slits filled with gleaming black, and the mouth—

It opened its mouth to take a breath.

The mouth was an intricate chasm filled with teeth far more wolf-like than human.

It stood unclothed, and it stank. Its genitals hung hugely at its groin, all that grotesque flesh flinching slightly as the black-gash eyes stared more intently at Clare.

"A spectacle of creation, isn't it?" Winster said, looking at it in sheer awe.

"I think I'm going to throw up," Clare blurted.

"Imperfect, yes, but as we learn more and more, and as our techniques continue to improve, just *think* what we'll be able to produce here. And you, Clare, will be part of it—in your own little way."

Clare gulped. "So you—"

"Created it," Winster snapped. "Right here. And it's less than a year old. What I told you earlier wasn't entirely accurate—there was one transfected fetus that we *didn't* destroy, the first one." Winster was ecstatic. "*This* one."

Clare could scarcely look at it.

"We'll perfect them, educate them, train them," Winster went on. "It already obeys simple commands, it's grasped a minor vocabulary, it's learned to perform minor tasks . . ."

She remembered the rat, and some of the specimens in the tanks—*Their heads, their skulls*, she thought. The brows seemed to suggest points that had never fully developed, almost like horns. This thing standing before her displayed a similar cranial feature. Then her gaze flicked to its arms . . .

She was looking at the bulging muscles. There were muscles groups she didn't even know existed. Her gaze followed the arm all the way down. Hook-like nails grew out of the ends of the stout fingers. Did the fingers have an extra knuckle? And then—

Wait a minute! she thought next.

She looked at the other hand.

The basic structure of the first hand seemed normal, but the other hand only possessed two fingers: a thumb and index finger.

Same as Stuart.

Winster seemed to see that she had just noticed this fact. "I cloned my son, after transfecting in certain *other* properties—to see what would happen. The transfection itself was one hundred percent successful, and so was the gestation. Regrettably, there were a few of Stuart's *defective* properties that filtered in as well."

"You took your own kid's chromosomes and made a mutant out of them," Clare realized.

"Yes, but soon enough we'll be making mutants out of *your* chromosomes."

It stood there, a mute hulk—

A *monster*, she thought.

Clare knew that she was looking at her future.

"So now you know," Winster said. "Selecting hosts with no family base, no siblings, and no real domestic roots was simple, with the military personnel records at my disposal. And I particularly wanted *you*, Clare. Dellin never even knew our past relationship when I sent him out to find you. The others, too—they were perfect. Joyce seems especially fertile—" He re-aimed the nozzle at her head. "Yes, right there—I'm really starting to get the knack of this." He seemed to be matching a matrix on one of the computer screens against an MRI scan of Joyce's brain. "The motor sulcus and rear-right quadrant of the temporal lobe are what we want to burn up—here we go, that looks like it . . ."

He reached for the discharge button.

"Wait!" Clare exclaimed. "What's that smell?"

Winster glanced back at her reprovingly. "Really, Clare. You've been biding extra time for your friend long enough. I'd expect something a bit more original than that—"

"Hey, Harry?" Adam sniffed the air. "I smell something too."

It was no ploy. Some vague acrid odor filled the air. Clare's eyes began to sting slightly.

"The closet," Adam said. "Want me to check it out?"

"No." Winster looked at the storage closet. Then he looked directly at the hulking clone. He spoke loudly to it, pointing to the door. "Dellin is in there. Get him. Kill him." Then, to Stuart: "Unlock the door for your brother, son."

Stuart approached the door with his key, his mutant brother right behind him. When the thing walked, its footsteps slapped against the tile floor. Stuart was reaching forward with his key when—

WHACK!

—the door flew open and cracked Stuart right in the face. He went down, wailing.

The room seemed to freeze. Everything happened in split-second flashes. Some deep phlegmatic sound rumbled up from the mutant's throat as Dellin—bloody-faced—leapt from the closet and tossed a beaker full of some oily liquid in the thing's primeval face. Then—

POOOF!

"Noooooooo!" Winster shouted.

The hideous clone burst into flames, black oily smoke pouring off the aura of fire. The bellow of agony that erupted from its throat nearly deafened Clare. Even though it had all happened in a fraction of a second, she saw what happened.

Dellin had ignited the fluid with a spring-loaded flint-igniter; Clare remembered using them to light Bunsen burners in college lab classes.

The thing tramped out of the room, bellowing and burning harder, then:

Pandemonium.

Dellin charged Winster, had his hand around his throat. "You should remember what you keep in your store rooms, Harry," he said, choking him. "It burned the wood out around the lock with sulphuric acid and just torched up your creation with phenol—"

Clare grabbed Adam's wrist and could think of nothing better to do than bite it. Adam shouted. He dropped the gun, and it clattered across the floor. She was reaching for the gun stuck in his belt with her other hand, but then he grabbed her throat with his big hand, began to squeeze.

Clare was shocked by his strength, instantly locked up in terror. His fingers compressed like vise-grips, were cutting off the blood supply to her brain. In just a few seconds, her vision was dimming. A thought struggled across her mind: *Can't let the fucker kill me—not like this—*

But she was going limp.

"Lights out, honeybunch—"

It was impulse rather than volition that sent Clare's thumb into Adam's eye. His hand flew off her neck and suddenly he was bent over, holding his face.

"You BITCH! You poked out my fuckin' EYE!"

"Clare!" Dellin yelled. "Get out of here while you can!"

More phenol on the floor had ignited—now the tiles were burning, the black smoke filling up the room. Clare ran, not to escape but to search for a weapon so she could help Dellin. She raced into the next room but before she could make an earnest search—

"Damn him!"

She heard Adam's footsteps right behind her.

The room was another lab; she noticed a table with several computer monitors on it—so she dove under it.

"You ain't goin' nowhere, you little blond bitch," Adam's voice rumbled. "I'm gonna do a job on you that'd make the devil proud . . ."

Clare squashed herself against the wall under the table. She could see Adam, from the waist down, coming closer, and her gun wasn't in his belt anymore, which meant that it was now in his hand.

What a stupid move, she realized in an instant dread. *Now I'm trapped under here*. All he needed to do was bend over and look down . . .

Think of something! she screamed at herself. She could see Adam's boots—they were walking right for her.

With both hands she grabbed a power cord to one of the monitors just above her; she yanked down hard several times. On top of her, she heard the monitor smack into the wall.

"There she is—"

That last yank managed to rip the cord's connections out of the monitor. Now she was holding the cord with its bare ends exposed, the other end still plugged into the wall.

"Come out, come out wherever you—"

Clare slipped out from under the table, was lying on her back between Adam's legs. He looked down, grinned, pointed the gun—

Then screamed bloody murder.

Clare had reached up with one hand, grabbed his

belt, while her other hand jammed the bare wires into his crotch. The raw electric charge crackled; she could see white-blue arcs jumping around his pubic area. He stood there, screaming and shuddering, and soon his groin began to smoke, the potency of the charge no doubt amplified by all those metal piercings in his genitals.

Eventually, Adam collapsed.

Terrific, she thought. Adam was dead, halted by electrocution, but when he'd fallen, the gun slid under a set of heavy shelves, irretrievable. She pulled herself up, gave him a final glance. His crotch was smoking. One eye hung out of the socket, the other was blood-red from hemorrhage.

"Go fuck yourself, Adam," she said to the corpse. "And pardon my fuckin' French."

She ran back into the other room where Adam had dropped the first gun but she could scarcely see now from all the smoke.

"Dellin! Where are you!"

There was no answer, just the crackling of flame. She edged in closer, squinted, and then she saw them.

Shit!

Joyce had regained consciousness, was screaming for help as she lay strapped to the table. Stuart Winster had Dellin backed up against the wall with a crowbar across his neck.

He's killing him!

Again, it was instinct more than any premeditation on Clare's part. She grabbed Stuart by the hair from behind, jerked him to the right with all her might. His head banged hard against the grooved metal table. Dellin lunged forward to help, pinned his shoulders down. Meanwhile, Clare had already brought the IRMT nozzle.

She jammed it right against the front of his forehead.

Then she smacked the DISCHARGE button.

The grotesque two-fingered hand reached up, grabbed Clare's throat and squeezed but Clare just gritted her teeth and took it, all the while Stuart began to shudder on the table as the device slowly cauterized random nerve centers in his brain. The pincer-like hand shuddered, too, around her neck, then slid off.

"I think he's done," Dellin said.

"Not quite. I want *this* sick son of a bitch *well*-done," Clare said. Stuart lay drooling, immobile but still quite alive. Dellin opened the desiccator hatch, and Clare just gave Stuart a little pull and he rolled right in.

Then Dellin closed the hatch.

"Come on, this place is burning up quick," he said.

Clare was unstrapping Joyce, helping her off the table. "Here, take her and get yourselves out of here!"

"Where are you going!"

Clare picked Adam's pistol off the floor, grabbed a flashlight.

"I'm going after Harry!" she shouted back and disappeared into the smoke.

It was either intuition or luck that told her which way Winster would go. When she got out into the hallway, she almost turned toward the exit door, thought about it for a second, then turned in the opposite direction and went for the ladder that descended into the great sewerpipe. Immediately, she saw the footprints in the muck, leading away.

She didn't waste time.

She ran.

When she got to the dead rodent, she leapt over its collie-sized carcass, not stopping to look too closely at the smaller vermin that were now feasting on it. But she did remember what Adam had said when they were down here earlier: *We're in its home. There's probably more of 'em, lots more.*

Clare hoped she didn't get the opportunity to find out if this was correct.

Winster's footsteps kept going straight when she arrived at the next ladder and outlet—the one that rose up into the basement of Mrs. Grable's cottage. *He didn't go up there—he kept going straight.*

So that's what Clare did, even though it had just occurred to her that she had no idea where the pipeway ended.

Her boots slopped through deepening muck. She'd traversed another hundred yards, but down here, in the stinking dark, it seemed like a mile.

Go back, a voice in her head tried to seduce her. *Go back, find Dellin and Joyce, get away from this place.*

"No," she answered herself.

She wasn't going to give up. She *couldn't.*

Winster had come down into this tunnel, and she wasn't going to stop until she found him.

But after just another few yards, something jeopardized her determination.

Damn!

The tunnel branched off into a fork.

By now she was walking in muck ankle-deep. It wasn't holding footprints.

Which way?

Just forget about it. Go back!

Another voice, then—not her own—made the decision for her.

"I'm here, Clare," Harold Winster said.

Where the tunnel branched to the right, Clare aimed

her flashlight. She could see him, just barely, about sixty or seventy feet away.

"Neither of us can run all night," his voice echoed, "and you know full well how dangerous this sewer is. I'm taking a big chance here, Clare, hoping that I'm a little bit out of range of your gun."

Actually he was. She had a bead on him now, but it was a real long-shot.

"Let's make a little deal," Winster said.

"You've got to be kidding me!" she nearly laughed. She cocked her pistol, held the bead his body's center of mass—the most practical target in a low-light long-range firing condition.

"Before you fire a volley of bullets at me, please hear me out."

Clare's finger was about to squeeze the trigger, but then she paused.

"I must seem like the most evil man in the world to you," he intoned.

"Yeah."

"But if you kill me, all you'll be serving is a rather foolish primal emotion: revenge. I'm not being trite when I tell you that I'm on the verge of a breakthough that can change out society—for the better."

Do I really want to hear this?

"Bullshit, Winster. If I kill you, I'll be making the world a safer place."

"You may *believe* that, to yourself. But you're letting your hatred obstruct your objectivity. You can't even *begin* to know the good things that can result from our research . . ."

But this was just more rhetoric, and all of a sudden, it struck her.

Why did he stop? Why didn't he just keep going? It didn't

make sense that he'd stop to confront her, knowing she was armed. Then she thought back to when they were in the clinic, how Clare herself groped for any distraction to keep Winster from hitting that discharge button.

He's doing the same thing to me now, she realized. *He's playing for time.*

But time for what?

Time for someone to sneak up on me from be—

Clare spun around and shrieked. She only had time to get off one round—into the middle of the huge, taloned hand that slammed down on her. The bullet went right through the hand but the thing that the hand belonged to didn't care in the least.

The gun was wrenched away, and Clare was grabbed by the throat and raised upward—

smack!

Her head was slammed into the top of the pipe.

She went completely limp, then was dropped into the muck.

"Well done!" Winster celebrated.

Clare was too dizzy now to see with any great clarity, but she didn't really *need* to see to realize that this would be an appalling end. The clone's abominable body odor was much worse now that it mingled with the stench of burnt flesh. The face, chest, and shoulders were crusted with char, but the black eyes gleamed wetly in their slits.

God in heaven . . .

The shot to the head was beginning to wear off, but this seemed the cruellest trust of all: she'd be regaining her senses just in time to feel the full force of this most monstrous rape.

The thing tore open her top. Then it reached down to tear open her pants—

"Look out!" Winster shouted.

Clare, in the horrid daze, didn't understand why Winster was suddenly bellowing. The monster's hands came off her body; the angled, blackened face looked up. Clare brought her hands to her ears, screamed at the nightmarish shock of muzzleflash and deafening shots—

The clone's huge head exploded into fragments before her eyes. Lumpy brain matter flew out of one side and splattered against the pipewall. Clare counted five pistol shots that had been fired.

It was who was helping her up.

"Come on," he said, "let's get out of this shit-hole."

Clare's life had just been inexplicably saved, but her emotions remained raw, inflamed. There was still one more thing to do.

Clare picked up her own pistol out of the slime, and grabbed the flashlight.

"Clare, forget it," Rick tried to talk sense. "He's too far away—"

Winster had turned back around, was running away. She could barely see him down range.

She took a breath, let half of it out, and—

BAM!

One shot. In the gun-sight, Winster fell.

"Jesus, you got him," Rick said. "*Now* can we go?"

But Clare ran forward, deeper into the pipeway. She had to finish him.

Rick was pulling her back when Winster started screaming. They were still several yards away from where the bullet had dropped Winster.

"Holy shit!" Rick shouted. "Look at those things! Clare, we've got to—"

"—out of here!" she finished for him, and they both turned and ran.

Winster's screams followed them all the way back to the ascending ladder, and when they climbed into the late Mrs. Grable's basement, and then ran like maniacs out of the house, jumped in the Blazer and spun wheels out of there, Clare thought she could *still* hear Winster's screams.

In that last glimpse of him down in the sewer, she and Rick had seen several hairless, collie-sized rats very meticulously eating Colonel Harold T. Winster alive.

They were driving off the grounds. Rick was at the wheel. They'd picked Dellin and Joyce up on the road just past the clinic.

The clinic was an inferno.

No one said anything for a while.

Joyce sat up front. Clare was sitting in back with Dellin, his arm around her as the shock wore off. It wouldn't *all* wear off—ever—but she regained a level head fairly quickly.

"Rick," she said. "I forgot. Thanks for saving my life."

"Sure," was all he said, Joyce hugging him.

"Winster showed us a tape from one of the security cameras. We saw Stuart give you both barrels in the belly."

Rick pulled up his shirt, showing the pocked Kevlar vest. "My mama didn't raise no dumbell. But I thought I was a goner for sure when the retarded kid threw me in the lake. That eel or snake or whatever it was had me around the neck, dragging me down. But it let go pretty fast after I shot its head off."

Thank God, Clare thought.

Joyce was still shook up. Clare knew it would take

her some time to get back to normal. Dellin's arm around Clare was almost desperate.

"I still can't believe what Winster was doing back there," she said.

Clare remembered the stink of the thing, and its sheer hulking weight on her back in the tunnel. "Believe it," she murmured. "What happens now?"

"I don't have a clue," Dellin said. "And to tell you the truth, I don't even want to think about it right now."

"But where are we going to go?" Joyce asked.

"I know a great place," Rick answered.

"Where?"

"Any motherfucking place but here . . ."

Even when they were back out on the main road, off the official grounds of Fort Alachua Park, they could see the fire raging in the woods.

Through her exhaustion, one last thought occurred to Clare:

I wonder what the master sample was. Winster never said . . .

But the thought dissolved, and she was asleep in Dellin's arms as they headed for the bridge that would take them to the interstate.

Epilogue

Federal Land Grid S27-0078
Central Florida
June 1995

"Professor?"

The voice seemed distant, but the face from which it came was a blur right in front of him.

"Professor Fredrick?"

Fredrick's eyes were wide open, focusing. He lay prone somewhere. *Where's the sun?* he wondered, though he wasn't quite sure why he would think that.

A hand gently nudged him.

"Professor Fredrick, don't be alarmed. You're going to be all right . . ."

More of his vision was sharpening. He looked down and saw that he lay on a cot, and there was a man kneeling before him, a fairly nondescript man save for the white arm band with the red cross on it.

A *doctor*, he realized, *or an EMT*.

The man could see that Fredrick was conscious now. "I said you're going to be all right, sir, but I regret to inform you that you're the only survivor. Everyone else was killed, I'm afraid."

Fredrick didn't know what he was talking about but even the grave message didn't set in. When he looked around he saw that he was in a tent. Several other medical technicians milled silently about, and there were other cots there too, but the people who lay on them were covered fully by white sheets.

"It's a miracle we were able to get you out."

Fredrick reached up through a wave of pain, grabbed the man roughly by the collar. "What in God's name happened! Where am I?"

"Sir, you're in an emergency field hospital," he was told. "Can't you remember anything? You were down in that cavern, with the other archaeologists."

His hand released the collar, and more shock bloomed.

The cavern. The cenote. We found an original Ponoye Indian cenote—and the mummified bodies . . .

"There was a cave-in, sir. The forward part of the cavern collapsed."

When Fredrick gulped, he swallowed ancient dust. "Dales, my assist—"

"I'm afraid he was killed, sir."

Tears sluiced through more dust on his face. "I had half a dozen students down there with me. They're all—"

"They were all killed, Professor. I'm sorry."

Fredrick stared at the ceiling of the tent, more tears welling. The mummies, be damned. Suddenly the greatest archaeological discovery in the history of the state of Florida meant nothing. Everything would've been destroyed in the cave-in but that didn't matter now. His students were like his children, and Dales was the closest thing he'd ever had to a real son.

Dead, came the bare thought. *Dead because of my obsessions*.

Fredrick only wished he could've died along with them.

A sudden jolt of adrenaline grabbed his heart when memories began to surface. They'd been in the cenote, past the dolmen on which the Indian girl had been sacrificed to some nameless god. But the priests of the ritual had been sacrificed too—manually dismembered. The 10,000-year-old scene had been too confusing, but Fredrick knew the trimmings of the ritual. *An incarnation rite*, he remembered. And then—

More memory. Dales had been looking at the readout screen of the magnetic-mass survey equipment. "It's just the opposite, Prof. I'm getting a triple zero reading at a meter and a half."

"What!" Fredrick had yelled.

"This *isn't* a rockfall. There's another room behind this."

Another room, Fredrick recalled now. *Another cenote*.

The mummified hand emerging from the fissure had indeed been clawlike. *Demonlike*, he thought. "Be careful!" Dales had yelled at him when he began to squeeze himself into the fissure.

And that's when he'd seen what was on the other side.

"Professor Fredrick?" The doctor again, in the tent. "Can you tell me what happened? Can you remember anything? Anything at all?"

Yes, the thought creaked like old wood.

He closed his eyes, thought harder, then began to see more. In another few seconds he remembered it all.

"Anything, sir? We need to know."

Fredrick looked more closely at the man. There was

someone else kneeling next to him, another doctor, he presumed.

"Who are you?" Fredrick asked.

"We're an air-mobile emergency medical unit, sir," he was told. "When the cave-in occurred, your people radioed the authorities on the federal distress band."

Fredrick, now, could hear helicopters in the distance. A *med-evac unit* . . .

"What hospital are you from?"

"The LeMay Air Force Med Center," the man said.

Air Force? Fredrick thought.

"We got the call because we could get out here faster than anyone else."

It was Fredrick's good fortune, or at least he thought so. He was alive, he was going to live, but—

Something's just not right . . .

The first man persisted: "You went into the second cavern, right, Professor? What did you see?"

Fredrick remembered, he remembered *everything* now.

"Nothing," he lied.

When he'd slipped through the fissure, he did indeed expect to find a second cenote, but that's not what it was at all. He'd just stood there in shock, looking around, not believing it possible, and he remembered thinking, *The priests outside thought they were incarnating a demon*. He'd stared down at the rest of the perfectly preserved body on the floor. *This is what they got instead.*

It was not another cenote he'd squeezed himself into, it was some sort of a rimmed door. Inside was a cramped oval full of myriad apparatus that had long-since lost its lights. He was standing inside some sort of craft . . .

And the mummy on the floor? It was no demon, and it was no Ponoye Indian either.

His eyes darted back to the two Air Force men kneeling before the cot. "I didn't see anything," he lied again. "I don't remember anything about a second cavern." He feigned a wince. "God, my head hurts. Can you get me something?"

"You may have a concussion, Professor, so we can't give you any medications yet. Just try to relax, get some rest."

Fredrick nodded, watched the pair of Air Force men rise and leave. It was the second one, the older one, who'd instantly given Fredrick the bad vibe. That's why he'd lied.

Just something scary in his eyes . . .

He'd never forget the man's nametag, either. A strange name, one he'd never heard of in his life. Winster.

ATTENTION BOOK LOVERS!

DISCARDED

Can't get enough
of your favorite **HORROR**?

Call **1-800-481-9191** to:

— order books —

— receive a **FREE** catalog —

— join our book clubs to **SAVE 20%**! —

Open Mon.-Fri. 10 AM-9 PM EST

Visit
www.dorchesterpub.com
for special offers and inside
information on the authors you love.

We accept Visa, MasterCard or Discover®.